AURORA CROSSING

Karl H. Schlesier

Aurora
Crossing

TEXAS TECH
UNIVERSITY PRESS

This book is typeset in Monotype Bembo. The paper used in this book meets the minimum requirements of ANSI/NISO Z39.48-1992 (R1997). ∞

Designed by Lindsay Starr

Library of Congress Cataloging-in-Publication Data

Schlesier, Karl H.
Aurora crossing / Karl H. Schlesier.
p. cm.

Summary: "The Nez Percé War of 1877 draws young John Seton, whose upbringing and ancestry cast him as an outsider in sharply contrasting worlds. His quest to find identity and place in the clash of cultures propels him on the historical 1200-mile Nez Percé march toward a last refuge in Canada"—Provided by publisher.

ISBN-13: 978-0-89672-636-9 (alk. paper)
ISBN-10: 0-89672-636-3 (alk. paper)
1. Nez Percé Indians—Wars, 1877—Fiction.
2. Nez Percé Indians—Fiction. I. Title.
PS3569.C5128A95 2008
813'.54—dc22
2008014376

Printed in the United States of America
08   09   10   11   12   13   14   15   16   /   9   8   7   6   5   4   3   2   1

Texas Tech University Press
Box 41037, Lubbock, Texas 79409-1037 USA
800.832.4042 | ttup@ttu.edu | www.ttup.ttu.edu

Cavaleries du songe au lieu des poudres mortes, ô routes vaines qu'échevèle un souffle jusqu'à nous! où trouver, où trouver les guerriers qui garderont les fleuves dans leurs noces?

Saint-John Perse, *Anabase,* VII

Dream cavalries in the land
of dead dust, oh futile paths
which a breath lightly blows towards us!
Where can we find, where can we find
warriors who will watch the rivers
on their wedding nights?

Sharon Nell and Margaret Haggstrom, translators

AUTHOR'S NOTE

Nez Perce, Suyapu, Numipu

As early as the 1790s, among trading parties of tribes from the western High Plains who attended the Hidatsa Fair on the Missouri River were people who came from across the Rocky Mountains. Their distant domain was in what is now north-central Idaho, northeastern Oregon, and southeastern Washington. Their main trade item, besides the horn bow, was their special breed of spotted horses, the appaloosa. French Canadian traders who brought goods of European manufacture to the fair wondered about the identity of the strangers. They were informed in the sign language of the Plains: the swift motion of the index finger of the right hand passed close to the nose from right to left. It meant brave people, people who do not flinch from an arrow, or from death.

The French Canadians read the sign differently. They thought it meant people who pierced the septa of their noses to insert an object of bone or ivory, and therefore called them Nez Percé—in French,

Pierced Noses (from the beginning, English speakers omitted the French accent and spoke and wrote the tribal name without accentuation, "nez purse"). None of the long-distance travelers actually displayed such an ornamentation, and it was not a custom in that tribe. Though given in error, the name stuck, and the Nez Perces have been called thus ever since.

The Nez Perces gave a name to the French Canadians also. They called them *suyapu*—in their language, Head Upside Down, a reference to the fact that these men were bald but sported wild beards and robust mustaches. They extended the term *suyapu* to all white people, including those who later invaded their country, first as a nickname, later as an insult.

The word for themselves was *numipu,* meaning The People, or Us. The term was given to them by Old Man Coyote, *nasawaylu*. He is the spirit who finished the creation that the Supreme Being had initiated. A trickster, a master of animals, an earth maker, a sacred person, it was Coyote who made the world so that animals and humans could live in it. When the monster *itswa'wltsix* threatened to destroy the animal people, Coyote killed it. From the heart of the monster he made the Nez Perces. He gathered blood from the heart and sprinkled it along the Clearwater, Salmon, Snake, and Imnaha rivers, and said, "The numipu will be a small people, but you will be very, very manly."

The heart of the monster can still be seen today. It is a pointed hill of red stones one mile southeast of Kamiah, Idaho, on the east bank of the Clearwater River.

The long ride of patriot Nez Perce bands in 1877 is historical fact. In this story of the long ride the author has been faithful to historical reality and attentive to detail. But it is a work of fiction, and though many of the figures have recognizable names, they are put to fictitious use, as are figures from the author's imagination. Any resemblance to actual persons known in history is purely accidental.

The author long ago knew and befriended persons like those who appear in this story. It was during the time he lived among Nez Perces in Nespelem, on the Colville Reservation. In search of their ancestors he has traveled in the tracks of the long ride and has camped on their campsites. Much of their presence, like the presence of their wonderful horses, can still be felt there.

For narrative purposes it was necessary to render conversation in English syntax and grammatical structure. Anyone who would try to translate Nez Perce language would be unable to do justice to its complexity, flexibility, and its highly poetic and metaphoric expressions. The versatility of this language, with its richness of nuances and shades of meaning, has no equivalent in English.

For clarity, place-names are here given as they appear on modern state maps. In special instances the correct Nez Perce terms for a location are added. It should be understood that the individuals in the story would use established Nez Perce terms for features in the land or would invent new ones when passing through territory new to them. Readers will notice Nez Perces in the story using two different words to refer to the "east country." When a Nez Perce spoke from Idaho (*alayntsix*, the west country), the term for the east country was *kusayna*; when he spoke from east of the Rockies (from *in* the east country), he would use the term *nakunikay*.

CAST OF PERSONS

John Seton, 18

Alex Elwekin, 24, Seton's half brother

James Aaron, 48, Alex's uncle

*The members of a wi-ses (camp), a sub-band of the
Lamtama band of Nez Perces:*

Hemene, 61, *wi-ses* chief

Dawn, 27, Hemene's daughter

Teeweeyownah, 32, Dawn's husband

Tsacope, 5, their daughter

Itsepit, 21, Hemene's daughter

Allultakanin, 35, Teeweeyownah's brother

Oyipee, 35, Allultakanin's wife

Atemis, 16, their son

Red Walker, 8, their daughter

Talooth, 50, Hemene's sister-in-law

Ayokka, 27, Talooth's son

Petolwe, 26, Ayokka's wife

Ilsoo, 6, their daughter

Thunder Eyes, 25, Talooth's son

Tamonmo, 24, Thunder Eyes's wife

Weasel Bear, 3, their son

Magpie, 2, their son

Tannish, 20, Talooth's daughter

Short Bull, 22, Tannish's husband

Wolf Blanket, 1, their daughter

Elk Blanket, 24, Petolwe's sister

Kywis, 25, Elk Blanket's husband

Tasshea, 3, their son

Others, as they appear

AURORA CROSSING

ONE

HE WAS LYING THERE, A BOY OF ELEVEN, ON THE bare, rocky ground. His mother, Wetah, had brought him. She was a woman of the Lamtama band of Nez Perces, and it was her duty. There was no one else to take him there. It was his second *wáyatin,* quest, in two years. Nothing had happened the first time.

He lay on his right side. For three days he had been out on that lonely place above Lake Waha. A grizzly claw, its upper part wrapped in red flannel, lay at his side. His mother's guardian spirit was the great bear, and she had given him the "eye" of her *ipétes,* the sacred bundle, to assist him, perhaps to encourage a grizzly spirit to adopt her son. He suffered from thirst and starvation, but nothing had happened. The sun had risen every day, as always, and traveled across the sky to disappear behind the mountains to the west. But on the morning of the fourth day, there was a coyote.

It came out of nowhere. No sound, no footstep, ever so slight, signaled its arrival. The boy had closed his eyes for a moment. When he opened them again, there was the coyote.

It stood on the ground four feet away, a large male, head high above the boy's eyes. It looked down at him, huge before the red sky of morning. Its coat was coarse and heavy, the outer hairs tipped with black, throat and underbelly buff in color. A dark line ran up the front of its forelegs. The pointed ears were yellowish, and the slender, pointed muzzle was open, showing tongue and teeth. The animal's posture was aggressive, head held high, shoulder and neck hair erect. Its amber eyes were slits.

The boy closed his eyes and opened them again. The coyote was still there, squinting down on him.

He remembered that he had been told not to be afraid, regardless of what happened. Something or someone powerful might notice him, come and take pity on him, bless him.

He was still frightened. Was the coyote just a coyote who considered him meat, or was it a spirit coming for him in disguise? Perhaps Old Man Coyote himself, the mysterious maker, transformer, creator, and obscene jester, who lived in the old stories. With a heavy tongue and a voice that rasped from fasting, he asked haltingly, "You . . . have you come for me?"

He stared into the piercing eyes and began to lose himself in them. The coyote slowly lowered its head and appeared to speak, but the boy heard nothing. In growing desperation he listened. No sound reached him. The coyote's face came closer and closer until it almost touched his. He fainted. Whatever answer or message had been given to him was lost. When he came to, the coyote was gone. He searched. There were no paw prints . . .

He never tried a third time. He grew up without a Nez Perce name and without protection by a *wéyekin,* a guardian spirit. He had not heard the coyote speak. Although his mother disagreed, he considered his fasts failures. He never mentioned them to anyone. He came to believe, as the white missionaries taught, that the animal that appeared during a wáyatin was only an apparition induced by hunger and thirst and fear, not a visitor from the spirit world.

His name was John Seton. He was named for his father, a white man, who left him and his mother when he was eight years old. He was rarely called John. Mostly he was called Seton. It sounded like a nickname. He had his mother's features, but his father's gray eyes. He was eighteen years old when the great trouble came.

T W O

ON MAY 1 THE WEST WIND SHIFTED AND THE RAINS ended. The gray, misty clouds that had rolled across the Blue Mountains and the Snake, hugging the smooth hills that framed the Lapwai Valley, drifted away and opened the sky on the blue tent of heaven and the yellow ball of the sun. The last patches of snow on the high slopes sagged under its fierce light. Lapwai Creek ran wild with meltwater. Grassy flats everywhere in the valley were dotted with puddles and pools of water.

In the early afternoon a small column of wet riders and horses came over the rutted road through the hills west of Fort Lapwai. They were the Wallowa group, the first delegation of the five nontreaty bands to arrive for the meeting at the fort set for May 3, 1877. They numbered about fifty people and were led by the chiefs, Joseph and his younger brother, Ollokot. The column was preceded by a handful of warriors. Behind the chiefs rode a few old men, some women, and a few more warriors. Women accompanied husbands and fathers, leading packhorses and horses dragging tipi poles. A few young men brought up the rear, driving a small herd of extra horses.

They had left most of their people in camp at the mouth of Joseph Creek, where it runs down into the Grand Ronde River in northeastern Oregon. That morning they had crossed the boiling yellow flood of Snake River below Lewiston, losing four horses in the roaring current. Southeast of the town of four hundred people they had taken tipi poles from a stash hidden for an emergency. When the advance riders reached the road that went north and south along Lapwai Creek and past the western façade of the fort, they swung south. Searching for a relatively dry campsite, they found one four miles below the post. Soon eleven tipis were raised, and the horses, most the spotted kind, appaloosas, had been turned loose and were nibbling on the new wet grass.

No other riders appeared by May 3, a Thursday, the day agreed to for the meeting. The other bands held back, waiting to see whether the Wallowas would come at all. On May 3, Joseph and Ollokot, accompanied by a few warriors, rode to the fort and informed the authorities that the other bands had not yet come in. They asked that the meeting be postponed. They blamed the weather, slippery mountain trails, and swollen streams for the delay. Reluctantly, the two men who headed the government group, Major General O. O. Howard, commanding officer of the Department of the Columbia, and John B. Monteith, U.S. Indian agent, agreed to a new date: Monday, May 7.

On May 4 the delegation of the Paloos band arrived on the nontreaty campground with its chiefs, Hahtalekin and Naked Head. Their territory lay in southeastern Washington on the Snake River between the mouths of the Palouse and Alpowa rivers, forty to seventy miles northwest as the raven flies. They had only the Clearwater to contend with, a mild river compared to the furious Snake. They made the crossing above Lewiston without incident.

On the next day the Pekonan and Lamtama groups came in together. The Pekonan chief was Toohoolhoolzote. The Lamtama chief, White

Goose. Pekonan territory was the mountain country between the Snake and the lower Salmon River along the western edge of north-central Idaho. The Lamtama's lay directly to the south of the Pekonan's, on both sides of the middle Salmon. Both delegations had made the crossing of the dangerous Salmon River together. They did so near the mouth of Rock Creek, fifty miles southeast of Fort Lapwai. The floodwaters had swept away about thirty of their horses. Twenty-some were recovered downstream. With anger in their hearts, they had ridden up through Camas Prairie. They were putting up their tipis on the south side of the camp circle when the last group arrived.

This was the Alpowai band. Its chief was Looking Glass. They came from the middle Clearwater River where their territory lay along the Middle Fork and extended east, up the Lochsa River toward the Bitterroot Mountains and Montana. With no serious obstacles in their way, their progress was leisurely, covering the forty miles from their camp in two days. Their tipis closed the northeastern section of the camp circle of the nontreaty delegations.

May 6 was Sunday. Religious services were provided at the fort for both of the troops stationed there—one company of the First Cavalry and one company of the Twenty-first Infantry. A crowd of Christian reservation Nez Perces also gathered to witness a meeting that was bound to have grave consequences for them.

A brief meeting was held in the nontreaty camp. Two men were appointed to speak for the five bands to the government representatives on the following day. They were Toohoolhoolzote of the Pekonan band and Naked Head of the Paloos, both great orators steeped in Nez Perce history and tradition. Toohoolhoolzote, a powerfully built man in his early fifties, was a noted warrior. He had led expeditions to the buffalo plains and traced his lineage through many famous war leaders. Naked Head, in his early thirties, was a respected *tiwét,* a ceremonial man of the old religion.

Fort Lapwai, May 7. There was a cool breeze from the north, with the sun veiled by a layer of cirrus clouds. There were horses on the parade ground inside the fort, about 140 Nez Perce horses. These were the best the bands could show off, all appaloosas, spotted horses of Nez Perce breeding. Their skins, still in rough winter fur, showed the patterns for which they were famous: black or brown spots all over on a white background; white quarters and loins on a dark coat; a few dark spots on a white background; roan with dark leopard spots; white spots on a dark background; white flecks all over on dark loins. And there were appaloosas whose coats displayed mixed patterns. Each horse was different, a fresh painting come alive.

The Nez Perce horses were decked out as for a festival. There were beaded pad saddles and martingale chest and forehead ornaments. Eagle and hawk and owl feathers had been braided into manes and tails. Buffalo robes with fancy strips of beaded designs were thrown over saddles. And there were horses painted with red, blue, and yellow stripes or circles or lightning-like lines in white.

This dazzling herd had been ridden up from the camp south of the fort by men and a few women dressed in colorful finery. The tipis and the extra horses and pack animals were left under guard. Each of the five bunches had traveled in a close group. They had ridden slowly, ceremoniously, and in silence past the stables of cavalry horses, the horse herd of visiting reservation Nez Perces, and through the gate of the fort. They dismounted on the parade ground, a wide rectangular space surrounded on all sides by wooden buildings or fences.

From there, the delegations walked past the guard house and the garrison headquarters building to where a big white hospital tent had been raised. The tent covers were lifted and braced, open to all eyes outside it. The nontreaties disappeared behind the unruly mass of reservation Indians squatting on the ground. Appaloosas had been left on the parade ground in the care of a few young men acting as horse holders.

Seton was one of them. He stood by the horses of the Lamtama band. The horse holders were dressed for the occasion, some looking as fanciful as their horses. But not Seton. He wore a plain deerskin shirt and leggings, a trade blanket breechclout, and partly beaded moccasins. His only adornment was a choker bead necklace around his throat. His hair was combed up above the forehead in the old Nez Perce style. His face, with its high cheekbones, strong nose, and wide mouth, was framed by black hair hanging loose over his shoulders. He wore no feathers.

He stood holding the double reins of his saddle horse, a roan mare with dark spots. The horse was without fancy gear and unpainted, but its reddish coat had been brushed until it shone in the sun. Seton stood outside the bunched group of thirty Lamtama horses. They waited quietly, sometimes shifting from hoof to hoof, lifting and ducking their heads. They exuded a warm, earthy smell fragrant with sage and herbs and grass.

The meeting had started at the white tent when Alex Elwekin walked toward Seton. Alex was his half brother from their mother's first marriage to Elwekin, a Nez Perce of Three Feathers' band. Alex had been adopted by James Aaron, Elwekin's brother, after Elwekin's death. Alex lived on the reservation on Aaron's twenty-acre allotment by the Clearwater River, a few miles upstream from the government agency. He was dressed in drab secondhand white men's clothes that had been distributed to Christian Nez Perce from the agency.

Alex was a sturdy man of twenty-four, built wider than his slender brother. But their facial features were similar. Alex had his parents' dark eyes. His hair was cropped short, the way the agent and the preacher at Lapwai Agency liked reservation Indians to wear it. The brothers had not seen each other for seven years.

They looked each other over. Alex's face was friendly, but there was a quizzical look in his eyes. He shook hands with Seton, then leaned back against the hindquarters of his brother's horse. The roan stomped and nodded and moved aside. "You are still around," Alex said. "I didn't know where you were. Down there on the Salmon or in the east country, living among the buffalo." He smiled.

"On the Salmon," Seton said. "The east country, that was years ago. We went with Eagle from the Light and Toohoolhoolzote. Lamtama and Pekonan went. Eagle from the Light stayed there."

He paused. "Too many miners in this country, he said. Too many white people running around everywhere. Eagle from the Light stayed in the east. We came back after two years. White Goose is the chief now. He is there, with the others."

Seton pointed with his chin toward the garrison headquarters and the top of the white tent beyond it. There was a silence. "You didn't come when our mother died," Seton said finally. "Last year. You didn't come to the funeral."

Alex turned uneasily. He looked toward the rounded heights of the hills east of the valley. "No. It was too late when I heard of it. You buried her the old way?"

"Hemene did, the Old Man," Seton said. "On the burial hill at lahmotta." Lahmotta was the old campsite in the gorge of White Bird Creek.

Alex nodded. He turned to face his brother. "Let's go over to that meeting. See what is happening. There is no need for you to stay here."

Seton hesitated. Hemene had asked him to stay with the horses, and he had said yes. There was one other man keeping watch over the Lamtama horses, Ayokka, a cousin. He stood with a Pekonan guard on the opposite side of the bunched herd, talking. Seton scanned the parade ground to the rows of the fort's barracks. Soldiers sat there in casual groups, unarmed. Everything seemed calm and peaceful.

"Come," Alex urged.

Seton called out to Ayokka. The man waved and nodded, hardly looking. Seton dropped the reins of the roan and stroked its neck. He talked softly to the mare and walked away. The brothers went between the guard house and the garrison headquarters building and came upon rows of reservation Nez Perces sitting on the ground. The large rectangular tent stood parallel to the buildings, its broad front facing west. It was surrounded on both ends and in the back by the dense mass of treaty Indians. There were many women among them, even some children. Around the corners of the tent, in the back and along the sides, stood a cordon of soldiers armed with rifles, butts resting on the ground.

Inside the tent, facing out, seven people sat on chairs. One was a woman. Behind this group stood three military officers and a few officers' wives. Two of the men on chairs were reservation Nez Perces. Alpowa Jim was a Presbyterian preacher. James Reuben was son of the head chief of the Christian faction and served as second interpreter.

Outside the tent, opposite the government people, seven nontreaty chiefs sat in a row. At their backs were the members of their bands. Together they numbered about 120 people. They all sat on robes and blankets on the ground. In contrast to the soldiers, they were unarmed.

Starting from the left-hand corner, the chiefs were Ollokot, his brother Joseph, Looking Glass, Toohoolhoolzote, White Goose, Naked Head, and Hahtalekin. There were two main spokesmen for the government. General Oliver Howard was one. The nontreaties called him Cut Arm because he had lost his right arm in the Civil War. The second was the Indian agent at Lapwai, John Monteith. Directly opposite these two sat Joseph and Toohoolhoolzote.

On that day the differences between the nontreaty and the treaty Nez Perces were brought into clear focus. While the latter were dressed in colorless white man's clothes, the nontreaty people displayed the stark beauty of the past. That morning, before leaving camp, the chiefs had said, "Those people up there do not know us. We must show them who we are." So the bands had dressed as if for a feast or for a funeral.

The women wore fringed and beaded and quilled leather dresses whitened with chalk, and high-top moccasins. Strands of fur were looped in their braids. Some wore old-style circular women's hats, called *neetscow,* woven from bear grass with geometric designs. Men wore their hair loose except for that above the forehead, which was cut short and stood straight up. Many had slivers of fur or strings of beads, shell, or bone ornaments attached to their hair. Most wore feathers or feathered caps. There were a few buffalo-horn headdresses. All were dressed in fringed buckskin shirts and leggings, breechclouts, and beaded moccasins. Many wore necklaces of beads, bone, or German silver.

Flesh sides of buffalo robes were painted or beaded or quilled with colorful designs. A few men held eagle wing fans in their hands, identifying them as ceremonial men, tiwét. Of the chiefs, both White Goose and Naked Head carried fans.

Seton and Alex walked past the throng of reservation Nez Perces huddled on the south side of the tent. They sat down where their files closed with the three rows of the Paloos band. The man in the middle of the government group had just finished reading from a paper. The man to his right started to translate from English into Nez Perce.

"Who is he?" asked Seton.

"Whitman," Alex said. "A white man who tries to speak our language."

"Who is the one who spoke before him?"

"John Monteith. He is the agent. He came here after you had gone to the Lamtama."

"Is that the Cut Arm general next to Whitman?" Seton pointed with his chin to the lanky, black-bearded man in uniform. A double row of brass buttons shone on his tunic and a single star gleamed on his shoulder straps.

"Yes."

"Who is the man on the other side of the agent?"

"This is his brother, Charles. He works at the agency."

Seton studied the white woman who sat next to Charles Monteith. She was dressed in a long white gown and wore a wide-brimmed white hat with a pink band. She sat stiffly erect on her chair and grasped a beaded handbag with both hands. She was tense and clearly uncomfortable.

"Who is the woman?" Seton asked. "She looks very young."

"She is called Frances. She is the wife of Charles Monteith and the daughter of Whitman."

For a while they listened to Perrin Whitman trying to convey the agent's message in Nez Perce. His voice did not carry far. Where the brothers sat, one could hardly hear him. Finally Seton asked, "Why are Alpowa Jim and James Reuben up there?"

"I don't know. I guess Jim because he is a preacher. He likes to preach." Alex chuckled. "James Reuben—I don't know why," he mused. "You know, his father died five days ago. They buried him yesterday. Maybe Reuben sits there for his father, the chief."

"The old Reuben died?"

"Yes." And after a pause: "James thinks that one of your *peléyc tiwét* killed him, witched him. Some others think that too.

"How did he die?"

"I don't know. It was sudden. They say it was not natural." He glanced at Seton sideways.

Seton did not respond. He studied James Reuben, sitting there in a formal suit, wearing a white shirt and tie. He had not seen him for many years. Young Reuben stared morosely over the ranks of the nontreaties before him. He was more carefully dressed than the white officials beside him. With his round, serious face and short hair parted on the right side, he looked like the model for a Christian Nez Perce that might be dreamed up by Henry Spalding, Sue McBeth, Henry Cowley, or the other Presbyterian missionaries. He knew his dour cousins watched him with scorn and amusement, marking every flicker of his eyelids and reading his every move, and he resented it.

"You have a new head chief now" Seton asked.

"I heard it is Jonah Hayes. The agent made him head chief at Reuben's funeral, they said. I don't know. I wasn't there."

Whitman had finished speaking. The rows of reservation Nez Perces stirred. There was talk among them. The nontreaties sat in silence. A gust of wind blew from the north and billowed the canvas flaps and tore at the stakes.

At last the general spoke. His voice was strong with authority, battle tested. The audience fell silent. Perrin Whitman translated after every sentence.

"We have met before," Howard said. "There have been many meetings. Nothing has been accomplished. You," he looked at the nontreaty chiefs, "are still arguing. You are still outside the reservation. You have heard Mr. Monteith. He is your agent. He has read the order from Washington to you."

He waited for a moment.

"There has been a treaty, duly signed. You belong on the reservation now. You must go there. The land that you still claim is not yours. Not anymore. The treaty says so. Washington says so. Washington says you must move onto the reservation."

He had moved forward on his chair as he spoke; now he sat back.

"There is nothing we can do about it. The order came from Washington. I cannot change it. Neither can he." He turned his head toward the agent who sat on his left.

There was a silence.

The nontreaty chiefs sat motionless. Finally Joseph spoke. Because he spoke away from them, Seton and Alex could barely hear him. They tried to listen to Whitman's translation into English. Seton's English was excellent. He had learned it from his father and neighborhood children when he and his parents lived for six years in Lewiston. Alex understood a little English from when he and Seton had attended the Lapwai boarding school for a few months in 1869 and 1870.

"You know me," Joseph said. "I am Heinmot Tooyalakekt. That is my name. We have talked about this before. Many times. To you," he pointed with his chin at the general. "To you," he pointed to the agent. "Many times. You have listened, but you do not want to understand." He paused. "We did not agree to the treaty you mention, the one of 1863. We never signed it. We never gave our land away. These did." He made a wide gesture with his right hand, indicating the body of treaty Indians surrounding the meeting place. "They did! But they cannot give away something that does not belong to them. They gave their land. Our land still belongs to us."

A strong murmur arose among the reservation Indians and ebbed away.

"We have gone over this before," the general said. Then he curtly dismissed Joseph's complaint as if he were a silly child. "We cannot

discuss it anymore. I cannot help it. You must move onto the reservation."

Ollokot cleared his throat.

"You ask us to give up what you call a million acres. For what?" he
asked. "For your allotments of twenty acres each? For the worst of the
land that is left on your reservation?"

He looked along the row of impassive chiefs to his right. "No part
of that reservation land ever belonged to us. It always belonged to the
downriver Nez Perces. It is their land. We have no claim on it."

He paused.

"It is already crowded with your Christian Indians. There is not
enough space left on your little reservation for us, even if we wanted
to go there."

His gaze went from the general to the agent.

"We have thousands of horses, hundreds of cattle. Where can we
put them? There is no place for them on your reservation, and no place
for us."

The agent shifted nervously on his chair. He glanced at the general
before he looked at Ollokot.

"There is room for you on the reservation," Monteith said. "You
can bring most of your horses, all of your cattle. You will plant gardens and raise vegetables and crops. Have your own houses, permanent
homes. Send your children to our schools. They will learn new ways,
good ways. We can live together in harmony. Your brethren here have
already proved that." He pointed with his right hand toward James
Reuben and the reservation Indians behind him.

"Once we are on that reservation, you will tell us what to do and
what not to do," Ollokot said. "You will not let us leave. You will
tell us that we have to stay here all the time. That we can't go to the
east country anymore, or to the Wallowa Valley, our home, or to the
Salmon country. You will deny us all the places we know, all the places
that have come to us through our fathers and their fathers, places that
always belonged to us. These lands were ours long before we ever saw
a suyapu, a white face."

"Once your home is on the reservation and you have moved your stock there, you can travel wherever you want," the general said impatiently. He pointed north. "Up there is a place you can dig camas. There is Potlatch Creek, where you can go as far as you wish. There is Weippe, where you can dig camas. There is a road open for you to go to the east country, to Crow country, and any other place."

"But we would have to tell the agent every time we want to go some place," Ollokot said angrily. "Even ask him for permission." He paused. "What about tepahlewam, Camas Prairie, where we have gathered for a long, long time. That part of the country is outside the reservation. White people are taking it over, plowing the earth, raising herds of pigs on the camas grounds. Could we go there? Would we not have trouble with the white people moving in there?"

Seton looked at Alex after Whitman translated. Alex nodded with a serious face. "You see . . ." he started to say, but he stopped when John Monteith spoke.

"The land outside the reservation is beyond my jurisdiction," the agent said. "I cannot protect you there. The white people have a right to be there. I can only protect you within the borders of the reservation. This is why you have to move on the reservation."

"We do not need your protection," Ollokot said. "We have always protected ourselves. I say your reservation is too small for us." He tried to get up. Joseph gently put his left arm on Ollokot's shoulder. A wave of movement ran through the nontreaty groups. The treaty Nez Perces sat in sullen silence. There was tension; everyone felt it.

"I am Peopeo Kiskiok Hihih," White Goose said. "I speak for Lamtama. Our people, numipu, have become two peoples. We," he lifted the right hand with the eagle wing fan and moved it slowly to his left and right, "we believe in the old religion. We do not believe in the white man's religion. We do not want it. We want to stay with the old ones, the people who were before us. We believe in hunyewat, the Creator, and in the spirit world. Hunyewat and nasawalylu gave us this land when the white faces were not even a dream. How could we give it up?"

He paused.

"The downriver Nez Perces on the reservation have become people different from us. They believe in the new religion. Your preachers, they talk bad about us."

He stared at the ground in front of him.

All eyes were on him. Everyone waited.

"How can we live on your reservation?" he asked. "There would be trouble all the time between us and the Christians. Look at them." He moved the fan toward the treaty Nez Perces. "They are not like us any more. They look different, they have become different. They will tell me that I have to bury my sacred things and this," he touched his buckskin shirt. "They will say that I cannot hold my ceremonies. They will tell me how to dress, how to have my hair, how to live." He paused. "They will try to make me over into a Christian. They will not leave me alone."

The agent moved uneasily on his chair, but the general spoke calmly. "You will not be forced to become Christians. You can practice your religion as you wish."

Again there was a silence. It was pierced by the shrill call of a bird from across the creek, once, twice. "We have asked Toohoolhoolzote to speak," Joseph said. "He speaks for all of us."

The chief from the lower Salmon River got up slowly. He was a tall, muscular man. In his younger years he was considered the strongest man of the tribe. He wore a single eagle feather tied horizontally to the long hair at the back of his head. As he rose, he grasped a handful of sand from the ground. Standing, he let the sand run through the fingers of his right hand. His gaze passed over the white officials in front of him and centered on Howard. He looked sharply into the general's eyes. Something passed between them. It was clear the men despised each other.

"What you have said, Cut Arm, I cannot do," Toohoolhoolzote said.

Perrin Whitman was visibly shaken. He stammered in his translation. Seton and Alex looked at each other, Seton with a thin smile. He had heard the chief speak before. He was not surprised.

"I will not come on the reservation," Toohoolhoolzote continued. "It is not my country. I will stay in the places that the Creator has given me. I have come from no other country, as have the whites." He paused. "Who is He who lives above? It is the Creator, First Person. You," he pointed with a finger at the general and the government people, "you are second man. I am second man. We are but children. I am a child. He who lives above set me down where the rivers flow, where the mountains stand. I must not make Him angry by going elsewhere."

He looked up to the sky. He turned his gaze back to the general and met his eyes.

"I have come from no other country. My people, my ancestors have always been here. The Creator placed us where we are. We cannot leave our country to the suyapu to raise pigs on and plow under. The earth is our mother. We do not harm her. We cannot harm her without harming ourselves. We come from the earth and we go back to the earth, our mother. The earth cannot be sold."

He paused again.

"When I was born, when I came from my mother into life, I was a baby. I grew to be a boy. I learned to use the arrow and bow. I hunted the birds and rabbits. I became a man and hunted deer and bear, and buffalo in the east country. When I shot and killed, I saw that life went out with the blood. This taught me for what purpose I am here. I came into this world to die. My body is only to hold spirit life."

The general rudely interrupted him. "What you say is true," he said. "We have gone over this before. Washington says that I cannot allow you to live where you are. You have to come on the reservation." He bent forward. "If you do not move onto the reservation, that means war between you and me. I want you to answer now whether you will move to the reservation."

There was a heavy silence.

Toohoolhoolzote replied, "I shall not move to any reservation. I will stay where I am."

The general stood up from his chair. "If you do not move on the reservation, I will send my soldiers to force you there."

Toohoolhoolzote answered fiercely: "Who are you to tell me what to do? I am a chief here, you are not. You may be a chief somewhere else. Go back to your own country."

The general's voice was cold. "I give you thirty days to move your people and your stock onto the reservation. After thirty days soldiers will come to your place and tie you up. Your stock will be taken from you."

"I hear you," the chief said. "I have wyakin, spirit power, that which belongs to a man. I am a man and will not go. I will not leave my home, the land where I grew up. Who can tell me what I must do in my own country?"

"I am that man," the general said with a loud voice. "If you will not come onto the reservation within thirty days, I'll send my soldiers."

"You brought a rifle to a peace council," the chief said. "If you mean but thirty suns for gathering our stock, yes, we will have a fight."

Seton watched the government people during this exchange. Howard was firm and angry. The agent, John Monteith, appeared shaken, disturbed. His brother, and his brother's wife, Frances, looked frightened. So did Perrin Whitman, who had stumbled a couple of times in his translations, groping for words, repeating himself. The two treaty Nez Perces sat rigid, flanking the whites. Alpowa Jim sat with a stony face, but young Reuben looked toward the soldiers standing near him, as if searching for protection. Some of the soldiers held their rifles half raised. Both treaty and nontreaty Nez Perces sat alert, listening and watching, missing nothing.

The general turned to his right. "Arrest the chief," he ordered the soldiers. None of the soldiers moved. Captain Perry, the post commander, who had stood behind the general, stepped forward and grabbed Toohoolhoolzote's arm.

"A last time," the general said. "Are you coming on the reservation or not?"

"Are you deaf?" the chief asked. "I told you. I will not change my mind."

"Take him to the guard house," Howard said. The tall captain hesitated. Toohoolhoolzote looked to his fellow chiefs.

"Go," White Goose said. "Go with him. We will get you out. This is a peace conference. We want no blood shed."

Joseph and Looking Glass grunted in agreement. "Yes," Looking Glass said. "We want no trouble here."

Howard took a few steps and grabbed the chief's other arm. The captain and the general escorted Toohoolhoolzote to the guard house, passing slowly through the tight rows of the treaty Nez Perces. The nontreaty chiefs spoke a few words to their people, calming them.

When the officers returned, the general asked, "What have you decided?"

There was a silence, and then Joseph said, "We will go with you to look over the reservation. See what there is. See if there are places for us. We will do that. But you must let Toohoolhoolzote go. He spoke for all of us. We feel much as he does." He paused. "We were told that this was a peace council, where we could freely say what we feel, what we think."

He looked into the general's eyes. "You broke a promise to us. You must let Toohoolhoolzote go."

Howard looked at the Wallowa chief and nodded. "Yes, I will do that."

He glanced along the row of chiefs. "Tomorrow? Can we go through the reservation tomorrow? Look for places there?" He turned to the agent.

Monteith nodded. Of the chiefs, first Joseph consented, then the others. Ollokot and White Goose said nothing. So the meeting ended. People got up slowly. They shook robes and blankets and folded them. Some stood stiffly, in silence. Others gathered in small groups, talking. Many started to walk away.

When Seton began to leave, Alex said, "Why don't you come with me to my place. This is over. There is nothing for you to do here. Not for a while."

Seton thought about it. "Yes," he said finally. "But I have to go to the camp first, tell Hemene and the others."

Alex nodded. "I'll get my horse and come down and get you."

The brothers parted. Seton reached the horses before the Lamtama arrived. He took the double reins of the mare and cut Hemene's and Teeweeyownah's horses from the herd and led them to the side. He mounted up.

Hemene was his mother's older brother-in-law, a man in his early sixties. Seton could call Hemene father according to Nez Perce rules, but he called him Old Man instead. It was more impersonal, but still a term of respect. Teeweeyownah was Hemene's son-in-law, married to his daughter, Dawn. Teeweeyownah was in his midthirties. He was known as a hard and fearless man.

The two looked for Seton when they came out between the buildings. They walked over, their faces grim. Behind them came White Goose and about thirty people of the band, a few women among the men. No one spoke. They took their horses and mounted. Hemene and Teeweeyownah accepted the reins from Seton, slung their robes over the saddles, and swung themselves up. Quickly the parade ground was filled with departing riders. The bands left one by one, the Lamtama bringing up the rear.

They passed through the gate of the post and through a lane formed by treaty Nez Perce standing quietly, shoulder to shoulder, faces raised. The riders turned south and, on the earth road that led past the stables of the cavalry, let their horses run. They were not running from something, they were running to something, back to themselves, to their own world. The appaloosas were glad to be free to run after the confinement of the fort. A stream of colors flowed beneath the midday sun. Swift and beautiful, the column poured into the circle of white tipis, dashed around the inside, and came to rest in a swirl of dust. Slowly the column disbanded as riders sought their own camps.

THREE

AT HEMENE'S TIPI HIS DAUGHTER DAWN AND HER
younger sister Itsepit had been preparing food on the outside fireplace.
Itsepit was twenty-one years old. She had been crippled by a fall from a
horse when she was thirteen. The fall had broken her hip, and she walked
with a limp. The sisters were being helped by little Tsacope, a happy,
round-faced girl of five, daughter of Dawn and Teeweeyownah.

The men rode up and dismounted. Hemene and Teeweeyownah
tied the reins of their horses to stakes, but Seton let the reins of the roan
drop to the ground. He went through the open door of the tipi. Some
clothing and pieces of equipment hung from pegs tied to tipi poles.
There were three rifles: two Winchester 1873 models, .44-40-caliber
centerfire, and one 1873 .45-70-caliber Springfield carbine. He took
his Winchester and a cartridge belt and slipped his leather belt with the
sheathed knife over his shirt and closed the buckle. He slid his rifle into

a buckskin scabbard. He wrapped two pairs of moccasins and the cartridge belt into a leather jacket and rolled it into his buffalo hide sleeping robe, securing the bundle with a rawhide rope.

When he came out of the tipi, Itsepit was feeding more wood on the fire. Dawn had walked to a neighboring lodge. Hemene and Teeweeyownah sat on logs near the fireplace, upwind from the smoke. They looked up when Seton took his bundle to the roan and tied it with the rifle scabbard behind the saddle. He bent and tightened the saddle girth, then walked over to them and sat in the grass.

"You are leaving?" Hemene asked. "Where to?"

"I saw my brother at the meeting," Seton said. "He wanted me to go with him to his place." He paused. "I haven't seen him for years."

"He is Aaron's boy, isn't he?" Hemene asked.

Seton nodded. Teeweeyownah looked into his face but said nothing. There was a silence.

"What happens now?" Seton asked. "Are you moving onto the reservation?"

"We don't know," Hemene said.

He looked into the fire. Itsepit knelt before it, stirring the flames. "We don't know," Hemene repeated. "First Toohoolhoolzote has to go free."

"Will you go with Cut Arm and the agent tomorrow?" Seton asked.

"Yes. It looks that way," Hemene said.

"It may not mean anything," Teeweeyownah said. "We might not see any place we like."

Seton nodded. He looked away to where little Tsacope was playing with a pretty leather doll. She saw him looking at her and smiled.

A rider came along the circle of tipis. He saw the three men and rode over. It was Alex. He dismounted and stood uneasily, holding his horse's reins. He raised his right arm. Hemene and Teeweeyownah did the same.

"How are things where you are?" Hemene asked.

"Good," Alex said. "We are doing all right."

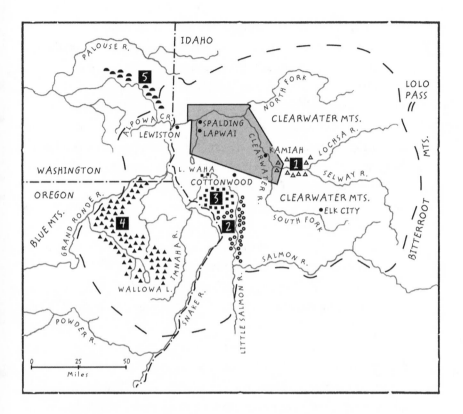

---- Nez Perce Reservation boundary by Treaty of 1855. For easier reading, con-
temporary state boundaries are included. In 1855, present-day Idaho was part
of Washington Territory but became an independent territory in 1863.

▓▓ Nez Perce Reservation boundary by Treaty of 1863, never signed by chiefs
of the five bands whose core territories were outside the new boundary, and
never recognized by them.

Core territories of nontreaty bands:

△△△ **1** Looking Glass's band

o°o **2** White Goose's band

▪▪▪ **3** Toohoolhoolzote's band

▴▴▴ **4** Joseph's band

⌃⌃⌃ **5** Hahtalekin's and Naked Head's band

"What happened to Reuben?" Hemene wondered.

"We don't know," Alex answered. "He wasn't sick or anything." He paused. "James Reuben said someone did something to his father." A quick smile flashed over Teeweeyownah's face.

"I doubt it," Hemene said. "We didn't do anything to him."

"He was one of Spalding's men," Teeweeyownah said. "Maybe Spalding came back for him." He chuckled. Everyone knew that Henry Spalding, who had ministered to the downriver Nez Perces off and on for years, had died in Lapwai in August of 1874. Reuben was one of his converts.

Alex said nothing. He looked to Seton. "Are you ready?"

Seton got up and went to the roan and mounted. Alex slipped the reins over his horse's neck and mounted also.

"When are you coming back?" Hemene asked.

"I don't know," Seton said. "I'll know where you are. I'll find you."

He pressed the appaloosa's flanks briefly with the inside of his thighs, and the mare walked forward. He waved to Itsepit and Tsacope and raised his arm to Hemene and Teeweeyownah. The brothers rode side by side across the open center of the camp circle. When they struck the road, they turned north toward Lapwai and let the horses run at an easy lope.

They passed the stables and the fort and reached the cultivated zone that extended through the bottomlands to the agency, three miles away. This was the old territory of the Chief James band, whose people were among the first Nez Perces baptized and pressured to farm. There were some twenty-acre family plots, separated by grassy areas where cattle were grazing. Most gardens had already been planted with vegetables. Tipis stood alongside wooden cabins and sheds, but lodge covers were made of canvas, not buffalo hides. The Nez Perces who lived there no longer joined hunting expeditions to the east country.

Halfway to Lapwai the riders left the road and crossed the turbulent creek and moved on along the foot of the range of barren hills that bordered the valley on the east. On the creek banks stood solitary cottonwood trees above brush and evergreens. Their ancient trunks and branches, ruined by weather and lightning strikes, were gray and withered. They looked dead but were not. Among bronze-colored dead leaves the green fluff of spring leaves had appeared. The trail led through thickets of tumbled branches and brush and dry, yellow grass. When they came to an open space near the mouth of the creek, they halted the horses and looked across to the agency.

A scattered array of wooden buildings, including a church, a wooden bridge, and two mills, sat on level ground above the rushing gray green waters of the Clearwater. Tall pines and a few cottonwoods were spread between the buildings.

"It's smaller than I remember it," Seton said.

"It's bigger, though, than when you saw it last," Alex said. "They put more buildings up. They built the church four years ago."

Seton searched for the school building and boarding house, built in 1868. In the fall of that year, school was open for two and a half months until a smallpox scare closed it. Of the fifteen boys who had attended school, two died from smallpox. From April to July 1869, and from September 1869 to March 1870, the school was open again. Seton and Alex were there with about thirty children. The smallpox passed, but tuberculosis became a scourge, killing adults and children throughout the reservation. Some died in the boarding house. To Seton the school had become a death house.

Seton remembered the school uniforms, frightening nights, excessive rules and punishments. Teachers lasted only for one brief session. There were constantly new ones and sometimes a new matron. Some were friendly but unfit. Others were hard and frustrated men who had failed elsewhere. They failed again, trying to teach Nez Perce children.

Sitting his mare across from Lapwai and scanning the agency grounds brought back memories to Seton, most of them bad—isolation, loneliness, harsh commands in English, a locked sleeping hall, the coughing of sick children. He wondered why he had come with Alex now. Was he looking for something? Was he trying to find something he did not yet understand? He shook his head as if shaking off a weight.

He turned the horse. Alex followed, and they took the trail that circled the edge of the hill and ran east on the south bank of the Clearwater. The trail widened, with the cuts of wagon wheels in it and hoofprints of horses unshod and shod. He remembered. As a boy he had been on this trail many times, on foot and on horseback. It was like coming back to the past. They rode in silence along the winding river and after four miles came to the first allotments scattered upstream on Cottonwood Creek. The creek rushed down from the great plateau that extended for sixteen miles southeast to the gulch of Big Canyon Creek. Aaron's allotment was the first they saw, spread above the river near the creek's mouth.

Seton pulled the mare's reins. She stopped, and he took in the sight. Two log cabins, three tipis in the back. The tipis stood near where the one in which he had lived with his mother had stood from the fall of 1867 to the summer of 1870. In that summer, the two left and went to live with Hemene and the Lamtama. Now there was a barn, a pole corral with five horses, and a wagon in a shed. Fences surrounded a large garden. Smoke from a fire curled up behind one of the cabins.

"Two cabins," Seton said. "I remember one."

"The one close to the river is the one I live in," Alex said.

"You have a cabin for yourself?" Seton asked. "You have a wife?"

Alex nodded. "Yes, Susan." He paused for a moment. "And a little girl. Mary."

"She is of our people?" Seaton asked.

"Yes, she is from Chief James's band."

"Mary is your stepmother's name," Seton said.

"Yes."

"How old is your child?"

"Two," Alex answered. He moved his horse forward, and they came to where a furrowed stretch of sand led to Aaron's place. Alex opened the gate and swung it shut after they rode through. They dismounted in front of Aaron's cabin and let the reins drop. The door opened, and Aaron came out, followed by his wife. The man stepped up to them and shook hands with Seton. "Come in," he said. The men walked past Aaron's wife and through the door. Mary nodded to Seton and went in after them. Aaron pointed to wooden chairs around a heavy, rectangular table. "Sit down," he said.

The men pulled chairs noisily over the wooden floor and sat down while Mary stood by the fireplace. Seton glanced around the room. It had changed little from when he'd last seen it. The cabin was about thirty by twenty feet, with the door in the middle of one of the broader sides, facing south. The fireplace was opposite the door. There were three windows: one next to the door, one each in the west and east walls. Two beds, one cupboard, some bundles wrapped in printed cotton cloth hanging from the ceiling, and a smaller table near the fireplace. A rifle on pegs above one of the beds Seton recognized as a .45-70 Springfield single shot. Nothing originally Nez Perce was visible in the room. A simple wooden cross hung on the wall above the fireplace.

Mary took water from a bucket on the floor and passed the dipper to her husband. He drank and passed it on. When Seton finished, Mary took it from his hand. "Thank you," Seton said.

"How are you?" Aaron asked. He masked his disapproval of Seton's bead necklace and buckskin clothing with a cautious smile. Christian Nez Perces no longer wore native accessories. He was dressed in woolen pants and a striped flannel shirt. Mary wore a long black dress she had made herself. The pattern had been handed around in Lapwai by the missionary, Sue McBeth, before agent Monteith removed her from the school and sent her to the Kamiah Mission.

Seton looked at the man he had regarded almost as a father. The relationship soured when Aaron began to quarrel with Seton's mother over the white man's religion. Aaron was a staunch Christian, while Wetah had held to the old religion. Aaron was in his late forties, medium sized, with a roundish face and short black hair parted on the right side. A mild-mannered man, they said, but perhaps deceptively so. He had a bland face, but his eyes showed a touch of shrewdness. In contrast, Mary's face was open and quiet, with keen, friendly eyes.

"Good," Seton said.

"Are you going to stay?" Aaron asked.

"I don't know."

Aaron nodded. He looked to Alex. "How did the meeting go?"

Alex explained what had happened at the fort and how it ended. Mary and Aaron listened attentively. "So they are coming on the reservation?" Aaron asked. He looked at Seton.

Seton shrugged. "It looks that way."

"Where will they go?" Aaron complained. "There is not enough room for all of them." There was a silence.

"Tomorrow the upriver chiefs come on the reservation and look for places," Alex said. "The general and white men from the agency will be with them. That was decided today."

There was a tapping sound on the door. Mary opened it. A young woman walked in holding a little girl on her arm. She nodded and examined the faces of the men around the table. She was a few years older than Seton, dressed like Mary and as slender. A smile was on her face. The little girl squirmed in her arm. The woman let her down, and she ran quickly to Alex who grabbed her and put her on his knee. She looked inquisitively at Seton, dark eyes unblinking.

"I brought my brother," Alex said. "This is Susan." He pointed with his chin toward his wife. "And this is Mary." He looked down to his daughter.

"I saw the horses," Susan said. "The food is ready. Come and eat."

Seton slept in one of the tipis by the willows, close to the river. Behind him the Clearwater plunged west toward its meeting with the Snake. Less than a stone's throw away was the site where he had once lived with his mother. The tipi was long gone, but it had left a slight indentation on the ground, overgrown with grass. He looked the site over, but found nothing to show for the almost three years they had been there, no trace of their presence.

The tipi he was in now had been partially emptied of stored equipment by Alex and Susan. Mary brought a tule mat on which Seton had put his bedroll. After the evening meal the two women had taken the remaining food away and washed dishes and joined the men by the fireplace. Talk had lasted until nightfall. Little Mary fell asleep and was bundled up and laid in the grass. When the fire burned down, they all went to their sleeping places.

Seton lay awake for a long time. A light wind stirred the tipi's canvas and rubbed it against the poles. When the moon rose, its ghostly light shone into the tipi and lit the area outside. Lying on his bedroll, Seton saw the shadow of his mare against the lodge wall, and through the open door he watched her move around softly. He thought of his mother. For the first time in years he wondered about his father and what might have happened to him. Before he fell asleep, he heard five wolves call from the plateau to the south. He dreamed something he did not remember later, though he thought it had been important.

He woke before sunrise. The mare put her head through the door and snorted, withdrew, and stepped away. When he got up, Alex came in carrying some white underwear, a pair of trousers, and a cotton shirt.

"Why don't you put these on," he said.

Seton was perplexed.

"These might fit you," Alex said. "We can get something better for you at the agency or in Lewiston." He paused. "Our people don't wear buckskin anymore. With these you won't look like a stranger to them." He dropped the clothing on Seton's bedroll and went outside. He turned and spoke through the door. "You can stay here with us, you know. You don't have to go back to the Lamtama. They will be coming here anyway." Seton heard his steps fade away.

He dressed slowly. Wool and cotton tickled his skin. The pants were too big but could be held by the belt. The last time he had worn white man's clothes was in 1870. He remembered the uniforms forced upon boys in the boarding school—dark gray pants, tight dark jackets with a row of buttons in front. In these, with their hair trimmed short, the boys looked like midget soldiers or tiny old men. He went to urinate in the brush and washed up in the river. The sun was coming up when he joined the two families at the fireplace behind Alex's cabin. He felt awkward, but they only nodded to him. Alex grinned briefly, satisfied with himself.

The two women sat on chairs by the fireplace, talking quietly, keeping watch over two suckers roasting on an iron grate set over the fire. The suckers were about two feet long, greenish silver in color, the first fish species coming up the rivers each spring. The men sat off to the side near a small table and waved Seton over. Alex's daughter sat on her father's knees. Aaron pointed to an empty chair. On the table stood a bucket with fresh water, a ladle hanging from its rim. Next to it were a stack of plates and a covered dish in enamelware.

"You had a good night?" Aaron asked.

Seton nodded.

"Have you gotten suckers in the Salmon River yet?"

Seton shook his head. "No. Not yet."

"We have been catching them in this river for two weeks," Aaron said. There was a silence. Mary came over and fetched the stack of plates. Aaron pointed to the covered dish on the table. "This is all of o'ppah we have," he said. He was referring to a kind of smoked bread made from kouse roots. "We planned to go into the hills today to get kouse. Get a good supply." He paused. "Are you coming with us?" He looked at Seton. "We will be gone for a week, maybe longer."

Seton nodded. "I'll come."

"We can do some hunting there too," Alex said. "Get some antelope." He paused. "What kind of rifle have you got?"

"A twelve-shot Winchester," Seton said.

"Where did you get it?"

"Elk City. Mother got it for me." He thought about that time they visited the mining town with a group of Lamtama. "She traded two good horses for the rifle and six boxes of cartridges."

There was a pause.

"It's time to eat," Aaron said. He moved his chair close to the table. Mary and Susan brought plates from the fireplace heaped with chunks of roasted fish. Mary took the cloth off the dish filled with slices of kouse bread. The women brought their chairs, and everyone moved to the table. There was a moment of quiet. Seton noticed that the adults sat stiffly erect, eyes closed. He looked at Aaron.

The man brought his hands together in prayer, resting them on the edge of the table. He spoke a long sermon in Nez Perce, as he had learned in Spalding's church. His voice was loud, self-assured, that of a man experienced in leading others in prayer. Seton listened, but the text meant nothing to him. His father had not been a religious man. His mother had believed in the old religion, although she rarely spoke about it. During the three years he had lived at Aaron's place, or in the boarding school, he had seen the daily routine of the Christian Nez Perces. During the seven years he had lived in Hemene's tipi among the Lamtama he had been part of the daily routine of the non-Christian Nez Perces. He saw no deeper meaning in the world of one or the other. He had not heard the coyote speak. Perhaps he was not supposed to hear, he thought. Perhaps what he himself saw of the world around him was all there was to it.

Finally Aaron ended. The adults said, "Amen." Mary handed a plate to Seton and passed the dish with the o'ppah to him. He took a slice of the hard brown bread and ate slowly. He remembered the taste.

"Is there any kouse down there?" Aaron asked with a full mouth.

Seton shook his head. "No." They finished breakfast in silence, the little girl's eyes still following Seton's every move. The women cleaned the table and washed the plates in the river.

"We better get ready," Aaron said.

"Where do we go?" Seton asked.

"To the hills north of Lewiston," Alex said. "We take the wagon and use the ferry to get across the river. There is a road up the big hill now. It was made three years ago."

Seton went to the tipi and got his things ready. He knew the Winchester was loaded, but checked anyway. He went to where the mare was grazing and put the saddle blanket on her back and rocked the saddle into place. He pulled the latigo up and fastened the backcinch. When the mare breathed out, he pulled the strap and buckled it. He slipped the double reins over the mare's lower jaw and let the ends drop to the ground. He brought out the bundle with his bedroll and buckskin jacket and tied it behind the saddle, then went to assist Alex in getting the wagon ready.

The wagon was about twelve feet long and five feet wide. Its top, bottom, and sides were made of three-quarter-inch hardwood planks weathered a dark gray. Up front was a footboard and a seat with a storage compartment underneath. At the rear were tie rings in case horses or cows had to be trailed. The rig rolled on twelve-spoke, iron-clad wheels.

"Where did you get this?" Seton asked.

"In Lewiston," Alex said. "Last year. For the wagon and the two horses to pull it, we traded over a dozen good horses." He paused. "We don't need many horses anymore." The brothers brought the two draft horses from the corral and backed them into place. Seton took his clues from Alex. They hooked up the shafts, ran the traces from the collar hames through the fills back to the doubletree, pulled the reins from the bits through the rings and tossed them over the footboard. Alex took the nigh horse by the bridle and led the span and wagon from the shed to the front of Aaron's cabin. One of the four saddle horses of Aaron's allotment was left behind to graze between the cabins and tipis. Two were saddled for Alex and Aaron, and one was hitched to a tie ring on the wagon. Aaron and Seton placed their rifles with the camping equipment on the wagon and covered them with tule mats. Alex owned no firearm.

When the party moved out, the two women were on the wagon seat, Mary holding the reins, Susan beside her with little Mary on her lap. Alex and Seton rode ahead; Aaron closed the gate and brought up the rear. They moved on the river trail to Lapwai, crossed the creek on the wooden bridge, and went through the agency compound to its southwestern corner where the road from Lewiston came in. They saw two white agency employees and a dozen saddled horses tied to a rail in front of one of the buildings. The road climbed the plateau to the west, overlooking the agency and the Clearwater River. The party moved through bright sunshine on a cool, windy day. They made the ten miles to Lewiston at an easy pace.

The road came down on the southeastern corner of the town, near where, in January 1864, three white bandits were hanged. It had been a great spectacle. People from all over had come to watch, including many Nez Perces from the reservation. Seton, not quite five years old, had seen the hanging with his parents. It had left an indelible impression.

Alex led the party on a side road to the river. There were a few wooden buildings and a white tent near the landing on the north shore. The ferry was a side-railed, flat-bottomed scow that used the river's strong current to move it. This was accomplished by means of a large hawser fastened to a tree on the bank upstream, and block and tackle playing freely on the rope attached to both ends of the scow. When the party arrived, the ferry was in transit from north to south, carrying one wagon and some milk cows. The scow arrived and was unloaded. Mary hollered to the span, and the horses stepped out. The wagon bounced onto the deck. The men rode up behind the wagon and dismounted.

Seton held his mare tight. She had not been on a ferry before. The ferryman was white. He demanded seventy-five cents for the passage. Aaron paid him. The man waved at his helpers, two Indians with short hair, probably from farther west. They laid to, working the ropes, and the scow eased slowly from the bank. The swollen river pushed the scow hard until it nosed to the north landing. The bottom crunched as it swung onto the landing, and Mary hollered and snapped the reins and the span moved out at a fast trot.

The road north up Lewiston Hill negotiated a two-thousand-foot ascent between the upper prairie and the Clearwater Valley below. It was built in 1874 to accommodate "a wagon and eight yoke of cattle." It was a dangerous road, five miles long, with hairpin turns and narrow curves spiraling up the face of the hill. The wagon proceeded slowly. A few times the men dismounted and pushed in support of the draft horses. It took a long time to reach the top of the hill. They halted there to look at the country before them, an immense prairie of rolling hills with evergreens in the breaks and on sweeping curves of ridgebacks. Finally, they moved on for another two miles and made camp in a sheltered nook on upper Hatwai Creek. There were four more camps of reservation Nez Perces within a few miles, people of the *yecéme* band from Potlatch Creek who had also come to dig for kouse.

For seven days Mary and Susan worked dry, rocky hillsides with digging sticks, unearthing a plentiful supply of the carrot-shaped roots. The roots were spread out on mats to dry, the brown outer skin was scraped off, and then they were ground to powder in a mortar. Some of the powder was made into a gruel for meals. Most was formed into square-cornered cakes and baked over a slow fire that transformed it into o'ppah, which remained edible for a long time. Seton and Alex went hunting, while Aaron watched the camp. Seton killed two prong-horn does with his rifle. The meat was a welcome addition to kouse, raw or cooked.

They broke camp on May 15. Traveling down Lewiston Hill with the loaded wagon was more perilous than going up. When the party passed the edge of Lewiston, Seton made a quick trip into town. He rode slowly down Main Street. The house where his father, a black-smith at the Lapwai Agency when he met Wetah, had run a little gun shop was still there. They lived there from the winter of 1861 to the fall of 1867, when his father went away. Behind the gun shop was a small room where his father repaired guns and loaded ammunition. And behind that were two small bedrooms, a living room, and a kitch-en where Seton had lived with his family. Turning around, Seton rode through the little Chinatown along C and D streets, passing the joss house, a secretive place of lanterns, incense, and brass gongs that he spied on as a child. He cast a long look at the places of his childhood, then rode out to rejoin the party.

They made Lapwai in the early afternoon. On the agency grounds they ran into two of the reservation chiefs, Timothy and James Levy. They waved Aaron over. He dismounted and they talked. Seton and Alex sat their horses by the wagon, waiting. When the talk had ended, Aaron mounted and rode up. His face was serious.

"I heard something," he said. "The chiefs who came to the fort,

Joseph, White Goose, Looking Glass, and them, they were on the reservation while we were away. They have agreed to come here. They have chosen areas for their bands. Yesterday they met here with the general. He told them they had thirty days to move here with their horses and cattle." He paused. "Thirty days. That is not enough."

"Where is Toohoolhoolzote?" Seton asked.

"The general released him a few days ago."

"Was he here, too?" Seton asked.

"No," Aaron said. "He stayed away." There was a pause. "More soldiers have come," Aaron said. "One company of horse soldiers under Captain Trimble, they say. Two more companies of horse soldiers are camped on the Wallowa River." He pointed west.

"What does that mean?" Alex asked.

"I don't know," Aaron said. After a pause, he added, "Four days from now, in the evening, there is a meeting here of people of the downriver bands. We'll go there and hear for ourselves."

On May 19, three men stood in front of the administration building. John Monteith, in the middle, was flanked on the left by Alpowa Jim, on the right by James Reuben. A thin, self-confident figure, the agent was dressed in a dark suit and a white shirt with a bow tie. His jacket was open and displayed the curve of a gold watch chain.

Monteith had been nominated by the board of the Presbyterian church after the U.S. government assigned the Nez Perce reservation to the Presbyterians, and had served as agent since early 1871. He was the tenth agent at Lapwai within a period of fifteen years, since the treaty of 1855. In his early thirties, he had a face with a high forehead and a receding line of thin brown hair, a long, lumped nose, and penetrating eyes, his small mouth hidden by a mustache and scrawny beard. Monteith's father was a Presbyterian minister in the Willamette Valley. The son was a religious zealot, committed to bringing the nontreaty bands under his control and stamping out their religion. He stood in a stiff pose, a white man representing a church and a faraway government, a hundred dark faces of reservation Nez Perces in a half circle before him. He stood as if looking in a mirror, arranging himself for a photographer.

They had come from all parts of the reservation, from Potlatch, Lapwai, and Lawyers creeks from upstream on the river as far as Kamiah on the middle Clearwater. They had come in wagons and on horseback, band chiefs and headmen, preachers and men to whom some significance was attached by others or who attached some significance to themselves. They had put up a temporary camp on the edge of the agency buildings, near the mill and the river. Aaron had come because he was a preacher in the Lapwai church and was looked to by others in the community near Lapwai. He had brought Alex and Seton because they were family. Seton had been scrutinized by some of the men because of his long hair. He was not one of them, but Aaron waved off any disapproval.

Monteith raised his right arm and began to speak. Talk among the men sitting on the ground in front of him ebbed away. It was a calm evening, and his voice carried well. Seton, perhaps the only one among the listening men who did not need Reuben's translation, spoke English better than the dead chief's son.

"You have asked me for this meeting," Monteith began. "You want to know what has happened. I will tell you." He looked around while Reuben translated.

"The chiefs of the nontreaty bands traveled through the reservation," he continued. "The general and I, we were with them. They have seen everything." He paused. "They are going to come on the reservation with their bands. They said that." He waited. "They have to hurry now. The general told them they have thirty days. If they have not come on the reservation in thirty days, the general will send troops to bring them in."

A murmur ran through the files of the Nez Perces. Aaron looked at Seton and nodded with a serious face.

"The chiefs have chosen where their bands will be located," Monteith said. He looked along the faces in the front row where the more prominent of the reservation chiefs sat. He tried to give his voice an official tone. "We worked locations out, I and the general. We came to an agreement."

He waited for the translation. James Reuben, flushed with the pride of his service at this meeting, spoke with a strong voice.

"I will tell you where these locations are," Monteith went on. He spoke slowly so that every word was understood. "The Paloos band will settle on the Clearwater just east of Lapwai. Joseph and the Wallowas settle on the middle Clearwater downstream from Kamiah. Looking Glass stays where he is, on the Middle Fork of the Clearwater. The bands of White Goose and Toohoolhoolzote settle upstream from Looking Glass."

The ranks of the reservation people began to protest even before Reuben finished the translation. There were a few shouts. Monteith raised his arm and waved, trying to get attention. A neighbor of Aaron's, Billy Owen, stood up.

"You said the Palooses will settle just east of here," he shouted. "They can't! That's where we are. We have our allotments there. You gave them to us. There is no room left for anyone else."

A strong murmur of agreement swept the crowd. Aaron stood. His face had hardened. "Billy is right. This is our land where you said the Palooses are going. You can't give them our land. They must go elsewhere."

After Reuben translated, Monteith shook his head. "There is no other place for them," he said over the din. "We have to move closer together so all Nez Perces can live on the reservation."

"We agreed to allotments, to stay on small places, when we made that last treaty," Aaron said. "Now you ask us to give away even more. We have given away all we can. We can't give away more. I tell you, there is no room for the Palooses where we are."

Seton watched his uncle, surprised. He knew Aaron as a man subservient to ministers and agents, who had modeled himself after white clerics, yet now he spoke in opposition to white authority.

Reuben was losing his earlier confidence. The debate unsettled him, and his translations became inaccurate, even false. He began to substitute terms that changed the meaning of sentences, and he knew it. So did Seton.

A young man who looked like a twin brother to Reuben got up. He was dressed exactly like Reuben. Both were clothed like the agent—dark suit, vest, white shirt and tie, even a watch chain. He had a smooth, round face, with short hair neatly parted on the right side.

"Who is he?" Seton whispered to Alex.

"Lawyer. Young Lawyer," Alex whispered back.

He was the son of the first head chief of the Christian Nez Perces, appointed by Governor Isaac Stevens in 1855. Old Lawyer had died in early 1876. One of Spalding's first converts, he was the downriver chief most responsible for the passage of the treaty of 1863 that created the rift between the Christian and the non-Christian factions of the tribe. The Lawyer band resided in and around Kamiah on the middle Clearwater.

"My father has done more for our people than anyone else," Lawyer said. "Because of him and a few others we live in peace on our land. We have farms and gardens. In Kamiah we have a church, a mill, and a school. We grow our own food. In most years we sell vegetables and grain to white towns. We are protected by horse soldiers. Our children grow up without fear." He paused. "If my father were alive, this would be his saddest day. He worked hard so that our people live by the holy book our brother Henry Spalding brought us many years ago, that we live by the laws Jesus taught, that we live the new life."

He paused again, waiting for Reuben to catch up.

"Now the heathens are upon us. They are going to surround us on every side. They are coming with their filthy ways and will laugh at us and our religion. They are evil and dangerous. Their horses will trample our gardens, their young men will assault our women and daughters. My father wanted this to be our country, our country alone, the country of people who accepted the Lord. He made the treaty with the government years ago to keep the heathen bands out. 'Let them stay where they are or go elsewhere,' he said to me. That's why he made that treaty. He wanted to protect us from them."

He stood looking at the ground. He seemed to be crying. Voices rose in support from the gathering. "We cannot live with them side by side," he said finally. "We will not change our ways, they will not change theirs. There will be conflict. They should not be allowed into our country." After a pause, he added, "If they come, we need protection."

The agent stepped forward and swung his arms. He reminded Seton of a crow flapping its wings. The man was visibly shaken. He had not expected dissent, had not understood the depth of antagonism between the two divisions of the tribe. It took some time before the crowd let him speak.

"That treaty," Monteith declared loudly, "was not for the downriver Nez Perces alone. It was for all the Nez Perces."

He waited for the translation.

"There is plenty of land on the reservation for all. When the nontreaty bands come in, they will have to change their ways. They must settle down, live in permanent homes, raise food from the earth, plant and harvest as we do. They will not be allowed to go to the buffalo country. They must stay here." He paused. "There are more and more white people coming to this part of our great country, building farms, building towns. If the nontreaty bands continue to roam over the country, there will be trouble. There will be war. This is why they must stay here."

He paused, waiting. Finally he said, "This is why we must make room for them on the reservation."

There were angry faces as Reuben translated.

In the front row Timothy stood up, son of Old Timothy, one of three downriver chiefs who had traveled to Washington in 1868 to sign amendments to the treaty of 1863. Lawyer and Jason had been the other two chiefs in that delegation. "I heard something at the agency," he said slowly. "I heard there are only sixty allotments of twenty acres each left on the reservation." He paused. "How can you split sixty allotments among the seven or eight hundred people that are coming here?" He sat down.

The crowd fell silent.

"We will work it out," Monteith said. "We have to move closer together, as I said before. We all have to give something."

Timothy stood again.

"They bring thousands of horses, hundreds of cattle," he said. "Where are these going to go? There is not enough grazing room for so many animals. What grazing there is we need for ourselves." He turned and looked over the gathering. Men nodded in agreement. He looked at Monteith again. "What will you do about this?" He sat down.

Monteith waited for the translation. It gave him time to think. He looked uncomfortable. "There won't be thousands of horses, hundreds of cattle," he said. "The nontreaty bands were only given thirty days to move their stock here. They can't do that. There is too much country to cover in that time. And the rivers are too hard to cross. They will have to leave most of their stock behind."

A voice said, "Herds they leave they can get later, when the rivers are down."

Monteith shook his head. "No," he said coldly. "What they leave behind now will be lost to them. Whatever animals they leave will become the property of whoever wants to take them."

"Thousands of horses," someone said in disbelief.

Monteith shrugged. "They won't need them here. Not anymore. You said yourself there is not enough space for so many horses and cattle."

There was a silence. Alex looked at Seton and shook his head. Seton whispered, "The suyapu planned this. They want trouble."

Once again Lawyer stood up in the front row. "I still say these people should not be allowed to come here. This has always been our country, ours, downriver people. These other bands never had any claim to it. We don't want to mix with them. There will be trouble if they come." He sat down.

"They will come," Monteith said testily. "It has been arranged. The government has ordered them to come here. There is a treaty. I cannot change it. The general will use his soldiers if there is trouble."

He looked at the sullen faces in front of him. "We have to move closer together. Washington says so."

There was a silence. Billy Owen, Aaron's neighbor, spoke again. "The Palooses cannot come on our allotments." He pointed east with his chin. "We have just enough for ourselves; we have no land to give away." He paused. "The Palooses have always lived way down on the Snake River, away from us. They belong there, not here. I say we won't let them in."

Billy Williams, a preacher who belonged to one of the lower Clearwater bands, cleared his throat. He was an elderly man, respected on the reservation. "The holy book says we should help each other in His name," he said. He made the sign of the cross over his chest. "The nontreaties are our people too. We used to be the same, they and us. Back in time, in the time of our grandfathers and our grandfathers' fathers, we were one people. We always shared with each other. No one ever went hungry. Now we are different from them. We have accepted the Lord. The Lord is with us. The Lord is with us now. The Lord says that we should help our brothers in their need."

He paused while Reuben translated. There was a murmur of agreement. "We shall help our brothers, our kin. We will give what they need. The Lord is merciful. He asks us to be forgiving. We will bring our brothers home. The Lord will help us to bring them into His house. Amen."

After a long silence Jonah Hayes spoke. He was the new head chief appointed by Monteith a month earlier.

"What Billy Williams said is true. We hoped it would not come true, but we have to accept what the government says. We must make room for those who are coming. They need our help. The Lord will bless us for what we give them." He paused. "I say we stop arguing among ourselves. We shall try to make it good for everyone. We will welcome them and teach them what we know."

The meeting ended. Monteith had prevailed, but two factions had developed among the people who watched and listened, one voiced by Lawyer and Billy Owen, the other by Billy Williams and Jonah Hayes.

Both views would be carried to the distant corners of the reservation to be debated over and over again.

As people began to disperse, one of the reservation headmen, a relative of Chief Joseph, an elderly man called Captain John, waved Alex over. The two talked while Aaron and Seton waited. Seton noticed that the headman observed him carefully. Captain John and Alex shook hands when they parted.

"Captain John asked me to do something for him," Alex said. "He has a contract with a Lewiston merchant to take a mule train to Elk City. He has to go to a funeral and can't do it. He asked me. I said yes. You can come too." He looked at Seton. "I told him you had been to Elk City." A pause. "We get money for this."

Seton bent and picked up a twig. He started to chew on it. Should he ride to the Salmon country and tell them what he had heard here? Wouldn't the Lamtama already know, or at least suspect? Hemene might need him. He thought of Itsepit and little Tsacope, all the older people and children who would have to cross the swollen Salmon River in hide boats pulled by ponies and steadied by young men swimming with them. He should be there to help Teeweeyownah. And yet it would be something to ride from Lewiston to Elk City, across and beyond the reservation, even with mules. Perhaps the Lamtama could wait. He heard himself say, "Yes."

FOUR

ABOVE THE DOCK ON LEWISTON'S WATERFRONT, IN a row of wooden buildings, sat the store and warehouse of the Lewiston Mercantile, Frank Robinson & Sons. A wooden sidewalk ran along the front of the buildings but left an open space at the warehouse. Lewiston was the last landing site upstream from Portland on the Columbia–Snake River route, and Robinson's was one of the main supply depots for mining towns and evolving cattle towns in the Idaho and Rocky Mountain interior. Goods delivered by steamboat were transported from here by mule trains and freight wagons to places near and far.

Alex and Seton arrived in the early morning of May 25. They tied their horses to a rail and walked up the stairs to the sidewalk and into the Robinson main office. The head of the company, Frank Robinson, a burly man in his fifties, looked up from his desk. He glanced at the two Nez Perces, Alex wearing a hat, dressed as a townsman but for moccasins, Seton dressed in woolen pants and a leather jacket. Robinson nodded to Alex, who had worked for him before, but looked Seton over, his eyes caught by the shoulder-length hair.

"Captain John told me that you would come," Robinson said, looking at Alex. "Who's this?" He tipped his head toward Seton.

"My brother," Alex said. "Seton. He is staying on our place."

Robinson nodded, measuring Seton. "Does he know how to work with mules?" He obviously didn't think Seton could understand him.

Seton spoke up. "No," he said. "But I've worked with horses since I was a boy. Alex can show me what I don't know."

Robinson raised his eyebrows. "Where did you learn English so well? In school?"

"My father was a gunsmith," Seton said quietly. "We lived here." He paused. "You might have known him. Gary Seton." He felt strange speaking his father's name.

Robinson thought for a moment. "Yes," he said. "I remember him. Tall man, a good man. Eight years ago, maybe nine." He paused. "I remember his wife too. Good-looking woman. Nez Perce." His eyes seemed to focus on something far away. "Your mother?"

Seton nodded.

"What happened to Gary?" Robinson asked. "He left suddenly, didn't he?"

"I don't know," Seton said.

"Your mother, where is she?"

"She died. Last year."

"Sorry to hear that." Robinson shook his head. "What brings you to Aaron's place?"

"Alex and I met at the fort. He wants me to live at his place."

"Were you at that meeting with the general?"

"Yes," Seton said.

"What band are you with?"

"White Goose."

"Robinson thought for a while. "White Goose. That's the band down on the Salmon, isn't it?"

Seton nodded.

"Well, everybody says they're coming on the reservation. They are, aren't they?"

Seton shrugged.

"They said they would," Alex said.

"The newspapers say so too," Robinson said. A quick grin flashed over his face. "If they say so, it must be true." Serious again, he looked at Alex. "It's all right if your brother goes along. But," he pointed a finger at Alex, "I hold you responsible."

Alex nodded. Robinson looked from one to the other. "You are paid fifteen dollars each for the drive. Is that all right? I'll pay when you get back."

The brothers nodded. "Yes, we know," Alex said.

"In the warehouse they're putting loads together," Robinson said. "Go help them. Leave your horses in the corral. The train leaves tomorrow morning."

He got up from behind the desk and shook hands with them, pressing hard, the white man's way. The two walked out and mounted. They rode a few hundred yards, going past the last house on the waterfront to where the pole corrals of the Robinson outfit stood, a smaller one for horses, a larger one for the mules. There were nine horses and about ninety mules. Alex opened the gate, and they rode in and closed the gate behind them. They dismounted and took saddles and gear and bedrolls and Seton's rifle scabbard with the Winchester to a saddle room. On one side of the mule corral was a long shed where pack saddles and equipment were stacked. An old man in blue overalls was working in the shed, repairing cinches. He recognized Alex and waved. The two Nez Perces looked over the quiet drove of mules and walked back across the road and through the bay into the warehouse.

This was a deep, two-story building, half filled with wooden boxes, barrels, gunnysacks, tools, tins, and smaller packages. Two men were working inside the bay, stacking loads of cargo from a large pile of merchandise behind them. One was a lanky, tough-looking fellow in his early sixties, the other a tall boy of fifteen with a freckled face and a wild mop of hair.

Alex knew both well and shook hands. He introduced Seton. The older man was Cyrus McNally, who had drifted into Lewiston after the gold rush of 1861, tried his luck on Orofino Creek, and, after the gold played out in 1867, worked as a pack master for the Robinson mercantile. The fifteen-year-old, already a skilled hand at chores around the warehouse, was Frank Robinson's youngest son, Cecil. He had been teamed with the experienced Cyrus to learn the art of running a mule train operation.

"Seton is my brother," Alex said. "We talked with your father. He said that we ride with you to Elk City." He glanced at Cyrus McNally.

"If it is all right with him, it's all right with me," Cyrus said. He turned and went back to work. Cecil Robinson looked with big eyes at Seton. Here was one of those wild Nez Perces, the ones who roamed the country with their pretty horses and rode across the Rockies to hunt buffalo and fight other Indians in the Plains. This was no reservation Indian. This was a cutthroat Indian. He stared at the elkhorn handle of Seton's belt knife, the blade hidden in the beaded sheath.

"Have you been to the Plains?"

Seton looked at him and nodded.

"You've hunted buffalo there?"

"Yes," Seton answered.

"You fought in battles with other tribes?"

"No." Seton paused. "I saw two battles, but I did no fighting."

"You speak English well," Cecil said. "How did you learn it?"

"I grew up in this place," Seton said brusquely.

The pack master had grown impatient. "Listen. You talk some other time. We have work to do. Tomorrow we have to be on the road. Get to it!" For the rest of the day Alex, Seton, and Cecil worked under the pack master's orders. The cargo for Elk City was divided into separate loads not to exceed 250 pounds. The cargo consisted of soft, canvas-covered packages, gunnysacks, wooden boxes containing a wide range of merchandise from tobacco products to opium or staples as well as exotic goods, and barrels with salt pork, salt fish, molasses, whiskey, flour, and other items. This would be the second mule train of the Robinson outfit going to Elk City that spring.

Elk City was a mining town in the Clearwater Mountains with a population of about two hundred whites and eight hundred Chinese miners. The Chinese had flocked to Elk City in 1870 and made it the largest Chinese community in Idaho. Work conditions were hard. Heavy snowfall in winter and high water in spring limited the mining season to the few months from June to October.

The four men finished in early evening. They had stacked loads for thirty-seven mules. Much of the cargo was destined for Chinese consumption and included imports from Asia. In the big kitchen back of the store the four were fed steaks, biscuits, and beans. Alex and Seton spent the night by the roaring river where their horses nibbled the new grass.

They broke camp at first light. They washed in the river, saddled the horses, and moved out. But the large double door of the warehouse was still locked. They sat on the stairs by the sidewalk and watched the river churn its yellow floodwaters toward the Columbia and the sea.

The town did not wake before sunup. When the golden rim of the sun cast its first rays over the plateau to the east and the town, Cyrus squeezed one wing of the warehouse door open and waved them in. Cecil already sat at the kitchen table. A heavyset white-haired woman served eggs and freshly baked biscuits. The men ate slowly, concentrating on the food; there would be no other meal until evening.

After breakfast the pack master and Cecil walked to the horse corral and saddled their horses and met Alex and Seton at the mule corral. Cyrus put a halter on one of the two bell horses provisioned among the mules, an old white mare, and went to the saddle shed and got the strap with the attached bell and put it over the mare's neck. The mules milled around and bunched in the far corner of the corral. They knew what was coming.

The men worked in pairs, one on the near—left—side of the mule, the other on the off side. Cyrus and Alex each cut a mule from the herd and led it to the saddle shed. Seton worked with Alex, Cecil with Cyrus. A saddle pad was placed on the animal's back before the blanket and the packsaddle were put on. The cinch attached to the lower end of the off side of the packsaddle was thrown under the animal's belly to the near-side packer. Alex slipped it through a ring on the lower end of the near side of the packsaddle, pulled tight, and tied it. The pack-saddle was further secured by the crupper, a leather band attached to the back of the packsaddle that ran around the mules' buttocks under the tail, and the front piece, a leather band attached to the front of the packsaddle and slung around the animal's chest. Together the bands served to prevent the packsaddle, once it was loaded, from slipping forward or backward.

Seton caught on fast. Forty-one mules were cut from the herd and saddled, thirty-seven to carry merchandise, the remaining four to carry supplies for the men, and canvas tarps to protect goods in case of rainy weather. It took the men one hour to saddle the mules. When they were finished, Cyrus took the halter of the bell mare, threw the gate open, and walked out. The mules followed the bell as they had been trained to do. Cyrus walked the train to the warehouse, the men passing him on horseback, Cecil leading Cyrus's mount.

It took another hour to pack the mules. Loads were secured with the diamond hitch. The lash rope that tied the load formed a diamond pattern over the packsaddle. When the packing was finished, blinders were placed over the animals' eyes. Before the train moved out, Frank Robinson took Cyrus aside for some final instructions. The men mounted. Of the four, only Seton had brought a rifle. Cyrus and Cecil carried holstered side arms. They waved. A few townspeople stood by, looking on. Cyrus took the long halter of the bell horse and led off, Cecil beside him, the mule train forming a line behind. Alex and Seton rode drag. With the jingling of the bell, the head of the train turned a corner and the line passed through Main Street and gained the road leading southeast toward Fort Lapwai.

On a cool, sunny day they climbed the plateau east of town. It took the train two and a half hours to cover the twelve miles to the military post. The mules were rested but not eager. Although they followed the bell, occasionally drag tails had to be pushed on by the drag riders. When they struck the Lapwai road, they turned south on Lapwai Creek on the rutted road to Kamiah. Near the mouth of Mission Creek they were passed by two wagons pulled by four-horse teams. The two white men driving the wagons stared coldly at the Nez Perces but talked briefly with Cyrus and Cecil. Seton learned later that they were teamsters who carried cargo from Lewiston to a store in Mount Idaho.

So far they had traveled through dense open grasslands with evergreens in breaks and ravines. Farther down the road they came into a ponderosa forest of tall trees with an open ground cover of grasses and occasional shrubs. After the train had covered twenty miles, Cyrus called them to look for a campsite. Camp was made by Lapwai Creek in a grove of cottonwoods. The air was sweet with the scent of pines and cedars.

The camp woke at first light. After breakfast the mules were brought in and packed. The bell mare was watered, horses were saddled. Cyrus and Cecil led the long line of heavily packed animals, with Alex and Seton again riding drag. They went back to the wagon road and turned southeast, still following Lapwai Creek. After eight miles they came to the knee of the creek where the road doubled back and climbed out of the ponderosa forest to the northern tongue of the Camas Prairie above.

The Camas Prairie was the heart of the old Nez Perce lands. The bands of the people lived in a circle around it. Annually in early summer they gathered in camps in the prairie to dig camas bulbs and celebrate life and the new season. The prairie was a high plateau thirty-five miles long in a southeastern direction, twenty miles wide. On average 3,500 feet high, the plateau was like a lake of grass embedded in mountain ranges that surged a thousand or two thousand feet over it. The plateau was famous for its patches of camas plants, the profusion of flowers, and its rich wildlife—antelope, deer, elk, wolves, and wandering grizzlies.

A dense grassland, the Camas Prairie was a land of low, swinging hills, the carpet of green grasses dotted with white, red, pink, and blue flowers, and the purple blossoms of camas lilies. The mule train moved in the great quiet of the prairie, the loudest sound the jingling of the lead mare's bell. Once Seton and Alex saw wolves running antelopes in the distance. They camped for the night by the headwaters of Big Canyon Creek, which flowed through the grassland from below Mason Butte. The sky had darkened, and fearing rain, they covered some of the packs with canvas. There was rain during the night, but morning came with a brilliant sun and blue sky.

On the third day they came to the fork in the road, the tracks to Kamiah running east, the wagon road to Norton House and Grangeville continuing south. They took the route south. On the next day they came to Norton House, a way station on the wagon road, but moved on without breaking gait. The house and tavern stood on a low hill, and below it, in a crease in the soft swing of the land, stood the one solitary cottonwood in all of Camas Prairie. Nez Perces called this special tree *cupcup*. Seton rode back to it after the mule train had passed. He went through a small herd of dark-colored cattle, dismounted, and placed a few beads in a hollow where a root broke through the surface of the ground. Once, years ago, when he had come by this tree with his mother, Wetah had shown him how to place a gift with a prayer. He did not pray this time, but he thought of his mother. When he rode back, Alex was curious about what he'd done, but didn't ask. That night they camped on the north shore of a little lake from which the thin rivulet of Cottonwood Creek emerged, meandering north and east toward the Clearwater River.

When they rounded the lake in the morning they came upon a broad trail cut only a few days before. Seton rode a ways along it. A hundred horses or more had passed this way, coming out of the coulee of Threemile Creek from the direction of the Clearwater, going southwest. Mixed with hoofprints were the drag marks made by tipi poles, deep cuts carved into the soft ground. Alex had stayed with the moving pack train. "Who were they?" he asked when Seton caught up with him.

Seton shrugged. "Looking Glass's band, I think. Must be them." He paused. "Perhaps they go to tepahlewam, Rocky Canyon." He was right. A mile later they saw riders in the distance, coming their way. Seton halted, waiting. The riders approached at a lope, then held in their horses and stopped before him. They were two older men and a young man, two middle-aged women and a girl of perhaps ten. The women were leading five packhorses. The two older men had rifle cases slung across their backs. The young man carried a bow-and-arrow case. The horses they rode were appaloosas, the packhorses were not. Seton knew the men. They were of Looking Glass's band. He raised his right arm.

One of the men, Kalowet, did the same. He shifted in the saddle, looking toward the string of mules drawing away. Then he looked at Seton. "Eh, cousin," he said. His face cracked into a smile. "What are you doing here? You are running mules now?" He chuckled.

Seton tried to smile. "No," he said. "I'm helping out my brother, Alex."

"Alex?"

"Alex Elwekin. My older brother."

"Elwekin—I knew him," Kalowet said. "I forgot about his son. Where does he live?"

"On James Aaron's place," Seton said. "By the agency."

"He had to be somewhere," Kalowet said. "He's not with us." He chuckled again. "You are with Hemene, aren't you? Or are you going to stay with your brother?"

Seton thought for a moment. "No, I don't think I'll stay." He paused. "Where are you going? I saw a big trail a mile this way." He pointed with his chin.

"Yes," Kalowet said. "Our people. They went to tepahlewam. All the bands are coming together. Our people went there four days ago." He paused. "We butchered two cows, and we're taking meat to the camp."

"What do you know about White Goose and Toohoolhoolzote and them?" Seton asked. "Are they at tepahlewam now?"

"I don't know," Kalowet said. "It will be hard for them to bring their horses across the Salmon. They will lose some." He paused. "Most of our horses are still on Clearwater. Where we are the river is not that rough." He paused again. "For the Wallowas it will be really bad. They have to get across the Snake."

The man next to Kalowet, Three Hawks, spoke up. "Where are you going with the mules?"

"Elk City," Seton said.

"Feeding the Chinamen, eh?" Kalowet said. He smiled. "We're leaving." He raised his right hand. Seton nudged the mare to the side and let them pass. One woman led two, the other three, of the pack-horses. The point rider urged his horse into a lope, and the others followed. Once the little girl looked back.

Seton pushed the mare into a gallop to catch up with Alex. Before them lay the hamlet of Grangeville, started a year before on Nez Perce land without Nez Perce permission. It consisted of a grange hall, a mill, a boarding house, a blacksmith shop, and two family cabins. The place lay at a fork in the road. One track led south toward the Salmon River country and the mining towns of Florence and Warren. The other track led east to the Clearwater on one of the old Nez Perce trails to the buffalo country; Elk City was on that track. It bypassed the hamlet called Mount Idaho, which had recently sprung up three miles southeast of Grangeville. Mount Idaho claimed a saloon, two general stores, and a new jail. Both towns served a few ranches that had infiltrated the southern corner of the Camas Prairie. The mule train wound through Grangeville and took the eastern spur.

For three more days they traveled on the trail until they reached Elk City. The ponderosa pine forest had given way to a dense evergreen forest of Douglas and grand firs. The train arrived in the early evening of June 2.

The town was spread along Elk Creek in a narrow valley beneath mountains rising to seven thousand feet. Snowfields still lingered. Among other major buildings, it had two general stores, two saloons, two boarding houses, a blacksmith shop and a gun shop; no school, no church, but a joss house for Chinese worshippers. A sprawl of cabins and shacks had crept up the slopes, interspersed with mine shafts and mounds of tailings. The Robinson cargo was destined for the John Cullen store. A crowd, including many Chinese, gathered when the train came to a halt in front of the store. There was cheering. People rushed out to assist in removing loads and taking them inside a warehouse. The mules and horses were corralled behind the store, fed and watered. It took hours for the storeowner, a bearded giant of a man, to match the cargo with the Robinson invoice. Long after dark he finished and invited the Robinson men to supper. He invited Cyrus and Cecil to stay in his house. He offered the saddle room in the corral to the Nez Perces. They slept there, close to their horses.

They stayed four days in Elk City, three days longer than expected. Alex and Seton were not told the reason for the delay. They guessed it had to do with receiving payment. Seton took Alex to the gun shop where Wetah had bought the rifle for him in 1875. The two walked the streets and looked at strange sights, strange faces, few friendly. They looked into the dimly lit saloons with their mirrors, bars, and hard-bitten prostitutes, and walked away, glad not to be part of this. Finally, on the morning of June 7, the Robinson mule train pulled out of Elk City on the trail back to Lewiston. Only a few mules were packed, mainly with the pelts of animals trapped during the winter. Cecil led one mule personally. Alex told Seton it carried the payment for the cargo, bags of gold dust and silver coins.

The return journey to Lewiston over the same route was a day shorter than the way out. Throughout the journey Cyrus and Cecil had stayed together by themselves, as if an invisible line was drawn between whites and Nez Perces. The two parties worked and ate together but hardly talked. The segregation was most obvious during the day. Cyrus and Cecil always rode together at the head of the train; Alex and Seton always rode drag. Cecil, although curious about Seton and the nontreaty Indians, did not seek another conversation with him. Cecil watched Seton and his sleek appaloosa horse, uncertain what to think. In his mind Indians were either cowards or killers, or both. Seton seemed neither one or the other, but how could one tell? Cecil saw Alex as a reservation Indian. Their teeth had been pulled by the authorities a long time ago. How else could they have agreed to let the gold and silver deposits in their country pass to white folks? Cyrus regarded the reservation Nez Perces as cowards. About the others he wasn't sure. Perhaps they were cowards too. After all, they had never raised a weapon against whites, even when some of their people had been murdered by white interlopers.

They reached Lewiston at noon on June 13, corralled the mules and stacked packsaddles and equipment. A nod, and Alex and Seton rode off. In the office of the mercantile Frank Robinson paid each of the brothers the fifteen silver dollars agreed upon. A handshake, a nod. They left and rode through town and took the road to the agency, reaching Aaron's allotment in late afternoon.

In the early afternoon of the following day Aaron rode to Lapwai Agency. He returned a few hours later, unsaddled the horse, and slapped it on the rump. When it walked toward the river, he joined Alex and Seton, who sat near Alex's cabin watching him. Aaron's face was pensive.

"The general has come back this morning," he said. "At the agency they said he came with the boat to Lewiston and went on to the fort." They sat in silence, thinking.

"What about the Paloos band?" Alex asked at last. "Where are they? Are they not supposed to come here?"

Aaron shrugged. "Yes. They are supposed to come here. We don't want them, but Monteith said they will settle here somewhere." He pointed with his chin in different directions. "There. There. Somewhere. I don't know where. On this side of the river there is no room for them. You were there when we talked about it at the agency." He looked from Alex to Seton.

"Where are they then?" Alex asked.

"They are at tepahlewam with the other bands, or so I have heard,"

Aaron said. He looked toward the river. Beyond the willows an osprey hovered above the water, then plunged, white plumage shining in the sun. "They came up the Snake and crossed the Clearwater near Lewiston. Maybe ten days ago. They took the road and went by the fort. We did not see them. They came with a big bunch of horses, someone said. They lost a few when they crossed." He paused. "We heard, though, that the Wallowas lost a lot of horses and almost all of their cattle. There are some bad white people over there. They drove the cattle off, many horses too. That was before the Wallowas could round them up. They left mares with young foals on the west side of the Snake. None of the foals would have made it across. All were stolen by whites. The river killed many horses in the crossing." He paused. "Maybe two thousand horses got through. That is half of what they had. The Wallowas are very angry." There was a silence.

"Why is the general here?" Seton asked.

Aaron shrugged. "I think tomorrow is the day the nontreaties have to be on the reservation. The general gave them thirty days to move, remember? I guess he is here to make sure that they do." He paused. "He said he would send soldiers after them if they are not here in time."

"What do they think at the agency?" Alex asked.

"About what?"

"Why they are not on the reservation yet," Alex said.

"No one at the agency knows. They know that the nontreaties are still at tepahlewam. They know that they are angry. They know that the general is waiting at the fort. That's all." The three men sat quietly, the rumbling of the river in their ears.

"They'll come, the upriver bands," Aaron said. "They know that they can't fight the soldiers."

Around noon on the next day, June 15, a rider galloped up the sandy track from the agency. At Aaron's place he halted the nervous horse briefly, delivered his message across the fence, and hurried on. The rider was Joe Albert, a young man who lived with his uncle near Fort Lapwai. His father, Weesculatat, was a member of Chief Joseph's Wallowa band. In his excitement Joe Albert struggled with words. "They are killing on the Salmon. The warriors are killing people. On the Salmon. Three men have come from the camp. They are at the agency." He pointed. "The general is there too. They want you at the agency! Hurry!"

Aaron, who had run toward the fence, stood stiffly, following the messenger with his eyes. There was a look of shock on his face when Alex and Seton joined him.

"What is it?" Alex asked.

"He said the warriors are killing people on the Salmon River," Aaron said. "He said there are men at the agency who come from the camp. He said we must come to the agency." He looked from one to the other. He bit his lip.

Alex shook his head. "I don't believe it."

"He said to hurry," Aaron said. "Come. We have to ride."

They went for the horses and saddled up. Mounted, they spoke briefly with the women. Under a bright sun they urged their horses to a fast lope. When they reached the bridge over Lapwai Creek they saw dozens of Nez Perces riding up the road. A crowd had gathered in front of the main agency building. Horses were tied up everywhere. Aaron, Alex, and Seton rode to the south side of the building and sat their horses, looking over people who stood in front of them.

On the broad porch of the office building, five steps above the ground, stood a group of white men facing three agency Nez Perces. Among the whites, Seton recognized the Cut Arm general, the tall captain, David Perry, who had arrested Toohoolhoolzote at the Fort Lapwai meeting, the agent, John Monteith, his brother, Charles, and Perrin Whitman. Off to the side stood an official-looking white man he did not know. He was Indian inspector Erwin Watkins, who had arrived with the general in the morning for an inspection tour of the reservation.

One of the three young agency Indians standing on the steps of the porch was talking.

"Who are they?" Seton asked Alex in a low voice.

"The boy is Nat Webb. The one in the middle is John Lawyer. Mitchell, he is the one who does the talking."

Mitchell spoke fast in the downriver dialect. Whitman bent forward and listened intently. He asked Mitchell to repeat some words. He nodded when the young man had answered. He began to translate.

"He says they visited the Split Rock camp of the nontreaty bands. They left there this morning. They could not have left earlier because they were afraid for their lives." He paused. "He says yesterday three warriors rode into the camp singing war songs. They had killed two white men by the Salmon River. They had been looking for a man named Ott, Larry Ott. They could not find him and killed two other men."

Whitman looked toward the general. "He says the three warriors are Wahlitits, Sarpsis Ilppilp, and Swan Necklace." He looked back to Mitchell. Mitchell nodded.

Alex bent toward Seton. "You know them?" he whispered. Seton said he did.

"Which band do they belong to?" the general asked, his cold voice suppressing anger. Whitman translated.

"White Goose band," Mitchell said.

"Of course," the general said. "What happened then?"

"The camp split up. Most of the people went east to the Clearwater River." He looked from the general to Whitman. "Only two tipis remained at Split Rock. The one of Chief Joseph and the one of his brother, Ollokot. Some warriors stayed with them. We stayed too. We were afraid to leave."

"Chief Joseph, what did he do?" the general asked. He waited impatiently for the translation of his question and the answer.

"He was not a part of it. He was not in camp when the three men went out to kill. His wife gave birth in that camp. He and Ollokot were away butchering some of their cattle for meat." There was a silence.

"The killing stopped after the two white men were killed?" the general asked.

Mitchell's hands flew in a gesture of frustration. He looked at the general. He spoke fast. Whitman translated slowly. "We don't know. We saw that a bunch of warriors went away with the three who had killed. They rode south."

There was a silence. The white men on the porch stood rigid, faces blank. From across the river came the piercing call of a red-tailed hawk.

At last the general said, "Where are Chief Joseph and his brother now?"

Mitchell waited for the translation.

"They went where the camp had gone, east. We heard the camp is at sapachesap, Drive In place."

John Monteith spoke up when Whitman finished. "This place is on the reservation! What does that mean? Does it mean the nontreaties have come in after all? Are the killings only acts of a few young bucks?" He looked at the general. "If it is true, what these men have said, it seems the chiefs have distanced themselves and their bands from the murderers."

"We don't know yet," Howard said. "We must find out. The killers must be apprehended and punished. I have two companies of First Cavalry ready. They'll move out as soon as I get pack mules from Lewiston."

Monteith was disappointed and angry. He had expected the inspector from Washington to witness his greatest triumph as an agent: the peaceful removal of the nontreaties, after years of futile disputes and bitter wrangling, and their arrival on reservation lands. Instead, the inspector might have arrived at the beginning of a war. Monteith tried to put a hopeful face on the situation. "Yes," he said. "But let me contact Joseph and the chiefs. If they don't want war, they must give up the murderers. Do you agree?"

"It won't hurt," the general said curtly. "But my soldiers will march."

Monteith nodded. He turned to Whitman. "Tell Jonah Hayes to come up here. I want him to ride to Joseph's camp." Whitman searched for the downriver head chief in the crowd. He had come with the general from Fort Lapwai and stood among the silent Nez Perces. Whitman called and waved him over. Hayes edged through the crowd and went up the steps of the porch.

"We should have one more man," Monteith said.

Captain John stepped out of the crowd and joined Jonah. He looked around and noticed Aaron above the people. "Aaron!" he shouted, "come with us! We can still make peace! Come!" Aaron signaled his acceptance. He turned to Alex and Seton with a stony face. "I'll ride with them. You better go home. This is over."

Before Alex and Seton backed their horses out of the throng of people, Seton heard the agent admonish Jonah and Captain John. "Tell Joseph and the others that no one wants war. Tell them to keep the murderers out. They will be arrested. The people have nothing to fear. Tell them."

The general and the captain pushed through the crowd to their horses and rushed back to the fort. The white agency officials disappeared into the building. But the gathering of Nez Perces did not break up. Some stood in silence. Others began hushed conversations. Something huge, a great shadow, had come and had neither passed or fallen. It hung over them.

Alex and Seton rode slowly back to Aaron's place, each with his own thoughts. They were sure it would be a long wait. They were wrong. Aaron rode through the gate less than two hours later. He let the reins drop and walked over to where the two men and the two women were sitting. His horse glistened with sweat. It had been ridden hard.

"It is over," Aaron said sourly. "We got to the mouth of Mission Creek when we ran into two men who came from Mount Idaho. One was a white man. The other was a Nez Perce from the Clearwater. I don't know him." He paused. "They had letters from Mount Idaho for the general. The nontreaties are killing white people everywhere, they said. They had seen bodies with their own eyes. On Camas Prairie."

He paused again, looking glum. "We rode back to the fort with these men. The horse soldiers are ready. Two companies. They don't have their mules yet. They are waiting for them."

He shook his head. "I don't know." He looked at Seton. "What will you do?"

Seton felt all their eyes on him. "I don't know." He looked straight ahead. "I think I should be with Hemene and them. They may need me."

"You are safe here," Aaron said. He stared at the ground. "Jonah and a few older men are at the fort. They'll ride with the horse soldiers. They still want to talk with Joseph and them, trying to end it before it becomes worse." He paused and looked at Seton. "I think the war is already on. Jonah can't stop it."

He paused again. "The officers are looking for Nez Perce scouts. You could go as a scout and leave when you are near the camp. They'll find it. You can't ride by yourself now. If settlers catch you, they'll shoot you."

"I can't be a scout for the soldiers," Seton said.

"It's a way to get back," Alex said. "If you must get back."

"Yes," Seton said. "But the soldiers would not take me as a scout. They wouldn't trust me. They can't."

"I am your brother," Alex said. "I'll go with you. They'll take you if you are with me."

They sat in silence. Finally Mary spoke directly to Seton. "You should stay here. This is not your war. Who knows what will happen. What can you do there?"

Seton nodded. In his mind he saw Wetah, when they had lived in the Salmon River country, Hemene, the Old Man who had been his father more than anyone, Teeweeyownah, hard and unblinking, his wife, Dawn, pretty yet remote, the crippled girl, Itsepit, pleasant and shy, and little Tsacope with her smiling eyes and face. He saw others, even Wahlitits and Sarpsis, the boy Swan Necklace. Many faces.

"I have to be with them," he said.

FIVE

THE CAVALRY AT FORT LAPWAI WERE READY TO
march in the early afternoon. The force consisted of Companies F and
H of the First Cavalry, with a total of 103 enlisted men and 4 officers.
Captain Perry was in command. General Howard waited impatiently
for the mules from Lewiston to arrive. Hour after hour passed with no
sign of them. When retreat sounded for the garrison in the evening,
Perry did not want to wait any longer. He asked Howard for permission to leave without a pack train. Permission was granted. Each soldier
carried rations for three days, a Colt single-action .45-caliber revolver,
and forty rounds of ammunition for their single-shot, breech-loading
.45-70-caliber Springfield carbines. The column moved out at 8 p.m.

Three hours earlier, Alex and Seton had joined a group of nine
Christian Nez Perces with the cavalry. Three chiefs were with the
group: Jonah Hayes, Frank Hushush, and Wishtaskat. The other men

were young and had enlisted as scouts. Seton knew only Joe Albert and Joe Rabusco, the latter serving as interpreter. Three of the scouts were armed with rifles. The Nez Perces went to the head of the column, and Seton heard the last exchange of words between the general and Captain Perry. The general's voice was precise.

"You are to bring relief to Mount Idaho and ensure the safety of the people living in the area. When you make contact with the hostiles, keep them occupied until we can deliver a crushing blow. Whipple is on the way with two companies of cavalry. I have sent Wilkinson to the telegraph station at Walla Walla to communicate my orders for troops and supplies to headquarters. By tomorrow or the next day the infantry from Walla Walla will come up the river. It will take some time until we have the strength I need."

He looked sharply into the captain's face. "Be careful. I don't want to feed the enemy with driplets."

"Good-bye, General," Captain Perry said.

"Good-bye, Captain. You must not get whipped."

"There is no danger of that, sir."

Perry saluted and barked an order. The troopers mounted. A few horses bucked and reared but were quickly brought under control. Under the general's critical eyes the column passed in twos, the Nez Perces pushing out in front. Alex and Seton rode with the chiefs when the scouts took the lead. They rode south on the wagon road that Alex and Seton had traveled twice with the mule train. Before nightfall it started to rain. A thunderstorm quickly drenched horses and riders. The gray dusk turned into a night lit by crackling streaks of lightning and booming thunder. The command moved according to the cavalry tactical manual, halting five minutes at the end of every hour to adjust equipment and tighten girths. Every third hour officers and troopers dismounted and led the horses for twenty minutes. Mounted, they alternated walk with trot.

Seton was amused but said nothing to Alex. He observed the practice with interest. With the possible exception of the horses of the two captains and the horse of one of the lieutenants, none of the mounts in

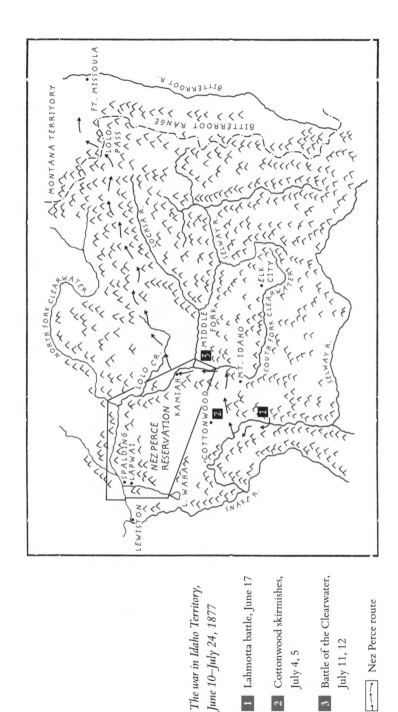

The war in Idaho Territory,
June 10–July 24, 1877

1 Lahmotta battle, June 17

2 Cottonwood skirmishes,
July 4, 5

3 Battle of the Clearwater,
July 11, 12

Nez Perce route

this outfit matched the stamina of a Nez Perce appaloosa. Still, at about two hours after midnight the column had climbed up to the Camas Prairie. The rain had stopped and the sky cleared, inflamed by brilliant stars. Taking a short rest, the companies unbit the horses and let them graze while the men stood in the wet grass and chewed hardtack.

They rode on into the heart of the Camas Prairie. Long before the sun appeared, a streak of green slanted across the plain from the east. Sunrise bared the quiet beauty of the grassland, low, swinging hills with new greens, and splashes of flowers in patches of blue, red, pink, purple, and white. The only sounds were the flutelike songs of meadowlarks, and from the horsemen, hoofbeats and the squeaking of leather. Once, two curious coyotes sat in the grass, watching the cavalcade pass.

The first sign of the conflict came at midmorning. Two burned-out wagons with trailers sat in the road, the horse teams missing. The wagons had carried goods for either Grangeville or Mount Idaho. Some gunnysacks, slit open, and smashed boxes had been thrown around. Among the litter was an empty whiskey barrel with the head knocked out. There was no trace of the teamsters.

Captain Perry ordered an advance guard out, a corporal and eight men. They galloped forward and took a position half a mile ahead of the column. Alex and Seton joined the scouts who kept well in front of the advance guard. The Nez Perces fanned out, riding on both sides of the road. Seton knew he was under scrutiny and acted like the others, watching for tracks. He also knew that this was not the place where the bands would make a fight.

By noon they reached the Norton House. The house and the tavern on the low hill had been set afire, but the thunderstorm had squelched the flames. The partly burned buildings were empty. A small herd of cattle was grazing near the lone cottonwood tree. After a watering call and a brief rest the column moved on.

By nightfall, four miles out of Grangeville, the scouts came upon an empty wagon with two dead harness horses. All around were tracks of shod and unshod horses. A faint smell of smoke was in the air. Seton thought it came from either east or southwest. To the east lay the ranch of a white man, Ad Chapman, married to a woman of the Umatilla tribe. Chapman had established a horse ranch in White Bird Canyon, on Lamtama land, in 1861. He sold it to the Manuel family in 1874 and moved over to a place on Cottonwood Creek, seven miles northeast of Grangeville. To the southwest lay two spreads recently set up by two white men, Overman and Johnson. Both were situated on ancient Nez Perce camas grounds and not far from tepahlewam, the favorite early summer camping place of the upriver bands. Seton had seen these men; he was certain that the three ranches had been destroyed by the warriors.

Pushing on to Grangeville, they found settlers and a few refugees fortified in the grange hall. They had built a log wall around the building and piled sacks of flour against windows in the upper story. The column made another halt while Captain Perry calmed the people. Jonah Hayes went there with the Nez Perce interpreter, Joe Rabusco. The scouts sat away from the troopers. Hayes and Rabusco returned with serious faces. "A lot of white people killed," Hayes said. "From Slate Creek up through Iahmotta to the prairie. Some were killed just north of town, where we saw the wagon. All the ranchers around are dead."

"One Nez Perce was killed here this morning," Rabusco said.

"Who?" Seton asked.

"Jyeloo. He was killed by men from Mount Idaho. Chapman was there; he recognized him. They said Jyeloo was drunk."

"You know him?" Alex asked.

"Yes." Seton looked at Rabusco. "Where are the bands?"

Rabusco shrugged. "They say the band of Looking Glass and the Palooses are on the Clearwater. Looking Glass warned the settlers before the killings. These two bands had nothing to do with this. They say it's the bands of White Goose, Toohoolhoolzote, and Joseph who do the killing. No one knows where they are. Their camp has not crossed the prairie to the Clearwater. They think they are somewhere on the Salmon." He looked at Seton. There was a question in his eyes, but he did not ask.

The night march continued. The column reached Mount Idaho around ten o'clock. Here the people had blocked the one street through town on both ends with wagons and logs. On a hill by the north end of town they had built a circular stockade for defense. Tents inside and outside the fortification housed refugees. In a darkness lit by torches and fires, the troops received a raucous welcome. Captain Perry ordered the command to a campsite on Butler Creek outside of town. Because men and horses were tired from the long march, stable call was sounded. Troopers unbridled, removed saddles, wiped saddles and bridles, groomed and watered the horses. The troopers settled down for the rest of the night in an open square, the open side facing the creek and its high bank on the opposite side. The horses were picketed inside the square where there was abundant grass. Sentinels were posted.

The two captains talked with leaders of the Mount Idaho defenders. They sat around a fire in front of the barricade blocking the north entrance into town. Jonah Hayes, Frank Hushush, and Joe Rabusco went to sit with them. Rabusco later explained what had been discussed.

"Ad Chapman was there. He said the camp of the three bands is in White Bird Canyon. Lahmotta. He said the Nez Perces are cowards. He said he and a few volunteers could whip them. He said the bands are getting ready to flee across the Salmon into the mountains, and they should be stopped before they can escape. He said the camp should be attacked at dawn. He said the war could end right there." The scouts were listening. They sat in a circle in the dark.

"What did the captain say?" Joe Albert asked.

"He said he had been ordered to protect the people of Mount Idaho and Grangeville. He had no orders to attack the camp." He paused. "Chapman said they were ready to protect themselves. He said there were plenty of volunteers to join the soldiers if they would attack the camp at daybreak. He said it could be a long war if the Nez Perces escaped and went into the Seven Devils Mountains. Or he said, the war could be finished with one blow."

There was a silence. Rabusco then said: "They talked more. At the end, the captain agreed. Wake-up is in three hours. The soldiers will attack the camp at first light."

"What about us?" Joe Albert asked. "They don't need us any-more."

"No. They want us with them." When the others went to wrap themselves in blankets to sleep a little, Alex and Seton stayed where they were. In the dark they could barely see each other's face.

"I have a bad feeling about this," Alex said. "What will you do? Are you going with us?"

"I'll go with you to tamon toyam, where the trail goes down into the canyon to lahmotta. No farther," Seton said.

Alex nodded. "You could leave now or come with us," Alex said. "These people are wrong. They should not have killed so many white people. It's not your war." They sat in silence for a long time.

"You don't know, brother," Seton said at last. "I've been on the Salmon and in these places for several years. The suyapu come and come, more and more. They take and take. They make a place for themselves here and a place there. They come and the first thing they do is build a fence. They fence something that does not belong to them. When a Lamtama tears a fence down because it is on his land, the suyapu kills him. That has happened here. Wahlitits's father was killed that way." He paused. "Of all the suyapu who came here there was only one who asked. He is called Cone. He came to White Goose and asked if he could have land on Slate Creek, build a ranch there. Just this man. He was given permission. He gave the chief a lot of money. He paid for the land."

He paused again. "The other suyapu never asked. They came and took. That is what Hemene and the others say. I have seen it. They killed Wahlitits's father. They killed others. I think this is how it started . . ."

They sat in silence. "Our tracks will take different trails tomor-row," Alex said. "Remember our home on the Clearwater. You can live with us." He wanted to add, the Lord be with you wherever you go, but he did not say it.

The command was awakened at 2:00 a.m. and made ready as quietly as possible. The officers explained to the companies what was expected of them. Along with a mere eleven citizen volunteers, who had chosen George Shearer as their captain, the cavalry moved off, the Nez Perce scouts leading. The column rode in silence below the long slope of White Bird Hill, on a dark night on rain-soaked ground. First light was breaking when it reached the draw that led straight south through the narrow gap below Bald Mountain toward the head of the *tamon toyam* trail. There was a short halt. Then Perry, with a low voice, called out an order, and the scouts and the head of the column started into the trees. They rode three miles through clusters of pines on a tight, well-worn trail and slightly dipping ground until they reached tamon toyam, the lip of the hill.

This was a high overlook that granted a view of some parts of the canyon below—miles and miles of waving slopes and mountain ridges curling toward the Salmon River, hidden from sight. At the edge of the canyon, the Nez Perce point riders held one more time. There was some hesitation, and then the three chiefs rode off to the side. Seton nudged his mare and joined them. Alex waited for a moment and followed him.

"I'm too old for this," Jonah Hayes said. He shook his head. "It's too late for me to do anything." He waved the scouts on. Seton watched them go.

Joe Albert and Joe Rabusco were in the lead, with four young men behind them. They had not stripped for battle. They wore their baggy white man's clothes. With weary faces, they disappeared on the steep trail down. They were followed by the small bunch of civilian volunteers and an advance guard of eight troopers led by a Lieutenant Theller. The lieutenant looked at Seton and Alex with contempt. Captain Perry rode stiffly ahead of his F company, his trumpeter at his side. Behind came Company H, two officers leading, Captain Trimble and Lieutenant Parnell, also with a trumpeter. A string of five pack mules formed the end of the column.

Before the last of the horsemen was swallowed by the depth of the canyon, a coyote howled to the right from the eastern flank of Chuck Mountain. Another answered from somewhere far below. Seton smiled.

The scouts of the lahmotta camp were not asleep; their eyes and ears were open.

There was a heavy silence. Wishtaskat's horse neighed, pawing the ground.

"I came to do something good," Jonah Hayes said. "It didn't work. This is stronger than I." He paused. "I'm going home," he said quietly. "Whatever happens now—I couldn't change it." He turned his horse and urged it into a canter, as if trying to leave this place fast. Frank Hushush and Wishtaskat followed, not looking back.

"What will you do, brother?" Alex asked. Are you coming with me, or will you stay?"

The two looked into each other's eyes. "I'm staying," Seton said. He paused. "I don't know what will happen." Alex nodded. He extended his right hand, palm forward, and Seton put his palm against it, stopping short of touching, the old way of greeting or saying good-bye. Alex turned his horse and rode off without looking back.

Seton sat on the horse, thinking, not certain what to do. A cold wind from the north brushed through the gap, making the pines shiver. The appaloosa jerked its head and nickered, ready to go. It stirred Seton into action. He dismounted and untied the bedroll pack from behind the saddle. He removed the rifle case and hooked it with the shoulder sling over the saddle horn. He took off the reservation pants and leather jacket and dropped the pants on the trail. Another episode of his life seemed to have ended. He slipped into leggings and breechclout and slung the canvas cartridge belt over his naked chest. He closed the pack and tied it up behind the saddle, checked the girth, and mounted. He took the Winchester out and levered a cartridge into the chamber, closed the hammer carefully on the shell, and pushed the rifle back into the case. He did not have a warrior's medicine objects with wéyekin power to protect him from enemy bullets, but he had a good rifle and was a good shot. He would defend himself.

He felt as alone as he had ever felt in his life. He felt like a person who belongs nowhere, as free as a black buzzard circling in the sky. He felt no kinship with those riding down. But what about those in the camp below? The time had come to decide. Or had it? He squeezed the horse's sides with his thighs. The mare turned left from the trail, east. He rode over a grassy ridge to a high, round knoll four hundred yards away that had a commanding view of the canyon and the valley and the rolling slopes to the east. He went around to its eastern side, dismounted, and tied the horse up in cover. He took the rifle case and climbed the steep incline to the top and sat.

Early dawn, and the canyon was directly south of him, hugging the sheer flanks of Chuck Mountain, the Knob, and the Giant's Nose, ending in the slim gorge, three miles downward, where White Bird Creek had cut through the shelf toward the Salmon River. To the east the canyon opened wide to a valley that merged with hills in yellow and green grass, rolling on, ridge after ridge. The valley was dissected by numerous ravines and draws. The canyon was also broken up by ravines and by a few rocky escarpments that blocked from view what lay behind. Perhaps four hundred Nez Perce horses were grazing in the valley and on the first of the slopes to the east. Seton saw a few tipis among the cottonwoods in the cut by the creek and smoke rising straight up in the still air. There would be more tipis, hidden by a rise of ground. To the left he saw the collapsed roofs of buildings of the Manuel ranch on Chapman Creek. The ranch had been sacked.

Of the cavalry, nothing was to be seen. Seton glanced along the swerving slopes and fastened his eyes on the two little buttes, half a mile above the lahmotta camp. They had served as favorite Lamtama burial places for a long time, containing many dozens of graves. Wetah was buried in the butte closer to the creek, the second one from Seton's location uphill.

Seton remembered the burial and the place, the day. Wetah's fragile body had been wrapped in a partly beaded Hudson Bay blanket, face and hands painted with red ocher. Her necklace with the grizzly claw was around her neck for the journey into the spirit world. The *ipétes,* the sacred bundle with her medicine things, was under her folded hands. Hemene had prayed and sung a mournful spirit song, touching her body with an eagle feather from head to toe.

Seton was deep in the grip of memory when something touched his hair. Not wind, perhaps a spirit's breath. Perhaps Wetah's. He was close to crying. He felt angry. Down there the camp, the graves—they were places that should be left alone. There was Wetah's place, sacred ground. Through his mother it was his place too. And now the cavalry was on its way. But where, suyapu? Where were they?

Seton watched and waited. The sky turned red in the east. He saw some movement among the tipis, and then the cavalry came into the open. It emerged from a ravine about a mile above the camp. In the great silence of dawn the whites tried to form a line, but the broken country made the maneuver difficult. They were grouped in three bodies: the civilians on the left flank, two companies of blue-clad soldiers to their right, their right flank close to the mountain slope. They moved forward slowly, hesitating as if waiting for something.

Five Nez Perce riders came up over a hill, one carrying a staff with a white cloth. They seemed to move rapidly toward the soldiers. There were two shots in quick succession. The riders turned away and vanished. A single shot answered from the direction of the camp.

Seton observed the deadly game from where he sat. In the company near the civilians, a trooper dropped from the saddle. The small bunch of civilians moved farther to the left and took up a position on a knoll, with a solitary tree on top, above the burial buttes. There were more shots beyond the soldiers, and ragged carbine fire from the left-hand company at targets Seton could not see. The horse herd in the valley and on the eastern slope galloped away from the thundering gunfire, a stream of animals running east. There were whoops from Nez Perce throats, salvos from the soldiers. The two companies converged toward the middle on a section of flat ground. The troopers dismounted, losing contact with the civilians on the knoll.

A few more salvos from the command, and then Seton saw them. A single file of mounted warriors came up a draw on the soldiers' right flank. Another suddenly appeared to the left of the knoll on the left flank. They came fast, guns booming, warriors hanging on the off sides of their mounts. The flankers on the left numbered less than twenty. On the right, perhaps fifty. The smaller bunch surrounded the civilian contingent, riding close. In minutes the civilians broke, leaving some dead on the knoll. What was left of the Mount Idaho volunteers mounted and raced away from the circling warriors. They ran up the steeply rising ground toward the canyon head, from where they had come.

On the flat ground the larger bunch of warriors pushed the right flank of the command inward. They were supported by the warriors who had dislodged the civilians and who now began to harass the command's left flank. The salvos of the cavalry became irregular, individual fire. Warriors dismounted and took cover, picking off men and horses. Seton saw the men in blue fall and their horses crumble. The roar of battle continued for a few more minutes, then the cavalry broke too. Panicked soldiers mounted horses that were still maneuverable. Some men rode double, firing revolvers as they broke away and fled, in disorder, uphill. They left blue-clad bodies and stricken horses in the yellow grass.

The warriors took to their horses, and the pursuit began. The soldiers were widely strung out by their desperate attempt to escape. It had become each man for himself. Warriors on the fastest horses closed with stragglers and shot them. Gunfire continued. Some soldiers, whose horses gave out, tried to escape into draws. They were surrounded and killed. Only once did Seton witness an orderly action. A bunch of soldiers made a stand in a ravine a mile below where Seton sat. A handful of warriors circled the ravine. After some shooting, the answering fire fell silent and the warriors moved on.

The first of the fleeing men on their way through tamos toyam passed on Seton's right as the golden rim of the sun came over the eastern mountains. This was the party from Mount Idaho. The men, some wounded, were brutally spurring exhausted, wild-eyed horses. Soon the first of the troopers came up to the lip of the canyon. One bunch, then another behind. The second, larger one seemed to be keeping together. Seton recognized the tall Captain Perry among them. They went by without stopping and disappeared on the trail. On the high slope toward tamon toyam the whooping of warriors continued, mixed with single shots from Nez Perce guns. The last of the troopers were no longer firing back, only trying hard to gain the heights.

Many did, some did not. There were bodies in blue strewn over the slopes for two miles from the initial place of battle to the exit from the canyon. Riderless cavalry horses ran wild. Some stood with drooping heads, wounded. Among the dead on the battlefield were cavalry horses as well as a few appaloosas.

Seton was amazed by how quickly the soldiers were defeated. And how cowardly their effort. They had outnumbered the Nez Perce warriors. He had seen two battles with Lakotas on the Yellowstone. Although the Nez Perces had been victorious, the Lakotas had been hard to fight. They had not run like these white soldiers.

A last bunch of troopers emerged below Seton's knoll and gained the trail through the gap below Bald Mountain. Seton stood and watched them clamber away. Their horses were worn out; most of the men had lost their carbines. Two in the back fired with side arms at their pursuers.

About fifty warriors chased them. They were strung out over five hundred yards when the front riders spilled over the edge of the canyon and into the gap. Their appaloosas were tired, too, but in better condition than the cavalry mounts. The men were stripped to breechclouts, their naked bodies glinting with sweat. A swirl of spotted horses and men leaning low in their saddles, feathers in floating hair, rifles held forward, piercing shrieks of bone whistles, whoops and yells, as they worried the last of the cavalry. A few unarmed single riders came after them, excited youngsters caught up in the thrill of the chase.

When Seton looked back over the canyon and the battlefield, two miles way, he saw that many people were riding up from the camp to the flat ground where the main fight had taken place. They had begun searching among the dead, gathering weapons and equipment left there. Some moved uphill to look at troopers killed on higher slopes and in draws. The horse herd had been brought under control by young herders and driven into the area around White Bird Creek close to the camp. Seton slung the rifle case over his shoulder and climbed down to where his horse was hidden.

He mounted and rode around the base of the knoll and west to where the trail dropped into the canyon. Twice he heard gunfire from the direction of the Camas Prairie. He pressed the mare with his thighs, and they went down the trail. On the first half mile he passed three dead troopers, one with two arrows in his back. Their weapons were missing. They had been snatched by the men who killed them. In the next half mile Seton saw four dead troopers and a few crippled cavalry horses. A little farther down, where the canyon opened eastward to the valley, he saw two Lamtama men and four boys dismounted above a ravine. They saw him, too, and one of the men, Sioux Blanket, waved to him.

He rode over and stopped on the rim. Looking down he saw the bodies of eight troopers at the bottom of the ravine, partly hidden by clumps of thorn bushes. Among the dead was Lieutenant Theller, who had led the advance guard into the canyon. The dead had not been stripped, but their weapons, gun belts, and carbine slings had been taken.

"You been in this fight?" Sioux Blanket asked.

"No," Seton answered. "I'm not one of the warriors. I came from Lapwai with my brother. I watched the fight from up there." He pointed with his chin.

Sioux Blanket nodded. "I was not in this fight either. Had no gun. Had too much drink last night." He laughed. "We got it from the suyapu store down there. That man Benedict, dead now."

A woman in her late twenties rode up from below, a baby in a cradleboard on her back. She looked at the dead soldiers, the flies buzzing around them. She turned to the men. "Has anyone seen my husband, Left Hand?" She was of the Wallowa band, and Seton didn't know her or her husband.

"No," Sioux Blanket said. "But don't fret. None of ours was killed here." He shook his head.

Two warriors were coming down the mountain, letting their tired horses walk. Their loose hair was knotted from sweat. Their faces were unpainted, but each had a single eagle feather tied to the back of his head. One of them, Two Moons, carried a captured cavalry carbine and a gun belt across the saddle. When the two passed the group on the rim of the ravine, the woman asked them the same question.

"He's up there chasing soldiers," Two Moons said. "By now they must be close to Mount Idaho." He chuckled and walked on.

Seton backed the mare away from the ravine and rode slowly down the slope. He had seen all he wanted to see. Another mile, more dead and crippled horses, more cavalry dead, and he got to the flat area, the main killing ground. Many women and children had ridden up to see the blue-belly bodies in the yellow grass. Among them were Itsepit and little Tsacope. Itsepit was a poor walker because of her hip injury, but a splendid horsewoman. She sat her appaloosa with Tsacope on the blanket in front of her. Itsepit looked at him with a shy smile when Seton rode up to them. Tsacope held out her arms, and he took her. She pressed her little body tightly against his.

S I X

SETON AND ITSEPIT RODE SIDE BY SIDE DOWN THE
draw through which warriors had attacked the Mount Idaho volunteers, past the burial buttes. Tsacope chatted eagerly about a new doll
Itsepit had made for her, and about her friends Ilsoo and Red Walker.
Little braids flapped around her face when she turned her head, looking up at him. Seton listened and smiled, happy to see her warmth and
innocence.

"We were wondering if you would come back," Itsepit said.

Seton thought about this. "A few times I wondered too. I wasn't
sure." He paused. "I went away with my brother without thinking—
after that meeting at the fort. But it was only a visit."

A few more women came riding up from the camp. Two nodded
to him when they passed. In their long, fringed, cream-colored deer
or antelope skin dresses, their moccasin boots, braids, and with their

cheerful faces they looked radiant. So different from the listless, subdued women on the reservation.

"Then I wondered why I was there," Seton said. "I think I wanted to see the other side again."

Once more he paused, listening to the hoofbeats of their horses, the swishing of the tall grass as they rode through it. He glanced sideways at Itsepit. She had a quiet, sensitive face framed by braids and a delicate throat above her white buckskin dress. She looked ahead of her over the appaloosa's ears. "I saw the other side," Seton said. "I should have known; I lived there once. It's not like this." He pointed with his chin toward the camp on the low ground before them. They had come over a rise and could see it clearly.

From the gorge through which the creek gushed to the Salmon River, stands of old cottonwoods extended for a quarter mile east along the stream. Tipis stood in irregular groups under the cottonwoods and eastward into open grassland. Most were buffalo hide lodges, but some had canvas or old-time tule mat covers. Hide and canvas lodges were white, smudged dark at the tops from the fires that burned inside during cold weather. They stood in contrast to the pale yellow of tule mat tipis. On a number of lodges, horse tails were suspended from the lifting poles to which the covers were attached. These reached higher than the poles of the lodge frames and the smoke flap poles. A few tipis were painted with dots and circles and bands in various colors, and with symbols and depictions of animals and birds and insects such as dragonflies. Horses were tethered around tipis among packs and piles of equipment and meat racks. The meat racks hung with heavy slabs of meat from butchered cattle. Fires burned outside lodges, the smoke rising straight in the still air. People moved between the tipis. Because of the warm weather, tipi covers were raised a few feet off the ground, rolled up and tied.

Seton noticed that the tipis were loosely concentrated in three clusters, each a little space from the next. The smallest group stood on the west side—twenty lodges. The group in the middle numbered nearly forty. The one on the east side, about fifty. "Three camps," Seton said.

"Lamtama in the middle, the Wallowa band east, the Pekonan west, is that right?"

"Yes," Itsepit said. "We chose first. Our camp is where we always were. Toohoolhoolzote's people are on our left, Joseph's people on our right." She paused. "The other bands did not come with us. They went to the Clearwater."

Seton nodded. Under the cottonwoods, beyond the Pekonan camp near the entrance to the gorge, he saw the smoke-blackened ruins of the Brown store above the north bank of the creek. Across the foot-bridge were the gutted remains of the Benedict ranch and inn. "What happened to the suyapu down there?" he asked.

"The warriors killed the men. Women and children were let go."

"I heard that the man Benedict is dead," Seton said. He remembered Benedict. Two years ago he had killed a Lamtama boy, Chipmunk, who stole a bottle of whiskey from the inn.

"Yes," Itsepit said. "A bad man."

They rode on, Tsacope rocking on Seton's saddle. "I don't see Hemene's tipi," Seton said.

"We did not set it up," Itsepit said. "Half the lodges were not set up. The chiefs said we would camp here only for a few days. My father and I are staying with my sister." After a pause, she added, "Many people are sleeping in the open."

Seton searched along the line of Lamtama tipis. Some were partly hidden by brush or the twisted trunks of cottonwoods. Finally he recognized the six tipis that usually stood around Hemene's: that of Teeweeyownah; that of his brother, Allultakanin; the lodge of Ayokka, a son of Hemene's brother, long dead; that of Kywis, a young man married to a sister of Ayokka's wife; and the lodges of Thunder Eyes and Short Bull, sons of Hemene's sister-in-law, Talooth, from a second marriage with a husband who died in the buffalo country.

Teeweeyownah's lodge was easy to make out because of the four blue circles painted on the cover in the four ceremonial directions. Allultakanin's lodge was painted with a walking grizzly in the back, but Seton could not see the bear figure from where they approached the

camp. The two brothers, both in their thirties, were among the domi-
nant warriors of the Lamtama band.

The six lodges, normally with Hemene's tipi among them, formed
a *wi-ses,* a camp or little band within the greater Lamtama band. Lamtama was an aggregation of eight wi-ses, each with its own chief. Hemene
was the chief of his wi-ses, which numbered twenty-four people,
including Seton. White Goose was head chief of the Lamtama, elected
by the chiefs of the wi-ses.

This was the ancient numipu band organization as it was still maintained by the nontreaty bands. On the reservation the system had been
dissolved by government agents and missionaries. From the time when
Wetah and Seton had come to live with the Lamtama, in 1870, they had
stayed in Hemene's wi-ses and in his lodge.

The camp was in a high state of excitement. People gathered in
groups, talking. Others rode to and from the killing places. Near the
lodge of White Goose, small groups of armed men came together, their
horses bunched nearby. Seton recognized Chiefs Joseph and Toohoolhoolzote among them. Later he learned that some of the men had been
in the fighting; others had never left camp.

Seton and Itsepit came down the slope above Hemene's camp and
rode into the creek. The swift waters reached to the forearms of the
horses. The appaloosas easily climbed the opposite bank and moved into
the half circle of tipis.

Three of the wi-ses women, Dawn, Petolwe, and Elk Blanket, sat
on logs between fireplaces chatting quietly. They kept the fires going and
roasted hunks of meat on cobblestones placed around the fires. They fed
the fires from piles of dry driftwood someone had brought in. The women
raised their arms in greeting as Seton and Itsepit rode up. They did not
seem surprised. Seton bent in the saddle and let Tsacope down. She ran
past her mother and joined the children playing behind the tipis.

Seton and Itsepit dismounted. He untied the bedroll pack from
behind the saddle. Itsepit pointed with her chin to Teeweeyownah's
lodge. Seton nodded and went inside. Itsepit followed and indicated
a place near the door, on the southeast side. He dropped the pack and

looked for an empty hook on the frame poles. He suspended his rifle case and cartridge belt from one that was close to his sleeping place. He glanced around the lodge. The early morning sun beamed through the tipi frame below the rolled-up skin cover. Everything was the way he remembered it. He nodded and walked out.

"Where is Atemis?" he asked. Atemis, Spirit Deer, was Allultakanin's son of sixteen. He and Seton often watched over the horse herd of the Hemene wi-ses, and the two shared with others in guarding the large Lamtama herd.

"He is over there," Itsepit said, pointing with her chin. "He is with the horses."

"I would like to see him," Seton said. He mounted and let the mare walk northeast along the creek bank and past another dozen Lamtama tipis. He saw people he knew well, and they acknowledged him. A few huge, wolflike dogs stared at him silently when he went by. He reached the gap that set the Lamtama and Wallowa camps apart and nudged the mare uphill on the first of a series of long slopes that crested two miles to the south. The slopes were cut by deep ravines. The herds of the different bands had been kept separate and were guarded, as expected, by a few young men and boys. The largest bunch of horses was in the valley above the Wallowa camp, perhaps 170 animals. The second largest bunch was on a slope behind a deep ravine behind a smaller herd. Seton recognized Atemis and one more herder with the second bunch. He went on, and his mare climbed through a brush-choked ravine to the Lamtama herd. Atemis rode a spotted-hip appaloosa, a horse with white flecks over the loins on a dark background.

"Greetings, cousin," Atemis said, raising his right arm, smiling. "You are back!"

Seton smiled too. "Yes. I couldn't stay away."

"Did you see the fight?" Atemis asked. "Were you in it?"

Seton shook his head. "But I saw it. I was way up on the mountain there, above tamon toyam. I did nothing, but I saw everything."

They dismounted and sat in the yellow grass, holding the reins of their horses. The second herder rode over and sat with them. Seton searched the Lamtama herd for the mares he owned and had left behind when he went with the Lamtama delegation to Fort Lapwai. One was a chestnut. The other, a snowflake appaloosa with white spots on a dark background. "Where are our other horses?" he asked. "These are just a few. I don't see my horses here."

"They are on the other side of the Salmon, up in the high country," Atemis said. "We only brought these to tepahlewam. The river was too high! We figured we could bring the rest over later." He paused. "The herds of the Pekonans and Wallowas are there too. A few men and boys stayed with them. The Wallowas lost lots of horses when they went through the Snake. Suyapu on the other bank stole many when the Wallowas were crossing the river . . ."

"Those suyapu on the hill there, they won't steal horses anymore," the other herder said, pointing with his chin. He was Nahush, half a year younger than Seton.

"How did you get here?" Atemis asked.

Seton explained where he had been and how he reached lahmotta. They listened in silence.

"How many horse soldiers were there in that fight?" Nahush asked.

"More than a hundred, and four officers. I saw one of the officers dead," Seton said. Then he grinned and described to his companions the order of the march of the cavalry from Fort Lapwai to Mount Idaho, the frequent halts, the poor horsemanship of most of the men, the domineering attitude of the officers, their lack of knowledge. "They thought it would be easy, that our warriors would not make much of a fight. That is what they had been told, and they believed it," he said.

Seton and Atemis chuckled, but Nahush laughed so hard that he wiped tears from his eyes. They talked for a while longer, and then Seton stood up. "I'll go back to our camp now," he said. He mounted and rode down the slope through the Wallowa herd in the valley and past the Wallowa tipis. He knew very few people of this band. No one paid attention to him. Only two dozen dogs watched him attentively when he rode by.

Hemene sat by himself in front of Teeweeyownah's tipi, bent and cross-legged, on a trade blanket someone had put down for him in the grass, probably Itsepit. His Springfield rifle rested against a lodge pole behind him, a cartridge belt dangling from the muzzle.

"Grandson," he said. "It is good to see you." His eyes sparkled above a wide smile. The white hair above his forehead was carefully combed, and strips of red cloth were worked into his braids. This was Itsepit's handicraft. She had taken care of her father since she was thirteen when her mother died eight years ago. Being unmarried, she devoted most of her energies to her father and her sister's daughter, Tsacope. She bestowed some on Seton, although he did not acknowledge or indicate awareness of it. Others did, and poked fun at Itsepit behind her back.

Hemene was dressed in breechclout, leggings, and a fringed buckskin shirt beaded on the shoulders and around the neck. His moccasins were simple ones without beads.

Seton dismounted. Itsepit came from where she had sat with the three women and led his mare away. Seton sat in front of the wi-ses chief and held the palms of his hands against Hemene's. "I'm back, Old Man," he said, speaking the ancient term of respect he always used. "I'm glad to be here. I'm happy to see you well."

"How is your brother, your uncle?"

"They are fine. They helped me get here," Seton said. He pointed with his chin to the rifle. "Did you do some shooting?"

Hemene shook his head. "No. We left the fight to the young men. We older men made ready to meet the horse soldiers if they came as far as the camps." He paused. "The warriors captured three of the Lapwai numipu. They were scouts for the soldiers. They were taken before the chiefs. They begged not to be killed. The chiefs took pity on them and let them go. But they warned them. If they help the soldiers again, and if we catch them again, they will be punished."

He paused again. "One of the Christian Indians said he was Joe Albert. His father is a warrior in the Wallowa band, Weesculatat. He said he knows you. He said you came with the soldiers from Lapwai. He said you and your brother left the soldiers before they came down."

"Yes," Seton said. "I came with the horse soldiers because I was told it was the safest way to get here. I also wanted to learn about the soldiers. My brother came because of me. He did not scout for the soldiers. When he thought I was safe, he rode back." He paused. "I saw the fight from up there on the mountain. I heard your scouts call in the dark before the soldiers went down tamon toyam. I knew you would be waiting for them."

Hemene's dark eyes looked straight into Seton's gray ones, piercing his soul, finding nothing hidden, no fear. "It is good, grandson," he said. "It is good that you are back. I missed you. Let's go and eat. When Teeweeyownah and our warriors are back, you must tell us what you learned in Lapwai, and about the soldiers."

The warriors of Hemene's wi-ses returned at midday. They appeared suddenly in the draw along the burial buttes and made straight for their camp. They were not alone. Most of the warriors who had pursued the enemy had come back. Some went to the Wallowa lodges, others to the Lamtama and Pekonan camps. Allultakanin, who at thirty-five was the oldest of the six warriors of the Hemene wi-ses, led them in.

The men looked as tired as their horses. Facial paint had worn off, eagle feathers hung limp from disheveled hair. Their naked torsos were smeared with sweat. Some had powder stains on their faces. They were all armed with rifles and *kopluts,* clubs. They had tied medicine pouches to their hair or belt or to thongs that hung from their neck. War whistles were tucked under their left arms on buckskin thongs looped over their right shoulders. Among them they had captured four cavalry carbines and two gun belts with revolvers. They rode through the creek to the fireplaces and dismounted.

All were back safely, none wounded. The wi-ses received them with smiles and calls in low voices. There was no loud clamor, no victory celebration. This one was not like fights with the Lakotas or Cheyennes in the buffalo country. Those fights could be broken off if something went wrong—they had no real consequences. Now they were in a war in their own country. Every suyapu had become their enemy. They had won this fight, but there would be more coming. The suyapu were like a flood that swept the land and never abated.

Atemis went to his father and took his horse's reins. His mother, Oyipee, walked up and touched her husband. Seton saw Allultakanin's worn face over his wife's shoulder. The other women stood with their husbands; the two with small children, Elk Blanket and Tamonmo, held them up to their fathers. "Where is my husband?" Dawn asked sharply.

Allultakanin stepped free of Oyipee. "He is over there," he said, pointing with his chin. "He went to tell White Goose that we have come back. There is only one man up there watching the soldiers. They barricaded themselves at the place the suyapu call Grangeville. We need men with fresh horses up there."

The men ate while their horses were taken behind the tipis. Roasted meat and *e'pine,* cakes made from cooked camas roots that had been gathered and prepared at tepahlewam before the killing started. Halfway through the meal Teeweeyownah arrived. He rode up on a blanket-pattern appaloosa, a horse with white quarters and loins on a dark coat. Tsacope rushed to take the reins when her father dismounted. Seton stepped forward and helped the child lead the mare to an open grassy spot under the cottonwoods behind the tipis where the other horses were bunched. When he and the child returned, Teeweeyownah, the leader of the warriors of the wi-ses, was standing by Hemene. He was talking, but acknowledged Seton with a nod. Tsacope put her arms around one of his legs and hugged him.

"We chased them to Grangeville, where they are hiding now. On Camas Prairie, they tried to make a fight near the Johnson ranch. They hid their horses in a draw and shot at us from a point of rocks. We went around and tried to drive their horses off. They got scared and took their horses and ran. Some of them rode double."

For a moment his stern face cracked into a grin. The hair on top of his forehead lay flat, and sweat-soaked braids hung stiffly down over his chest. He wore no feathers in his hair, but there was eagle down on the war whistle under his left arm. The whistle was carried there so as not to interfere with the firing of his rifle. His war whistle was made from the wing bone of an eagle. The choice of a wing bone for a war whistle was personal. Some men chose crane or pelican. The selection of a whistle that gave a degree of protection from real danger was always made in agreement with a warrior's wéyekin, his guardian spirit. From Teeweeyownah's right wrist hung a kopluts, a short-handled war club, on a buckskin thong. He had a light cut on his right arm from a scuffle with a soldier, but the bleeding had stopped.

"None of our men was killed," Teeweeyownah continued. "I heard that two were wounded. I saw Chellooyeen shot through the right side when he wrested a gun from a soldier. I heard that Auskehwush was shot in the belly. He lives—his mother is doctoring him."

"It is good," Hemene said. He touched Teeweeyownah's arm. "You fought well, all of you. Because of you we are safe here. Go and eat. Your wife and daughter want to be with you."

As the men were finishing their first meal of the day, a crier rode by, calling all warriors and wi-ses chiefs to the lodge of White Goose. He told them to bring captured weapons and ammunition. Hemene went with the men. They took the firearms they had seized from the soldiers. Before they walked away, Hemene asked Seton and Atemis to care for the warriors' horses.

The two worked from horse to horse, including Seton's mare. They unbridled, removed saddle blankets and saddles, and groomed and watered each. Then they took the tired mounts across the creek to graze on the slope opposite the camp. They kept their own horses on halters on good grass close to the tipis, in case fast riding or herding was needed. They sat together, talking, until Hemene and the men returned.

Allultakanin was the only one who carried a Springfield carbine and a canvas cartridge belt. He made a sign to Atemis. Atemis got up and walked to him.

"I took this for you," Allultakanin said. He handed belt and carbine to his son. "A gift from the suyapu," Allultakanin said with a grin.

Atemis said nothing. He slipped the cartridge belt over his head and held the carbine away with both hands, looking it over. He stood like this for a long moment, then brought it closer to read the stamping on the breechblock. Next to the hammer was a U.S. eagle. To its right it said, "U.S.," and below that, "Springfield" and "1873." Atemis let his hand glide over the twenty-two-inch barrel, turned it over and examined the metal butt plate. He looked back at his father and smiled and walked over to Seton. Seton nodded to him and touched his shoulder when he sat down.

Hemene motioned, and the wi-ses slowly formed a circle in front of Teeweeyownah's lodge. The men sat in a first circle; women and children formed a second circle behind them. Atemis sat with his father, the carbine laid across his knees. Seton sat with Hemene. "Numipu warriors made a good fight today," Hemene said with a quiet voice. "A fight that will be remembered. The dead soldiers have been counted, thirty-four. All our men came back; only two were wounded. Many of the suyapu were wounded; some of them will die."

A murmur ran along the women's circle. Tamonmo, a boy of three in one arm, a boy of two in the other, shook them to keep them still and bent and talked to them softly.

"We captured sixty-three of the horse soldiers' short rifles, forty-seven six-guns, fifty-two saddles, nineteen soldier horses that are not injured, five mules with food. We took one of the rifles for Atemis." He nodded to the boy. "We didn't take anything else. The six-guns went to boys and a few women. We didn't want any of the horses. They are not as good as ours."

He paused. "We got two trumpets too. Otstopoo took one. He killed the first bugler. He said he would learn to play the signals as the soldiers do, confuse them." He grinned.

There was laughter around the circle.

"For the first time in many years there are no suyapu in the lands of the Lamtama and Pekonan," he said with a sober face again. "It is like old time." He paused again. "But it is not like old time. The suyapu will be back; there will be more soldiers. We will have to fight again. They will not leave us alone."

There were uneasy sounds from around the circle, people sucking in their breath, sighing heavily.

Hemene nodded. "Yes, there is trouble ahead. It has been coming for a long time. We knew, but we ignored it. We should never have welcomed the suyapu, never helped them survive in our country as our grandfathers did when I was a child." He paused again, looking at the ground. "It started with those suyapu who came over the Lolo Trail when I was young, men sent by Washington, Clark, and this man Lewis. They would have died if the numipu had not taken them in and fed them and kept them alive."

He continued to look at the ground, tossing a piece of broken twig. "This is how it started. After them came other suyapu, and still others, and those missionaries in their black coats who turned the downriver numipu away from us, who made them sign the thief treaties. Now others are still coming."

He looked around the circle. Eyes burned into his.

"And now, after all these years, we are in a war with them. When we were strong and they were weak, we welcomed them. Now they are strong in numbers and we are weak. Now they fight us for our land." He fell silent, looking down between his knees. A hush fell over the people. One of the little children began to cry. The mother cradled him in her arms and calmed him.

Hemene looked to the side. "Seton has come back from the reservation. Perhaps he can tell us things we should know."

There was a silence, and then Teeweeyownah said, "What should we know?" Seton swallowed. All eyes were on him. "I'm not sure," he said.

"What did you see?" Teeweeyownah asked, his eyes hard.

"I have been to Lapwai," Seton said. "I stayed near Lapwai on my brother's place. I saw how people live there. I've been to Lewiston. I've been to Elk City with a mule train. I and my brother and two suyapu." He fell silent. He felt foolish being questioned like this.

"What did you learn?" Teeweeyownah pressed him.

"Not much."

"What?" Teeweeyownah insisted.

There was silence.

"They dress like suyapu," Seton said at last. In his mind he went back to where he had been, mixing what he had seen recently with what he remembered from earlier years. "Men and women dress like that. They get their dry goods from the churches. It all comes from people in the east. They go to church every Sunday. The reservation chiefs are preachers in the churches. They speak about Jesus and the holy book. They tell the people how to live."

He paused, looking around.

"They are told not to wear leather. When a man is baptized, or a woman, they are told to dig a hole in the ground and put their skin clothing in the hole and burn it. They also burn feathers and medicine things. They keep nothing of the old things. Old things must be burned. They have a new life now. They cannot have feathers, keep ipé-tes, or medicine bundles. Nothing of the old ways." He paused again. "Their preachers are strict. The suyapu ministers and the suyapu at the agency direct them."

He waited, thinking. "If they do everything they are told, they have no trouble. They raise pigs and cattle, a few horses for their wagons. They have gardens and grow food. The only things they do as they used to do are fishing and digging kouse and camas. They are not starving, but they cannot leave the reservation."

He looked at Teeweeyownah. "They treated me good, my brother and his family. They wanted me to stay."

There was a silence. "But you didn't stay," Hemene said at last.

"Why not?" Teeweeyownah asked. "We are in a war now. You had nothing to do with that."

There was a pause.

"I was thinking of all of you," Seton said. "I was thinking of my mother. Where she is buried, over there." He turned and pointed with his chin toward the cemetery buttes.

He waited, remembering. "I didn't like some of the things I saw. I don't think I want to live like that."

"You came with the soldiers. What did you learn?" Hemene asked.

"When we left Fort Lapwai, the Cut Arm general said he was calling soldiers in from far away, horse soldiers and foot soldiers. He said he wanted to destroy us."

He bent and gathered earth from the ground, raised and opened his hand, letting it fall like dust. "He also told the tall soldier chief who led the horse soldiers against us that he should not get whipped."

There was movement among the listeners, some laughs.

"I heard Cut Arm say that. It was the suyapu rancher Chapman, the man who used to live here, who talked the soldier chief into attacking the camp. He was not supposed to do that."

"How is that?" Teeweeyownah asked.

"Chapman said that the camp would cross the Salmon. That you should be beaten before you could do that. He said, once you were across the river, you would go into the high mountains, toward the Snake."

"He was right," Teeweeyownah said. "We might do that."

There was a silence. "What did the Lapwai numipu think about all this?" Hemene asked.

"Most of the ones I saw were angry about the killing of suyapu, or sad. Three reservation chiefs came with the soldiers. They wanted to talk to you."

"Who were they?" Allultakanin asked.

"Jonah Hayes, Frank Hushush, Wishtaskat. They came as far as tamon toyam. When they were sure the soldiers would attack, they gave up and rode back to Lapwai." He paused. "The reservation numipu won't help us, not in anything. They are afraid of the government, the ministers, the soldiers, and the suyapu who live around them. Some of them will help the soldiers fight us."

"We knew that. We don't need their help," Teeweeyownah said grimly.

"Next time soldiers come, there will be many more than today," Seton said. "And Cut Arm will be there too." He looked at Teeweeyownah. The warrior nodded. They left it there. Nothing more had to be said.

After a while the meeting broke up. Seton and Atemis saddled their horses, took rifles and bedrolls and meat from the racks and a water bag.

They rode out to spend the night watching over the Lamtama horse herd, replacing other watchers. Before darkness fell they started a fire in a depression on the slope, horses milling all around them. Joined by other young Lamtama and Pekonan herders, they roasted meat on wooden spits and talked until the half-moon stood directly above then, a white, curved blade in the breathless sky. Toward morning they heard wolves and coyotes call from across the valley, quarreling over the dead horses on the killing grounds.

In the morning, ravens, crows, and magpies discovered the carcasses on the battlefield. The wolves and coyotes had been at them during the night. These were the first winged scavengers, and they took to the bloated, torn, dead flesh. They were three dozen birds altogether, hopping, running, tearing and pulling, briefly lifting into the air. And arguing, with the hoarse rasping of ravens, the cawing of crows, and the harsh notes of magpies.

A little later the turkey vultures arrived. First there were six, soaring in a wide circle below the blue canopy of sky. They saw their smaller cousins feed unchallenged and swung down, one after another, and glided to the ground among the scattered cadavers. Once they began feeding, two more groups flew in front out of nowhere and joined them—red-headed, brown-feathered ministers of death.

From near the horse herd, Seton and Atemis had seen a scouting party of eight men go up past the battlefield and into the canyon to check on the soldiers at Grangeville. Another party came back from there. But by midmorning a new band of riders came down the trail from tamon toyam. Hidden by folds in the canyon, they emerged into the open above where the main fight had taken place. They rode unhurriedly, stirring agitation among the nervous birds, looking at the carnage as they passed without slowing.

Two men rode ahead of a group of seven men. Behind them came a few women leading packhorses. Two had cradleboards hanging from saddle horns. Older children rode by themselves. Two more men rode drag, looseherding about two dozen appaloosas before them. All the men were armed with repeating rifles and all carried, in addition, either bow-and-arrow cases or lances.

"Buffalo hunters?" Atemis said, wondering.

"Yes," Seton said. The party rode closer.

"I know who they are," Seton said. "The two in front are Rainbow and Five Wounds."

The names conjured up memories of warfare in the buffalo plains where these two warriors had led upriver numipu bands in clashes with Lakotas and Cheyennes. The last time was in 1874, before a lasting peace was made between the Lakotas and numipu later that year. This peace had not included the Cheyennes. Rainbow and Five Wounds had a wide reputation as skilled and successful leaders in war. Originally of the Lamtama band, with their handful of followers they had lived for years on the High Plains of southern Montana. Seton was an eyewitness to the last fight with the Lakotas. It was near the Pryor Mountains, south of the Yellowstone River. Rainbow and Five Wounds had led the warriors of the Lamtama, Pekonan, and Alpowai bands.

"They have come back to us!" Atemis said jubilantly. "They'll help us."

The riders came through the draw along the cemetery buttes and made straight for the lodge of White Goose. It was easily distinguished by the horse tail on its lifting pole and the paintings on the hide cover—a solid red border near the ground and four dragonflies in the four directions, the signs for whirlwind. Seton and Atemis mounted and rode down to their wi-ses camp and left their horses behind the lodges. People gathered in front of White Goose's lodge. There were many people, some from each of the three bands. White Goose and Toohoolhoolzote stood together. Joseph and Ollokot wound their way through the crowd from the direction of their camp and joined the other chiefs as Rainbow and Five Wounds rode through the creek and up the south bank. The men and women of their party stayed on the ridge behind, sitting on their horses.

The two warmates dismounted. They were in their thirties, medium sized, hard and lean. They wore leather shirts, no feathers. White Goose, tall and stately, quick, even though he was in his early seventies, stepped forward. "Welcome," he said formally. "It is good to see you again. It is good to have you here."

He extended his right hand, palm forward, and first Rainbow, then Five Wounds, stretched their palms toward his. Toohoolhoolzote greeted them the same way. White Goose introduced the two warriors to Joseph and Ollokot.

He pointed with his chin to Rainbow. "Wahchumyus," he said, and, "Heinmot Tooyalakekt," indicating Chief Joseph. "Pahkatos Owyeen," he said, introducing Five Wounds. "Ollokot, Heinmot's brother," he said. The men greeted each other. They knew about each other, but the Wallowa men and the two warmates had not met before. The formal introductions over, the leaders sat down in the grass, the newcomers facing the band chiefs.

"Why have you come back?" White Goose asked.

"We heard you had serious trouble with the suyapu," Rainbow said.

"Who told you?" White Goose asked.

"Lean Elk. He was camped in the Bitterroot Valley with seven lodges. He heard it from a suyapu trader, McDonald." Lean Elk was the leader of a small band of numipu buffalo hunters who lived in western Montana.

"How did you come here?"

"We came over Lolo Trail," Five Wounds said. "We came by the Paloos camp on the Clearwater. They are close to Kamiah. They have a hard time with the reservation people. They are waiting to join you. Naked Head said so."

He paused. "We stayed for a day in Looking Glass's village. The Alpowais are split among themselves. Some want to join you, some don't. Looking Glass is mixed up too. He doesn't want to fight the suyapu, but he feels bad that he hasn't helped you."

"Did you run into soldiers on the way here? Did you see enemy scouts?" Ollokot asked.

"No," Five Wounds said. "I guess they are hiding." He and Rainbow laughed. "We did run into your scouts. They told us about the fight."

"The valley stinks of death," Rainbow said. "We saw buzzards long before we got to tamon toyam." He paused. "When are you moving camp?"

White Goose nodded. "We will move tomorrow."

"Where?" Rainbow asked.

"Across the Salmon," Toohoolhoolzote said. "Most of our horses are still there. We will round them up and wait to see what the Cut Arm general does. If he comes after us, we let him come and make him cross the river. When he's across, we cross again north," he pointed with his chin. "We'll move to the Clearwater."

He paused. "There we have to decide what to do, where to fight, where to go. We could stay here, in the mountains between the Salmon and the Snake. We know this country. Cut Arm can't hurt us here. We can hurt him, no matter how many soldiers and big guns he brings."

There was a silence. Finally Rainbow said: "We will go with you wherever you decide to go. We will fight with you—that's why we came. Why don't we cross the Salmon first and see what happens. We could fight Cut Arm there or someplace else. It's up to you to decide." He paused. "We have come a long way. Where can we camp for the night?"

"Anywhere," White Goose said. "Pekonan camp is there." He pointed with his chin down the creek. "Wallowa camp is there." He pointed east. "We are here, Lamtama. Make your place anywhere you want."

Rainbow and Five Wounds nodded.

"You and your people come to my lodge tonight," White Goose said. "We'll eat together and talk." He turned to the other chiefs. "You should come too."

The two warmates and the chiefs got up. "Yes," Rainbow said. "We'll be there."

The crowd slowly broke up, and people returned to their camps.

S E V E N

AT FIRST LIGHT THE NEXT MORNING THE LAHMOTTA
camp broke up. Seton and Atemis went up to the Lamtama herd on
the high slope and cut the horses of the Hemene wi-ses from the herd.
Riders from the other wi-ses came and got theirs. A few horses had
strayed to the Pekonan herd and were taken out.

For the camp move of the Hemene wi-ses, eighteen saddle horses
were needed, one for each of the seventeen adults, including Seton and
Atemis, and one for eight-year-old Red Walker. Each of the seven tipis
required three packhorses, one for the lodge cover and the tipi poles,
the other two for the possessions of the people who lived in the lodge:
robes, skins, basket and rawhide bags, camping equipment, supplies,
bundles containing many items, tools for cooking, riding, and hunting, and things useful or necessary for various parts of life. Most of the
saddle horses were already behind the wi-ses tipis, but the packhorses

and a few extra horses had to be brought in. When Seton and Atemis herded them in, the lodges were coming down. The work was done fast with the experience of generations.

First the anchor rope, which tied the four-pole foundation to crossed stakes in the center of the lodge floor, was loosened. Next the wooden pins that had held the cover together in front were removed. For the top lacing pin under the smoke flaps, boys shinnied up the front pole. Then, in succession, the lifting pole with the attached cover was brought down, the frame poles were removed in reverse order from which they had been laid into the crotch, and the four foundation poles were lowered and untied. The poles were taken aside, and the lodge cover was unfastened from the lifting pole and rolled up.

Most of the lodges were built on either a ten-pole or twelve-pole frame, not counting the two smoke-flap poles. The buffalo hide cover of such a tipi weighed around one hundred pounds, a canvas cover of the same size half of that; a tule mat cover was lighter but bulkier than the others.

Next, horses were brought up and saddled. The packhorses got either a special saddle built on a deer horn frame or saddle pads made of blankets or skin. For transporting lodge cover and tipi poles, a sturdy gelding was chosen. First, the lodge cover was slung over the gelding's saddle. The lodge poles, either twelve or fourteen, including the smoke flap poles, were tied up in two bunches with rawhide ropes laced through grooves cut around the upper ends of the poles. The two bunches of poles were hitched to ropes around the outside of the folded cover on both sides of the horse and allowed to drag on the ground. The packhorses were loaded; bedrolls and saddlebags were attached to the saddles of mounts to be ridden. The bands were ready to move.

Because Iahmotta was in Lamtama territory, White Goose led the march from the campsite. A handful of scouts galloped ahead, and a screen of warriors followed the chief when he rode upstream along the creek and turned south, upslope, past the waiting column of the Wallowa band. The Lamtama wi-ses swung in behind the advance guard, coming on in file. Hemene's wi-ses was the third behind White Goose and the advance guard, with Hemene at the head. Itsepit rode beside him. Teeweeyownah and Allultakanin rode at their backs. Behind came the men and women of the wi-ses with the packhorses. One woman, Tannish, carried her one-year-old baby, Wolf Blanket, in a cradleboard. Seton and Atemis rode drag, looseherding the few extra horses.

The fiery rim of the sun peaked over the mountains that closed the valley to the east when Seton reached the foot of the slope. Riding up, the column cast long shadows across the grass. When the Rainbow and Five Wounds contingent behind the Lamtama wi-ses had moved past, the Wallowa band swung into line in the same order, Joseph and Ollokot leading. They went with the rumble of many hoofbeats, the cadence of unshod hooves hitting earth, and the creaking of lodge poles as they dragged over the ground. Reaching the crest of the slope, Seton looked back. There was the canyon, the killing ground. There too, the two burial buttes with many graves, including Wetah's. He nodded. The line of the column behind him was about a mile long, the Pekonan wi-ses bringing up the rear. Ahead were a few depressions to cross and a few ridges to climb.

White Goose and the men around him reached the valley of Skookumchuck Creek, four miles south of Iahmotta, and, after one last hilltop, the trench the Salmon River had gnawed into the mountains lay before them.

Running up from the south, mostly through narrow canyons, north of the mouth of Slate Creek, the river passed through a wide bowl and swept into a horseshoe bend. Benches around the horseshoe were covered with yellow grass turning green and sprinkled with white and yellow flowers. The knobby hills on both sides of the bowl were dotted with dark ponderosa pines and shrubs between open patches of grass. In the distance behind them rose jagged lines of high blue mountains. Some of their peaks were still crowned with white splashes of snow. The horseshoe had been a favorite crossing point of numipu bands during high or low water.

White Goose went down the rolling slope and led the column upstream to a place where the river ran hard and straight against the first sharp bend, the southern curve of the horseshoe. From there, the current took any object from the east bank into the bend and pushed it against the opposite shore. For a crossing from west to east, the entrance was in the middle of the horseshoe, where the pressure of the current fell on the other side. In either case, the river itself helped a crossing here.

The bands gathered on a half-mile stretch, unsaddled and unloaded the horses, and bunched them nearby. Men had cut green shoots from such tall shrubs as willow, sumac, chokecherry, and dogwood on the creek near Iahmotta the evening before. They continued when they passed through the Skookumchuck Valley, and some cut along the Salmon until enough were secured to build hide boats.

Women built them. They made a frame by tying shoots together around which dressed, watertight buffalo robes were fitted. The rim hoop was measured from a woman's eyes to the ground, forming a round frame. The rim hoop was connected with lower hoops secured by crosspieces. Robes were stretched around the frame, hair side in, and tied to the rim hoop.

A numipu hide boat took ten to fifteen minutes to construct. The finished boat was carried to the river, tied to a stake, and set into the water. The load was carefully fitted inside while it sat in the water. Because of the strong current, hide boats were bunched, up to a dozen riding downstream together, the gunwales joined by thongs. Experience taught that tightly bunched boats rode through a choppy current more safely than a single boat. Elderly people and women with small children rode in the boats on top of the packs. The bunched boats were held steady by men swimming alongside, and were hauled toward the opposite bank of the river by horses guided by swimmers.

The bands crossed in the same order as they had observed during the march. Nine boats of Hemene's wi-ses made the first crossing together, six of the women riding with their little children. Seton swam on the side of one of the boats, holding the rim hoop fast. Tsacope rode in it, held by their mother. Dawn focused on the churning river. Tsacope watched Seton earnestly, grimacing only once when the current pushed him under for a moment and he swallowed water and came up coughing. They made for the crooked curve of the first bend and hit the bank, the lariated horses, already out of the water, holding the boats against the sweep of the current and pulling them ashore. The boats spilled parts of their loads as they were dragged to safe grounds. Some of the women and children were thrown out, but it did not matter. They had made the crossing.

Hemene, Itsepit, and Talooth, Hemene's sister-in-law, crossed on their own, swimming with their horses. The young men recrossed to the east bank to assist another hide boat run. Not everyone was needed. Others floated the tipi poles across, tied up into rafts pulled by horses maneuvered by swimmers. One by one the bands crossed. Last came the horses, driven into the river in their hundreds, struggling, wild-eyed, but gaining the western bank without any losses.

After a brief rest on benches above the river, the horses were ready to move again. The column marched on, Lamtamas still leading. It passed downstream along the curving river, on flats below knobby hills. Two miles farther on it swerved west and crossed a ridge and went into the valley of Deer Creek where camp was made among tall ponderosas on ground with good grass. Everyone knew this camp would not be for long, so fewer than half the lodges went up. Cool mountain weather prevailed, but there was no rain. In the mornings the sun came up and walked unhurriedly across the sky.

The chiefs thought it necessary to round up the great herds of horses and the smaller herds of cattle that were widely dispersed over the plateaus and broken country between the Snake and Salmon rivers. Parties of men and older boys went out to do it, while groups of scouts recrossed the Salmon to search for the suyapu soldiers who were surely coming.

The Lamtama party, to effect the roundup, left on the second morning of the Deer Creek camp. Of the Hemene wi-ses, Seton, Atemis, and the young warrior Ayokka went. They took supplies for four days. Men of the Wallowa band had gone before them because they had the farthest to travel.

Deer Creek flowed from the slopes of Wildhorse Butte, six miles away, and ran through a pleasant valley northeast toward the Salmon River. On the trail of the Wallowa party, the Lamtama men and boys rode up the valley on rising ground and turned north and climbed Horse Ridge in front of Wildhorse Butte. They stayed on the high ground, following the contour of the plateau, and angled northeast until they reached the Doumecq Plain, seven miles north of their camp on Deer Creek as the raven flies.

The plain, with an average height of four thousand feet, was a high plateau ten miles long and four miles wide, surrounded by the deep trench of the Salmon to the east and north and the equally deep furrow of Rice Creek to the west. Rice Creek separated it from the Joseph Plain, four times the size of Doumecq but identical in vegetation.

The herds of the Lamtama had roamed free on the Doumecq Plain during the past winter and spring. A handful of men and older boys had patrolled the area, mainly against wolves and suyapu intruders. No suyapu had come so far yet, although a few were working two small mines on the Salmon's west bank below the rough slopes of the plain.

The Joseph Plain was shared by the Pekonan and Wallowa bands. Although the plain was part of Pekonan territory, Toohoolhoolzote's band had allowed the Wallowa people to bring their herds to the plain after crossing the Snake River in mid-May. In this crossing, executed near the mouth of the Imnaha River just north of Hells Canyon, the turbulent stream swept away and drowned hundreds of Wallowa horses and nearly a hundred head of cattle. Mares with newborn foals had to be left behind in Oregon. None of the foals would have survived the river. Hundreds of horses still on the Oregon side, and held by a few youthful herders, were stolen by suyapu ranchers. The Wallowa people, already on the other riverbank, watched with heavy hearts, unable to stop it.

The Pekonan herds were concentrated on the southern part of the Joseph Plain, the Wallowa herds on the northern part. Despite the great losses, the Wallowa horses still totaled over sixteen hundred, including those by the Deer Creek camp. The Lamtama herd numbered above a thousand. The Pekonan band had about six hundred. Together the three bands still held well over three thousand horses.

Seton and the others rode through scattered clumps of horses from the moment they crossed the narrow tongue of land that connected the ridge country with the Doumecq Plain. Among those they passed were many that had never known a human's touch. Breaking was not the numipu way of persuading horses to accept a saddle or pack. They were not tamed. Their spirit was not broken. They were gentled by patience and care to accept humans and to partner with them. The appaloosa's strength, endurance, and courage required the same qualities of a rider.

Seton and the Lamtama men looked at the herds with pride as they rode toward the smoke flag coming from the campsite a few miles ahead. There were two tipis under the ponderosas, and saddle horses grazed close by. A handful of herders rushed to greet the riders, eager for news. They had been isolated for three months. They knew nothing of what had happened away from the plain. The news sank in slowly. There was a silence. There were questions. Some could be answered, some could not. The herders reported that they had seen no other people, but three grizzlies were on the plain. None had bothered the horses. They had shot at wolves, though, and killed two pumas who had killed foals. Beyond that, they said, the horses were well. So was the small bunch of cattle. The springs had good water. It was early afternoon when Seton's group rode away.

For five days the riders searched every ravine and nook. They traveled the length of Center Creek, which cut through the north face of the plain toward the Salmon. With thundering hoofbeats, wave after wave of skittish, unshod horses was gathered on the wide flat in the middle of the Doumecq Plain. They were held by a ring of riders. The few horses that could not be found had probably been chased away or killed by wolves. Three old white-faced bulls refused to be removed and were left behind. The rest of the cattle, about sixty head, were also assembled and held near the horse herd.

Horses of the different wi-ses were kept together within the large gathering. Seton found his two mares, the chestnut and the snowflake appaloosa. He loved these days in the mountains—the earthy smell of the horses, their restless bustle, the smell of sage, juniper, pine, and dry grass, the grousing coyotes, the singing wolves, a wind full of messages, night's friendly campfires, slow, long stories told while the stars stood still.

In midafternoon on the fifth day, June 26, a group of eight teenage boys arrived to replace the men in the herders' camp. They had been called back to the main camp. Scouts had reported that the Cut Arm general and his army had arrived on the battlefield above Iahmotta and buried their dead. When the men left, the wind was changing. Heavy clouds rolled in from the northwest, ominous, threatening.

Before dark fell, it started to rain, a hard, pounding rain that turned to snow. The herders huddled in the two tipis, smoke flaps set away from the wind, and tried to keep a fire going in each. The newly arrived teenagers had brought o'ppah, kouse bread, and a good supply of fresh beef. They roasted meat on spits and listened to the wind hurl itself at the tipis, making the poles groan and covers creak.

Riders had come in soaked and told them that the herd had drifted south about a mile, seeking shelter in an area where ponderosas stood densely above the plain. Beside Seton, only two herders were eighteen, Moositsa and Antelope. One was nineteen, Kowtoliks. They were not warriors yet, but they soon would be. Like Atemis, they had received captured Springfield carbines after the Iahmotta fight. The other boys were between fifteen and seventeen. Leadership was expected from the oldest, including Seton. This bunch of fifteen teenagers would drive over seven hundred wild and skittish horses and a small cattle herd wherever was demanded of them.

With Kowtoliks and Antelope, Swan Necklace had been among the new arrivals. A good-looking boy of seventeen, he was a nephew of Wahlitits and a cousin of Sarpsis Ilppilp. He had served as horse holder for the two when they started killing whites on the Salmon on June 13.

He had been given a new Winchester 1873 repeater for his service, taken from one of the victims. Everyone in camp knew about his role in the raid, but no one spoke of it. Seton, who had not seen him since before the Fort Lapwai meeting, acknowledged him when he rode in with the others. Their eyes had met, and both had smiled. They knew each other well. Nothing had to be said. Swan Necklace moved into the same lodge as Seton, along with Kowtoliks and Moositsa.

Rain mixed with snow continued through the night. Two of the younger boys by the door kept the fire alive for a while, but the wet wood they brought in caused so much smoke that they let it die. Toward morning the temperature fell below freezing. When Seton peeked through the door flap at daylight, the ground was white under a gray sky.

The day before, he had turned the roan mare loose and taken the snowflake appaloosa out of the herd for his saddle horse. The mare was a gift from his mother. He had ridden slowly into the herd with a rawhide halter. The horses were milling nervously, and he had not looked at them. He moved the roan forward with his knees, and when he came to the snowflake he slipped the halter over its head and clucked to her and talked her gently out of the herd. He had taken the mare to where the tipis sat and tied it up and rubbed the animal's nose and ears and back. He walked around it, touching, talking, and when he ran his hand down the mare's foreleg it had lifted its hoof. He had cradled the hoof between his knees and pulled out his knife and pared back the hoof wall where the edges were splayed, then walked around and pared the other hooves. The mare's hooves were dark with heavy hoof walls, the kind of horse one should have to run in the mountains.

Looking out from the lodge door this morning, he found a white and cold world. The saddle horses stood bunched among the pines with hanging heads. They were wet and miserable, but patient, their hindquarters against the wind. It had stopped snowing, but the wind was still from the northwest. Seton walked barefoot in the snow to keep his moccasins from getting wet. He relieved himself and walked to the mare and rubbed the water off the silky skin of her back. He went inside the tipi and broke off a chunk of o'ppah and came back and broke it into smaller pieces and fed them to his horse one by one.

It started to rain while he stood there, a thin, soft rain that drizzled down from the leaden sky. It continued for a long time. Inside the tipis, water ran down along the poles, coming in through the open crotch at the top where the poles jutted out. It dripped on packs and bedrolls, and the boys sat hunched around cold fires. Like Seton, most of the others shared their o'ppah ration with their saddle horses, but the horses of the great herd had to fend for themselves. They had done so through many a winter. The boys and the horses spent another miserable night, but early next morning the sky cleared and the sun returned.

A few of the boys rode out to check on the herd and found it spread out on the southern edge of the Doumecq Plain, feeding, cattle mixed with the horses. Under a fine rising mist, the snow melted fast, leaving pools and slippery places on the broken surface of the plain. Around the camp the boys spread bedrolls and clothing and moccasins on brush and tree branches to dry. They lifted the lodge covers for the same reason. They had just managed to build a fire when they heard gunfire.

It came from the direction of their camp, seven miles due south. First there were rolling salvos from the suyapu army. Then a scattering of irregular rifle fire that petered out quickly. The army salvos crashed on a few more times before falling silent.

The boys stood, listening. "Sounds like a fight," Kowtoliks said.

No one moved. "If it was a fight, it is over," Moositsa said. They kept listening but heard nothing more.

"This was close to our camp," Seton said. The others nodded with serious faces.

"We must get ready," Kowtoliks said. "The chief said he would send someone to tell us when to bring the herd in."

No messenger came that day. They used the time to separate the dams and their two-month old foals from the herd and drive them to the northern part of the plain. They left them there with heavy hearts. The foals were too young to swim the Salmon. The Doumecq Plain was the safest place for them to stay. Perhaps they could be brought out later.

The messenger arrived in the early afternoon on the following day. He was Eshawis, a warrior of White Goose's own wi-ses. Half the boys were with the herd, holding it to a large but confined area on the southern part of the plain. Eshawis talked to Moositsa and Antelope, the oldest herders in camp. The others listened attentively.

"Cut Arm is crossing the river," he said. "He has horse soldiers and foot soldiers with him. He has big guns. He has many suyapu civilians with him, some people we know. We did not touch these people. Now they are fighting us too."

He paused. "He tries to cross at the horseshoe bend. The suyapu cannot do this well. They have lost horses and mules. He has many soldiers there. We rode at them at the crossing and scared them. They shot at us, but no one was hurt."

He grinned briefly. "We moved the camp up into the mountains where the medicine trees are, *pottoosway*. The women were afraid of the big guns and the soldiers. We are some distance this way." He pointed southwest. "The Wallowas and Pekonans are ahead of us. We wait."

He paused again. "We wait until all the suyapu have crossed to follow us. Then we will move north and cross at the big bend, at Pah-kayatwekin's cabin."

He waited, letting the information sink in. He looked at Moositsa and Antelope. "We will tell you when to bring the horses. We talked about the cattle. We agreed that you should leave them here. They would slow us down. Leave the mares with foals here too. We'll have to move fast."

He paused. "You understand?"

The boys nodded. "When do we bring the horses?" Moositsa asked. "When will this be? Tomorrow? One day from tomorrow?"

"I don't know," Eshawis said. "It depends on the suyapu soldiers." He frowned. "Maybe two days. They are slow. Maybe more. We will let you know." He nodded to the boys and turned his horse and rode off.

No messenger came the next day, but at midmorning on the day following, Eshawis rode up again. This time he met with Kowtoliks, Seton, Atemis, and Swan Necklace, who were guarding the herd. "Cut

Arm and the army have crossed the river and are moving past our campsite on Deer Creek. It is time to leave."

He paused. "Wallowa and Pekonan bands left at sunrise. Our band,
Lamtama, is leaving now. The chief says to bring the horses in behind
us. Follow our trail."

The boys nodded. "Yes," Kowtoliks said. Eshawis turned his horse.
He looked back once, raising an arm as he galloped away.

"Go, tell the others," Kowtoliks told Atemis. "Break camp, hurry!
Leave the lodge poles. When you come up, cover the flanks and the tail
of the herd. Seton and I will ride point. You and Moositsa ride at the
tail, agreed?"

Atemis nodded and backed his horse away. "Wait," Kowtoliks said.
"When you break camp, we'll cut the cattle. Hurry!"

Seton and Kowtoliks and Swan Necklace and four boys rode
into the herd slowly and separated sixty head of cattle from the horses, moved them out, and drove them a short distance north. It took a
while, and when they were done the rest of the herders came up, leading packhorses with the lodge covers and equipment. They halted and
waited.

Kowtoliks raised his arm, and he and Seton rode to the southern
edge of the herd and took the point. When the flank and the drag riders
called out, yipping, they rode slowly south. An old mare took the lead
of the herd and followed the point riders. A tremor ran through the
great mass of horses as they started forward, slowly at first, thinning
out into a file three to four animals wide. They gained speed as Seton
and Kowtoliks urged their mounts into a lope. And then the surge of a
stream of bodies came on with a powerful churning of hooves.

The rear guard waited at the empty campsite on the southern edge
of the Joseph Plain, twelve heavily armed men. Beyond them were still
others, scouts hugging the advance of Howard's army, but they were
miles away. The rear guard stood by their horses in silence as the clamor
of thousands of hooves drew near.

Finally the herd came into view, Kowtoliks and Seton riding point,
rifles across their backs, looking wild and distant, absorbed in their task.

The wave of animals lapped forward behind them, coming on, nostrils flaring, manes waving, wild-eyed with flashes of spotted skins in bay, roan, pinto, black and white. Along the flanks of the remuda were the teenage riders, yipping, occasionally slapping their thighs, or singing with high-pitched voices. It seemed the stream of horseflesh was endless. The point riders reached the campsite and swung north, acknowledged the raised arms of the warriors but kept moving, concentrating on the trail in front and on the horses behind them.

The trail was a deep furrow plowed into the highland meadows by hundreds of horses and countless tipi poles. It meandered through a thin spread of pine forests, staying on the high ground, evading ravines and depressions filled with brush and debris. A few miles farther on the Joseph Plain, the point riders slowed the herd down and let the animals walk. A few times small bunches of horses branched off and tried to escape, slipping into the pines only to be headed off by flank riders and moved back. The herd had covered about ten miles, half the distance to the river crossing. Another run on a slow canter, another walk. On the last leg of the trail, the run went along the ridge that jutted into the great oxbow of the Salmon and plunged down the east side of the ridge to the narrow belt of grassland by the river. Near the first curve, where the river twists sharply north, Seton and Kowtoliks turned the herd upon itself and brought the rushing flood of horses to a nervous standstill.

Looking north toward the apex of the great bend nearly two miles away, Seton saw the Lamtama people on the opposite shore getting the packhorses ready after crossing. The current had driven their hide boats, their swimmers, and their camp horses against the north bank between the mouths of Maloney and Deer creeks. The Wallowa and Pekonan bands were not in sight. They had crossed earlier and gone on. To the northwest, beyond the river, the heights of the Craig Mountains stood against the sky.

It was late afternoon. The herders gathered, sitting their horses in a circle. They gazed glumly at the blue gray waters before them. Four of the boys were away, searching for shoots to build two hide boats to ferry across lodge covers, weapons, bedrolls, and clothing. "We'll give the horses a rest," Kowtoliks said, "until our people over there are gone to the hills." He looked along the faces around him. "Let's unload the packhorses."

Packs, saddles, and every piece of clothing but breechclouts were put on a pile by the river. While the others took up positions around the herd, three of the boys, led by eighteen-year-old Antelope, began to build the hide boats. They were not as skilled in this as their mothers, but they managed to produce boats that would float.

The sun broke through the clouds and walked toward evening. Finally everything was ready. First, six of the boys swam across with the boats, four horses pulling, struggling, the boys' naked brown bodies and wafting black hair bobbing in the waves among their horses. The current took them by Pahkayatwekin's abandoned cabin and orchard on the south bank and pushed them into the curve of the oxbow against the bank where they got a hold and scrambled out of the flow of the river.

Next, the herd was lined up against the bank, and with Seton and Kowtoliks forcing their mounts into the wild waters, the head of the remuda, with yells and the slapping of thighs, was pushed to follow. In a great rush, the long line of horses, like an avalanche, splashed into the river. The animals were immediately taken by the current, swimming, struggling, their heads bounced up and down by the waves. The remaining herders swam along with them, holding the necks of their mounts.

Seton and Kowtoliks and their horses hit the north bend of the oxbow first, clambered ashore and mounted up. Behind and around them, along a stretch of half a mile of shore, horses fought for footholds and climbed out, wild-eyed, breathing heavily. About three dozen animals drifted past but made landfall farther down the bend. None was lost. The herders unloaded and dismantled the hide boats. They dressed and saddled up, rearmed themselves, brought the herd under control, and moved off. Kowtoliks and Seton were still at point.

They followed the broad trail before them. It climbed to higher ground, the westernmost corner of the Camas Prairie, and turned east. This was dry grassland, sparsely dotted with evergreens. They rode on for eight more miles, once crossing the upper reaches of Deer Creek.

When dusk came, they smelled smoke and saw the fires of the camp glowing in the distance below Moughmer Ridge. This was the old *aipadass* campsite. One big herd of horses was spread out north of the camp, another to the south. They moved their herd to a position west of the camp and let the animals disperse to graze. Water was available at Telcher Creek and a spring to the west.

Kowtoliks signaled to the boys, and he and Seton rode over to the camp. No tipis had been pitched. Saddle and packhorses were held close to the packs piled in the grass. Dogs howled when the two approached. People sat around cooking fires; some got up to watch them. The camp was behind Telcher Creek, stretched west to east along a tributary. They rode through the creek and came up to the Lamtama part of the camp. Someone called out to Kowtoliks. He waved his arm and rode up. Another call. Teeweeyownah suddenly stood in their path. He raised his right arm, glancing from one to the other.

"We are looking for White Goose," Seton said. "We brought our horses."

"Yes," Teeweeyownah said with a rare smile. "We saw you. Did you lose any?"

"No," Kowtoliks said proudly.

"We had to leave mares and their foals in the high country," Seton said. "We could not take them with us." Teeweeyownah nodded. He pointed with his chin. "White Goose is over there." He stepped aside to let them pass. He touched Seton on the leg as he rode by. "Later, come and eat with us. And Atemis."

They found the chief sitting by a fire with three men beside him: Wottolen, Five Wounds, and Rainbow. The group looked up when the two herders dismounted. White Goose got up and waved them over. He stood straight and tall, still muscular despite his seventy-three years. He wore neither feathers nor ornaments. Carefully braided hair hung down his chest. His usually somber face showed a friendly smile.

"You brought the horses," he said. "Thank you. You must tell us. Come, sit with us." He pointed. He looked behind him and called to a woman in the shadows. "Bring food. These men are hungry."

EIGHT

TSACOPE HAD BROUGHT TWO PAIRS OF MOCCASINS over and set them in front of Seton. The moccasins were of soft, cream-colored deer skin uppers with stiff rawhide soles. Below the tongue, in the middle of each front piece, was a beaded six-pointed blue star about two inches in diameter, and above the soles ran a beaded band in transverse stripes of white and blue, all seed beads.

Seton had spent the night in Hemene's camp. Men had guarded the horse herd, giving the teenage drovers a rest. In the morning Seton and Atemis had enjoyed a good meal with the families, and later the people of the wi-ses sat around the fire, talking. One of the young men, Kywis, was away on scout duty. Ayokka had replaced Seton and Atemis guarding the horse herd.

Seton looked from the moccasins to Itsepit. She sat across the fire, next to Dawn. "Thank you," he said. "They are good. I needed them."

Itsepit smiled. "Make use of them," she said. "Your footsteps will be soft on the ground. The suyapu and the deer won't hear you." She was teasing him, looking coy. Everyone present knew. She had made moccasins for him since his mother had died, but not with such a design.

"So pretty, these moccasins," Teeweeyownah said, pointing with his chin, teasing his sister-in-law. "You should have made them for me. I could be your husband. I would be a good husband for you."

"You have my sister," Itsepit said. "You don't need two wives."

"But I see you are looking for a husband," Teeweeyownah said. "I know that you had your eyes on Seton for some time, and now that he is back, this is getting serious." It was a joke. Everyone knew that Seton and Itsepit should never be a couple because they were parallel cousins.

All around the circle people were smiling. Seton looked bashful and tried to avoid meeting anyone's eyes.

"Sometimes you speak too much, brother-in-law," the girl said, smiling. "You are jealous and you're not that good-looking. I wonder what my sister sees in you."

"Oh," Teeweeyownah said. "You are bad. I have other qualities. You should ask your sister."

"I did," Itsepit said. "She wouldn't tell me."

"See," Teeweeyownah said. "It's a secret. But if you were my second wife, you would know."

"Thank you," Itsepit said, "but I don't want to know."

"I think there is something to what Teeweeyownah said," Thunder Eyes cut in, continuing the teasing. "I also noticed how Itsepit looks at Seton when she thinks nobody sees it."

"Be quiet," Itsepit said. "I don't tell what you try to do to me when your wife is not around."

"Tell us, girl," Tamonmo, Thunder Eyes's wife said. "I think we already know." With a wicked smile she looked around the faces of the other women in the circle. They laughed.

"Sometime I'll tell you," Itsepit said. All this had been done in good humor. She had held her own, but now she had had enough. She stood and beckoned to Tsacope. The little girl went to her, and they both walked away.

Seton would have liked to disappear too, but that would have made things worse. Sitting next to Hemene, he was eager to change the topic of the conversation.

"Where are we going from this place?" he asked. "To the Clear-water?"

"Yes." Hemene nodded.

"The Alpowai and Paloos bands—will they join us there?"

"The Alpowais will. The Palooses, I don't know," Hemene said.

The people around the circle stopped talking among themselves and listened, their faces serious again.

"Looking Glass sent two men yesterday. They talked with the chiefs. Horse soldiers attacked their village two days ago. A Captain Whipple, they said, with two companies of bluecoats and a bunch of suyapu civilians. It was a surprise. The Alpowais were in their village on reservation land. The suyapu should never have attacked them there."

He paused. "The Alpowais lost most of their lodges. They barely escaped with their lives. There was a lot of shooting. The village lost everything of value. Their cattle and all their horses were stolen—over seven hundred horses."

His voice was angry. "One woman and her little child drowned in the river along with their horse, trying to escape." He shook his head. "Looking Glass is waiting to join us, his men said. They wanted to stay away from the war, but the suyapu did not let them. Now they want to fight. They want their horses back."

There was a silence. "What happened to the horse soldiers?" Seton asked.

"We don't know," Teeweeyownah said. "We have scouts out looking for them."

The answer came from an unexpected source. They were still sitting there, thinking of what had been said, when they heard someone singing. A chant sung by a single voice drifted across the camp. A rider had come west across the Moughmer Ridge and began to sing when he passed the Wallowa camp. It was the high-pitched halloo of a warrior who has met an enemy and killed him, a victory song. The warrior rode a bay horse and continued singing until, by the Pekonan camp, his horse was halted by men of the three bands, who quickly surrounded him.

Seton went there with the men of his wi-ses. The rider was Seeyakoon Ilppilp. He held a captured Winchester repeater and a cartridge belt high above his head. "Some white men almost killed me," he called out. "They were scouts, two suyapu men coming this way. They saw me and came for me. They fired at me. I killed one of them. Shot him through the head. The other man got away."

An excited murmur ran through the men around him. The band chiefs had come up behind the men. "Soldiers are close," Seeyakoon said, now with a calmer voice.

"Where are they? What are they doing?" White Goose asked.

"They are on a hill by the Norton place, where the cupcup tree stands. They are camped there. They have dug rifle pits and trenches. They are ready for war."

"Let us go and see," Rainbow said. "Let us make three bunches of warriors. I will take a few. Who is going with me?" He looked around. Arms rose.

The meeting broke up. Three bodies of men rode out, led by Five Wounds, Rainbow, and Two Moons, about forty warriors altogether. They gathered and galloped off, and the three groups spread out. The left and right wings were under the two warmates. Two Moons and the men with him took the center.

Back in camp people talked and waited. Teeweeyownah, Allultakanin, and Short Bull of the Hemene wi-ses had ridden with Five Wounds. Plenty of warriors remained in case the camp had to be protected or moved. The men were called back from the herds. Teenage guards resumed their duties there. Seton wore his new moccasins when he rode out. He looked for Itsepit but did not see her.

Seton, Atemis, and Swan Necklace sat on the ground in the space between the Lamtama horses and the Wallowa herd. They were talking, holding the lariats of their horses, when the sound of rifle fire reached them from the east beyond Moughmer Ridge. The boys mounted. The firing continued for some time, seemed to move away, became weaker and ended abruptly. They sat their horses and listened. The camp lay quiet. The horses of the vast herd grazed undisturbed. No more sounds came. Then gunfire erupted once more, closer this time, and to the northeast. First it was irregular rifle fire, then rapid bursts of a different kind the boys had never heard before. There was more rifle fire, more of the strange rapid fire, then silence again.

Seton did not know what to think. "Strange sounds," he said. "I think there was a running fight, and then there was that sound."

"They'll tell us what happened," Atemis said. But no one came. Perhaps an hour had passed when they saw two of the warrior groups streaming back over the ridge, yipping, riding fast, holding rifles high above their heads.

"Go and see," Seton said to Atemis.

Seton and Swan Necklace looked toward the camp, half a mile away. There was movement, horsemen riding back and forth, people standing in groups. Finally the horsemen dismounted and the people settled down. When Atemis returned, a few more herders had joined Seton and Swan Necklace. Atemis was laughing.

"They killed an officer and twelve men," he said, excitement in his voice.

"How did it happen?" Moositsa asked.

"They met those soldiers and chased them. They had been sent to look for us, Rainbow said. The soldiers ran. They dismounted and left their horses. They fought on foot. They took cover behind rocks in a bad place. All were killed."

He paused. "After that our men rode around the soldiers on the hill. The suyapu were afraid to come out of their holes. They shot at our men with rifles and with a big gun that is mounted on wheels. That gun shoots fast. It is called a Gatling gun, Rainbow said. He knows about it. It shoots on and on, fast, but it doesn't shoot far. None of our men was hurt."

He looked along the faces around him. "Two Moons and some men are still out there," he pointed northeast, "watching the bluecoats."

"What are we going to do?" Seton asked. "Are we staying here?"

"No," Atemis said. "I was told to tell you that the camp moves tomorrow. We are going to *piswah ilppilp pah,* the spring at Red Rock."

During a cool, quiet night, scouts came from all directions. One scout, arriving from the Salmon, reported that Howard's army was still on the other side of the river, but was approaching the big bend where the camp had crossed two days before.

Before sunrise on July 4 the camp repacked and moved out, the Wallowa band leading, Pekonan and Lamtama coming behind. The horse herds were driven alongside the bands, but at a distance. Each was steered separately, surrounded by drovers who made sure their animals did not mix with other herds. Small groups of warriors acted as advance and rear guards and rode cover along the flanks of the column. The column was about five miles long and went east with good speed. It traveled fourteen miles through low, green hills, the heart of the Camas Prairie, to the spring on Red Rock Creek. They passed as close as three miles from the entrenched soldiers at the ruins of Norton House, but they were out of sight.

As the column marched away, a scouting party of a dozen young men clashed with a slightly larger force of civilian volunteers who rode up from the Salmon. The skirmish lasted for hours, well into the afternoon. It took place in full view of the military, which offered no assistance to the civilians. A few of these volunteers were killed; more were wounded. The numipu scouts disengaged when one of theirs was badly wounded, Weesculatat, the only middle-aged man among them. He was the father of Joe Albert, one of Captain Perry's downriver scouts in the lahmotta affair. Weesculatat was brought to the camp by the spring, where he died during the night. He was the first casualty the bands had suffered in combat. He was buried the morning of the following day.

Seton was with the horses and did not see the burial. He saw from a distance that a crowd of about four hundred people had gathered, forming a tight circle. Because Weesculatat was of the Wallowa band, a

Wallowa ceremonial person conducted the parting ceremony. After the grave was closed, the Wallowa herders ran horses over the grave so that all trace of it was obliterated.

After a quick meal the bands continued the march east. They followed Red Rock Creek for four miles to where it joined Cottonwood Creek and went down the broad green valley of that stream for another seven miles to the Clearwater River. There, on the west bank of the river, on the ancient campsite called *peeta auüwa,* tipis were raised again. The horse herds of the three bands, well over three thousand animals, were held on six miles of Cottonwood Creek valley and on four miles of a valley branching off into the hills to the north.

While the camp settled down by the river, Ollokot, with about thirty warriors, rode back over their trail. They passed the Lamtama herd and waved to the boys watching the horses. Seton recognized a few men of the Lamtamas, but no one from his wi-ses was in the party. They were dressed for battle: the sun glinted on their floating black hair, their brown bodies were naked above the waist. They held their rifles ready and rode up a yellow slope and vanished.

Later he saw them come back, waving as they rode by, apparently satisfied with themselves. They had surrounded Captain Whipple's dug-in force at Norton House, which had been strengthened the day before by the arrival of Captain Perry with a supply train and an escort of cavalry. They had harassed the troops with dashing displays of numipu horsemanship and accurate fire from captured Springfields. Although the troops outnumbered Ollokot's little war band five to one, their officers had not dared to charge the enemy on the open prairie. The only losses on the numipu side had been two horses killed under their riders, including Ollokot's splendid cream-colored war horse.

The boys had set up a tipi on the upper reaches of Cottonwood Creek, beyond the perimeter of the herd. In the evening, five of them sat around a small fire under gnarled cottonwood trees. They were talking when they heard a rider approach at a fast lope. It was Kowtoliks. He dismounted and patted his horse on the rump. It walked away and began to graze. Kowtoliks sat by the fire, legs crossed.

"The Alpowais and Palooses have come in," he said. "They said they had had enough. They are going to fight. They have lost most of what they had, both bands. Not much more left, only the horses they ride. They were robbed by the suyapu, bluecoats and civilians." He plucked a blade of grass and put it in his mouth. He chewed and looked into the fire.

"What are they doing now?" Swan Necklace asked.

"They made camp north of the Wallowa people, on the flat by the river." He swallowed. "It's a poor camp. Many of the Alpowai tipis were burned by the soldiers. The Palooses still have their tipis, though."

"What did you find out about us?" Seton asked. "Will we stay here?"

Kowtoliks shrugged. "No one told me. I guess no one knows."

The meeting was held at midmorning near the west bank of the Clear-water in the space between the Pekonan and Lamtama lodges. A stone's throw away the river churned north, its banks framed by mountain alders, willows, dogwood shrub, and chokecherry thickets.

The band chiefs had taken their places according to the ancient geographical distribution of their bands. Hahtalekin and Naked Head sat in the north position, representing the Palooses. Clockwise the circle continued in the east with Looking Glass, Alpowai; southeast, White Goose for Lamtama; southwest, Toohoolhoolzote, for Pekonan; and west, Joseph and Ollokot for the Wallowa people. Rainbow and Five Wounds sat on the Lamtama side close to the Alpowais. The band chiefs had a few of the wi-ses chiefs of their bands beside them. Behind them were a handful of warriors. Seton sat behind Hemene with Tee-weeyownah and Allultakanin. Hemene had wanted Seton there in case someone wanted to know what had transpired at Lapwai Agency and the fort prior to Captain Perry's march to lahmotta.

When all were seated, White Goose, the oldest among the chiefs, opened the meeting.

"Finally, we are all together," he said, looking around the circle. "I welcome the Alpowais and Palooses to our camp. They have had difficulties, but now they are with us. They make us stronger."

A murmur of agreement came from the assembled men. "We are safe for the moment," White Goose continued. "The soldiers back there by the cupcup tree are no danger to us. Since we killed some of them, the others are afraid to come out of the trenches they dug into the hill. We tried to get them to come out and fight us, but they won't."

He paused. "Last night one of my men came in. Sarpsis Ilppilp. He had watched the suyapu army on the other side of the Salmon." He shook his head. "Cut Arm and his soldiers tried to cross the river where we crossed, at the great bend. They couldn't do it. They built a raft from the logs of Pahkayatwekin's cabin, but the raft turned over. Sarpsis said some men on the raft didn't come back. Maybe they drowned."

He paused again. "The suyapu army has moved back south. Maybe Cut Arm is going to cross at the horseshoe bend near Iahmotta. It will be many days before he comes close to us."

He touched his chin with the tip of the eagle wing fan he held in his right hand. "We are safe for the moment," he repeated. "But we have to know what we are going to do. We cannot stay in this camp for long."

There was a strong murmur of agreement.

Looking Glass raised his right hand. The Alpowai chief was the only one at the meeting to wear a head decoration—a black felt hat with beaded bands tied around the top and an eagle plume above the brim on the right side. In his early forties, he was a lean, muscular man of medium size with a sharp nose and high cheekbones. His mouth could turn quickly into a smile or a smirk. Looking Glass had a reputation for having fought Lakotas and Cheyennes in the Plains, but he was also known to be self-centered with a streak of vanity. Seton, who had known the chief during the three years he spent in the buffalo country from 1872 to 1874, watched with curiosity. He was not surprised that Looking Glass spoke humbly on this occasion.

"My relations and friends," the Alpowai said. "I sit before you a fool. I trusted Cut Arm when he said we would be safe on his reservation.

We were not. Five days ago my camp on the Middle Fork of the Clear-water was attacked by soldiers and civilians, some of whom we thought were our friends. Two of my people were killed, the woman Bear Blan-ket and her little one. Our horse herd was stolen. Our cattle were driven away. Our lodges were destroyed, and our gardens were trampled to dust by suyapu horses."

He paused. "We lost almost everything. We barely escaped with our lives. When the soldiers came, we weren't worried. We were in the place where Cut Arm knew we would be. I sent Peopeo Tholekt across the river to explain to the officer. He did not listen. They shot into our camp with rifles and Gatling guns. We could not defend ourselves. The bullets hit like hail among us."

He looked around the faces before him, bitterness in his voice.

"My father's warriors fought many battles as friends of the suy-apu. We had friends and relations killed fighting beside the horse sol-diers. The people we fought were more our relations than the suyapu. Hunyewat, the Creator, had given them the land they lived on. It was the suyapu who came from far away. But we were blind. For them we fought Cayuses, Yakimas, Umatillas, Spokanes, and others. The suy-apu turned us against them. Their preachers lied to us. Their chiefs lied to us. Cut Arm lied to us. We are not safe on the reservation."

He paused again. "We will fight the suyapu with you. They shed our blood. We will take theirs. We will punish them. We want our hors-es back."

There was a silence, then sounds of approval. Silence again.

"I was asked to speak for Palooses," Naked Head said. The tiwét held an eagle wing fan in one hand. He laid the fan across his chest, the tips of the feathers touching the shirt over his heart. "We were deceived too," he said. "We left the lands where our people are buried, all that country in the northwest, by the Snake River. We left because we didn't want a war. We were not afraid for ourselves, warriors; we were afraid for our women and children. The suyapu always try to kill them first. We have seen this many times. Remember the Cayuses, the Umatillas,

Yakimas. Remember what happened to them. We looked the other way. We should not have looked away."

He paused. "We, Palooses, moved on the reservation as we had promised Cut Arm. We made our camp downstream from Kamiah. We thought there would be peace."

He shook his head angrily. "We were wrong. After we heard that horse soldiers had been defeated at lahmotta, suyapu civilians began to hang around our camp, spying on us. Our women were afraid to leave camp. Our own people, downriver numipu, spied on us. We saw that we had made a mistake. We wanted to join you," he looked to White Goose, "but we are only a small band. We could not have fought our way through the soldiers on Camas Prairie and through Cut Arm's army. We waited. We waited for you to come here."

He paused again. "Five days ago, on the same day the Alpowai camp was attacked, suyapu horse thieves drove our horse herd away. Three hundred horses, all the horses we had not tied up around the lodges. We could do nothing about it."

He moved the wing fan back and forth in front of his face. "We took the lodges down and moved upriver until we met the Alpowais. We had come past their camp. Lodges were still burning. At least we saved our lodges."

He stared blindly in front of him. "We are all together now, the ones who were told to give up their lands. We are of one mind. We will fight."

Again there was a murmur of approval from around the circle, then heavy silence.

"My heart is glad we are finally together," Ollokot said with a hard, unforgiving voice. "I hope we are of one mind. If not, we will lose."

He sought the eyes of Looking Glass, but the Alpowai chief looked away. "We must decide what to do," he continued.

He paused. "I see three choices. We take most of our warriors and hit Cut Arm when he is crossing the Salmon. He will not expect us there. Or we wait here until he comes to us and fight him on ground

where we have an advantage. Or we go back to the Snake River country, put our camps and our horses in the mountains where the soldiers
cannot reach them, and drive all the suyapu around us away. At least we
would fight in our own country. The trail is still open. Nobody would
stop us if we crossed Camas Prairie now."

He waited. "We must decide today."

Teeweeyownah, next to Seton, moved. He bent forward and put
his hand on Hemene's shoulder. The wi-ses chief leaned back. "Ollokot
is right," Teeweeyownah whispered. "We should take the best warriors
and attack Cut Arm when he is crossing the Salmon. We can destroy
him and his army there."

Seton looked past Hemene to the west side of the circle, toward
the Wallowa chiefs. He studied Ollokot's youthful face, normally open,
generous, and fair; now passionate, probing. Beyond, the yellow and
green slopes rose from the valley floor and rolled away west, hiding the
Camas Prairie behind their knobby heights. The sun lay full on those soft
slopes, the yellow grass, the green of other grasses, larches, and pines.
How beautiful, he thought suddenly, with the cream-colored lodges
and friendly curls of smoke of the Pekonan camp in the foreground.

"Yes," someone said, "we could do any of these things Ollokot has
described." The speaker was Looking Glass, his voice smooth, genial.
"If we move away to the Snake River, we and the Palooses will never
get any of the horses back that were taken from us. If we stay here, we
can."

"You can get more in the Snake River country and the Wallowa,"
Ollokot said brusquely. "We lost a thousand horses there. The suyapu
have become rich from what they stole from us."

There was a heavy silence. "Why should we run after Cut Arm?"
Hahtalekin asked. "He is coming to us! Let's wait for him. Let him
exhaust himself and his soldiers, then fight him in a place that is best
for us."

"We are of one mind concerning Cut Arm," White Goose said
slowly, trying to reconcile the differing opinions. "We want to give him

battle. We all agree on this." He paused. "And it seems we agree to decide what to do later, after the battle."

The chiefs sat in silence, thinking about what had been said. Finally Rainbow spoke. "There is one other choice," he said. His voice was quiet, but it reached all present. "We wait for Cut Arm and beat him. Then we move through the mountains to kusayna, the east country, the buffalo plains. We leave all our trouble here. Make a new life there. Last year the Lakotas and their allies beat two armies of bluecoats. The Lakotas are in control of the buffalo country west and north of the Black Hills. They would welcome us. We can live there. The Crows would also welcome us."

He paused. "We leave the bad things here. We know the suyapu in the east country. They have never troubled us. We," he motioned to Five Wounds, who sat next to him, "we left there three moons ago. The Crows and Lakotas are our friends. There is room for all of us."

Silence again. Finally Joseph spoke. "You came here from the east country to help us fight the soldiers. I respect that." His voice was calm, unemotional, but powerful. "Why should we fight Cut Arm and then run away from our own country? This war is about our country, the land that holds the graves of our ancestors. I have been to the land of the buffalo. It is beautiful. But it is not our country."

He waited. "Perhaps the Lakotas and the Crows would like us to join them, help them fight their battles. We have plenty of battles to fight here, for what belongs to us. If I die, I want to die here, not in a faraway place."

He paused. "I have heard what has been said. Perhaps Hahtalekin is right. We could wait for Cut Arm to come to us. His men will be tired. We are rested. We must prepare ourselves for the fight to come. This fight will decide what we should do after that."

He stared at the ground in front of him. "This battle with Cut Arm—we must be ready for it."

Around the circle solemn faces nodded. There were throaty sounds of approval. Movement stirred the rows of men sitting on the ground.

But everything stopped when Toohoolhoolzote spoke; everyone listened.

"Heinmot Tooyalakekt is right," the Pekonan chief said. "This battle is important. Let Cut Arm come to us."

He looked across to Rainbow. "I have been in the east country many times. I have hunted there and I have fought there, from the Bighorn Mountains north to the Blackfeet country. I have fought there together with you, Wahchumyus," pointing with his chin to Rainbow, "and with you, Pahkatos Owyeen," pointing to Five Wounds. He laughed. "I have some scars from Lakota and Blackfeet arrows." He laughed again, touching his broad chest. "I like to remember those times. It's a great country, kusayna."

He paused. "But it is not our country. This is our country, numipu. For this I fight. For this I die. It is as Heinmot Tooyalakekt says: when I must die, I want to die here. In this land," he bent forward and pulled a small plug of grass from the ground and tossed it into the air. "This land, my father's land, I want to be buried in it."

He looked across the men into the green spread of the willows by the river. "This is all I have to say."

There was a long silence. Dark words had been spoken. Finally White Goose cleared his throat. "We are of one mind," he said, looking thoughtful, content. "We agree that we let Cut Arm come to us. We agree that we decide after the battle what we do next."

He paused. He looked toward Naked Head across from him. "I ask Husishusis Kute to speak a prayer for us."

Seton watched as the tiwét stood. He placed his fan in the grass before him and turned, facing east. He stretched out his arms, palms up. He closed his eyes. All around men bowed their heads. Seton didn't. He kept watching as the tiwét began with a voice heavy with feeling:

Waila yawixne
wine nisu
wax metu weineke
avitsnatsaka
. . . .

It was a long prayer. Naked Head swayed back and forth with his upper body, as if in a trance. He ended crying, overwhelmed by the sacredness of the prayer, of the moment. Heads rose again. Like a long-drawn growl, thanks were given by many voices.

The meeting broke up. Men rose stiffly, stretching their legs and folding the robes or blankets on which they had sat. Seton followed Teeweeyownah when they walked away behind Hemene, back to their camp. Itsepit sat on a log near Hemene's lodge. The sun lay on her pretty oval face, the long black braids, the fringed buckskin dress and beaded moccasins. Her shiny eyes passed over her brother-in-law and focused on Seton.

"I hardly see you anymore," she said, with a smile.

Seton nodded, surprised.

Itsepit looked full into his eyes. "There is a dance tomorrow night. I want you to come."

"Yes," Seton heard himself say. He was suddenly aware that Teeweeyownah stood close by, watching with a grin on his face. "Yes," Seton repeated quickly. He was embarrassed. He was angry with himself that he was, and that it showed. He tried to get away fast. He marched past Itsepit around the lodge, untied the snowflake mare and mounted, riding off to his post with the Lamtama herd without looking back.

After sundown the tomtom of a tiwét drum sounded from the top of the hill above sapachesap, Drive-in, the cave on Cottonwood Creek a mile above its mouth. There, in the year White Goose was born, 1804, a party of over one hundred Bannock raiders from the south had sought shelter after killing Nez Perces on the Clearwater. They were smoked out by enraged Nez Perce warriors and entirely destroyed. The drum continued for half the night. Occasionally, the wind carried the thin voice of a singer into the valley, to the listeners and the dreaming horses.

NINE

IN THE MIDDLE OF THE AFTERNOON, SETON, Atemis, and Kowtoliks were sitting on the rim of one of the hills that was part of a chain that formed the northern boundary of the Cottonwood Creek valley. Their saddle horses were at their backs. They were in a spot six miles upstream from the mouth of the creek and the Lamtama camp, the southernmost camp of the five bands along the river. Below them, the horses of the Lamtama herd grazed quietly, covering four miles of the valley. Behind them, the outlier of the Camas Prairie, a high, broken plateau, ran north toward the deep canyon of Lawyers Creek. Two prominent hills pushed upward from the plateau, partly covered with mixed stands of larches and ponderosas. To the west, beyond Red Rock Creek, the sweep of the Camas Prairie could be glimpsed. This section was a rolling grassland furrowed with sudden dips and shallow ravines.

They were talking quietly when they saw the lone rider meander through the herd and past the tipi and angle up the slope toward them. His horse stretched out, climbing, bobbing its head. Swan Necklace reached them and dismounted, letting the mare walk. "They are starting the paxam," he said, sitting down.

"Where?" Kowtoliks asked.

"In our camp," Swan Necklace said. "Maybe in the Pekonan camp too. I don't know about the others."

Seton thought about the paxam. This was a warriors' dance. He had seen it a couple of times. Only males participated. Sometimes boys were encouraged to dance when they were not yet warriors but had acquired a wéyekin, a guardian spirit, on a wáyatin, a thirsting quest. Seton knew they would let him dance, too, even though he had not been blessed by a wéyekin. But he would have to remain silent because he did not own a personal wéyekin song. Everyone knew about his impediment, and many were sad. Although people respected his mother and his family, and liked him because of his helpfulness and his quiet dependability, some thought his misfortune was because he had a suyapu father. He was not ashamed of his father, but he was ashamed that his wáyatin ordeals had achieved nothing. When he thought about it, the humiliation was stronger than his fear of going through life unprotected by a wéyekin.

He recalled the *paxam* with envy. Men arranged themselves, painted and fitted as for war. They formed two lines about fifteen feet apart, facing each other. The leader of the dance stood at one end in the middle between the lines. He held an elk horn scraper as a musical instrument. The piece of horn, a foot long and two inches thick, was carved into a snake's shape with a head and a tail. On the back of the snake, grooves had been cut about half an inch apart. The snake was covered with a buckskin bag when not in use, with dewclaws of deer sewed to it.

In the paxam the leader, keeper of the scraper, held the snake's tail in his left hand and rubbed an antelope leg bone back and forth over the snake's back. Seton did not know the purpose of the snake or the meaning of the sounds it made. The leader always started with a song. The men joined in, their two lines dancing slowly toward each other and back. When the leader ended, one man began with his wéyekin song. The men on his line joined in. Next a man from the opposite side chanted his wéyekin song. The two lines swayed back and forth. The paxam continued this way, sometimes for hours, until all or most of the men in it had sung their personal songs.

Swan Necklace interrupted Seton's reflections.

"They are still gambling there, too," he said. "In the morning some held horse races. At noon some started gambling." He chuckled. "They'll probably gamble till midnight."

"Who?" Kowtoliks asked.

"Mostly people from the Paloos and Alpowai bands," Swan Necklace said. "They don't have much to lose. They are playing the stick game in our camp and the Pekonan camp. Most of the women are watching the paxam though." He paused with a smile, raising his eyebrows.

"The owl dance starts after sundown. Hamolits told me that I have to remind Seton to be there. If he won't come, she'll come get him herself." They looked at Seton, smiling.

Hamolits, a sturdy woman in her forties, was one of three Lamtama whip women. With their male counterparts, they monitored the social dances, watching the dancers closely. In the owl dance, which was a woman's choice dance, a man was not permitted to refuse. If a man twice turned a girl down, the whip woman was called and she forced the man to the dance ground, using her whip if necessary.

This was Itsepit's doing. Seton was embarrassed and could not hide it. "Yes," he said. "It seems I have to be there."

In late afternoon, two women rode up with food to the herders' tipi west of the horse herd. They brought ep'ine, cakes of camas bread, and a kettle with a thick beef stew made with wild onions, wild carrots, corn, and cucumbers. There were only six herders on watch, and they gathered for the meal in a circle near the tipi. Later they cleaned bowls and spoons and the empty copper kettle in the creek and sat and talked while the early July sun slowly sank beyond the Clearwater Mountains. Before it got dark they built a fire outside the tipi. Soon after, the wind carried the rapid tomtom of a big drum upstream from the camp by the river. Seton reluctantly got up. He walked to his horse and mounted and rode off without saying a word.

"He looks as if he is going to his death," Swan Necklace said. They all laughed.

Seton rode slowly through the dark mass of horses. When he came out at the mouth of the valley and crossed the creek, he saw the Lamta-ma camp lit with many fires. He heard a single drum resound with a commanding voice. He rode past empty lodges until he found Hemene's with the painting of a white wolf in the four directions on the buffalo hide cover. A fire burned in front of it, but no one was there.

He dismounted and slipped the mare's bridle over the tip of a log lying on the ground. Four unsaddled horses stood there, nibbling on the grass. They nickered, greeting the snowflake. When Seton took his rifle case and cartridge belt into the lodge, he noticed clothes laid out on the south side, the place where he used to sleep. Itsepit's bedroll, along with parfleche and rawhide bags, was assembled in an orderly fashion on the north side of the lodge. Hemene's possessions and medicine things were in place on the westernmost tipi pole and below it.

Neatly folded, a pair of leggings and a breechclout made from a blue trade blanket lay next to a fringed, long-sleeved buckskin shirt with a red disk on the chest in quillwork. It was a gift to him, Seton assumed. Itsepit must have made it. He stood for a long moment, looking down, then put the weapon aside and undressed. He put the new leggings on, wriggled the new breechclout into place, and slipped on the shirt with the sun disk. He brushed his shoulder-length hair and was ready. He was thankful to Itsepit, but he dreaded the dance and the teasing that would come later.

He walked slowly through clusters of quiet lodges and bunches of tied-up saddle horses toward the dance ground. The tempo of the drum and the voices of the singers indicated that the eel dance was taking place. Twice he passed groups of gamblers playing the stick game, entranced by their challenge songs. They sat on blankets behind tipi poles laid flat, striking them with sticks, swaying their torsos, cajoling, taunting their opponents, laughing. Groups were made up of men and women. Bright fires burned between the opposing teams, around which bets were heaped. The flames cast shifting shadows over lodge walls behind the gamblers.

The dance ground was located between the Lamtama and Pekonan camps. A wall of people surrounded a circular space about five hundred feet in diameter. They were three rows deep, men standing in the back while women and children sat in front facing four huge fires in the four corners. In the center of the dance ground, six men sat around a big drum. To the thump of the drum, the high-pitched voices of the singers, and the shuffling of many moccasined feet, Seton walked behind the back row, searching for the men of his wi-ses. He found them on the southeast side of the circle. Teeweeyownah and Ayokka moved aside so he could stand between them. He saw Hemene sitting to the left and some of the wi-ses women on both sides. Some places covered with blankets were empty. The people who had sat there were in the eel dance.

A long file of dancers—men, women, and children—swerved across the dance ground, twisting and turning to the drum beat and the singing, imitating the movement of eels. Each dancer had both hands on the hips of the person in front, forming a human chain. The head of the eel was a male dancer who wore a buffalo horn headdress. Men and women were dressed in their finery, especially the women. They were beautiful in their beaded and quilled buckskin dresses, beaded headband or basket hats, colorful moccasins, and long braids. Many held fancy feather fans or bear grass bags in their hands. Children were as dressed up as adults, their clothes imitating those of their parents. The dancers moved on, shaking the ground with their feet until suddenly the drum and the singing stopped and the dance formation came to a halt.

There was a pause, the dancers letting go for a moment, laughing, shuffling around. Then the drum spoke again, the voices of the singers rising high above the thunderous beat. The dancers grasped each other once again and the eel moved forward. Seton looked for Itsepit and her sister and finally saw them. Itsepit followed Elk Blanket. Tsacope was wedged between Itsepit and her mother. Seton touched Teeweeyownah's arm and pointed with his chin. The man nodded curtly. His face was serious. His thoughts were elsewhere.

Meandering round and round between the fires and the drum, the human chain rushed on until the drum and the singing came to an abrupt end. This time, when the dancers stood resting, there were three tapping sounds from the drum, a signal that the eel dance was over. The long file slowly broke up. The dancers returned to their seats.

Dawn emerged from the crowd first. Behind her came Itsepit, holding Tsacope by the hand. Their faces were flushed from excitement and their physical exertion. The women fanned their faces with hawk feather fans, smiled to Teeweeyownah and Seton, and sat down. Tsacope stretched her arms toward her father. Teeweeyownah bent and grabbed her and held her on his arm. She turned sideways, facing Seton. She leaned forward, round black eyes smiling. She touched Seton's forehead with the beaded headband on her forehead. She pulled back and smiled. From the corner of his eyes Seton saw Hemene turn around and glance up. When he saw Seton he briefly raised his right hand. Tsacope shifted restlessly on her father's arm. He put her back down, and she settled onto her mother's lap.

The crowd was noisy, expectant. Some young men fed the fires, stacking logs diagonally across the flames. Two women took water bags and dippers to the singers. The singers joked and laughed with each other, then grew quiet. There was a delay, then one of the singers threw his head back and made the call of the great horned owl, seven low hoots. The drum beaters struck out with a fast beat. The singers' voices joined the drum with the beginning sequence of the first song. As the drum and the song went on, the hoots of the owl were repeated twice.

Dawn got up and turned around, looking at her husband. Teeweeyownah shook his head, but Dawn nodded, insisting, and he edged forward and joined her. Itsepit stood and faced Seton, a smile on her face. He knew what was expected. He walked past Hemene to Itsepit's side. They followed Dawn and Teeweeyownah, walking toward the center of the dance ground. Behind them, from all along the rows of people, couples came and began forming a long file.

As they half faced each other, Itsepit took Seton's left hand in her right. She placed her left hand on his right shoulder. He put his right hand around her waist. Her pretty face beamed at him from under a headband beaded with geometric designs in white and blue seeds. He smiled back, feeling awkward. The file of couples began to move forward in step with the drum. Seton and Itsepit had been in this dance once before—almost the only time they had ever touched each other. He felt her hand in his and the hand on his shoulder, light as a feather. He held her hand firmly. He thought she squeezed his a couple of times, but maybe not on purpose.

Wedged between Teeweeyownah and Dawn in front, and three couples from their wi-ses behind them, they went slowly round the circle. Stomping the ground with their mocassined feet, the dancers drowned the rumble of the drum. But not the voices of the singers. Sometimes Itsepit's body pressed against his. He felt it, a sudden new sensation, unexpected, yet comfortable. He was so close to her he smelled the fresh fragrance of her hair, the perfumes of her throat.

"You look pretty," Itsepit said with a twinkle.

He looked into her eyes, then down his shirt where the sun disk stood out. "Thank you for this," he said. "You made this beautiful." He looked down again. He wanted to tell her she was beautiful, too, in her white buckskin dress beaded around the throat and on the shoulders. He could not bring himself to say it. She seemed to know what he thought, though, and laughed.

The dance went on until suddenly the drum stopped. The couples halted. No one left the dance ground. The couples let go of each other and stood, talking. They waited. The owl called again, and the drum and the singers started out once more. The couples linked with each other and the dance continued.

"You seem to like the horses better than the Old Man and me," Itsepit teased. "You spend all your time with them." Her left hand now lay heavily on his shoulder.

Seton did not know what to say. He concentrated on the dance, trying not to look into her face. "No," he said finally. "But I am not really needed in camp." For a long moment he was silent. "I am not a warrior. I can't ride with the warriors and do what they do. Guarding the horses is the best I can do." He fell silent again. They danced, hand in hand. "I think about them a lot," he added. "You understand."

Itsepit squeezed his hand. "I know," she said. "Remember where we are. That's your place too."

"Yes," Seton said. Nothing more was said. When the dance ended, they walked back to their places in the rows of spectators, Itsepit holding his arm. The slight limp in Itsepit's gait had never bothered him. He took his place next to Teeweeyownah, who looked at him and nodded but said nothing.

The next dance was a circle dance, repeated twice, followed by the rabbit dance. Then came a recess lasting an hour. Freshly cooked food was served. After people had eaten and cleaned up, the drum sounded again. There was a new group of singers. Another owl dance, repeated again. Once more Itsepit and Seton danced as a couple, holding each other, feeling comfortable. When he brought her back after the dance, he looked full into the girl's eyes. "Thank you for this," he said, touching the sun disk on the shirt. "Thank you for the dance. I will go now."

Itsepit smiled. "Just remember us." Seton turned and made his way back to Hemene's lodge. Two dogs growled at him from out of the dark. It was close to midnight. He changed his clothes, folded the blue breechclout, the leggings, and sun shirt and placed them on his empty sleeping place. He took his rifle and went for his horse, mounted, and rode slowly through the camp and up the valley through the restive horses. A low whistle came from the slope to the south. The watchers did not sleep.

Around noon the next day, July 8, Seton, Kowtoliks, Swan Necklace, and Moositsa were sitting at their lookout place on the rim of the hill above the valley. Under a fervid sun they had stripped to their breechclouts. They were watching a golden eagle lie motionless on the air, a six-fingered hand at the end of each brown wing. The breeze carried him east toward the Clearwater Mountains. When he saw the horses massed in the valley below, he swung in a circle and called once, *kya*. He soared on, and when he saw the camps by the river he called and circled again. His cry, because it was seldom heard, was considered a good omen. The eyes of the herders had followed him. When they turned back they saw a rider come in from the west. He came racing up Cottonwood Creek and passed the mouth of Red Rock Creek. Moositsa saw him first. He stood up and pointed. "Look!"

The herders jumped to their feet and waved. "A scout coming back," Kowtoliks said. The rider saw the youngsters on the hill and waved a red blanket over his head without slowing down.

"Enemies close by," Kowtoliks said. They knew the signal. They mounted on the run and urged their horses down the slope. They converged on the scout west of their tipi, pulling up in a cloud of dust. He was a warrior of the Wallowa band, jerking the war bridle of his nervous appaloosa. He was coated with sweat; his hair, with a single eagle feather, hung wet along his face. He wiped his forehead. His words were hurried.

"Suyapu. A hundred. Not soldiers. They're looking for us." He pointed with the barrel of the Springfield rifle. "West of here half a mile. They are riding north. Get ready to move the horses."

He swung his horse around. "They're riding north, but they'll see our trail." He clicked his tongue and loosened the bridle, and the horse jumped into a lope.

"What will we do?" Moositsa asked.

"Tell the others," Kowtoliks said. "But don't start the herd moving until we give the signal. Three shots. Go!"

"Where do we drive them?"

"I don't know," Kowtoliks said. "Down to the river, I think. Yes, to the river." He looked at the faces around him. "The chiefs will know what to do." The boys nodded agreement. Moositsa turned his horse and left.

"Let's see what the suyapu are doing," Kowtoliks said. The three of them rode swiftly upstream along the creek. They plunged into the waters of the mouth of Red Rock Creek and went up the valley on the deep trail the camps and herds had left three days before. They rode to the first bend, where the creek and the valley made a wide circle, dismounted, and left their horses in cover. They crept up the escarpment to the north. When they peeked over the crest they saw a long, irregular file of horsemen silhouetted against the great span of the Camas Prairie. It moved north, slowly but deliberately, half a mile away. They wore civilian clothes. A few packhorses were with them. No flank riders were in view. Apparently the men were not concerned about ambush or surprise attack.

"How many, you think? A hundred?" Kowtoliks asked.

"A few less, maybe," Seton said.

"I don't understand," Kowtoliks said. "They crossed our trail; they must have seen it. But they go on." He shook his head. "What are they after?"

The three kept watching. "They have no scouts out," Swan Necklace said. "These are ignorant men. They go to war, but they know nothing about war."

The column moved silently through the great empty prairie as if drawn by an invisible string until it disappeared behind an upward curl of ground. A meadowlark rose from the grass a dozen feet from the watchers and warbled its loud, flutelike song. The herders stood, looking at each other. They heard hoofbeats below and behind them and turned to see.

About twenty-five warriors rode up fast along the creek. They were painted and held their rifles ready. The sun lay shiny on their naked bodies. They came to a halt when they saw the youngsters on the hill. Ollokot was in the lead. The three pointed northwest.

"Suyapu riding north," Kowtoliks yelled, hands held to his mouth like a megaphone. "Two miles that way." He pointed again. Ollokot waved and the warriors rode on, now at a slow lope. They rounded the bend and disappeared but came back into view half a mile farther up.

Soon they halted, and the watchers saw two climb the slope to search for the white riders. Nothing happened for a long time.

"Why don't they go after them?" Seton asked.

"I think Ollokot is waiting," Kowtoliks said. "I think the suyapu will be attacked from the north first; then Ollokot will cut them off from the south." He grinned. They kept watching. Finally the two men slid down the hill and the warriors moved out, climbing up through a crack in the escarpment. When they reached the flat ground they formed a ragged skirmish line and galloped north, soon swallowed by a rise in the prairie. Once more the grasslands lay still, immovable under the fiery sun and the dome of the blue sky.

"We're not driving the horses today," Kowtoliks said. The others nodded. They went down to their mounts and rode back to guard the herd. They heard nothing for some time. It seemed they had been forgotten. In late afternoon Atemis rode up from the camp. "Those suyapu," he said. "Rainbow and Five Wounds hit them from the north, Kamiah way. When they saw Ollokot's bunch come from the south, they fled to possossona, the big hill way up there." He pointed. "I heard they left their horses and ran up the hill. They dug holes to hide in, like badgers."

"They are still there?" Kowtoliks asked.

"Yes, our warriors are all around them. They took the suyapu horses. Most had been stolen from the Alpowai camp."

"What does Hemene say? What do the chiefs say?" Seton asked.

I don't know," Atemis said. "I heard that our warriors are going to starve them. They will keep them on possossona until dark, then go back tomorrow morning to fight some more."

"Are we going to stay here?" Kowtoliks asked.

Atemis shrugged. "I don't know. I think so. Nobody told me anything. The camps are staying."

No more news came during the evening. Twice during the night, around midnight and before first light, a wolf pack howled in the hills to the south. The boys took turns calming the nervous horses, riding slowly through the herd, whistling, talking, singing. In the morning, shortly after sunrise, a scout from the Pekonan camp passed by. He told them the suyapu had walked away from *possossona* during the night.

The three, Kowtoliks, Seton, and Swan Necklace, stood in silence for a long moment, thinking. "Where is Cut Arm?" Kowtoliks blurted out.

The scout shook his head. "We don't know. We searched for him west and south. We have seen nothing of his army. They must be hiding somewhere." He clicked his tongue, and the horse whirled and sped away. He raised his right arm with the rifle in salute but did not look back.

Why the suyapu army had not followed the broad trail to the numipu camps was a puzzle to everyone, and the puzzle was never solved. When, two days later, the army came into firing range, it was not by design but by accident.

T E N

NOON, ANOTHER HOT DAY. SETON WAS BATHING in the creek, lying naked in a shallow basin below the coiled roots of a cottonwood with only his head above the water. He closed his eyes and enjoyed the cool swirl of a side current. Something boomed to the northeast, followed by a dull explosion much closer. Seton sat up. Silence. Another boom, another explosion. A suyapu cannon! He rushed out of the water and slipped into moccasins, belt, and breech-clout. He heard shouts from somewhere. Kowtoliks and Swan Necklace stood beside the tipi, thirty paces away. Seton ran toward them. They were looking in the direction of the sounds. The blasts seemed to come from a single gun five or six miles away, firing from the heights above the east bank of the river. The explosions were shells falling near the northernmost of the camps along the west bank. The chatter of Gatling guns mixed with the boom of the cannon.

"Cut Arm has found us," Kowtoliks said.

The herd moved uneasily, jumpy because of the strange noises. The boys mounted and rode out to quiet them. The shooting stopped. A rider galloped up from the camp. He found Kowtoliks and Seton, who had pulled away from the herd. He was Alikkees, a warrior from White Goose's own wi-ses. "The camp will be attacked," he said. "The chief said you must take the horses up on Red Rock Creek where the big guns cannot hit them." He paused, looking hard at the two. "You understand?"

Kowtoliks and Seton nodded. "Yes," Kowtoliks said.

"Hurry," Alikkees said. He turned and raced back.

Kowtoliks called out to Swan Necklace. "You and Antelope ride drag. Tell the others! Seton and I will take point. Leave the tipi here. We'll come back for it if we can."

Swan Necklace waved and rode off. They heard the dull thunder of hoofbeats as the great mass of Wallowa horses surged up the side valley to the plateau above, and on, followed by the Pekonan herd. Now the Lamtama flank riders set the herd in motion. Pushing from behind, the drag riders yipped and whistled. Kowtoliks and Seton once again took point, and the flood of horses flowed forward at a slow canter, thinning to three to five sleek bodies abreast.

After two miles the head of the long file reached the mouth of Red Rock Creek. They followed the point riders through the swift waters and into Red Rock Creek valley. They continued five more miles in a half circle around the first of the upward thrusting hills below Lawyers Creek. Kowtoliks and Seton led the herd out of the valley and east onto the high plateau between the high hill and the hill possossona, directly north. There, protected by higher ground to the east, they brought the herd to a halt and let the animals scatter. Soon the appaloosas began feeding on prairie grass. The Wallowa and Pekonan herds were already there, spread out on the plateau in the direction of Kamiah, the main downriver Nez Perce settlement on the Clearwater. It lay seven miles beyond the Lamtama herd as the raven flies. The Wallowa herd was in the northern position, Pekonan center, Lamtama south. They were safe for the moment, but no one knew what might come next.

For a time there was an odd, numbing silence. Then, once again, the sound of cannon fire. Two big guns, now, and Gatling guns. The muffled sounds of rifle fire could be heard too, in volleys and irregular reports. They stood listening. Finally Kowtoliks said to Swan Necklace, "Take someone and go back and get the tipi skin. Leave the poles." He paused. "Seton and I will go up the hill and see what is going on over there."

The two climbed the north face of the hill, with a few youngsters from the other bands scrambling after them. They went up a few hundred yards on an easy climb and found an open grassy area where the larches stood back. They had a clear view to the east. They could not see the camps, hidden in the trench of the Clearwater River valley, but they could see parts of the plateau above the bluffs that framed the valley on the east side. Blue dots, soldiers were on a tongue of rolling land wedged between the south and the middle forks of the river and the gash cut by Clear Creek as it ran into the north fork. The tongue of land was about a mile wide. The soldiers had taken up defensive positions in a line about a mile long, stretched south to north. They seemed to be surrounded on all sides. Their rifle fire, cannons, and Gatling guns were directed all around them.

From where the boys watched, the distance to the battlefield was about seven miles. They could see only part of it. Much was hidden by clumps of pines and depressions in the ground. One of the Wallowa herders pointed to an area two miles north of the battlefield. "See that round bluff with deep ravines on both sides, north of where the soldiers are now? Three big pines on top. See it? That's where the big gun shot from at first. I saw it there. I saw the powder smoke as we drove the horses. I saw the cannon balls fall into the river or on the mountainside."

"Yes," another Wallowa boy said. "I saw it too. A few balls came down on the Paloos camp. People were running everywhere."

"Our warriors must have pushed them back," a Pekonan boy said. "The suyapu are in a different place now. They can't shoot into our camps now." He paused. "Look, our warriors must have surrounded them." The boys grunted in agreement. They listened to the steady

chatter of the Gatling guns, the rattle of hundreds of rifles, the report
of the howitzers, explosions.

"I don't understand," Seton said. "Why did the general take his
army way up there, on that side of the river?"

"It's hard to believe," Kowtoliks said. "Maybe he got lost."

"Maybe he planned it that way," another boy said. "Maybe he
didn't want to fight us. Maybe he wanted to kill us with his big guns
from a distance."

There was a murmur of agreement. "This is a hard fight over
there," a Pekonan boy said. "Lots more soldiers than we have warriors.
And they have the big guns and plenty of ammunition. Always plenty
of ammunition." Everyone knew that the suyapu had an inexhaustible
supply.

There was a silence, and then someone said: "The suyapu soldiers,
they have no old people to protect, no women and children, no pony
herds. They can go anywhere they want. They have all the guns and all
the ammunition they want."

Again there was a murmur of agreement. The fire slackened, and
the boys saw a wild charge of numipu horsemen against the southern
part of the army line. The line broke, soldiers running toward the center of the army's position. The Gatling guns and the howitzers fired
furiously, and the charge ebbed.

"The suyapu are running," a boy said.

They sat and watched, and the fire slackened once again. Most of
the shooting was done by the soldiers. By evening, the soldiers' positions were unchanged. They had made no effort to drive the numipu
snipers away.

"The suyapu are in a bad place for water," someone said. "There is
no spring up there, and they can't get to the river. The creek up there
is dry. I have seen it." The others agreed. Cut Arm had marched his
army into a self-made trap. On the rugged, rocky terrain, despite his
vast superiority of men and weapons, he was at a disadvantage once he
lost the initiative. While his forces had become immobile, small groups
of numipu marksmen moved around them at will, striking where they

wanted. Only howitzers and Gatling guns saved the general's army from destruction.

A whistle sounded from the foot of the hill. Seton looked and elbowed Kowtoliks. Swan Necklace had returned leading a packhorse on a lariat. The bulky form across its back was the buffalo hide cover of the tipi. Kowtoliks waved and pointed toward the Lamtama herd. Swan Necklace rode that way.

From the hill Seton looked over the host of horses below, three thousand held in three separate units. They covered the plateau for about four miles north to south. It's good that we have water, the creek and the spring, he thought. He looked north, beyond possossona, to the broken hills along Lawyers Creek. He looked west, into the wide swing of the Camas Prairie. He searched warily but saw only a small herd of antelopes feeding quietly. No riders, no trace of humans. What if Cut Arm had a second army that would attack from the west while the camps sat by the river and the warriors fought the first army up on the east side? He shook his head. The threat was only in his mind. There was no second army. He looked again to the west. The prairie lay silent and empty, miles and miles of grass, flowers, low hills, and hidden pockets of mysterious beauty, all the way to a distant horizon.

The battle across the river continued as the sun came to rest on the peaks of the Clearwater Mountains. The army was in the same defensive position as in the beginning, unable to break out. Seton nudged Kowtoliks, and they walked down the hill to their saddle horses. They rode to a slight rise near the Lamtama herd where the tipi cover and some equipment and foodstuffs had been dropped. Swan Necklace and Moositsa and two others sat there, chewing jerked beef. Seton and Kowtoliks dismounted and joined them. Swan Necklace tossed a rawhide bag toward them. They helped themselves to jerked meat, thin slices, hard as a board. "What's happening over there?" Moositsa asked, pointing east with his head.

Kowtoliks chewed and swallowed. "I don't know. From what I could see the suyapu have taken cover. They are hiding and use their big guns. Our men are all around them." He took a small bite and chewed.

"Nothing has changed over there since the fight started."

"Once our men made a charge on horseback," Seton said. "They pushed the soldiers back a little way."

They ate slowly, in silence. "What do we do with the horses? Do we stay here?" Swan Necklace asked.

"We stay until the chief tells us what to do," Kowtoliks said.

When they finished eating, they went to the creek for water. Dozens of horses stood in the narrow channel, drinking. The boys went upstream, away from the herd, dismounted and knelt down, using their cupped hands. "I have a bad feeling about this place. What if more soldiers come from there?" Seton said, pointing west. "I'll ride out there and have a look."

Kowtoliks looked at him with surprise on his broad face, eyes curious. But he said nothing, only nodded. Seton mounted and rode through the creek, up the bank, and into the vast prairie. He patted the mare's neck and talked softly to her. He called her by her secret name, *Toga,* Sunflower. She pricked her ears and rotated them backward so she could pick up the sound of his voice. In the gathering dark they made nine miles to a hillock that overlooked the dirt track that led to Norton House, Grangeville, and Mount Idaho and Elk City, eventually all the way to Fort Lapwai and Lewiston. It was the track he had traveled with his brother, Alex, and the pack train. It lay empty and silent. There had been no movement on it recently.

Seton dismounted and sat in the tall grass, his cased rifle across his legs, letting the mare graze behind him. Where had the suyapu civilians gone when they fled from possossona? The warriors had never told the boys after they found the hill empty. Seton thought about his brother, Alex, and his family, including wide-eyed and curious Little Mary. His downriver relations had taken Alex in. Dignified Aaron and Mary were quiet and efficient, kind of heart. He thought of the tipis and the cabins by the river on Aaron's place. They had wanted him to stay. Would he ever go back there? Then he thought of his mother, Wetah, gone on the path to *ahkunkeneko,* the spirit world. Would he ever stand by her grave on the butte at lahmotta again?

He sat in the same place for most of the night. The only sounds were the call of the great gray owl, twice, and the wind swishing the tall grass. Before first light he fell into a deep, worried sleep. He woke with a jerk. His mare had snorted close to his face. He sat up, and in the early light saw five wolves sitting quietly a hundred yards away. They casually walked away when he got up. He checked the road but saw nothing human. He relieved himself and mounted and returned to the Lamtama herd just as the sun peeked over the horizon. He drank from the creek and let the mare have her fill. No fires were burning.

The distant sound of battle came again, accompanied by the crashing of artillery. Seton dismounted at the campsite where three of the boys were listlessly munching jerked beef. "You see anything?" Swan Necklace asked.

"No," Seton said. "Where is Kowtoliks?"

"Up there," Swan Necklace said, pointing with his head. "On the hill. He's watching."

While Seton and Atemis rode together circling the herd, two other boys went to join Kowtoliks and watch the battle. Action seemed to have slowed. Sporadic gunfire was followed by periods when the guns were silent. At noon Kowtoliks and Swan Necklace came back down. Seton met them at the campsite. The boys sat in the grass. "It's the same as yesterday," Kowtoliks said. "The suyapu are in the same place as yesterday."

They sat in silence for a while. Finally, one after the other rose and mounted and circled the herd. The distant battle seemed unreal, but the horses with their many markings and colors were real enough, sleek and muscular, smelling of the earth. In the early afternoon the gunfire intensified for a short time, then died down. Swan Necklace and Antelope came tumbling down the hill, shouting. They mounted and rode to meet Kowtoliks, Seton, and Atemis.

"The suyapu army," Swan Necklace said, breathing hard, "it has come out of its shelter. Masses of foot and horse soldiers are on the bluffs above the camp." Gunfire resumed and reached a new crescendo.

"They are probably shooting into the valley," Kowtoliks said.

"Into the camps," Seton added.

"What do we do?" Swan Necklace asked.

There was a silence.

Finally Kowtoliks spoke. "We wait. The chiefs will call us." He looked from one to the other. "We must get ready. We can't stay here." Everyone agreed. They cut a horse from the herd and loaded it with the tipi cover and packs. They staked it out and rode out to circle the herd. The Wallowa and Pekonan boys were doing the same. When the order came to drive, the Wallowas would go first, Lamtamas last.

It didn't take long. The order came with a warrior of the Pekonan band. He had a blood-soaked bandage on his upper right arm. His horse was fresh, but the man looked dirty and tired. "The fight is over," he blurted out. "We are retreating to nahush, Fish Trap, the crossing in Kamiah. You bring the horses. We'll be there." His face was haggard. He looked at the boys with a fierce expression, waiting for them to confirm that they understood.

"Yes," Kowtoliks said. "We will meet you in Kamiah." The warrior nodded and rode on to inform the Pekonan and Wallowa herders.

They waited, tense in the strange quiet. And then the Wallowa herd started out, the boys whistling and yipping, and the mass of horses converged into a stream pouring north. The Pekonan went, and then Kowtoliks and Seton took point and the Lamtama herd followed across the seven miles of plateau to the bluffs above Kamiah. When they reached them and spilled over, the flat below Lawyers Creek was already filled with Wallowa and Pekonan horses. The two point riders took their herd down and settled it in the valley south of the creek's mouth.

There were a few cabins and productive gardens of downriver Nez Perces of Chief Lawyer's band in this location. Lawyer and the missionary, Henry Spalding, had conspired to force the so-called treaty of 1863 that had led to the war. The Lamtama herders had no reason to protect Lawyer band property. They watched without emotion as their horses flattened gardens and crumbled wooden fences. A few owners protested, but when wild-looking boys trained rifles on them, they turned away.

The horses had arrived before the bands. The first people to come in were the advance guard, experienced, grim-looking warriors. They passed through the herds and took possession of the ferry that belonged to James Lawyer, son of the dead chief who had been a fanatical convert to Spalding's religion. Lawyer was hiding, but they found him and he promised to ferry the people over on the following day.

Next the bands arrived, Palooses in the lead, Lamtamas at the tail of the column. They made camp by bands south of the Lamtama herd, strung along the river. No tipis were set up. Many tipis had been left standing when the people fled from the army's sudden push through the thin screen of numipu marksmen. Some tipi covers had been saved, but pole frames were lost. From now on the people would sleep under the open sky or build lean-tos when it rained.

Cooking fires went up quickly. The sky blazed at sundown. That was when Itsepit and Atemis's mother, Oyipee, rode in. They brought cooked food for all the Lamtama herders, twelve boys in all, but they were mostly looking for Seton and Atemis. The two women stayed only a short time. They seemed disheartened but determined. "What happened?" Seton asked.

"Not enough men fighting," Oyipee said bitterly. "Too many young men stayed in camp. They said, 'Why fight up there? Our camp has not been attacked. We can all escape without fighting.' That's what they said." She paused.

"Fewer than a hundred warriors did the hard fighting. My husband was in it, my brother-in-law was in it, all the men of our wi-ses were in it."

"Yes," Itsepit said. "Our men all fought. At noon today, our leaders wanted to finish the fight. Cut Arm would not move. He only sat there. Teeweeyownah, Allultakanin, Sarpsis, Wahlitits, Wottolen, Toohoolhoolzote, Ollokot, Rainbow, Five Wounds, Strong Eagle—they called on all the young men to get their horses and fight. To make this the last fight. But many hung back."

She paused. "Teeweeyownah went where they were sitting, talking, smoking. He told them, 'You cowards. I will die soon! You will see hardships in bondage. You will lose your freedom. You will be slaves.' That's what he said."

"Yes," Oyipee said. "My husband heard him say it." They sat in silence.

"My brother-in-law, he said he would die soon," Itsepit said. She swallowed. She nodded her head a couple of times, close to tears.

They sat with their heads down. Finally Itsepit said, "He, my brother-in-law, Teeweeyownah, went back to the fighters and said, 'Let's quit and go to camp.' That's what happened. They left and the soldiers found out and charged. That's how the fight ended." She paused again. "The soldiers came to the bluffs and shot into the camps, and we ran."

Again there was a long silence. Finally Swan Necklace asked, "How many of our men died?"

Oyipee and Itsepit looked at each other. "Three died in the hard fighting in the hills. Wayakat, Red Thunder, Lelooskin," Oyipee said. "Wayakat and Lelooskin could not be brought back. Their bodies were too close to the soldiers."

"One more, Yoomtis Kunnin," Itsepit said. "He was badly shot and was carried back to camp. He died in camp." She looked down at the ground. "Some men were wounded. Only Yoomtis Kunnin was wounded so badly."

The two women stood and mounted. Itsepit looked squarely into Seton's eyes. He thought she wanted to say something, but she didn't. She nodded at him, ever so slightly. Before they rode away, Oyipee said, "We had to leave much in the camps when we ran. Now the suyapu have it."

The messenger came at first light. He told the boys to move the herds east across the river and take them to the middle of Weippe Prairie, twelve miles away. The crossing was at nahush, the ancient fish trap site for catching salmon near the mouth of Lawyer Creek. There was an island in the middle of the stream, the midpoint of a good ford. The

Wallowa herders waited in the dark by the river until there was enough light. The Pekonan and Lamtama herds followed.

When the herds were across, the bands broke camp and moved up. Across the river they passed cabins and a few canvas tipis of downriver Nez Perces. The homes were grouped around the white-painted wooden structure of the First Presbyterian church. Built in 1871, the church was marked by a bell tower above the entrance stairs. The cemetery of Christian Nez Perces behind the church held the grave of Chief Lawyer, first elder of the Kamiah church, nemesis of the nontreaty bands now passing the site.

Half a mile farther downstream, the bands passed the site where the heart of the monster *itswa'wltsix,* cut out by nasawaylu, Old Man Coyote, had turned into a small, circular hill of pale red stone. The people passed this place slowly, in veneration, many praying.

There was no reason to hurry. The rear guard reported Cut Arm's army had crossed from the east bank to the west bank and plundered the camps. The general had let soldiers and packers have all they wanted. The rest, great stores of food, clothing, robes, and equipment, was burned. The army had buried its dead on the battlefield. Sixteen, the scouts reported. About thirty wounded had been taken by wagons to Grangeville. Wayakat's mother went with the scouts and buried her son on the battlefield. They had not found the body of Lelooskin. Instead of pursuing, the army had spent the night near the wrecked camps, while the bands were south of Kamiah, only eight miles away.

While the army lingered, the bands moved up to nahush and prepared to cross. Skin boats were built, and old people and women with small children were ferried over. Camp and saddle horses swam across. James Lawyer's ferry was not used after all. The ferry was cut from its mooring and set adrift. Why Cut Arm took so long to follow them remained a mystery. Perhaps he did not want another fight. It was late afternoon when a numipu scout waved the blanket signal from a distant butte. The army had moved at last and was approaching nahush. By then the bands were encamped by a small stream four miles east of Kamiah.

In the established order of travel, Kowtoliks and Seton rode point for the Lamtama herd behind the herds that had preceded them. Three miles east of Kamiah they turned north and climbed a ridge studded with larches and ponderosas. After another three miles, they went down into the canyon of Lolo Creek. Before them lay Weippe Prairie, a dense grassland of bluebunch wheatgrass and Idaho fescue. Its open spaces, here and there, were broken by islands of open forests of tall evergreen trees dominated by ponderosas. Moist meadows in the prairie held camas grounds so dense that in springtime wide stretches were entirely colored blue violet.

Like Camas Prairie to the west, Weippe Prairie was bordered by mountains. South to north it stretched from Lolo Creek to Orofino Creek, a distance of fifteen miles. West to east it reached from the ridges along the Clearwater River to the vast belt of the Clearwater Mountains, eighteen miles away. Some of those peaks were still snow-covered in mid-July. Since ancient times Weippe Prairie had been a favorite camas-gathering place for downriver bands and a gathering area for Nez Perce expeditions to *nakunikay,* the east country, the buffalo range across the Continental Divide. On the eastern edge of Weippe Prairie the Lolo Trail began. The famous track to nakunikay, was said to have been initiated by nasawaylu, Old Man Coyote himself.

They descended into the canyon at sunrise. Kowtoliks and Seton sloshed through Lolo Creek and led the way up a side valley to the grasslands above. They took the horses another five miles to a small stream that cut through the center of the prairie, upstream of the other herds, and turned them loose to graze. They had passed a grizzly mother with two one-year-old cubs. The sun lay a golden fleece on the shoulders of their silver gray coats. The adult stood on her hind feet, viewing the passing remuda. The furry youngsters imitated their mother's stance. Seton had watched as the grizzly mother went down and galloped away, the cubs tumbling after her. A hundred yards farther the mother turned and stood again, the cubs following suit for a while, still as rocks, before they all walked away.

The boys had been told to keep the herds under control and wait for further instruction. The Lamtama boys made themselves a campsite on an insignificant rise near the creek, dropping the tipi cover on the ground without poles and with no intention of raising it. But it was sort of a gathering point. Small herds of elk foraged on the prairie. Swan Necklace and Antelope went out and shot an elk cow. They dressed her out and brought meat and the hide to the campsite. The boys built a good fire and enjoyed the early morning meal.

In the evening a Wallowa rider passed by and told them that the bands were still in camp east of Kamiah and ready to fight if Cut Arm crossed to meet them. The rider also told them that the rear guard had fired across the river at the cavalry when it approached the crossing place, throwing it back in confusion.

On his way back he reported that there was a small numipu camp on the stream beyond the Wallowa herd. He said it was a wi-ses led by Chief Red Heart, just arrived from the Bitterroot Valley over Lolo Pass. The people of this wi-ses numbered thirty-three. They had been friendly to both sides in the conflict. They spent most of their time in the Bitterroot Valley.

The Lamtama herders talked about them. Seton remembered something. "Red Heart is the father of Teeweeyownah and Allulta-kanin," he said. The brothers had married into Hemene's wi-ses and stayed there with their wives.

"Yes," Atemis said. "Red Heart is my grandfather. I'll visit him in the morning."

They had a quiet night. The horses were content with the good grass. Once again they had a red sunrise. Later clouds drifted in and a light rain fell. They heard nothing all day. They spent another peaceful night, and by midmorning the bands began coming in. Seton watched them.

The file of people and horses was over a mile long. A handful of warriors rode ahead of the first band, the Alpowais. Then came the Palooses, Wallowas, Pekonans, and Lamtamas. Everyone, young and old, was mounted. There were no travois for the old ones. Bunches of warriors rode along the flanks of the column. Women led packhorses, children looseherded extra saddle horses and camp horses. Camp was made by bands at the head of the stream south of the Lamtama herd in the order in which they arrived.

After they settled, Seton rode over to Hemene's camp. There were only a few cooking fires going among the bands because of a lack of firewood. Hemene waved when Seton dismounted. The families of the wi-ses sat loosely grouped among packs, saddles, and tipi cover bundles, eating cold meat and camas bread. Their horses were spread out, grazing. Hemene pointed to the ground next to him, and Seton sat down. Itsepit, who sat on her father's other side, prepared a plate with food for Seton and handed it to him. Seton looked to Teeweeyownah, who was fifteen paces away with Dawn and Tsacope.

"Your father, Red Heart, is camped down there with his people," Seton said, pointing downstream. "Farther than the Wallowa horses, on this creek. Atemis went to see him yesterday morning. He has not come back."

Teeweeyownah looked to his brother. Both were surprised. "We thought he was still in the Bitterroot Valley," Teeweeyownah said. "What is he doing here?"

"Let's go see him," Allultakanin said. They ate in silence. Finally Seton asked, "Where is Cut Arm?"

Hemene laughed. "He's on the other side of the river." He paused. "We teased him to come over and fight us, but he didn't come. He won't fight us again. We waited all day yesterday."

Again they sat in silence. After they finished eating, Teeweeyownah and Allultakanin left to see their father. Teeweeyownah had his little daughter sit on the saddle in front of him. Seton watched them go. He remembered what Itsepit had said. Teeweeyownah had told those unwilling to fight that he would die soon. How could he know? Why should it be him? Teeweeyownah didn't let anyone see what he seemed to know. He acted the same as always, or did he? Seton wondered, uncomfortable with the thought.

When Seton mounted to leave, Hemene called out to him. "This evening the chiefs meet to decide what we will do, where we will go. We'll let you and the others know." Seton looked at the chief for a long moment, then glanced at Itsepit. She had been gathering plates but stopped and returned his look. He raised his right hand and rode.

The rider came after dark and reported that the chiefs had decided to cross Lolo Trail to nukunikay, to the country of the Crows, their friends. Looking Glass had spoken for it forcefully. White Goose and Hahtalekin agreed, as did Rainbow and Five Wounds. The Wallowa chiefs, Joseph and Ollokot, had spoken against it but accepted the will of the majority. Joseph and Ollokot had wanted to return to the Salmon–Snake River country and fight there. At first they had been supported by Toohoolhoolzote. In the end, the three chiefs reluctantly acquiesced.

"Tomorrow morning we leave for siwishnimi, Mussel Creek, high up in the mountains," the rider said, pointing east. "The trail begins there. You have been there. But we will move differently from now on. The horses of each band will run with their band, follow their band. This has also been decided."

He looked at them, trying to make sure they understood. "The Alpowais go first. It was decided that Looking Glass will lead us on the trail. Then the Palooses. Then the Wallowas, their horses behind them. Pekonans then. Finally, Lamtamas, and you will follow them with the horses. You know the trail. In some places it is narrow, only one horse wide. Do you understand?"

"We will be the last?" Kowtoliks asked.

"No," the rider said, shaking his head. "There are warriors behind you, watching the back trail. No suyapu is going to ride up on you."

He paused. "Do you understand?" he repeated. The boys nodded.

"You wait here until the bands have gone by you, then close up on your band." He raised his right hand and rode away to inform those guarding the other herds.

The boys looked at each other. They had expected the move east sometime, but it still was a surprise. They had all been to nakunikay and had only good memories of the Plains country. They had never been troubled there as in their own country. They looked forward to it. But there were five mountain ranges to cross on the trail to nakunikay. Old Man Coyote had put them there a long, long time ago.

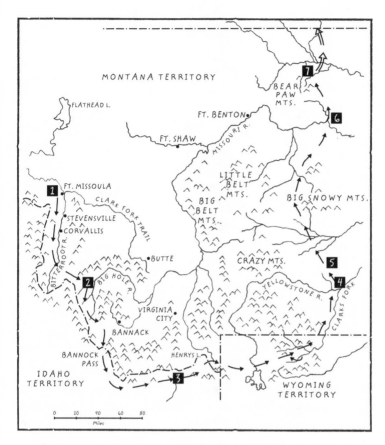

The war in Montana territory, July 26–October 5, 1877

1 Fort Fizzle, July 26

2 Battle of the Big Hole, August 9–10

3 Battle of Camas Meadows, August 20

4 Battle of Canyon Creek, September 13

5 Battle with Crows, September 15–16

6 Cow Island crossing, September 23

7 Battle of Snake Creek (Bear Paw Mts.), September 30–October 5

Nez Perce route

Route of White Goose and refugees on their escape toward Lakota camps located in the Cypress Hills, Saskatchewan

E L E V E N

THE FOLLOWING MORNING, JULY 16, CAME WITH a drizzling rain. To some in camp it was as if the sky was weeping because the people were leaving. For others the rain was merely a nuisance. From first light on, people from the three bands who still had their herds exchanged running horses for those better suited for mountain riding. Seton had cut his roan mare from the herd for his saddle horse and turned the snowflake back in. The herd boys, wrapped in buffalo robes, had to wait for the bands to move. They started out at daylight, the sun hidden by dark gray clouds.

Seton stood by his horse on the southern edge of the herd, feet in wet moccasins, leggings up to his calves wet from the tall grass the rain had soaked. He chewed jerked meat, grinding it slowly, deliberately, savoring the smoky taste, the hint of sage. He watched the column approach.

First came a dozen riders of the Alpowai band, the advance guard. Under furry brown robes, worn flesh side in, only their stern faces were visible. After they had passed the Wallowa band, farther up, they turned to the northeast and the mountains veiled by rain. Next came the rest of their band. It numbered about 150 people. Looking Glass rode at the head, a few older men, wi-ses chiefs, behind him. Women and children followed in file, leading packhorses. The Alpowais had become poor from Captain Whipple's surprise attack and the plundering of their camp on July 1. A few women held cradleboards close to their bodies under the shelter of the robes. The Alpowais rode as families, the old people alongside their grown children and their children's spouses and their grandchildren. The remaining fighting men covered the flanks of the column. It was the established numipu way of travel in territory where hostile action was possible.

Seton stood by his horse and watched them pass. A gap of two hundred yards, and the Palooses rode up, a small band of about 65 people. The two chiefs, Hahtalekin and Naked Head, rode point. Although their horse herd had been stolen on the reservation, they still had their pack and saddle horses and much of their camp equipment. This group passed in the same fashion as the Alpowais, a dozen warriors riding guard.

Another gap, and the Wallowas approached. This was the largest of the five bands, numbering about 240 people, including the boys with the herd. The two chiefs, Joseph and Ollokot, rode ahead of a few wi-ses chiefs and a handful of warriors. Joseph, although a tough and fearless man, had become known as a philosopher and protector of his people since he inherited the burden of the Wallowa chieftainship from his father. As the civil chief, he left military matters and leadership of the warriors to his energetic younger brother. The column went by with a dull thudding of hoofbeats on the trampled trail left by the preceding bands.

Next the Pekonans passed, a band of about 120, all counted. Old Toohoolhoolzote was leading, civil chief and chief warrior of the band. He was a great orator and a man of enormous physical strength. With fewer than twenty warriors, he had stopped General Howard's army on the first day of the Clearwater fight. His small force had held the troops on the high plateau away from the camp until midmorning of the second day. He rode with three warriors beside him.

The Lamtama were last. White Goose rode at the point, civil chief and tiwét, two war leaders at his side. Rainbow was on his left, Wottolen on his right. Seton waved when Hemene and his wi-ses went by. Tsacope was cuddled under her mother's robe and waved back at him. Five Wounds, and the companions and their families he and Rainbow had brought with them from the buffalo country, rode at the end of the column. With them the Lamtama numbered around 220 people.

And then they had passed. If Seton had counted, and added to those who had ridden by the boys guarding the herds, two scouts on the back trail, and the rear guard of five warriors, he would have known the total number of people of the nontreaty bands on their way to exile to be between 805 and 810.

Seton mounted. The mare circled under him, and he worked her around. Kowtoliks rode up to him from the west. That day, and during the days crossing the mountains, the two would ride drag behind the Lamtama herd. Ahead, the train of the Pekonan and Lamtama bands had halted. Standing up in the stirrups, Seton saw that a mile away the mass of Wallowa horses swung in behind the Wallowa band and was thinned into a continuous stream of animals. It took a while for this to be accomplished, and then the Pekonan band moved up and their herd was brought in behind. After another wait the Lamtama band was set in motion. The point riders of the herd, Antelope and Moositsa, drove the head of the herd up to about two hundred yards behind the Five Wounds contingent. Yipping, whistling, slapping their thighs, sometimes using their whips, the flank riders pushed the herd into a controlled string of eight to a dozen animals wide. The boys let them walk, holding the pace of the people in front of them.

Seton and Kowtoliks closed in at the tail of the herd. Looking over the backs of horses to the front of the moving cavalcade, they saw that it stretched over a distance of about four miles. The grand total of horses on this trek came to nearly 4,500. Never before had a numipu expedition to the east country taken such a multitude of animals across the mountains.

They rode on steadily. The rain fell harder when the column snaked around the ridge that juts into Weippe Prairie from the south beyond Lolo Creek. They made for Brown Creek as the rain pummeled the flats along its banks, water splashing down its bed white and fast. They crossed it and made for higher ground to the east and marched on. Before them, the mountains were dressed in mist, green flanks glistening in the gray light. They rode three more miles and into the draw of Mussel Creek where it runs down from the mountains, and they went through the turbid, angry current and turned north above the east bank and climbed the high slopes toward Hemlock Butte. The butte, on the six-thousand-foot level, lay shrouded in clouds ten miles away. They would not ride that far. They passed through thickets of pines and larches, where the ranks of horses thinned out further, and then, with the thunder of hooves, they flowed into open space, the meadow of *siwishnimi,* Musselshell Meadow, where the rain stopped.

It was about noon, and they had covered thirteen miles as the raven flies. The meadow was a well-watered green bowl of grass on the first outlier of mountain ranges that climbed east to the Bitterroot Divide. In better times people had come here to dig camas and hunt elk, mule deer, and mountain goats. Camp was made on the forest edges of the meadow, and the herds were turned loose to graze. Cooking fires were quickly started. Plumes of smoke from wet wood rushed east, driven by the wind.

The three herds were kept separate on the meadow. The Lamtama and Pekonan boys, who knew each other well, camped together in the space between the two herds. A few of them were sitting around a small fire when they saw one of the scouts ride up from below and press through the widely spread horses. The boys stood and watched.

"He is wounded," Kowtoliks said. The rider had been shot through the upper left arm. His leather shirt was red with blood on the left side. He held a rifle up in his right hand and passed by without a glance.

"He is in a hurry," Seton said. "Who is he?"

"He is Wetyettamaweyun," Swan Necklace said. "I know him."
"There is trouble," Kowtoliks said. "Maybe the bluecoats are following us." The boys stood for a while, listening, uncertain what to do.
No more riders came over the back trail. But a body of warriors rode
down from the camp and hurried through the horses toward the edge
of the meadow, to the mouth of the trail. About forty men. The boys
recognized the leaders: Rainbow, Five Wounds, Ollokot, Teeweeyownah, Two Moons, and Naked Head. Nothing more happened. There
was only the sound of the wind and the usual sounds made by many
horses moving around, cropping grass, neighing and sneezing.

Later, Atemis returned from a visit to the main camp with an
explanation. "Horse soldiers and suyapu civilians came upon the scouts
and the warriors behind us. There was shooting. Wetyettamaweyun
was shot through the arm. They didn't miss killing him by much." He
paused, looking around the faces in a half circle before him. "Warriors
have gone back a ways to prepare for enemies. The chiefs said we move
on tomorrow morning."

A little later, a woman of Swan Necklace's wi-ses brought food—
smoked salmon and warm kouse bread. When night fell, half of the
warriors who had gone out returned to the camp. The others stayed
with the rear guard. It was a cold, clear night, the moon a curved blade
in the sky.

Nasawaylu pahkatos maqsamna pa'yawnana was the numipu term for the
Lolo Trail, "Old Man Coyote five mountains he crossed over." This was
the North Trail of the nasawaylu stories. There was also a South Trail to
the east country. It ran southeast from Camas Prairie through the Red
and Selway rivers and through a pass in the Bitterroot Mountains to the
Nez Perce Fork of the Bitterroot River. The mining town of Elk City
in Idaho Territory was on the South Trail. Seton and Alex had passed
over a part of it in May and June when they went with the mule train
to Elk City. After the Clearwater fight, the warring bands were forced
to use the North Trail because General Howard's army blocked access

to the other. Since both trails went into the Bitterroot River valley of Montana Territory, it did not make much difference whether they took the northern or the southern trail.

The North or Lolo Trail was named by whites after two Lolo creeks. One Lolo Creek ran out of the Clearwater Mountains in Idaho Territory, curved through Weippe Prairie, and flowed west into the Clearwater River. The other Lolo Creek ran east from the watershed of the Bitterroot Mountains of Montana Territory into the Bitterroot River. Lolo Trail, or the nasawaylu trail, went from the creek of that name in Idaho to the creek of that name in Montana, a distance of seventy miles as the raven flies. West to east the trail passed through the Clearwater Mountains, with elevations between five thousand and seven thousand feet, and through the Bitterroot Mountains, with elevations from seven thousand to nine thousand feet.

Both mountain ranges were based on a few great branches, which in turn expanded into a vast mass of curving, winding, peak-covered spurs within which lay the sources of the Clearwater River. The major divides gave rise to many lateral spurs that formed a bewildering maze of ridges. The crests of the ranges were composed of a succession of sharp peaks and hogbacks with long east and west swinging curves alternating with deep saddles from which canyons ran out. While the peaks reached heights to nine thousand feet, a few even ten thousand feet, the deeper saddles were between five thousand and seven thousand feet in altitude.

The trail followed the tops of saddles and hogbacks, sometimes open and grassy, often covered with scattered pines or patches of pine forests. It meandered back and forth five to eight miles north of, and almost parallel to, the Lochsa River, one of the main tributaries of the Clearwater. The narrow gorges of the Lochsa and other mountain streams below the trail were utterly impassable, choked with brush, boulders, and fallen timber. Due to the erratic course of the trail, its length on the ground was between 110 and 120 miles.

Numipu parties traveling to or from the buffalo range generally needed six days for the crossing. In 1866 white road teams had tried to improve the trail in an attempt to link the mining towns on the lower

Clearwater (Orofino, Lewiston, and Pierce) with the mining centers of Virginia City and Bannock in Montana Territory. The conditions on the trail defeated the effort. It remained what it had been from ancient time on, a foot trail before the time of horses, a pack trail after.

The march began well after sunrise on the morning of July 17. That gave the horses more time to graze. First the Alpowais and Palooses moved out. Many of the warriors of the Wallowa, Pekonan, and Lamtama bands stayed back when the families left to help the herd boys keep the horses on the trail. The going was slow, a walk. The trail went northeast toward Hemlock Butte and followed the high ridge above Gold Creek. It snaked along near the crest of the ridge over open ground and through clumps of pines, around windfalls and dense pockets of hemlock and red cedar. A pair of snowbanks near the peak of Hemlock Butte glistened in the morning sun.

Kowtoliks and Seton rode at the tail of the infinite file of horses moving before them. They kept watch for strays and rushed in when horses broke away and branched off into the trees. Sometimes looking behind, Seton saw only the empty trail, a fresh, deep gash in the ground cut by many hooves. But around noon, after the drive had covered about eight miles, a dozen riders came up behind. Seton saw Rainbow, Five Wounds, and Teeweeyownah among them. While the others passed, Teeweeyownah fell in beside Seton.

"We had a fight with Cut Arm's scouts," Teeweeyownah said. "Downriver numipu. Christians. They wore blue soldiers' coats." He paused.

"We killed one." He looked sideways at Seton. "You know him, I think. John Levi, son of the preacher chief. We wounded two, one badly. Brooks, Abraham Brooks. The other was not hurt so bad. Jim Reuben. You know them?"

"Yes," Seton said. He remembered James Reuben from the Lapwai meeting. The man had dressed as a minister. He had a round, serious face, short hair, carefully parted. And an arrogant bearing. John Levi he had known in the Lapwai school, a thin boy, one of the minister's favorites. The other one, Brooks, he did not remember. "Yes," he said. "Reuben and Levi I know, sons of treaty chiefs."

"There were six or seven of those scouts," Teeweeyownah said. "They rode off fast when we hit them. We took four rifles. Later we saw horse soldiers and civilians a long way out there, riding back to Kamiah." He raised his eyebrows. "When you see horses coming up behind you, it will be Naked Head and some Palooses. They went down to raid for horses along the Clearwater."

Seton nodded. Teeweeyownah touched the horse's hindquarters with the rawhide lashes of his wooden quirt. He rode off at a slow canter, passing along the walking file of horses.

"What did he want?" Kowtoliks asked, riding up close.

"He said they had a fight with scouts, downriver men working for Cut Arm. They killed one and wounded two. Some others got away."

Kowtoliks grunted with satisfaction.

"He said to watch for Naked Head and some Palooses," Seton said. "They went to raid for horses and will follow us."

They rode three more miles and drove the tail of the Lamtama herd around the shoulder of a mountain into the open slopes between the head of Belle Creek and Beaver Saddle, one mile southeast of Hemlock Butte. There the column halted for the day, letting the horses have grass and water. The herds stretched over nearly two miles, and camps were set up between them.

In the cold mountain night, the herd boys took turns guarding the horses. There were no enemies within fifty miles. The rear guard reported that the horse soldiers were not following. But horses might wander away in the dark or be spooked by a grizzly, a puma, or wolves. The boys rode slowly through and around the herds, talking softly, singing.

The march continued after sunrise on a cloudy but rainless day. The column moved southeast from Beaver Saddle toward Lean-to Ridge, Soldier Meadows, and Squawberry Spring. There a brief rest was taken to let the horses graze and drink. Past Snowy Summit they went over a rough trail to the ridge above Yoosa Creek and turned northeast, following the Rocky Ridge to its wide curve east and, beyond Rocky Ridge Lake, to Weitas Meadow. This was one of the best grazing and camping grounds on the trail, called *woutokinwes tahtakkin,* Meadow Camp, in numipu language. They covered twelve miles that day.

More days of hard riding were ahead. Continuing straight east in the established order of march, the column moved over Green, Deep, and Sherman saddles past Chimney Butte and Sherman Peak to Noseeum Meadows, where camp was made in the early afternoon after traveling another twelve miles. For long stretches on the trail the riders, except for the old and very young, dismounted and led their horses.

Between Noseeum Meadows and the next camping place near the stone cairn of the Smoking Place ridge, the trail crawled past Bald Mountain and Castle Butte, both on the 6,500-foot level, and switched to the northeast. On this day the column often had to push through a dense hemlock and red cedar forest where parts of the trail were blocked by fallen trees. Here, a few horses were hurt—injuries to pastern bone, wrist, cannon bone, or coronary bone—and had to be left behind. When Kowtoliks and Seton approached the camping site, having advanced eleven miles from morning to midafternoon, they had the feeling that something was following them.

They circled their mounts around and halted. The herd before them walked away. In the sudden stillness they heard the hoofbeats of many horses coming over the back trail. Who was this? Not the rear guard. Horse soldiers? They waited. The hoofbeats became louder, and then a point rider on a tired appaloosa came in sight, leading a file of worn-looking horses at a trot. The man was a Paloos warrior. He had a leathery face, three eagle feathers standing upright at the back of his head. He raised his right arm, a bone quirt with a beaded wrist strap hanging from his wrist. An unsheathed rifle lay in the crook of his left arm. When he was close, Kowtoliks and Seton worked their horses around and rode on as the warrior fell in with them, slowing his horse to a walk. Behind, the file of horses fell back, walking.

"Good to see you," the Paloos said. "Who are you?"

"Kowtoliks," Kowtoliks said. "He is Seton." He pointed with his head. "Lamtama. We are the back riders. The bands have stopped to camp."

"I am Curlew," the man said. "We went back onto the reservation and took a couple of hundred horses. Some were our own, stolen from us one moon ago."

He paused. "Seven of us. Palooses. We had a fight with a bunch of civilians and some downriver men in blue uniforms." He shook his head. "Our own people." He was plainly angry, but then he laughed. "They didn't fight hard. We got away with the horses."

He paused again. "We lost horses on the trail. We drove them too hard."

"Where is Cut Arm's army?" Seton asked.

"We didn't see any soldiers," Curlew said. "I don't know where they are. Maybe they went back to Lapwai." He shrugged.

Before them the trail opened to a high divide above lower saddles running east and west, all covered with thin grass, some fields of huckleberry shrub, and a few stunted trees. The high ground was fringed below by a dense forest of hemlocks and white pines. North-facing slopes still held discolored tracts of snow. The grand view all around revealed mountains upon mountains, the peaks to the east in mantles of snow. An open place in the timber along the flank of one of the saddles held a deep, round sinkhole full of water, surrounded by a small marsh with tall grasses and herbal plants in pale green. The herds had spread over the open spaces, feeding. The camps were clustered below the crest of the divide, the Lamtama camp the nearest.

Kowtoliks and Seton rode aside and halted. Curlew nodded to them and led the file of new Paloos horses down to the forest edge and around the Lamtama herd to the camp of his band. Five of the raiders took the flank to keep the horses from breaking out. Seton guessed they were nearly 250 animals, some of them appaloosas. The chief, Naked Head, rode drag. He passed without a glance, a faraway look in his eyes. He wore no feathers. A sheathed rifle and a tiwét's drum hung from his saddle horn.

During that cold night the herd boys stayed in camp. They needed a rest too. Guard duty was not necessary in this place. The march continued after sunup. They made twelve miles that day on a rising trail past Devil's Chair and Moon Saddle to Indian Lakes. There camp was made in a basin with good grass.

To spare the horses, they made only nine miles the next day to Cayuse Lake, past Spring Mountain clad in snow, ten miles next to the camp on Papoose Saddle in the heart of the Bitterroot Mountains. And finally, on the following day, marching in heavy rain on a slick trail, they went through Lolo Pass and into the wide valley of Lolo Creek. They made camp on the West Fork beyond Wagon Mountain and the Snowshoe Falls.

Thus they left Old Man Coyote's trail behind. Now they were in Montana Territory. It had taken them eight days to reach this campsite after leaving siwishnimi, Musselshell Meadow, above the Weippe Prairie. Perhaps two hundred horses or more had been lost or left on the trail, but the bulk of the precious herds had been saved.

There were dances in camp that night while the herds fed on excellent grass.

Camp broke early next morning, and the bands moved out joyfully toward *nasook nema,* Salmon Creek, the last camp on Lolo Creek before reaching the Bitterroot River and the great valley. Even the horses, in their thousands, after the tense constraints of the trail, were eager to run. The column hastened down Lolo Creek past the hot springs. They made the thirteen miles to nasook nema, the Grave Creek Meadows, a famous campsite for long-range travelers, by noon on July 25.

While the camp settled down and the herds spread out over the wide, tree-lined meadow, an Alpowai scouting party was sent forward by Looking Glass to explore the valley to the Bitterroot River. One man soon returned at a gallop. Blue-coated soldiers, civilian militia, and Flathead tribesmen were erecting a barricade across the narrows of the valley eleven miles downstream. The route east was barred.

T W E L V E

IN CAMP THEY HELD A BRIEF MEETING. THEY DECIDED
to parley with the soldiers and civilians before the barricade was com-
pleted. Three of the band chiefs would speak for all: Looking Glass,
White Goose, and Joseph. They rode in the early afternoon. Each of
the three was accompanied by two or three wi-ses chiefs who rode in
a loose group behind them. They carried no weapons. Behind them
came a heavily armed protective force of forty warriors led by Rainbow and Wottolen.

Seton rode beside Hemene. He had been assigned to translate.
Hemene had proposed it during the meeting. Introducing Seton
to those of the Wallowa and Paloos bands who did not know him,
Hemene said, "This is my sister-in-law's son, Seton. He knows suyapu
language as well as any suyapu, perhaps better than some. He went to
Lapwai school. He has lived in Lewiston and on the reservation. He has

165

lived with us, Lamtama. He has been in the east country. His mother, Wetah, was of our band. So is he. This boy will speak in suyapu language everything the chiefs want said. He will translate accurately every word. We cannot trust the interpreters the suyapu bring with them. They are careless with words. Often they do not understand our language well. They don't speak for us. This boy, Seton, he belongs to us. We trust him."

So the chiefs agreed. Before the party had left, rawhide parfleche cases were taken from the packs and opened. The chiefs dressed in the badges of authority the whites would recognize—war bonnets and painted buffalo robes. Looking Glass wore his plumed hat. Joseph and White Goose put on headdresses of golden eagle feathers. Some of the wi-ses chiefs wore bonnets of the same kind; others sported feathered caps or buffalo horn bonnets with short tails. Hemene's headgear was a long-tail bonnet with split buffalo horns and a piece of buffalo tail wrapped with quills. Seton was awed by it. He had seen Hemene dressed like this only a few times for important formal occasions. In this company Seton looked out of place. He wore no decoration, only long black hair floating beside his face.

As the party rode down the valley, the bewitching display of the chiefs' finery stood in sharp contrast to the bland, cold efficiency of the warriors behind them. Few feathers were visible there. The men had bandoliers with cartridges slung across their chests or carried ammunition pouches on their belts. Their unsheathed rifles lay across their saddles.

Passing through the narrow valley along Lolo Creek at a slow lope, they met the Alpowai scouts west of the barricade in front of a scattering of pines that gave them cover. Nine men were standing by their horses, waiting for the chiefs. When the party halted, the sounds of trees being cut with saws and axes could be heard close by.

"What are the suyapu doing?" Looking Glass asked.

"They are building a corral," one of the scouts said. "You can hear them." He pointed with his chin.

"How many are they?" Looking Glass asked.

"We went behind them and counted. We went through the hill

on the north side. We saw between thirty and forty soldiers. There are many more civilians, between 150 and 200. Behind the corral some are digging rifle pits."

The man paused. "There are Flathead warriors with them," he continued. "Maybe twenty. Arlee is there, the chief from the Flathead camp by the mission. They have white cloth tied around their heads and arms." He laughed. "Flathead warriors with soldiers!"

White Goose said angrily. "The last time I saw them they said they were our friends."

There was a silence.

"All their horses are farther down," a scout said. "We could get around their camp and run them off."

"No," Looking Glass said. "We will do that if we must. But we don't want any trouble here. We don't want to fight. We left the war in the west country." He touched his horse with a quirt and the party rode on, the scouts mounting up and falling in with the warrior band. Briskly they rode the short distance until the barricade came into view. It was a two-log corral, nearly finished, spanning the narrows and reaching across the creek from the north hillside to the south hillside. On the steep and heavily wooded south hillside, some men were felling trees. Others, below, were chopping pine trunks into logs. Behind the corral, a system of rifle pits was being excavated. Beyond, plumes of smoke from cooking fires climbed into the calm sky. There were men in blue and men in civilian clothes with few Flathead tribesmen mixed in. The numipu took it all in, measuring the slopes on both sides. The one to the south was impassable, the one to the north was not. Its gently rolling rise was treeless and covered with tall grasses.

When they were seen, axes and saws fell silent. Behind the corral, men climbed out of the pits and stood, holding rifles. White Goose turned in the saddle and searched for Seton. "Go tell the suyapu chiefs that we want to talk," he said.

Seton edged the roan mare forward and urged her to a fast lope. Behind him the group of chiefs advanced and halted about two hundred paces from the suyapu position. A hundred paces back of them, the warriors formed two skirmish lines and sat their horses.

Seton rode to the center of the corral just south of the creek. The upper of the two horizontal logs was as high as his horse's head. He stood in the stirrups and looked over, seeking an officer among the blue-coats. A man came forward. "I am Captain Rawn," he said. "I am the commanding officer."

"The chiefs have come to meet with you," Seton said in English. He did not wait for an answer, but turned his horse and rode back. The chiefs had dismounted and spread their fancy robes on the grass. They sat in a half circle, the three band chiefs in the middle. Seton dismount-ed and, following a gesture by White Goose, sat next to the Lamtama chief.

One by one seven men slipped through the log fence and walked toward the chiefs. They were unarmed. They walked slowly, some clearly apprehensive, others hiding it. The seven sat in a row. Two were officers in soldier blue with captain's bars on their shoulder straps. Three were civilians. Two were Indians. One of the Indians was dressed like the white civilians; the other wore a white-cotton cloth turban on his head and a white cloth strip around his left arm. At the corral men pressed against the logs to watch in silence. They formed a dense, unin-terrupted line.

One of the captains, a tall, bearded man, cleared his throat. "I am Captain Charles Rawn," he said, "commanding officer of Fort Missou-la." He waited for a moment. "This is my interpreter, Delaware Jim." He pointed to the middle-aged Indian in white man's clothing.

"We don't want him," White Goose said in the numipu language. "We brought our own interpreter." He tipped his head to Seton, the feathers of his bonnet making a rustling sound. Seton translated. Dela-ware Jim looked at him, bemused and annoyed. Seton was embarrassed to be the focus of a disagreement.

"Very well," Rawn said. If he was dismayed, he didn't show it. He pointed to the captain next to him. "Captain Jonathan Livingstone of my command." The officer nodded toward the somber chiefs. Rawn went on, introducing a John Humble of Missoula, captain of volun-teers from the Missoula area, a Jerome Brown, captain of volunteers from Stevensville and the upper Bitterroot Valley, his lieutenant, Amos

Bird, and the Indian with the white cloth markings. "Chief Arlee of the Flathead tribe," Rawn said. "You know him."

The chiefs looked at the slender man with the white turban, the wrinkled face framed with braids. He wore a beaded vest over a dark cotton shirt, leather trousers, and beaded moccasins. The chiefs' faces remained stolid, without expression. "We know him," Looking Glass said coldly. "We are surprised he is here." Arlee sat, wooden, his legs crossed, his face showing no emotion. "He has dressed up to meet with us," Looking Glass said.

He looked at Captain Rawn. "I am Ippakness Wayhayken," he said.

"Chief Looking Glass," Seton said.

Looking Glass nodded toward Joseph. "Heinmot Tooyalakekt."

"Chief Thunder Rolling in the High Mountains," Seton said.

Looking Glass nodded toward White Goose. "Peopeo Kiskiok Hihih."

"Chief White Goose," Seton said.

"We speak for all the people of the five bands," Looking Glass said. Seton translated.

"I am glad to meet you," Rawn bowed his head slightly.

"You are from Fort Missoula?" Looking Glass addressed Rawn. "Since when is there a fort? We don't know of a fort there."

"Since three weeks," Rawn said. There was a pause. The two delegations eyed each other, studying their opposites.

"What are the bluecoats and the civilians doing here?" Looking Glass asked.

"I have been ordered to inform you that you must surrender your arms and ammunition to me if you want to go on. These volunteers," he glanced at the civilians at his side, "they have joined me and my soldiers because they are afraid of the Nez Perces. You fought with soldiers in Idaho Territory and killed many settlers there. The people of this valley are afraid for their lives and their livestock." Rawn might be worried, even afraid, but he showed a brave face.

"The war in the west country," Joseph said quietly, "it was not of our making. Our land was stolen. Many of our people were murdered by miners and settlers. We went before the suyapu courts, but they did not give us justice. They did nothing. Everyone cheated us. Your government cheated us. The agent cheated us. Thousands of our horses and cattle were stolen by white bandits."

He paused to give Seton time to translate.

"We did not want that war," he continued. "We were forced to defend ourselves. We had never before made war with the whites. We welcomed them in my father's time. We thought the land was big enough for all. But they kept coming and coming, like a flood. We became strangers in our own land."

There was a silence. Rawn said nothing. The other whites appeared nervous.

"We have left the west country in order to have no more war," Looking Glass said. "We had cause to fight. My camp was attacked on the reservation without provocation. Some of my people were killed. We lost almost everything. This is why we had to fight."

He waited for the translation.

"We left the war behind. We are on the way to the east country. We have not come here to make trouble. In the past, for time beyond memory, we have come through here on the way to the buffalo. We have never harmed a white child, woman, or man in this valley. The men from here know this to be true."

When Seton ended, the three civilians nodded in agreement. "Yes," Jerome Brown said, "the chief is right."

"One band of our people lives permanently in this valley, by the town called Corvallis," Looking Glass continued. "The band of Chief Eagle from the Light. Some of our people live with the Flathead by the Catholic mission. They have never made trouble with the white people. We always thought of the white people of this valley as friends. We always made good trade in Fort Owen, Stevensville, Skalkaho." He waited.

"We pledge to pass through the Bitterroot Valley without doing harm. We will trade and ride on to the buffalo country."

Seton had translated the speeches carefully, trying to find the right expressions in both languages so he would not change meaning or intent. There was a long silence. Finally Rawn spoke. "I have my orders; I must follow them. I have been ordered not to let you pass unless you give up your weapons and your ammunition. Surrender them to me, and I'll let you go through unhindered."

White Goose looked at Rawn. He rested his right hand with the eagle wing fan on his knee. There was anger in his voice when he spoke. "You were a boy when a war took place on the Columbia River. White soldiers fought against Yakimas, Umatillas, Cayuses, Spokanes, and Coeur d'Alenes. Colonel Wright was the big chief of the soldiers. After many battles the Indians were defeated. Colonel Wright told the Indians that if they would surrender, he would treat them well and hurt no one but the murderers."

He paused. The eyes of the whites were on Seton when he translated.

"Under these conditions the Indians surrendered," White Goose continued. "Then Colonel Wright hanged many innocent Indians. Some Indians deserved hanging, but the others' hands were clean of white men's blood. How do we know that you and your soldiers are not like Colonel Wright? If we give up our arms, we will be at your mercy." He paused. "We want no fight. But we will not give you our weapons. How could we hunt buffalo without weapons?"

Before Seton finished the translation, the Flathead chief interrupted. "I am Arlee. My Nez Perce friends; I am here to help. We, the Flathead, are sorry to see you in this trouble. You cannot win against the government. Lay down your guns and quit fighting the soldiers. You will all be killed or wounded, and maybe hanged, if you continue fighting. Put down your guns. We will help you."

He had spoken in Salish language, and neither Seton nor the whites understood what he said. Only Looking Glass and White Goose knew. Looking Glass looked at Arlee and brought his hands up. He addressed him in sign language, throwing these signs: "I am numipu. I am chief. When a Chinaman travels he carries no arms. Do you think I am a Chinaman? It is foolish to think that five bands of numipu are going to the buffalo without a single gun."

Then he spoke in numipu for Seton to translate. He was still talking to Arlee. "You are a fool," he said. "Your head chief, Charlot, the one the suyapu made head chief over you, has already put his mark under a treaty that gives the Bitterroot country to the suyapu. That was five years ago. I was told by Lean Elk of Eagle from the Light's band. He knew it from your chief, Adolph. Soon they will force you to go north to the reservation. What happened to us will happen to you, too. You will lose this land as surely as we lost ours. So what are you doing here?"

The officers and volunteer leaders sat in stunned silence as Seton translated. Before Arlee could respond, Looking Glass turned brusquely to the civilians. "Go home to your families," he said. "You are in no danger from us. We will only pass through. We left the war in the west country. Go home! You will be safe. I do not lie. I give you my word."

The three men looked at each other. Two of them nodded. The army officers tried to look calm. Rawn's gaze trailed beyond the chiefs to the silent lines of hard, unforgiving warriors. His position was weak. Even if the volunteers stayed with him he would have little chance in a fight. The Nez Perces could put sharpshooters above and around the barricade and pick off his men one by one. If the volunteers accepted the chiefs' assurances and left for home, he and his few soldiers would be lost. But he had received orders. Defiantly, he made a last desperate effort. "I must insist you surrender your arms," he said.

There was a stubborn silence. Finally the volunteer captain from Missoula, John Humble, raised his right hand. He looked at Looking Glass. "Chief, you give your word that the people in the valley will be safe?" he asked.

"Yes," Looking Glass nodded.

There was a pause. Jerome Brown stood up, the volunteer captain from Stevensville. "All of the chiefs agree to that?" he asked. Then, "Can you control your young men?"

"Yes," White Goose said. "They will do you no harm."

Looking Glass stood, the rest of the chiefs following. Rawn and the men with him also got up. "We do not want to fight," Looking Glass said. "I tried to surrender on the Clearwater. My offer was rejected. We will not surrender our arms. If the captain wishes to build corrals for the numipu, he may, but they will not hold us back. If we are not allowed to go peaceably, we shall do what we must." It was a threat, and it was understood by all.

The Wallowa chief spoke. He had let Looking Glass be the speaker because they had given him the responsibility for the march to the Plains. "We want peace," Joseph said, "more than you can know. But if we are not allowed to pass this fence, we will fight our way through."

White Goose had the final word. He pointed to the sky with his eagle wing fan. He looked along the faces of the white men in front of him. "With the mawie, the morning sun, we will ride out from here."

The meeting broke up on those words. Nothing more was said. Captain Rawn's delegation returned to the flimsy barricade, the chiefs and warriors to their camp. They left three scouts behind to watch the soldiers. Back on nasook nema the chiefs explained what had happened at the meeting, and that they had pledged that no suyapu would be harmed if the suyapu did not start a fight. They also, to the warriors' clamorous assent, announced that the camp and the horses would pass the corral the next morning.

Before Seton returned to the horse herd and his companions, the chiefs thanked him for his performance at the meeting. It was the first time they had noticed him. Hemene and White Goose were proud that a Lamtama boy had handled the difficult assignment well. Seton himself was glad to be back where he felt most at home. He rode slowly through the great herd, breathing the smell of warm, earthy bodies and hearing their familiar sounds.

Toward evening one of the scouts came in. Half of the civilian volunteers, perhaps more, had left the corral and gone away.

During the night the sky opened to a drizzling rain. The horses stood patiently in it. In camp the people woke among the packs they had spread on the ground. They wrapped themselves tighter into robes or blankets or built little shelters by stretching skins across packs, creating nooks that the rain did not reach. Seton, Kowtoliks, and Atemis, lying on beds of pine needles under low-hanging branches of pine trees, covered themselves more securely with their buffalo robes. The rain stopped toward morning. When first light crawled pale and gauzy over the eastern sky, birds began to sing and horses and people shook themselves from the memory of the dark.

A rider passed and alerted the boys that the march was about to begin. They and the horses drank the clear water of Grave Creek. The boys saddled up and chewed a few bits of jerky from their saddlebags. It took well over an hour until the bands and the other herds had gone and the Lamtama herd could advance. Again Kowtoliks and Seton rode drag.

There was no one behind them but the five young men of the rear guard who covered the Lolo Trail. Before them, the stream of horses flowed smoothly over the wet grass of the narrowing valley. Twice they crossed the twisting creek, and after covering ten miles they reached a point where the valley made a loop to the south. There a shallow draw ran down from the north. Rawn's corral stood behind the loop, only half a mile away. The ranks of the horses thinned out as they walked up the draw into the hills on a trail that would lead the column east. Wottolen and Teeweeyownah and about forty Lamtama warriors, including most of the men of Hemene's wi-ses, stood guard by their horses at the edge of the draw. The men mounted and swung in behind them after Seton and Kowtoliks had passed.

The trail dropped and climbed as it wound eastward a mile north of the valley and almost parallel to it. It was hidden by hills above the northern boundary of the valley. Its existence was unknown to the soldiers and volunteers at the corral. No one there heard or saw the numipu pass by until the column dropped back into the valley three and a half miles farther east.

When the drag riders neared the area due north of Rawn's corral, Seton noticed a bunch of saddled horses in a pine thicket below the crest of the highest hill to the south. He heard the piercing cry of a peregrine falcon from close behind him and turned in the saddle to see Teeweeyownah wave toward the hill. He saw nothing there, but as he rode on, two dozen warriors slid silently down from the crest and caught their horses. He later learned that they were sharpshooters. They had taken up positions overlooking Rawn's trenches. The whites never knew they had been there. Half a mile farther east, this group came up behind Wottolen's and Teeweeyownah's band.

At the head of the South Fork of Sleeman Creek the trail dipped south, following the drainage of the creek to the valley floor. There another body of warriors stood guard and closed in with the others as they passed. Another two miles of marching east and the drag riders and guards came into the wide opening to the Bitterroot River valley. It stretched from five to ten miles wide and was a verdant green. The shiny blue river was framed by tall stands of ponderosas and Douglas firs. The valley was edged by high mountain ranges, the Sapphire Mountains in the east, the Bitterroot Mountains in the west. The tallest peaks of both ranges were still snow capped on July 26, while the lower slopes were coated with the emerald green of ancient fir forests.

At the mouth of Lolo Valley the column turned south and advanced on the broad belt of grassland west of the river for four more miles to McLain Creek where camp was made. They had traveled twenty miles that day, and it was only early afternoon. While the bands settled down and the herds were let loose, groups of women went out with *tuk'es,* digging sticks with crosspiece handles, to dig in the rich meadows of blue violet camas and pink bitterroot. The yellow roots of *bit'an,* bitterroot, would be peeled and eaten raw. They also made a good tea. Camas bulbs were not eaten raw. They had to be cleaned and stored for baking in a pit, an earth oven. Because it took three days to bake camas correctly, they did not begin on this day. The opportunity came two days later, after the camp had reached Indian Prairie, where it remained until August 1.

While women dug for camas and bitterroot, small parties of men hunted in the foothills. Until dusk, reports of their rifles echoed across the distance. They brought in a few moose, three black bears, and about a dozen each of deer and elk.

Shortly after their arrival on McLain Creek, a band of fifty suyapu volunteers rode up on the Lamtama herd where it was spread out north and west of the camp. These were the last contingent of Bitterroot civilians who had held out with Rawn's soldiers at Fort Fizzle, as the corral had already been dubbed. They were on their way home. Seton saw them approach and rode close, unsheathing the Winchester and levering a shell into the chamber. He was quickly joined by Antelope and Kowtoliks, both holding Springfield carbines ready. From the south end of the herd, Moositsa whooped and hollered and came up at a gallop. The whites halted in confusion, watching the wild youngsters, casting nervous glances toward the distant camp, unsure whether they should continue or turn back. The boys sat their horses between the herd and the whites. When Moositsa arrived, whirling his horse and unslinging his rifle, they sat four abreast, blocking the whites' path. These strangers would not get close to the herd. There was a shout from the camp, and Looking Glass and two men rode out and the chief waved the whites on.

Still the boys did not budge. They were Lamtama protecting the Lamtama herd. They owed nothing to the Alpowai chief. Under their hostile eyes the whites pulled back and rode in a wide circle to the border of the camp where they were allowed to pass.

During the night Atemis returned from the camp to the boys' fireplace and sleeping place and brought news. At a meeting in the evening the chiefs again quarreled about which route to take. White Goose and many of the wi-ses chiefs proposed that they go north through the Flathead Reservation and Tobacco Plains to Grandmother's Land, Canada. It would be a short and safe route, away from white settlements.

There were three men, just arrived, who knew the route and had volunteered to guide the camp there. These men were Bad Grizzly Bear Boy, his brother Tepsus, both numipu from the Clearwater, and Owhi, a Yakima. The three had worked as scouts for General Miles and had fought Lakotas and Cheyennes in the northern Plains. They had deserted Miles when they learned that war had broken out in Idaho Territory and that their people were coming to the east country. They had made it to Missoula when the bands reached nasook nema, and had waited to join them.

But Looking Glass spoke eloquently of his old allies and friends, the Crows, who had pledged their unwavering support. He had, once again, argued for the long route south and east, past the Yellowstone, to the lands of the Crows and the buffalo. Rainbow and Five Wounds and some of the wi-ses chiefs supported this plan. Chiefs Joseph, Toohoolhoolzote, and Hahtalekin made no serious objections. They wanted to keep the bands together at all cost, so they let Looking Glass have his way. The Alpowai chief argued that the war had been left in the west country, and that the peace with the Bitterroot whites had been confirmed in the meeting at the corral. And so, Atemis said, Looking Glass had won out and was given leadership on the trail to the Crows.

The slow march through the Bitterroot Valley started the next day. In cool but sunny weather the column moved south on the wide, grassy flat west of the river. Hunting parties of men worked the foothills and the river bottom, and groups of women dug for bitterroot and camas in a sea of flowers. Blooms in white, red, blue, yellow, lavender, and purple were woven into the deep green of short bluebunch wheatgrass, fescue, and needle-and-thread grasses. The boys riding the herds had an easy, worry-free time. The horses needed no prodding. The column made nine miles to the bend of the river where Bass Creek runs in from the west. Behind the bend lay ponds surrounded by reed marshes over which clouds of ducks and geese and wide-winged trumpeter swans rose and swirled and fell. The boys remembered the place but were impressed by the great swarms of waterfowl.

On the march they had passed four or five ranches. The plain wooden buildings lay deserted, but there were cattle and a few horses grazing on pastures. Nothing was touched, no cattle driven off and butchered, although the temptation was undeniable. The ranchers had fled for shelter to Fort Owen. It was an old trading post built of adobe bricks located a mile north of the little town of Stevensville.

They passed it the next day. The square structure with its brownish walls and two squat towers was barely visible through the brush on the east bank of the river. Half a mile below it, on the outskirts of Stevensville, lay the narrow, white, wooden St. Mary's Church, its slim bell tower topped with a white cross. This had been the Catholic mission to the Flathead of the Bitterroot Valley since 1841; many of them had converted to Christianity. Off to the side stood a small circle of white-canvas Flathead tipis. Stevensville, a cluster of wooden houses along four short streets, appeared lifeless behind a wooden bridge wide enough for one wagon. The column went past two miles southwest and made camp near Chief Charlot's Flathead camp on Indian Prairie.

They stayed for three days. Finally the women had time to bake camas and lay in a good supply. They bought wheat flour from the flour mill near Fort Owen. There was much trading between the two camps. The numipu traded horses or paid with silver coin and gold dust for Flathead dried food and other essentials, including ammunition. They also bought goods from white men who came to the camp. On the last day of their stay, Seton took Itsepit, Dawn, a few of the women of Hemene's wi-ses, and all the children on a ride to Stevensville to visit the two general stores of the town. He still had the fifteen silver dollars he had been paid by the Lewiston Mercantile for the Elk City trip.

They rode in a happy group. The women were dressed in white leather and beads; the children were less fancy. They sang and laughed as they rode. Their mood seemed to convey itself to the horses. They strode elegantly, ears pricked, snorting and nickering with excitement. Seton and Itsepit rode point. Tsacope sat on Seton's saddle in front of him.

When singing stopped for a moment, Itsepit touched his right knee with her left knee and looked at him sideways. "You are chief now, Seton. Chief Seton. It sounds good." She giggled and looked back over her shoulder to Dawn and Petolwe who rode side by side behind them. Petolwe's six-year-old daughter, Ilsoo, rode on her mother's saddle.

"He leads us to do battle in the stores of this town," Petolwe said. "He takes care of us. He protects us. We will take many trophies." The women laughed loudly. Seton looked straight ahead.

"Our chief has many silver coins," Elk Blanket called from the back. "He buys anything we want."

"He promised us," another woman said. "He did say we could have whatever we wanted." There was laughter.

"No," Seton said. "I didn't say that."

"Yes, you said that," Itsepit said. "We all heard it."

"We did," Petolwe said.

Seton looked at Itsepit. Her knee was still touching his. She had a devilish twinkle in her eyes. "You always start this with me," he said, half seriously.

"The chief is arguing with Itsepit," Petolwe reported to the women behind her. "Who knows what will come from that."

"First we raid the store, then we'll see about that," a woman called from the back. Again there was loud laughter.

"Stop it," Dawn said. "Leave him alone. He has taken us and the children. That's more than some others have done."

"We will, we will," Elk Blanket shouted. "We are just happy to ride to town." She burst into song and the others fell in. The hooves of the horses clattered on the wooden planks of the bridge, and they entered the town. Dogs barked hysterically, but no white person was in sight. A few young Pekonan men were hanging around Reeve's saloon. They could buy whiskey there.

"Let's look for the general store," Dawn said sternly. There were two general stores in Stevensville. One had the name Jerry Fahy painted over the door. This store was empty. The owner had fled town. The second general store sat on the northeast corner of Main and Third Street, the Buck Brothers' store. At first the Bucks had removed their merchandise to Fort Owen for safety, but, after encountering friendly Nez Perces at the flour mill, they decided to bring most of it back and open for business. Two dozen Nez Perce horses stood in front of the store. The women with Seton dismounted and tied their mounts to the rail.

Inside were women, children, and two men of the Wallowa band. They had gathered a pile of merchandise on the counter. The people of the two bands mingled easily, laughing and joking. The Wallowa men eyed Seton with interest. The children he had brought with him converged upon the tall glass containers on the counter. Most were empty, but two were still half filled with white crystalline rock candy and suckers in orange and red. Two of the Buck brothers stood behind the counter, viewing the vibrant assembly with suspicion and a little apprehension. Itsepit pushed through the cordon of the seven children of the wi-ses and, with one of the Bucks assisting, made two little piles of rock candy and suckers. She went on to search the store's shelves with the other women, while Seton stood and watched the "raid" progress.

The Wallowa women paid with gold coin and left noisily. The women of the wi-ses checked for food but found only a little sugar and molasses left. They took a small cloth bag of sugar, three cans of tobacco, a bag of coffee, and had two jars filled with molasses. They went through rolls of dry goods and had lengths of fabric cut. A little would go for dressing their daughters' dolls. They inspected shawls and took some. Sewing needles and thread, some enamel cups and plates, and a hatchet were added to the stock until Dawn said firmly, "This is enough. He will have nothing left of his money." But after the merchant added numbers on paper with a stub of pencil, it turned out that Seton still had two dollars.

They rode home, continuing to sing and joke, making up a thank-you song for Seton and his generosity. After they crossed the bridge they met another group of women on their way to the store. A serious-faced Looking Glass led a handful of Alpowai warriors on their way to gather up the drunks at Reeve's saloon.

The next day the march south continued. The bands, under Looking Glass's leadership, still traveled slowly over the grassy flats along the river. They made camp after twelve miles across from the hamlet called Corvallis. There a few settlers had thrown up a primitive fort, stacking green sod twelve feet high and two feet wide for the outer wall. They had known Nez Perces ever since they came to this valley, but now they were afraid. The Nez Perces ignored this foolish gesture and went fishing in the river and hunting in the foothills.

While they were in this camp, six tipis of the Eagle from the Light band joined them. The newcomers had been residents of the Bitterroot Valley for a few years. These were crack buffalo hunters. They spent much of their time in the Plains, but their winter camp was south of Corvallis. Originally from the Salmon River country, they were angered by the lawless encroachment of white settlers on their old domain. They had abandoned the west country permanently. Not all the people of this band joined. The ten men and their families who did were led by a subchief, Lean Elk. When the bands moved on after sunup the next morning, Lean Elk's group were the only ones who dragged tipi poles with their horses.

In the following days they camped on Horse Creek, on Rye Creek, in one of the last wide openings in the narrowing, steadily rising valley, in Ross Hole, and on Trail Creek. They crossed the Continental Divide at 7,264 feet before they reached *iskumtselalik pah,* Place of Ground Squirrels, on August 7. This was their ancient campground on the trail to the buffalo country on the North Fork of the Big Hole River.

In two of the camps there had been voices of warning, premonitions. In the Horse Creek camp it was Wahlitits, fearless fighter of the lahmotta and Clearwater battles. He rode through the stunned people shouting, "My brothers and sisters, I am telling you! In a dream last night I saw myself killed. I do not care. I am willing to die. But first, I will kill some soldiers. I shall not turn back from the death. We are all going to die!"

In the Trail Creek camp it was Peopeo Ipsewahk, also a warrior of distinction. On a gray horse he rode around and around, crying his lament: "Why do these chiefs travel slowly? Maybe our enemies are overtaking us. Maybe we will get beaten! We should keep going. We should hurry. We should keep watch everywhere. Each chief should look after his own warriors! Be ready to fight any time! Keep going! Move fast! Death may be following on our trail!"

Both men were known to have strong wéyekin powers. But Looking Glass insisted that the bands were at peace here and dismissed the warning. Camp and herds traveled no more than nine to twelve miles a day on ground where they could have made forty miles with ease.

THIRTEEN

THE BIG HOLE WAS A HIGH VALLEY ENCASED IN
mountain ranges that rose to over ten thousand feet. From an eagle's
view it looked like the top of a giant buffalo skull, facing east. The skull
part between the horn cores was twenty miles deep west to east. From
there the massive horns, fifteen miles wide and tapering to ten miles,
stood out for forty miles each toward the northeast and the southeast.
In the southeast the tip of the horn rested against the Big Hole Divide;
in the northeast the tip of the horn pointed to the low-lying valley of
Clarks Fork, hidden behind the mountain wall. Snowcapped throughout the year, its lower flanks heavily laced with fir forests, the Anacon-
da Range framed the Big Hole in the northwest, as did the Beaverhead
Mountains in the southwest and the Pioneer Mountains in the east. The
Big Hole River wound through the valley, circled the Pioneer Moun-

tains, and escaped through a gap between Mount Fleecer and Round Top Mountain to empty into the Jefferson River.

Nearly seven thousand feet high, the valley was uninhabited because it was extremely cold during much of the year. Lower areas were carpeted with lush medium to tall grasses and countless colorful flowers. Rich stands of camas grew in moist areas along the river and its tributaries. Higher benches were covered with bluebunch wheatgrass and sagebrush.

When the column descended into the Big Hole, Seton and Kowtoliks, riding drag on the Lamtama herd, were the last to cross the divide. The rear guard, which had faithfully shadowed the retreat across the Lolo Trail, had been pulled in during the second camp in the Bitterroot Valley. Now, coming down Trail Creek, Big Hole opened before them, green and beautiful and inviting. The river ran through it like a silver strand. Where Trail Creek reached the valley floor, it was joined from the south by Ruby Creek. The two creeks started the North Fork of the Big Hole River. The North Fork hugged the foot of the western mountain for a few miles until it swerved east and ran through the flats into the river. On its course it meandered through a narrow, swampy marsh with stagnant pools among reed grass and thickets of willows.

When Seton and Kowtoliks had a chance to look beyond the stream of horses, they noticed that the bands had converged on a dry meadow along the east bank of the North Fork, less than a mile above the juncture of Trail and Ruby creeks. There packhorses were unloaded and band and individual camps were being set up. The Wallowa and Pekonan herds had been run downstream beyond the campsite and onto the benchland to the east. The Lamtama herd was taken west and moved through stream and marsh and up to the wide, grassy slope of Battle Mountain that offered excellent pasturage. While the bulk of the herd was already spreading out on the green side of the mountain, Kowtoliks and Seton plunged through the river and drove stragglers through the marsh toward the slope. Then they rode slowly uphill until they reached the border of the dense forest of lodgepole pines running along the crest. The boys who had ridden point and flank were there, searching for a good campsite.

Looking east they had a grand view of the North Fork below, the camp, the Wallowa and Pekonan herds, the wide flats to the distant river, and the snowy mountains beyond. The boys made camp in a clearing inside the forest edge that protected them against the fierce northwest wind. Later, they built a fire there when they returned from an evening meal in the big camp. They had learned that Looking Glass planned for the bands to stay in the Big Hole camp for a few days and prepare for the next leg of the journey east.

During the night a thin layer of ice formed on standing water. Before first light two packs of wolves called, one from across the valley, the other, closer, from the north. A few dogs answered from the camp, then fell silent. After sunrise, parties of men and boys left to hunt for game. Groups of women went out to dig camas; others took horses to the forest edge closest to camp to fell trees for tipi poles. The sound of crashing trees and of axes chopping into trunks and cleaning trunks of branches continued into early afternoon. Horses dragging poles plowed through the river; then poles were laid out near camp to dry. The first tipis were raised by midafternoon, and by early evening a total of thirty-four stood on the campsite—about half the tipis the bands had left after the Clearwater affair.

Most of the tipis stood densely clustered in a small area next to a sharp bend of the North Fork at the southern end of the camp. The remaining tipis were spaced across an open meander to the next bend, which marked the northern end of the camp. From Red Scout's tipi in the south to Wottolen's tipi in the north the camp stretched a thousand feet. By nightfall about a hundred people were sheltered in tipis, while around seven hundred people camped in the open.

The camp of Hemene's wi-ses was located in front of the open meander of the river about four hundred feet below the northern perimeter of the camp. The women had cut lodge poles for three tipis, but when darkness came none had yet been raised. Camps of Lamtama and Wallowa wi-ses were directly to the north, east, and south. A peaceful sight, but Seton wondered about the premonition Wahlitits and Peopeo Ipsewahk had voiced on the road to Big Hole. Why had the chiefs ignored it?

On that first morning in the Big Hole, Seton and Atemis left the herd after sunrise to hunt downstream along the North Fork. They brought one extra horse in case they had to pack out game. Riding downhill, they cut diagonally through the grazing horses past twin pines halfway up the hillside, the only trees on the slope. They crossed marsh and stream north of the camp, the frigid water reaching to the forearms of their horses, and passed through the Wallowa herd where it was spread over two miles. To their left, across the stream where the forest edge slanted down to the marsh, a dozen women were cutting tipi poles. From the timber to the north came the first echoes of rifle shots. To the south they saw riders chase antelopes in the flats by the river, trying to drive them into a surround. There were fresh hoofprints in the wet grass. They judged that two parties were ahead of them. They followed the stream turning northeast and, close to its mouth, came to a marsh miles wide, parted by the Big Hole River. Two deer bounded away as they rode in. When they tied their horses up, they heard two shots half a mile away.

They checked the wind direction and stalked into the northwest breeze. Eighty yards apart they walked slowly into the tangle of brush and willows, setting their feet carefully on the spongy ground. There were tracks of deer and moose, the pug marks of a puma. They went on and heard three shots in quick succession ahead to their right. In the distance a voice called in their language. Then silence. Seton and Atemis looked at each other and stood for a while, listening. They moved on. Something dark and heavy crashed through the brush, a moose breaking away from their right. It was fifty yards away and seemed as big as a log cabin. It moved across their front at an angle. Atemis had one good shot with the .45-70 Springfield. Seton got two poor shots with the Winchester. And the moose was gone, splashing through a pond and tearing through brush and on and on, until there was silence. The boys stood for a long moment. The silence faded, filled by the voices of insects.

The boys went to where the moose had been when they fired at it and knelt and touched the grass. They found sprinkles of frothy blood, light orange red in color.

"Lung," Atemis said, looking at Seton.

Seton nodded. They knew they would find the animal dead. They traced the spoor and, after two hundred yards, came upon a cow moose lying on its right side. The eyes were filming over. It was huge, bigger than a horse. There were two bullet holes. The lung shot had come from Atemis's rifle. One of Seton's shots had been high and a little back, not high enough to strike the spine. His other shot had missed.

Atemis slit the animal's throat to let the spirit go, and both knelt and gave a prayer of thanks. Seton went for the packhorse. The heavy work of butchering began. They used their knives and a hatchet. Even for boys as skilled as they were, it took two hours to skin the carcass and place the internal organs—liver, heart, kidneys, and lungs—with the pile of meat stripped from the bones. Twice they had to resharpen their knives with whetstones they carried in their belt pouches. Each of them ate a thick slice of liver, crunchy, still warm. The parts they took were packed into the fresh hide, bundled, and tied up on the pack-horse. The horse complained and stepped nervously, edgy from the smell of blood. The remainder of the carcass was left to the wolves and ravens that always spotted Indian hunters and expected a share of the kill. Seton and Atemis took their time on the eleven-mile ride to the big camp.

The smoke of many fires stood over the camp like so many flags. Long before they reached the Wallowa herd, they saw women and horses in the flats, working the camas meadows. They rode the two miles through the Wallowa horses and came to the northern edge of the camp. Tipis had not yet been raised, but meat-drying racks were set up. Young boys and girls were racing ponies east of the camp, and small children were playing among the packs, parfleches, baskets, and the many hobbled horses. A dog barked. A few old men sat together, smoking. The sound of axes rang from the timber edge. The late morning sun lit up a busy camp. Women worked on hides or cooked or cut up game. Some women prepared earth ovens for baking camas; others fed children or the few men left in camp. Some old women sat together, mending leather clothes or sewing moccasins. Although he had seen such scenes many times before, Seton later remembered how he had taken it all in, trying not to forget but not knowing why.

Four wi-ses camps down was Hemene's. The old man sat by the one fire that was going well. Thunder Eyes and Short Bull sat beside him, their little children on their knees. They had come back earlier with an elk cow they shot high up on Trail Creek. Only three women were in Hemene's camp; the others were away with axes or digging sticks. The three worked on the elk, slicing chunks of meat into long, thin flaps and spreading them over the limbs of the drying rack. They were Elk Blanket, Petolwe, and Petolwe's mother-in-law, Talooth. They were talking and joking and laughing. Seton and Atemis dismounted and carried the heavy green hide bundle to the women. They nodded to the boys but kept on cutting. Seton looked for a moment, marveling once again at how skillful and fast they were with their knives.

"Come, sit with me," Hemene said from the fireplace.

A night without a moon but lit by countless stars, cold with a freezing wind. The boys lay around the fire in the clearing high up in the tree edge of Battle Mountain, wrapped in their sleeping robes. Earlier they had gorged themselves on deer and elk and moose and listened to the sound of the activities in the camp almost a thousand feet below. There had been singing and drumming down there for quite some time, but it died down around midnight. The fires burned down at the same time, and quiet settled over the camp and the mountain. On the hill below their herders' camp the horses moved slowly, cropping the good grass, shadows in the night.

But a few hours after midnight the horses began to drift upward and north along the slope, neighing and snorting, unhurried but determined to get away from something. Some dogs barked from the camp for a while, then fell silent. But the slow drifting of the horses continued. Seton heard it, but was not sure if the sounds were part of a dream or real. Swan Necklace tossed the buffalo robe away and sat up, listening.

"The horses!" he said. "They are spooked by something."

"What?" Kowtoliks said, sitting up. "A grizzly?"

"We better go and look," Swan Necklace said. The boys made their rifles ready and went to their horses. They took the hobbles off and mounted. They rode slowly south along the forest edge where horses were gathering, still drifting up from below. Whatever troubled them seemed to be at the bottom of the hill. The boys walked their steeds through the herd, talking to the horses, trying to calm them. Three of the boys stayed back when Seton and Swan Necklace went beyond the herd and crossed the empty hillside as far as a pine-covered draw that came down from Battle Mountain and ended in a timbered fan above the floodplain. In the star light on the dark mountain they saw nothing disturbing. Down to their left some of the fires of the camp still glowed. Because of the curvature of the slope, they could not see where its bottom stood against the floodplain.

"There is nothing here," Seton said. He coughed. "The horses must have smelled something down there they didn't like."

"Maybe a grizzly walked along the river," Swan Necklace said. "Or is looking to get to the meat on the drying racks." He chuckled. Then serious again, he said, "I have seen two sets of grizzly tracks on the creek south of here."

Seton grunted in agreement. "Let's ride back." They turned their horses, and when they reached the herd they noticed that the animals were slowly spreading out downhill again. The other boys looked at them. "Nothing," Seton said. "We saw nothing."

"The horses are not scared anymore," Kowtoliks said. "I'm going back to sleep." They all went. Kowtoliks put more wood on the fire, and the boys rolled themselves into their robes. The wind from the northwest brushed through the trees and sucked all night sounds in. The sky spun toward first light.

From down the hill, beyond the herd, came the crack of a gunshot. Two more followed. Then, in rapid succession four more. Quiet again. The boys sat up, listening. A rolling salvo from many rifles. Another. A third. Loud shouting, whites' voices. Soldiers. They were drowned out by a stampede of the panicked horses that raced uphill and wheeled to the left and right as they came up to the timberline.

The boys sprang to their feet. "Soldiers!" Kowtoliks shouted. "They are attacking the camp!" They grabbed their rifles and ran to their saddle horses. The horses bucked and neighed and spun around, but the boys were able to mount and bring them under control. Above the tumult made by a thousand terrified Lamtama horses, they could still hear the sound of gunfire below, irregular now, and the shouting of many suyapu voices.

And then there was gunfire from Battle Mountain itself, from the northern end of the grass slope where the forest edge slanted east and down to the floodplain. The horses on that side streamed back over the slope, wide-eyed, running away from the new threats. The whole herd pushed toward the pine-covered draw and the timber on the southern end of the hill.

"They are trying to drive the horses off!" Kowtoliks called over the din. The boys held their horses and waited. When the last of the herd had passed, they rode out and swooped over the empty hill. They were five. Before them were a dozen white men in civilian clothes spaced over a distance of two hundred yards, walking toward them, still firing their rifles into the air. The whites stopped when they saw riders coming on in the uncertain light. They were caught by surprise. Where had these Indians come from, and how many more would follow? The boys whooped and circled, firing their rifles with both hands, directing their horses with their thighs. The two with repeaters, Seton and Swan Necklace, fired as fast as they could lever shells into the chambers. The whites broke and ran away down the hill. The boys followed a short distance to make sure that they had cleared the hill, reloaded, and rode back.

They sat their horses in a row. First light was breaking, and they could see what was happening below. The cries and shouts continued, partly drowned by the thunder of the guns. Infantrymen in blue and men in civilian clothes had broken into the southern part of the camp, the place where most of the tipis stood close together. A few tipis smoldered. The fighting continued. Some of the whites were trying to torch the tipis, but they would not burn because the skins were wet from dew.

The boys looked at the carnage with burning eyes. "We must save the horses," Kowtoliks said. "We must drive them away from here, down across the river and north where the Wallowa horses are. We must round them up and do that now."

"Yes," Seton and Atemis said. The others nodded. The boys rode south and circled the herd where it had packed against the timberline. The animals had run as far from the noise as they could. The boys rode into the herd talking, singing, and after a while were able to get around the milling, frightened mass and set it in motion back across the face of the hill. The flank riders had the most difficult task because the horses tried to break away from the sound of gunfire below. Calling and hollering, they drove the herd toward the northern timberline until Kowtoliks, riding point, switched it east and down and into the marsh and through the willows and took it dashing across the North Fork. Now the gunfire was south of the herds. The animals were getting away from it, and they ran hard to get farther away.

Seton had ridden drag. When the last of the herd splashed through the river, he turned around and rode back up the hill. Swan Necklace joined him. They knew the horses would be safe. They rode to the twin pines halfway up the bald slope and dismounted, tying their horses. They stood and looked down. In the east the sky was lighting toward sunrise. From where they stood they could see the camp and the battle clearly.

The whites were now concentrated near the southern end of the village but had been driven away from the tipis. They were no longer the attackers. They were on the defensive. Above the sound of the guns, the boys heard the rallying call of a chief and the whooping of warriors. Most of the whites had recrossed the river and were drifting into the marsh, shooting at targets all around them. Apparently numipu marksmen had encircled them. The willow thickets shielded much of the fighting in the marsh from their view, but the boys saw that soldiers and civilians were mixed together. Once they glimpsed a man on a horse, probably an officer. They saw his horse go down. They saw a few warriors slip around the marsh to the rear of the troops. Now the last of the whites had recrossed the river and followed their men into the willows, moving away to the southwest.

For a few minutes the boys saw them bunched in an open glade. Despite the distance, about 450 yards, the boys brought their Winchesters up and emptied the under-barrel magazine tubes into the crowd, adjusting elevation for bullet drop. By the time they thumbed fresh shells into the loading gates of their repeaters, the men in the glade were gone. If the boys had done any damage, they did not know it.

They watched as the troops slowly made their way through the marsh under fire from different directions. The boys were mesmerized by the struggle in the willows. Suddenly Seton understood. "They are getting away to the trees," he said. The two mounted and rode along the slope to the timbered draw that ran down from the top of the mountain.

They put their horses in cover and scrambled down along the trees. The pines here were two hundred yards wide. Farther down they converged to a neck, a narrow belt, before widening out onto the fan. The fan, densely covered with young pines, was five hundred feet broad at the upper end and three hundred feet at the lower. The lower end, a few feet high, stood directly above the marsh. When Seton and Swan Necklace, rifles ready, passed the neck, they heard a low whistle ahead to the right. They knelt and looked in the direction from which the sound had come. A warrior was lying behind the trunk of a pine in the upper part of the fan, waving them down. Down. Seton raised his hand in response. The young men crept forward, close to the ground, and took cover when they reached the fan. Twenty feet apart, they lay in

the cover of trees. They were seventy feet to the left and a little below
the warrior who had signaled.

In the marsh the gunfire was intense and moving slowly toward
the fan. Seton half raised himself and looked around. He saw two more
warriors in cover behind the first one, spaced unevenly fifty to seventy feet apart. He lay down again. He wondered if the soldiers would
break through in this place. He did not think so. The crashing of rifles
came closer. He could distinguish the muzzle blasts made by the .45-70
government-issue rifles from those of the lighter-caliber Henrys and
Winchesters. The numipu rifle assortment included all of these. The
soldiers carried only .45-70 Springfields. Most of the civilian volunteers were armed with underlever repeaters. Although the soldiers no
longer fought in anything resembling a formation, Seton could tell
from the reports where groups of soldiers stuck together. And they
were coming up against the bottom of the fan.

He heard a commander's voice order the troops to get onto the
fan and build a defense there. Almost immediately, a bunch of soldiers
and civilians climbed the outer edge of the fan and moved up among
the trees. Rifles cracked to his right as the warriors started shooting
at them. The whites went to ground and returned fire. More whites
came up behind them, a few dragging wounded men. Seton heard
Swan Necklace's rifle to his left. Seton took aim at a tall man in civilian
clothes who had come up through the mouth of the draw. He missed,
hitting a tree behind the man's head. The man hunched down. Seton
got him with the second shot. Though he had just shot his first man, he
felt nothing. His target slumped and lay still.

At this moment the sun flooded the tops of the trees. More and
more suyapu came over the lip of the fan and, fired on from behind,
surged forward. In a frantic rush, many started digging with trowel
bayonets and hunting knives, while others, lying prone, fired at the
few numipu punishing them from the front. In the narrow space the
crashing of guns was deafening. Seton took two quick shots at the line
of soldiers less than two hundred yards away. Then he lay back, hugging the ground, his head flat on the needle-covered surface between

the roots of a tree. He thought he might have hit another man. It was hard to see through the tangle of tree trunks, and dangerous. Bullets careened off trees and ricocheted wildly. There was a steady fire from the soldiers, answered sporadically by the few warriors and the two young men. Once Seton saw an officer's horse come up among the soldiers. He fired at it, and it plunged and went down.

The soldiers and volunteers were hemmed in on all sides. They could go neither back nor forward. Although they vastly outnumbered the snipers around them, they made no effort to break out. They had dug pits and trenches over an area about a hundred feet in each direction, located above the lip of the fan. In this small area about 180 soldiers and volunteers were squeezed together. These were all who had survived the attack on the village and the fighting in the willows. Many had been dragged in wounded. Seton had heard some of them cry for water. More were wounded or killed as they worked to excavate shallow trenches and rifle pits. Some were killed or wounded in the trenches when they raised their heads above the ground to shoot. The rocky ground had been hard to penetrate. The digging had to be done while lying on one's side. A man standing or kneeling became an immediate target.

Seton fired five more shots, waiting patiently, taking careful aim. Once the suyapu were lodged in the ground, their fire slackened. Perhaps they were running short of ammunition and saving what they had for the charge they expected. Seton looked to Swan Necklace. He had heard his friend's rifle bark a couple of times and had seen bullets from enemy guns whack splinters from the tree above the boy's head. Seton waved to him, and Swan Necklace waved back.

Seton listened to the groaning and crying of the wounded men in the soldier trenches for some time. But then a terrible noise rose from the camp across the river, about five hundred yards away. High-pitched wailing of many women's voices merged with the angry whooping of men. Sounds of grief and rage about a horror Seton had not yet seen and could not imagine. He looked at Swan Necklace. Stunned, the boys listened helplessly. The guns had fallen completely silent. Everyone seemed to listen to the cries of despair from the camp.

Seton saw the warrior to his right, the man who had warned them when they came in, push himself back, flat on the ground and, when he could not be seen from the soldiers' position, crawl away. The wailing continued. For some time the sniper's place was empty. Then another warrior crept up and took his place. Seton recognized the man by his face and his headdress of short-eared owl feathers. Ten Owl. The man stared at Seton for a moment, then sighted over the barrel of his rifle. He called out, angry and upset, but softly so his voice could not be heard by the soldiers. "You better go back to camp. Hemene is dead."

Hemene dead? Seton started to raise himself, but Ten Owl snarled and made a quick gesture with his hand. Down, stay down. Seton looked at him. Ten Owl shook his head and pointed behind him. Go, he gestured. Seton breathed out heavily. He put his head down. When he raised it again, he looked at Swan Necklace. "Go," Swan Necklace whispered. "They need you in camp. The suyapu are not going anywhere. We'll keep them here."

Seton nodded. He placed the rifle on his belly and inched backward on his back, moving slowly, pushing with his feet. He was only 150 feet away from the closest soldier trench. Ten Owl and Swan Necklace each fired a round to keep the enemy down, and Seton was able to get away without a shot being fired at him. He ran to where the horses were tied, loosened the double reins of his roan mare, and mounted and galloped across the face of the hill. He rode down to the floodplain, crossed the river almost opposite from the camp of Hemene's wi-ses, and went into the willows.

The great, piercing wailing from the camp had ended, but individual crying and sounds of despair continued. Seton saw the first bodies lying among the willows. Three soldiers, one an officer. One civilian volunteer. Two warriors. There were people kneeling above a ditch, a dry arm of the stream. They were crying, looking down. He rode by and saw five women and a little boy there lying dead. He rode up from the marsh to the dry meadow on which the camp was located. There stood an isolated birthing tipi with a dozen people around it, crying. The tipi was partly destroyed, the hide torn by bullets. Women brought out two bodies and the corpse of a newborn baby. A man stood there, tears streaming down his face. Seton knew him: Wetahlatpat, a brave warrior. A woman said that Wetahlatpat's wife and baby had been killed, as was his sister who had been the midwife. The woman said that civilians with the soldiers did it. They had gone into the tipi. The baby's head had been crushed with a rifle butt.

Seton edged his horse away and looked for Hemene's camp. There were a few dead and crippled horses around him, a huge dog with one leg shot off. People stood near something on the ground. He recognized the familiar faces. He dismounted and ran over. Teeweeyownah was bent over Dawn, her leather gown bloody in front. She was wounded but alive. Three bodies were laid out nearby, surrounded by family members and kin. Elk Blanket, dead. Her little son, Tasshea, dead. And Ayokka, dead. His wife, Petolwe, sat next to him in the grass, her hand on his chest, their little daughter, Ilsoo, by her side. But Hemene? Itsepit? Where were they?

Seton searched, desperate. Another group of people stood in a circle around something on the ground. He squeezed himself through. Itsepit was kneeling in the bloodied grass, holding her father's head. Blood seeped from a gunshot wound high in his chest. Hemene's eyes were open. He was alive.

F O U R T E E N

SETON KNELT BY HEMENE'S SIDE. THE OLD MAN CLOSED his eyes for a moment. He breathed in with difficulty, and when he breathed out, foamy blood trickled from the bullet hole under his collarbone. The bullet had gone through the top of the right lobe of the lung. Seton looked at Itsepit, a question in his eyes. She understood. "The bullet has gone through. It broke his shoulder blade," she whispered.

Hemene sighed and opened his eyes. "Seton," he said. He smiled and held his right hand out. Seton took it. The Old Man was in pain, his breathing irregular and strained, but his face did not show it. "You did well," he said. "We heard from Atemis. You ran the white men off who tried to steal our horses."

Seton was embarrassed. "There were five of us." He didn't think they had done much. It didn't compare with what had happened in camp. Hemene guessed what he meant to say. "Atemis brought fresh horses in," he said. "Look around. Many of our horses in camp were killed or hurt."

"Don't talk, father," Itsepit interrupted. She turned to Seton. "Get Talooth. She knows how to bind wounds."

He stood up and walked past two young women of the wi-ses, Tannish and Tamonmo. Tannish, Short Bull's wife, held her one-year-old daughter, Wolf Blanket, on her arm. Tamonmo, the wife of Thunder Eyes, knelt to take Seton's place at Hemene's side. Both their husbands were somewhere fighting the soldiers.

Seton searched for Talooth. He looked over the wi-ses camp. Among packs, smoldering fireplaces, and two toppled drying racks he found eight horses down. A few others limped or stood still, crippled, shocked by their injuries. The adjacent wi-ses camps looked the same. The few tipis to the north seemed mostly intact, but those in the southern part of the camp, where they stood packed above the river, were in tatters from the soldiers' salvos. Dead and injured horses were everywhere. So were torn equipment and bundles and packs that had ripped and spilled their contents over the grass. There were dead dogs. Smoking earth ovens still cooked their loads of camas. A smell of wood smoke, burned flesh, gunpowder, burned hides, sweat, and something else hung over the camp. It was death, Seton realized. Groups of women and children surrounded the dead or dying and those who suffered from their wounds. Sounds of grief and lament from across the river mixed with the crackle of rifle fire where the soldiers were pinned down in their holes, waiting for death to claim them too.

Seton stood for a moment, looking at the destruction. His eyes glazed. He remembered the soft words of the ministers and missionaries in Lapwai, in churches on the reservation and in the Lapwai boarding school. They spoke of the path of redemption, the Savior. He remembered the prayers they had learned, Alex and Aaron and Mary and the others. The road of the cross, the suyapu road, the good road. But in this place the Jesus people had crawled out of the dark like snakes and tried to kill everyone—men, women, and children. How could this be? He shook his head. He remembered his father. He had not been a cruel man. He would not have done anything like this. Or would he? Seton shook himself and went to find Talooth.

Talooth had cleaned and dressed Dawn's wound while Teeweeyownah held her. The bullet had come from a civilian's small-caliber rifle and had gone through Dawn's lower right side, injuring a rib but not touching the lung. There was a clean exit wound in the back. Talooth had cleaned both punctures and taken herbs from a pouch in her medicine bag. She chewed and pasted the mush on both wounds. She wrapped Dawn's rib cage tightly in order to hold the rib in place. There was nothing more she could do. Dawn had not flinched during Talooth's treatment. But she had lost blood and was tired. Teeweeyownah laid her gently down in the grass, putting a robe under her head and spreading one over her body.

"Itsepit wants you to come," Seton said. "Hemene needs you." Talooth nodded and closed her medicine bundle. She was a stout woman in her early fifties. She had been married to Hemene's brother, killed years ago by Bannock or Shoshone raiders on the lower Salmon. Ayokka, the young warrior who had died defending the wi-ses camp, was her son. When she reached Hemene and knelt down beside him, he touched her arm.

"I heard about your son, sister," he said. "He was brave. He was good." He stopped, gasping for air. "He died fighting for us." He paused again. "He has gone ahead. We'll all follow him."

Talooth nodded. "Don't speak," she said. Itsepit was holding Hemene's head. Seton and Tamonmo grasped him deftly around the shoulders while Talooth cut his shirt with her belt knife and stripped his chest. She looked at the ugly punctures in front and back. They had been made by a heavy lead bullet of .45-70 caliber. She felt for the broken shoulder blade around the exit wound and plucked a bit of leather from it. She looked at Tannish and said, "Get me water." The young woman hurried off and came back with a small bucket of river water. Talooth opened the medicine bundle and retrieved a roll of cloth. She tore off a piece and, after dousing it in water, began cleaning the edges of the punctures.

Hemene's eyes were open. He gave himself in to Talooth's hands.

She took one small bag from her bundle and opened it, taking pounded dried root from it. Seton remembered from his mother's medicines that this was bloodroot, a medicine against bleeding. Talooth wetted it in her hand and put the paste as a poultice on both wounds. She covered them with cloth and secured everything with a long wrap-around of deer leather tied around his upper chest. Slowly Seton, Tamonmo, and Itsepit laid Hemene back on the grass. Talooth handed pinches of bloodroot to Itsepit. "Make a tea with this. This could stop the bleeding from his lung."

She turned away. "I have to go to bury my son." She got up and walked away to where Ayokka had been laid out along with Elk Blanket and Tasshea.

Hemene looked at Seton and Tamonmo. "Thank you son," he said with a tired voice. "Thank you, Tamonmo. It is good. I will rest now. Go and help Talooth and the others."

A howitzer boomed to the southwest. A cannon ball came down in a high arc and thudded into the ground south of the camp but did not explode. Seton stood stock-still, looking southwest, searching for the location from which the shell had come. He saw a white puff high on the hill below the timberline, three-quarters of a mile away. A boom and a second cannon ball hit near the first one. It also failed to explode. Seton watched for another puff of smoke, but none came. There was a distant rattle of gunfire, then silence. The cannon did not fire again.

While the fight continued, the sad work of burying the three dead of the wi-ses began. The slain—the young warrior Ayokka; Elk Blanket, the wife of Kywis; and their little son, Tasshea, three years old—were carried in blankets to the plain east of camp. Kywis and Seton cut the deep sod with axes and removed it in rectangular lumps. These were stacked, and a grave about four feet deep was dug. Talooth had prepared the bodies by washing and wrapping them in blankets to their armpits. She had brushed their hair and painted their faces and hands with red ocher. A personal object and stems of sacred sage were placed into each blanket. Talooth, the oldest present, spoke the invocation. Each of the bodies was covered with a robe. They were placed side by side in the grave. Until this moment the people had stood in silence.

When the grave was filled with earth, the women started the death wail, their voices rising and falling. Theirs were not the only ones. Other burials were taking place up and down the flat. Voices of grief rolled like a great wind across the valley.

So that the dead would not be disturbed by the suyapu or Cut Arm's Bannock scouts, Kywis and Seton tread the earth hard before they put the sod back in place, trying to leave no sign of the grave. They stood until the wailing ended. In camp, Kywis and Seton mounted their horses and ran the wi-ses horses over the grave to further hide its location.

Later, Seton and Itsepit were sitting by Hemene when they heard hoofbeats behind them. Allultakanin, Short Bull, and Thunder Eyes dismounted. Their leather shirts and leggings were caked with wet earth. They looked angry, tired, despondent. Short Bull had a cloth wrapped around his upper right arm that was stained with dried blood. They walked up and looked down at Hemene. The Old Man raised his left hand and smiled.

"How are you doing?" Allultakanin asked.

Hemene shook his head slightly. "Not so good," he said. "You can see. But I'll be better." He smiled again. "How is it with the suyapu?"

"We have trapped them," Allultakanin said. "They are in a small place. They can't get away. They have dug holes to hide in. They can't get to water. We are making them suffer." He grunted angrily. "We lost many, mostly women and children. Some older men, some young boys."

He paused. "We lost some of our best men, too. Rainbow is dead. Five Wounds is dead. He threw his life away at the soldiers' trenches. He did not want to live after Rainbow was killed. Wahlitits is dead. Sarpsis Ilppilp is dead. The best warriors we had. Hahtalekin is dead, the Paloos chief. His son died fighting at his tipi. Wookawkaw is dead."

He paused again. When he continued his voice filled with bitterness. "These suyapu! They love to kill women and children. They love to kill the unarmed! These whites of the Bitterroot! They made a treaty with us at the corral by Lolo Creek. It was a lie. Our words were good. They had two tongues. They traded with us for our silver and gold. For our horses. Here, at this place, they tried to steal them all . . ."

Hemene raised his hand again. "Yes," he said. "You speak truth. We lost many good people. The suyapu are liars and cowards. They are what they are. We should have known not to trust them. But we, you, must go on."

Allultakanin nodded. He tried to control himself. His wife, Oyipee, had come up behind him, their little daughter beside her, Red Walker. Tannish had also come over and touched the wounded arm of her husband.

"Seton did some fighting in the trees," Allultakanin said. "We saw him, him and Swan Necklace." He looked at Seton. "We heard they saved our horses when the whites tried to run them off."

Hemene looked at Seton and smiled. "You did well. I knew you would." Seton said nothing. But Itsepit looked at him with a strange expression.

"These soldiers, who are they? Is this Cut Arm?" Hemene asked.

"No," Short Bull said. "They are from the east country, mostly foot soldiers, a few horse soldiers without horses. A prisoner told us. He said the main officer is Colonel Gibbon. He is from a fort in the north, Fort Shaw. The prisoner said that Cut Arm and the soldiers from the west country are coming after us, too. They are already in the Bitterroot Valley."

"Where is the prisoner?" Hemene asked.

"He is dead. Otskai shot him after he told us."

"Did I hear a cannon?" Hemene asked.

"Yes," Allutakanin said. "The cannon was destroyed. Lean Elk rolled it down the mountain. Seeyakoon Ilppilp, Tenahtahkah, and Yellow Wolf killed some of the cannonmen. The others ran away. Espowyes captured a packhorse loaded with rifle ammunition. They broke the boxes open. The ammunition fits one kind of rifles—those we took from the soldiers. Plenty of ammunition, over two thousand cartridges."

"My father is tired," Itsepit interrupted. "He should rest."

"You have to make ready to move," Hemene said before the three warriors left. "These soldiers over there are no longer dangerous. But with Cut Arm on our trail, too, we must get away from here."

A little later Teeweeyownah came over. He looked distant when he sat down. He did not speak for a while. During the attack in the morning he had killed the officer, Lieutenant Bradley, who led the northern wing of the troops and the volunteers. With a few warriors he forced the attackers back into the marsh. After that he did no more fighting. He had gone back to care for his wounded wife and his horrified daughter, Tsacope.

"Dawn is asleep," he said. "The bleeding has stopped." He looked into Hemene's eyes. "This is Looking Glass's fault. He kept us from scouting the back trail. If we had done that, this would not have happened. Wahlitits warned us. He is dead. Peopeo Ipsewahk warned us." He shook his head. Hemene's eyes closed.

"Please," Itsepit said. "He is still losing blood."

"Yes," Teeweeyownah said. He stood up and looked at Seton. "I want you to stay with him," he said. "With us. From now on, the small boys have to drive the horses. We need you here." He looked sharply into Seton's eyes. Seton nodded. This was unexpected, but it seemed right.

Later a crier rode through the camps calling to the people to prepare to leave. He was Buffalo Stone, of the Wallowa band. The chiefs had sent him, he shouted. There was a new leader of the march, Chief Lean Elk. Lean Elk would ride ahead with twenty warriors, the herds following. Next, the wounded would be dragged on tipi poles. Last, the families would come in the same order as before. Ollokot, he told them, had stayed behind to keep the soldiers in their holes. "Get ready," he called out. "Get ready, Palooses, Alpowais, Wallowas, Pekonans, Lamtamas! Get ready!"

Itsepit and Seton set to work on a travois to transport Hemene. They selected two tipi poles of equal length and laid them side by side. They tied them firmly together six feet below the tips and spread the ends out. The upper parts of the poles crossed where they were tied, forming a fork. Eight feet below the fork the first of two crosspieces was tied to the poles, connecting them. A second one was seven feet below the first. Between the poles and the crosspieces a buffalo robe was stretched, hair side up. Additional robes were piled on lengthwise to make a comfortable bed, and a robe was added for a pillow.

While Itsepit and Seton finished the travois, Teeweeyownah and Oyipee, his sister-in-law, worked on one for Dawn. A call went out, and they saw Lean Elk and a bunch of warriors ride out and take the trail south. In the camps, horses were saddled and packed, and the travois with the incapacitated were readied. Itsepit picked a strong old mare for Hemene's transport. She and Seton put a thick buffalo robe on the mare's back and cinched it. They added a horse blanket and put on Itsepit's saddle. They lifted the fork of the travois over the saddle to ride in front of it, the poles along both flanks of the horse rubbing against the thick robe. The transport for Dawn was also finished, Oyipee riding the draft horse.

The camps waited for the herds to move out. They came and passed and flooded like a wave over the bench east of the camp and went on in a cloud of dust, cutting a trail hundreds of yards wide. Seton saw Atemis riding drag on the Lamtama herd. When the dust cleared, the first travois started out. Seton and Teeweeyownah cautiously lifted Hemene upon the travois bed and tucked him in. He was in great pain, but he smiled. Itsepit mounted and took the reins. She touched the mare's hindquarters with the quirt and guided her slowly through the tall grass toward the broad trail south. Seton followed on his roan mare, leading Hemene's saddled horse and Itsepit's unsaddled horse, watching the ends of the drag poles and Hemene's bundled figure with only his face showing. Oyipee came behind them, riding Dawn's travois horse, with Teeweeyownah back of Dawn. Tsacope, on his saddle, led Dawn's and Oyipee's horses on a rawhide lariat and a pony with Oyipee's daughter of eight years, Red Walker.

The small procession of wounded who were incapable of riding numbered fourteen travois. Among them rode White Goose, whose wife had been shot through the left side, and Chief Joseph, who went with the travois of Fair Land, the older of Ollokot's two wives. She had been shot three times and was close to death. He was there because his brother led the remaining warriors at the soldiers' trenches. One warrior, Husis Owyen, rode beside a travois that carried both his wife and their two-year-old child. In the confusion of the early attack the baby toddled toward the soldiers. His mother ran after him, but before she reached him, he fell to the ground, shot through the hip. Snatching him, she ran away from the soldiers and was shot through the back. On another travois lay a twenty-year-old, also called Dawn, generally recognized as the prettiest girl of the five bands. She had been shot twice during the attack while she cared for the wounded and dying around her. She was not expected to live.

Seton looked back once when their little group reached the benchland. The camps were preparing to move but were not ready yet. He imprinted the sight into his memory: the stricken camp on the wide meadow below the green slope of Battle Mountain. The gunfire had died at the point of trees where the soldiers were entrenched. Perhaps they were all dead.

Slowly the travois and escort riders continued along the western edge of the Big Hole in front of the snowcapped Beaverhead Mountains. Here and there a travois stopped to give the wounded a rest or minister to their needs. Eventually the small column was stretched over three miles. Twice Hemene called for a halt. He had been unconscious part of the way. The bands passed them in midafternoon when they crossed Rock Creek. After six more miles, having covered a total of twelve, they reached the site on Lake Creek selected by Lean Elk for the night's camp. The place was called *takseen* in their language, meaning "willows." The date was August 9.

Before nightfall, White Goose came over from his wi-ses camp. Itsepit and Seton, who had sat with the Old Man, got up and moved a few paces away so the chiefs would have some privacy, though the cousins would still be able to overhear what the chiefs said. White Goose sat down slowly. He had his hair cut short as a sign of mourning for the dead. He had brought a pipe bag and laid it across his legs. His voice, usually resolute and confident, sounded different. He touched Hemene's arm lightly. "I smoked a pipe for you, brother," he said. "I asked the spirits to help you. I smoked for my wife too and for the others of our band who are sick from bullets."

"Thank you," Hemene said. "How is your wife?"

"She has a bad wound, but she says she will be getting better." He paused. "How is it with you?"

"Not so good," Hemene said. "Talooth has been working on me." He paused. "I caught a bad bullet." He coughed into a cloth with blood stains on it and wiped his mouth. "We need more cloth and bandages," he said weakly, but with urgency in his voice.

"Yes," White Goose said. "There are a few ranches farther down the valley and up on Horse Prairie. I'll send our young men to take all the cloth and linen they have." He paused. "It won't be enough."

They sat in silence. "How many of our people died?" Hemene asked at last.

"We're not sure," White Goose said. "From all the bands, some say, forty-three women and children; some say forty-six. Men, twenty-seven or twenty-eight, mostly old men and young boys who were unarmed. A dozen were warriors who did much of the hard fighting." He paused. "Some of our best men died in this place. Rainbow and Five Wounds . . . They had come all the way from the east country to help us. Two of their men. And Wahlitits and Sarpsis Ilppilp of our band. Hahtalekin. Two of Lean Elk's men."

He paused. "They are gone. We must continue without them."

"Where are you going from here?" Hemene asked. He coughed again.

"We thought we were safe," White Goose said. "We weren't. We thought we had made a peace with the suyapu. But civilians came to fight us and soldiers we had never heard of. Now we have found out that Cut Arm and his army are still following us, too."

He paused. "We were fools to think we would be safe with the Crows. What Looking Glass told us was wrong. We are not safe anywhere in the American country. We have to go to Grandmother's Land, Canada, to be safe. This is where Sitting Bull and Gall and the Lakotas have gone. Bad Grizzly Bear Boy told us. He saw it as a scout for the white general, Miles, who was fighting the Sioux."

He paused again. "It's a long trail. We will have to fight to get there."

There was a long silence. "It is too long a trail for me," Hemene said. "I may not get there with you."

The two chiefs looked into each other's eyes. They had grown up together, grown old together. They had seen much. They did not lie to each other. Both understood.

"The One Above be with you, brother," White Goose said. "I will smoke for you again tomorrow." He touched Hemene's arm and got up slowly, as if he carried a heavy load, and walked away.

A little later a crier rode through the camp announcing that the bands would move out at first light in the same order of march as on the day before. Lean Elk was to ride ahead south toward the mountains at the end of the valley. No cooking in the morning. After midday they would rest to prepare food and let the horses fill up on grass. Then the march would continue until early evening.

The fires were burning down around midnight when Seton awoke to the low hoots of a great horned owl calling from the willows. He lay still, wondering whether the owl had awakened him or the dream.

He had seen his father in the dream, dressed in boots and suyapu clothes, wearing a white hat, stiffly holding a rifle across his chest. He stood there, face stern, looking at Seton. Then his mother stepped in front of his father, a big smile on her face. She looked young, energetic, and handsome. She wore a wide blue suyapu skirt and a red and blue blouse, her long black hair loose around her face. She was barefoot. She rushed forward with a quick, floating movement and grabbed Seton's hand and ran with him. They ran fast, the dust beneath their feet speeding past. Then they were on Main Street, Lewiston, wooden buildings on both sides, a few empty wagons, a few tethered horses, but no people. They ran, and there were many people—men, women, and children, horses and wagons—packed around a scaffold. On the scaffold were a hangman and three men with ropes around their necks, black hoods over their heads, and hands tied behind their backs. The hangman stood there as a man climbed the ladder to the platform. The man wore dark clothes with a gold watch chain on his vest. He had a thin beard with white streaks under a strong nose and piercing eyes and a wide, bald forehead. The Reverend Spalding of Lapwai! He went from one condemned man to the next, removing the black hood from each head. Over each man he made the sign of the cross, then turned around and made the sign of the cross over the crowd of onlookers. He began laughing hysterically, his mouth round and puckered between beard and mustache, laughing, laughing, bending over laughing. And behind him the three prisoners began to laugh until they laughed so hard that tears ran down their cheeks.

And then Seton and Wetah fled. They were running again. First it was dust under their feet, then yellow grass, then they flew over round mountaintops and across a blue lake. There was the rocky place above the lake. His mother knelt by him and held out the grizzly claw. Only the tip of the curved dark blade with the yellow inner side thrust from the red flannel wrapping. She held the claw with a serious face, intense eyes. He took it from her hand. "There," she said. "There, look." She was gone, and he saw a coyote trotting toward him, huge, eyes ablaze. The coyote threw back his head and howled, more like a wolf than a coyote, and in that instant Seton heard howling from the west, from the foot of the mountain wall.

He rose to a sitting position and listened, looking around. No more calls came. People lay huddled around the fires. Itsepit and Allultakanin lay close to him. They did not stir. Hemene lay to his left. When Seton looked toward him he saw the glint of the fire in the Old Man's eyes. Was Hemene sleeping with open eyes, or had he died? But then Seton saw him blink and bring a hand up and wave him over.

Seton rolled out from under his blanket and got up, careful not to wake anyone. He sat next to Hemene. The chief's eyes had a feverish shine, or perhaps it was the dying fire reflected in them. He coughed and wiped his mouth. "Bring me some water," he said. Seton went to a water bucket behind the fireplace and filled a dipper. He returned and held it close to Hemene's mouth. The Old Man took it and, raising himself a little, put the dipper to his lips. After he had taken a few sips he set the dipper in the grass and lay back. He looked into the starry sky without saying a word. Seton thought the Old Man wanted to be left alone and started to get up. But a hand gripped him and the Old Man said, "Stay with me." He turned his face to look at Seton.

"You had a dream," he said. "I saw it. I heard you speak in the dream."

He moved his head and looked back into the canopy of stars. "I worry about you," he said after a while. He coughed again, a rasping sound. "You are becoming a warrior, but you have no protection."

Seton swallowed. He knew what the Old Man meant. He had no wéyekin, no guardian spirit that every numipu child went on a quest to find, or to be found by, and blessed. He had tried twice but failed. Yet his mother's wéyekin, the grizzly spirit, had not prevented her early death. His white father had had neither Jesus nor a wéyekin, and had not wanted either one. He was probably still alive somewhere. All those dead or dying from the attack half a day ago had had a wéyekin, but their guardian spirits had not stopped the bullets or made the bullets miss. Neither had Jesus protected the whites from numipu bullets. Seton did not know what to say and said nothing. He did not want to slight the Old Man.

"You have no protection," Hemene insisted. "You need a wéyekin."

Seton grunted just to make a sound. He was not sure whether he agreed or disagreed. It was true that he felt like an outsider sometimes because he did not have a guardian spirit, no song and no object or objects connected with it. He felt this most acutely during the *wee-kwetset,* the guardian spirit dances held over a week or two in wintertime, when tiwéts performed remarkable, inexplicable feats, and when everyone danced and sang his and her spirit songs. Seton sat stoically through these performances, night after night, a lonely figure uncertain about what was going on, uncertain about himself.

He wondered, though, why he of all those around him had been ignored by the spirits when he submitted himself to them. Was it because his father was a white man? He did not think so. He was not the only mixed blood among the bands or on the reservation, and the others had not been left out as he had. Finally he had given up thinking about it. The Jesus people had not reached him, and he stayed aloof from the tiwéts. He did not confront mysteries. In the world he saw, he regarded some things or acts as wrong, others as right, but when decisions had to be made dealing with these he left them to others, to the chiefs or warrior leaders or elders or simply individuals, even tiwéts. He came back from his thoughts through Hemene's voice.

"I should have asked you earlier," Hemene said. "Maybe it's not too late." He coughed and breathed heavily. "You went on two wáyatin, did you?"

"Yes," Seton said.

"What happened there?"

"Nothing happened there," Seton said. "Nothing."

"Something must have happened," Hemene said. "Maybe you didn't notice. What did you see? Did something or someone come?"

Seton thought for a while. "The second time a coyote came."

"A coyote," Hemene said. "What did the coyote do?"

"He walked up to me."

"What happened then?"

"He seemed to speak to me, but I heard nothing. I passed out."

"You say 'he,'" Hemene said. "The coyote was a male?"

"Yes, a big male."

Hemene coughed again. There was a pause. "Tell me what he looked like," Hemene said. "Be precise. Leave nothing out."

Slowly, haltingly, Seton began to speak. He saw the coyote in front of him and described him to the Old Man. The animal had stood there, looking down on him, huge before the red sky of morning. His coat was coarse and heavy, the outer hairs tipped with black, throat and underpart yellowish in color. A dark line ran up the front of his forelegs. Pointed ears. Pointed muzzle open, showing tongue and teeth. He stood aggressively, head held high, shoulder and neck hair erect. Yellow eyes, slits. Seton remembered that he had stared into those eyes. The coyote lowered his head and seemed to speak, but Seton heard nothing, no sound. The coyote's face came closer and almost touched his. This was the last he saw. He must have fainted. When he came to, the coyote was gone. There were no paw prints. "This is what I saw on my second wáyatin," Seton heard himself say, coming back from his memories as from a trance. "I never heard the coyote speak."

There was a long silence. Seton looked at the Old Man. His eyes were closed.

At last Hemene spoke. He spoke slowly but with a voice that would accept no argument. "I should have known. I think what you saw, this he-coyote, was not the spirit of itsayaya, the little brother of the wolf who is always around us. Him you would have understood. I think what you saw was Old Man Coyote himself, nasawaylu, he who gave us life, who gave us our land, the salmon, camas, all the things and places we need. He who showed us the way to the buffalo. He who brought death into our world so that our spirit becomes free and goes home to the spirit world. Where we come from. He taught us that death belongs to life, that the spirit is what matters, not so much the body."

He coughed. Seton sat stunned, trying to comprehend. What did this mean?

"There is a reason why you didn't hear nasawaylu talk. You were not supposed to. I would not understand him either. His language is spirit language. It is called isxí-p timt, and only one kind of tiwét understands it, the one called isxí-p."

He paused. "There are only six of these tiwéts among us now."

"Why did the coyote speak to me in spirit language?"

"Nasawaylu. Yes, he always plays tricks on people. He played a trick on you. You passed out because his spirit language is very powerful and you were not qualified to hear it."

He fell silent. "Here is something important, though," he said. "Nasawaylu almost never visits a person on a wáyatin. And he knew that he was too powerful for you. Why didn't he send you itsayaya's spirit? Why did he come by himself?"

He paused. "It is strange, but it is good. He did something to you. You may have fainted, but he did something to your spirit. You will find out when the time is right."

He searched Seton's face. "I'm glad I know this. I think I can do something for you. We'll talk about it tomorrow. I'm tired now."

AT FIRST LIGHT THE CRIER RODE THROUGH THE CAMP
and told the people to get ready to move. Before Lean Elk and the
advance guard left, two small groups of scouts went ahead to scour the
valley south to the Big Hole Divide and east to Big Hole Pass, the gap
in the mountains that led to Grasshopper Creek and the mining center
of Bannack. When the herds were driven south, two travois fewer than
on the day before were readied. Ollokot's wife, Fair Land, and a woman
of the Pekonan band had died. The two travois of the Hemene wi-ses
pulled out as the burial song for the Pekonan woman began. The Wallowa people waited for Ollokot and the rear guard to come in so that
the chief could attend his wife's funeral.

Dawn's condition had improved a little, but Hemene's had not.
The bleeding had stopped, but he had a fever. The tea Itsepit had boiled
for him toward morning had not reduced it. His broken shoulder blade

made lying on the bed of the travois painful, regardless of how skillful Itsepit was in guiding the draft horse and dragging poles around rougher spots. As on the day before, Seton followed Hemene's travois with Itsepit's and Hemene's saddle horses on lariats. Dawn's travois came behind. The four travois of the most seriously wounded Lamtama were led by White Goose, who rode by his wife's travois. The injured who could still ride a horse went with their kin groups in the bands.

The journey to kusayna, the east country, had become a sorrowful affair. So many people lost, more than a hundred wounded, some of those sure to die. Much equipment and baggage was lost also. Over a hundred horses had been killed or left behind because they were injured. Of the small number of dogs that had made it to the Big Hole, nearly all were gone, either killed or missing. Before the bands lay a trail beset with danger, with enemies on every side and no one to help them. And the trail to Grandmother's Land was long, perhaps six or seven hundred miles from where they were now, with mountain ranges and canyons to traverse and mighty rivers to cross. Finally, in the wide country of the shortgrass plains, they would be open to attack by fresh armies from places they had never heard of. But, with their wounded, weak, very young, very old, and their thousands of horses, they rode on.

Leaving the takseen camp, the group with the travois continued south on the broad trail cut by the horse herds. With a cold wind at their backs, under a partly cloudy sky, they rode slowly along the edge of the foothills of the Beaverhead Mountains through the great stillness of the Big Hole. Three times Seton, who watched Hemene from his place behind the travois, called for a halt when he thought the Old Man needed it. They were passed by the bands a mile before they reached Miner Creek, the location selected by Lean Elk for the midday rest.

Cooking fires went up quickly, and the herds were allowed to spread over the rich grassland. The wi-ses women put together a hot meal, and Talooth treated both Dawn's and Hemene's wounds. Hemene took only a little broth and Talooth's herbal tea. Itsepit fed her father with a spoon while Seton held him up. Later Hemene lay down on his left side and, a thick robe propped against his back, fell asleep. When he awoke the fever had gone down. He was troubled by something but did not speak of it. He asked for White Goose. When the chief came, the two talked for some tine. As White Goose left, he cast a long, inquisitive look at Seton before he walked away.

When the march continued, the column made nine more miles to Pioneer Creek, on the first bench toward Selway Mountain, rising to nine thousand feet, and the southern pass through the Big Hole Divide. There, camp was made for the night. It was early evening when White Goose and another Lamtama tiwét, Bear Shield, a man in his early sixties, came to see Hemene. The Old Man was sitting up against a pile of two lodge covers. He had asked Itsepit to bring his ipétes, the medicine bundle. It lay unopened at his side. The two tiwéts had brought their personal bundles also. They sat on blankets, with crossed legs. Hemene had gestured that the three should be left alone, so the wi-ses members had moved out of earshot.

The three men talked briefly before Hemene called Seton over. Seton was astonished. Hemene pointed to a blanket beside him, and Seton sat down. They waited in silence for a while, Seton feeling edgy in their presence, apprehensive. Finally Hemene looked at him and spoke with a slow, raspy voice. "I told White Goose what we talked about last night. He wants to know more. He brought Bear Shield with him. Bear Shield is a isxí-p tiwét. You know him."

The two tiwéts looked at Seton as if seeing him for the first time. "Tell us," White Goose said. "Tell us what you told Hemene."

Seton coughed. He looked at the ground and told the story of his second quest for a guardian spirit. He started with Wetah and his leaving Lapwai and riding to Lake Waha, twenty miles southwest of the agency. He told how his mother had taken him to the high place in the rocks, her instructions, the "eye" of her medicine bundle she had given him, the grizzly claw. He told of praying, how thirst had made his tongue feel like a heavy snake in his mouth, how he had seen unknown lands in the clouds, strange forms of animals and persons, how he had heard the soft taptap of deer hooves walking by closely. And finally he told about the coyote. When he finished and looked up, the eyes of the tiwéts were fixed on him.

There was a silence.

Finally Hemene spoke. "I think it was nasawaylu who came to him. I think that is why he did not hear him speak. He was just a small boy. He was not qualified to hear spirit language."

They sat thinking. If the tiwéts were surprised, they did not show it.

"I don't know," Bear Shield said. "It could have been Old Man Coyote or it could have been the coyote we hear every day, itsayaya. Old Man is in him too. He is part of him."

He paused. "You know that nasawaylu went back into the spirit world after he had finished here. Since then we have only his kin in this world, itsayaya. It is true that nasawaylu comes back sometimes for a reason, for something special. If there was a reason to come for him," he pointed with his chin to Seton, "I wonder what the reason was."

He paused. "I have seen nothing that would show me a reason. "This man," again he pointed to Seton, "has shown me nothing that is special about him."

He looked away. "He, Old Man Coyote, is a spirit who created much of what we see in this world. And much we usually don't see. He is powerful and dangerous. It is true, sometimes he comes back to play. When he does, be careful. He could be deadly to the person who claims him if he doesn't want to be claimed."

"Seton does not claim him," Hemene said. "I thought of nasawaylu when he told me. It is me. Seton knew nothing of this."

"There is a puzzle here," White Goose said, stepping in. "Seton did not hear the coyote speak although he almost touched his face. He either could not, or dared not, or was not supposed to. In any case it was not a mole or a rabbit. It was a coyote. A coyote who spoke to him." He paused.

"It is important that Seton passed out when the coyote spoke. That could be nasawaylu's mark. It is true that Seton has not shown anything special yet. But he is just a boy becoming a man. It could still happen."

They sat in silence. "It was a coyote," Bear Shield said finally. "If it was Old Man, we don't know yet. Now that we know he saw a coyote we still have to do something about it. I think it is up to me."

He paused. "Seton is the only one his age who does not have a numipu name. I think he should have one. I want to give him a name. Itsayaya pa'na, Coyote Spoke to Him. This is good for now. If something important happens through him, we will give him another name. This is up to nasawaylu."

He looked at Seton.

"His mother would approve of it," Hemene said. "She always believed that something good happened to him on that mountain. But he asked her not to speak about it. He felt bad."

"Most of the times I ask the spirits for something, they do not seem to answer me either," White Goose said thoughtfully, uneasy. "They live by rules different from ours. They also like to play." He looked from Bear Shield to Seton. "This is a good name. Itsayaya is the intelligent one. He is fast and he understands the ways of this world. It is good to have him for a wéyekin."

Seton had listened as if the three men were talking about someone else. He had sat, tense, staring ahead. Now it was necessary to say something. He looked at Bear Shield, fearsome isxí-p, caller and handler of spirits, a tiwét whom no numipu dared deny. This man had given him a name. "Thank you," he heard himself say.

Bear Shield nodded curtly. "You have to make up a song about itsayaya. The one you saw, your itsayaya. A short song. Hemene will help you make it. He will tell you when you use it."

He looked at Hemene. The Old Man nodded. "I have something for you," he continued. He opened his medicine bundle and brought out a leather pouch tied with a string. "Red paint," he said. "Red paint mixed with deer kidney fat. Deer and coyote go together." He handed the pouch to Seton. "When you need it, before you go into fighting or a ceremony, or when you want itsayaya to be with you and protect you, paint your forehead above the eyes with this paint. It is the way nasawaylu taught us to paint for the coyote. If you do it right, it gives you the coyote's wisdom to survive danger."

Seton looked at the pouch and felt strange. All his life he had seen numipu paint themselves, but he had never been painted and had never owned paint himself. Now he was being given paint to mark himself for an animal spirit these men said belonged to him, or he belonged to it. Or both belonged together, both becoming or being the same. This was too hard to comprehend quickly. It had to be learned.

"I have something for you too," White Goose said. From out of nowhere he produced a necklace and handed it to Seton. It was a leather string with eight coyote claws attached. Seton recognized them, the claws from the toes of a coyote's front paws. "You should wear this necklace at all times," White Goose said. "I prayed over it. To make it alive for you, you must smoke it with sweetgrass. Hemene will teach you."

Before Seton could say anything, the two tiwéts stood up. "We have been close to your mother," White Goose said. "She was one of us. You were not really of us. You have always been different, distant. We thought the suyapu had messed you up, turned you away from us." He shook his head. "Now you are one of us. The coyote brought you back to us. If it was nasawaylu or itsayaya, we will see. Either one is good."

"Be careful with this," Bear Shield said. "This is good for you. But if you do not treat it right, or if you try to let it go, it will destroy you."

The two tiwéts walked away without another word. Seton's eyes followed them until they were hidden by the early dark. He turned and looked into Hemene's eyes.

"You heard them," Hemene said. "What they said is true. That much I know." He coughed. "You have your protection. I am glad about that."

He paused. "We have to give each of them a gift. They will try to refuse it, but we must insist. This is the way."

He paused again. "I have something for you too. I'll give you my war whistle and my war club. You need them; I don't. You have to smoke them with sweetgrass to make them yours." He coughed. "Now let me rest."

Later Hemene helped Seton to make up a coyote song, a two-liner ending in a yipping call. He taught him how to smoke the necklace, the war whistle, and the kopluts to make them Seton's. Later still he called the people of the wi-ses together and told them Seton's coyote name and what they had to know about it. Not everything could be told. What they learned was enough.

Seton lay awake for half the night. When he finally fell asleep, he dreamed about his mother and a coyote who spoke to him with his mother's voice. This time he understood every word. But when he awoke to the camp crier's call at first light, he could not remember what was said.

Two more of the wounded died during the night, two elderly men, Gray Eagle and Red Heart. The group with its shrinking number of travois heard the keening of the burial songs when they moved out. As on the day before, Lean Elk and the advance guard had left ahead of the herds. The number of warriors with him had been increased to thirty because they expected the march to reach Horse Prairie. The center of Horse Prairie was less than fifteen miles southwest of Bannack, a town large enough to organize a force of civilian volunteers that might try to attack. Horse Prairie had been selected as the evening campsite. Only small children and the wounded were fed—leftovers from meals prepared the evening before. The rest of the people rode on empty stomachs until the midday rest high up in the mountains beyond the divide.

The trail went south to the headwaters of Big Hole River, Dark-horse Creek, and upward to the seven-thousand-foot level. Black Mountain and Selway Mountain, two miles to the east, stood snowcapped and shiny in the morning sun. So did Goldstone Mountain, three miles to the west on the Continental Divide. The climb into the heavy pine forest on the Big Hole Divide was as fatiguing as the hardest stretches on the Lolo Trail, more so for the wounded. But the travois crossed the divide behind the horse herds, and on Bloody Dick Creek, around seven small lakes in a glade near where Selway Creek ran in from the north, they came to the area chosen for their rest.

Hemene swallowed some broth and fell asleep. Although in pain, he had endured the ordeal of being dragged over bumpy ground without complaint.

"I think we are going to lose him," Talooth said quietly. The adults of the wi-ses sat by a fire near the uppermost of the lakes. Only Atemis was absent. He was staying with the Lamtama herd. Talooth looked at the serious faces around her. They all had the same fear, but no one else had dared to say it aloud.

"What can we do?" Itsepit said, close to tears.

There was no answer. Finally Talooth spoke again. "He needed quiet, to stay in one safe place. No moving around. The others needed that too."

"Yes," Teeweeyownah said. Leadership of the wi-ses, although not sought by him, had fallen to him since Hemene was incapacitated. "This is the one thing we do not have, a safe place. We are forced to keep moving. If we stay somewhere too long, the suyapu will come on us from every side. We know that now."

They sat in silence. "They'll do that anyway," Short Bull said at last. "You'll see."

"What are you saying? We should give up?" Teeweeyownah asked.

"I don't know," Short Bull said. He was only twenty-two years old, but had shown his bravery in all the fights, from lahmotta to the Big Hole. "The chiefs have to think about that. We will have to fight again and lose more of our people."

Seton looked on. He remembered what Teeweeyownah had said at the end of the Clearwater fight, that he would die soon. He looked at the warrior's hard, uncompromising face. If he somehow knew that he was about to die, if he was certain, did this mean that all their fates had already been decided? What did Teeweeyownah know that the others did not? Wahlitits and Rainbow both had said that they would die soon, and they had. Teeweeyownah was still alive. What did this knowledge do to him? Seton saw no sadness in his face. Whatever Teeweeyownah knew, he had accepted. Perhaps, it occurred to Seton, he should also accept what was to come—to Hemene, to himself . . . And then?

"If we surrender, the suyapu will put us in prison," Teeweeyownah said. "They'll never let us be free again in our own country." Some of the men and women nodded in agreement.

"Yes," Short Bull said. "It would be so. But my wife and my little one would live."

Teeweeyownah looked to the ground between his crossed legs. "Maybe," he said. "Maybe."

There was a long silence. "About my father," Itsepit said. "Is there nothing else we can do?"

"Pray," Talooth said in a low voice, almost a whisper.

"We are doing that," Teeweeyownah said, getting up. He went to his wife who lay nearby with Tsacope sitting next to her, talking.

A little later the crier rode through the camps and called out to get ready to move. The trail wound south downstream along Bloody Dick Creek, through thick pine forest, past some marshlands wedged between mountain slopes, past Pyramid Hill to the right, and, ten miles down, the riders with the travois came to the edge of Horse Prairie. It was a high grassland like another, smaller, Big Hole, surrounded with mountains. When they arrived, the sun was sinking in the west, a red, fiery disk.

Itsepit brought the draft horse to a halt. The Old Man's eyes swept the valley before him. "Horse Prairie," he said. He coughed, holding his chest. Seton and Short Bull lifted him from the frame and carried him to a place under a pine Itsepit was preparing for him. Gently they laid him down.

"Horse Prairie," Hemene said. "There used to be buffaloes here. When I was young, we sometimes came here to hunt them. Bannocks came too, Lemhi Shoshones, Flatheads, even Blackfeet. Sometimes we had to fight." He smiled weakly.

Later during the night, fires still burning brightly throughout the camps, Itsepit and Seton sat at Hemene's side. They sat in silence, thinking their own thoughts. They believed the Old Man was asleep, but he was not.

"I must tell you something," Hemene said suddenly, making an effort to speak clearly. "I will be going away tonight, maybe early in the morning."

Itsepit tried to speak, but Hemene raised a hand and shook his head. "No. Hear me." He paused, breathing hard. "It is time for me to go. I am setting my feet on the trail to the other place."

Again Itsepit wanted to speak, but Hemene gestured for her to listen. "It is best this way," he said. "I had a good life. I had good people around me."

He paused. "They are waiting for me there."

Itsepit burst into tears, but Hemene shook his head. "No. I don't want you to be that way. It is my time. Your time comes too."

He turned and looked at Seton. "And yours," he said softly. He coughed. "My bundle, daughter," he said. "You know what is in it. What these things mean. You have helped me with it, prayed with me when we opened it."

He paused again. "If you want to keep it, keep it," he continued. "You know what you have to do if you keep it. If you don't want to keep it, bury it with me."

Itsepit sat, bent over, crying quietly.

Hemene looked at Seton. "Son of my wife's sister," he said. "Itsayaya pa'na. I am glad that I could do something for you. It took a long time."

He fought for breath. "The wéyekin will help you. It is not as the missionaries say. They know nothing about this. They are birds of death. They lie for the suyapu world, a dead world. When your time comes, the wéyekin will take you where we are. We'll wait for you. You'll come to our place. No suyapu can get there."

He paused again. "My wéyekin is the wolf. When I'm about to leave, you'll hear wolves call. They call for me."

He was still looking at Seton. "I want to ask you for something. When I am gone I want you to look out for this girl." He pointed with his chin to Itsepit.

Seton looked into the Old Man's eyes and nodded. "I will," he heard himself say. He said it firmly.

Hemene nodded, satisfied, a shine in his eyes. Or was it a reflection of the fire? "Leave me now," he said. "All has been said. I am grateful to you." He turned his head. When Itsepit bent over him, he waved her off. Seton and the girl sat for a long time without speaking. Itsepit was still crying, tears dripping from her chin. Finally they went to their sleeping robes and lay down near the fire.

When sleep finally came, it was a fitful sleep. Then Seton dreamed that he was running with wolves. Fast. They ran over a wide plain, the wolves looking at him, recognizing him, their yellow eyes wide and passionate, strangely familiar. Then the pack stopped and stood in an irregular group. They lifted their muzzles to the sky and howled. He stood among them, naked, filled with a feeling of elation, an unknown awareness.

Seton woke with a jolt. He raised himself and looked around. The fires had burned out. People lay wrapped in robes. To the east the faintest touch of first light crept over the dark sky. Wolves were calling from the high ridge to the north, less than half a mile away.

Seton went to the Old Man's side. Hemene patted his hand. "You heard them," he said. "They have come for me." He coughed. "Raise me up a little." Itsepit was there and placed blankets and robes against her father's back. She called, and one by one the men and women of the wi-ses gathered around the chief. He looked once along their faces, knowing them, not knowing them anymore. His eyes glistened in the vague light. He looked forward at something, something the others did not see.

"Hiyatommon," he said. "Wettiwetti Seeyakt. You too, Hoyouw-erlikt. You, Koolkooltami." Now there were tears in his eyes, tears of joy. "Diskowkow, my wife." One more time he coughed. "There is my horse. Let us ride."

His head fell back. Teeweeyownah bent over him and closed his eyes. "He is gone," he said. The keening began, the high-pitched wailing by the women. On the hill, the calling of the wolves had ended.

S I X T E E N

HEMENE WAS NOT BURIED IN THE PRAIRIE. HIS BODY, rolled in a blanket, was taken up to a place in the pines where a shift in the soil had exposed roots of a tree and a cavern behind. The cavern was widened, and he was placed inside. The opening was closed with earth and rocks and sod, and camouflaged. White Goose spoke the invocation and sang a tiwét spirit song. After the keening, the grieving wi-ses pulled themselves away from the hidden grave. Dawn had not been able to reach the place. The proceedings were hardest for Itsepit. She had kept her father's bundle. Back at the campsite, all the people of the wi-ses who had not already done so after the burials of Ayok-ka, Elk Blanket, and Tasshea in the Big Hole, cut their hair short in mourning. Now their attention centered on Dawn.

Two more people had died during the night and early morning. One was the pretty young girl also named Dawn. The other was a

Wallowa woman who had been shot through the stomach. Neither death had been easy.

In camp, Dawn's travois had been prepared for travel. Itsepit replaced Oyipee to ride the draft horse that dragged the travois. Seton was helping load packhorses when Swan Necklace and Kowtoliks rode up.

"We are going to look for suyapu," Swan Necklace said. "You want to come with us?"

Seton hesitated. "Who is going?"

"Us and Tababo," Swan Necklace said. "White Thunder is the leader."

Seton glanced at Itsepit. She nodded to him. Teeweeyownah was hitching the cinch of a packhorse. He pulled hard and tied the lash rope to the top of the pack. He looked at Seton and nodded. "Go," he said. Seton went to his roan, already saddled, the rifle scabbard attached to the saddle horn. He mounted and joined his friends. Working together during the past weeks, keeping a thousand Lamtama horses moving, they had developed a strong bond.

"We heard about the coyote," Kowtoliks said, glancing at Seton's claw necklace. Seton nodded but said nothing. He wore the necklace as White Goose had told him to do, but Hemene's war whistle and war club were in his saddlebags. These two objects could be brought out only before a battle or when he was in deadly danger. He had been instructed in their use but felt very self-conscious, even worried at possessing them.

White Thunder and Tababo were sitting their horses at the edge of the Wallowa camp. White Thunder, twenty-two years old, kin to the Wallowa chiefs and a proven scout and warrior, looked Seton over. Kowtoliks made the introduction. Tababo was a cousin of Kowtoliks and, like White Thunder, a member of the Wallowa band. He was a mixed blood, raised by Bannocks, but had come and married a Nez Perce woman. He was a few years older than White Thunder, a tough and reliable warrior.

"He speaks suyapu too," Kowtoliks said, pointing with his chin to Tababo.

Tababo, with a quick smile, said, "Only a little."

"He speaks suyapu like a suyapu," Kowtoliks said, nodding toward Seton.

"We know," White Thunder said. "We saw him with the chiefs at the Lolo corral."

Seton was surprised that they knew him. White Thunder, despite his youth, impressed him as a man with a strong, independent personality. He was medium sized, trim, with keen, observant eyes in a face with high cheekbones, a strong nose, and a wide mouth. Like all present, his hair was cut short in mourning for a dead relative. Among the bands there were few left who had not suffered a personal loss.

White Thunder was aware that Seton had sized him up and approved of him. He nodded to Seton and, without a word, turned his dun mare. She was painted with a white zigzag line on the left shoulder, the symbol of lightning. He urged her into a slow lope. Heading northeast into the depth of Horse Prairie, the companions followed. From behind them came a thunderous sound as the herds moved out, their waves surging southeast along the edge of the valley toward Bannock Pass. The advance guard was already on its way. Ahead of it a scouting party explored toward the pass and was expected to scan the Lemhi Valley beyond.

Horse Prairie Creek dropped out of the Beaverhead Mountains. It ran north into the valley for thirteen miles, turned east and southeast, and, after another twenty-four miles, emptied into the Red Rock River. Within the bend of the creek lay four ranches. Farthest south was the Donovan ranch, five miles below Bannock Pass. The Montague-Winters ranch sat near the center of the prairie, the Pierce ranch lay five miles beyond it to the north, and the Barrett was five miles farther east.

White Thunder's party rode in a loose group, the riders scanning the valley as they went. They noticed horses and cattle grazing around the Pierce and Montague-Winters ranches, but no human activity. The high valley, covered with bluebunch wheatgrass and sagebrush, with willows strung along Horse Prairie Creek and its tributaries, lay quiet under a cool wind from the northwest and a mild sun. The ridge to the north that separated Horse Prairie from Grasshopper Valley lay empty. Yellow dots and white flecks in three areas were distant herds of antelopes feeding on sagebrush.

Seton rode along with the others without thinking of their purpose. He was still numbed by the events of the last days—the slaughter of innocents, all the deaths, especially the death and burial of Hemene. The Old Man had been his closest link to his mother, a role that somehow made him a surrogate for two other persons Seton had lost or never known, his father and grandfather. He had never had the feeling of belonging until Hemene gave it to him. Hemene and Itsepit had become his real family, with little Tsacope and Itsepit's sister, Dawn, next. Slowly his half brother, Alex, and Alex's adopted father, Aaron, had become distant. Now, blurred by what had happened, they were people from a different world, a world ruled by the white men, a world turned hostile. Anger built in Seton.

They rode down on Bloody Dick Creek and followed its course north to northeast. As they passed along a narrow marsh by the creek, they heard a clatter of gunfire to the southeast, from the Montague-Winters ranch. They halted, circled, and faced the direction of the ranch. A few more shots. Silence. Then they saw a handful of Nez Perce riders round up horses from the ranch, close to two hundred animals, and prepare to drive them toward the column of people starting out from the campsite. A few more riders began to gather the cattle.

"We'll have beef tonight," Swan Necklace said with a sly smile. White Thunder grunted in agreement and pressed his dun forward. The party fell into a fast lope and, two miles on, below Red Butte at the mouth of the creek, crossed Horse Prairie Creek and made for the Pierce ranch. The horses ran smoothly in the rich grass of the flat. They passed through amber-colored cattle and about eighty horses spread out on the prairie by the creek. White Thunder gestured to Kowtoliks to circle the wooden buildings on the right, Seton to circle them on the left. They did, fast, and they met in front where a low staircase led to a veranda and the door of the main house. White Thunder and Tababo went in with rifles ready while the others watched a bunkhouse and a shed. "No one here," White Thunder said, coming out. Kowtoliks held the horses while Swan Necklace and Seton searched the other structures and found them empty too. "Let's take the other place first," White Thunder said. "We'll come back here later."

They mounted and rode to the Barrett ranch. The people there had fled too and taken their animals with them. The scouts took linen, bedspreads they emptied of feathers, and any materials suited for bandages. They found biscuits in the kitchen and jelly in a glass on a shelf. They sat down on chairs and ate, looking through a window. They left everything else.

They took their time riding back to the Pierce ranch. There too they rifled the place for bandage materials. They left the buildings and interiors intact, but outside they rounded up the horses and moved them south, experts at this task. They left the cattle alone. White Thunder expected that the bands would cross Bannock Pass by early evening. He knew that the steers could not be driven there in time. Lean Elk had decided that the bands should camp for the night two miles below Bannock Pass to rest the herds after the hard climb over the Big Hole Divide. That would give them time to process the meat of the steers taken from the Montague-Winters and Donovan ranches.

Each member of White Thunder's party selected one of the captured horses for himself. The others would be given to the chiefs for distribution. Seton chose a gray mare, a horse five years old with clean lines, a fine runner. He put her on a lariat before they reached the camp in the afternoon.

Lean Elk had chosen a good site. In the range of hills rolling upward to the wide opening in the Beaverhead Mountains that is Bannock Pass was a pan of flat ground near where Divide Creek falls into Horse Prairie Creek. Files of firs climbed the hills around it. There was firewood and good water. The bands had settled down in the pan, and cooking fires were going when the party arrived. The steers had been parceled out and were being butchered. The horse herds grazed on the hills around the camp.

White Thunder held the eighty captured horses outside the camp. Because his party was made up of Wallowas and Lamtamas, the horses would be split among these two bands. White Thunder sent Tababo and Swan Necklace to inform the chiefs. Joseph and White Goose came with a few men and took charge. The herd was divided into equal parts and moved to the Wallowa and Lamtama camps. There the chiefs gave out animals according to need and invited some persons to take a horse of their choice, honoring them. Four horses went to the Hemene wi-ses. Called by White Goose, Teeweeyownah chose a chestnut stallion, fast and strong, but high spirited and nervous. He put it on a halter and led it to the wi-ses camp, talking to it, introducing himself as its new owner. He tied the stallion with a long rope and brushed and fed him. Finally he cut his property mark into the stallion's right ear. Seton did the same with the gray mare, marking her as his with his mother's property sign.

The loss of Hemene, Elk Blanket, Ayokka, and Tasshea lay like a dark shadow over the wi-ses camp. The mood was somber, even among the children. The good news was that Dawn's condition had improved. She would be able to ride a horse in the morning. She no longer needed the travois. Seton's arrival was greeted with approving nods, and later, when he was asked to tell the story of the scouting ride, faces lightened for a moment.

He asked about the gunfire they had heard coming from one of the ranches. He was told that four ranch hands had put up a fight there and been killed. There was not much talk after that. They ate the evening meal in silence, even though the roasted beef was something special and the smell of sizzling fat on the fireplace was a reminder of happier days.

Seton sat by Itsepit, both very much aware that the third person who had for so long been beside them would never be there again. They had no desire for small talk. Each was thinking of other times. Itsepit had laid Hemene's bundle next to her, part of her father, a presence. Tsa-cope came over from her mother's side and sat down between the two, reaching out to them, her round black eyes probing theirs. Finally, a smile stole over Itsepit's face. She bent and embraced the little intruder, holding her fast.

Three hours after midnight they heard keening in a camp nearby. One voice, another, still more. Sounds of despair slicing the stillness of the night like knives. All the camps woke, people stirring uneasily, helpless. On the hills, in the dark, the horses stood in their multitude, listening. Then, keening from another place, the two blending together as if responding to each other. Two more dead, Seton thought, sitting up. Tsacope, between him and Itsepit, was deep in sleep, her moccasined feet sticking out from the robe. Itsepit reached over to cover them. They sat listening.

A figure came through the tethered horses and stacked packs into the wi-ses camp, searching. Although the fire had died, Seton recognized Swan Necklace. He whistled. Swan Necklace knelt beside him. "We will look for suyapu again," he whispered. "Are you coming with us?"

"Who?" Seton asked.

"I and Kowtoliks and Tababo and White Thunder. We go north in the next valley. See what the Shoshones are doing. Tababo knows these places. White Thunder is talking with Lean Elk." Despite the dark, Seton saw that Swan Necklace looked at him expectantly.

From Seton's right, behind Itsepit and Dawn, Teeweeyownah asked, "Who is going? Where?"

"Me, Swan Necklace. Kowtoliks. Tababo. White Thunder is the leader. We go up to the Shoshone reservation. See what we can find out. Lean Elk says it is good."

There was a silence. "Who has died?" Itsepit asked.

"Husis Owyen's baby, the one who was shot through the hip," Swan Necklace said. "The other, I don't know."

"I want to go," Seton said in the direction of Teeweeyownah.

"Yes," Teeweeyownah said. As an afterthought he added, "Don't stir the Shoshones up. We don't want to fight them too."

"No," Swan Necklace said. "Lean Elk said that also." Seton got up and folded his sleeping robe. He took off his moccasins and walked barefoot through the wet grass and the shuffling horses toward the creek. He urinated at the edge of a fir thicket, then stepped into the icy creek and splashed water in his face. He drank deeply. While the roan looked on, he saddled the gray mare he had taken from the captured ranch herd, slipped the rifle scabbard over the saddle horn, and adjusted saddlebags and sleeping robe behind the saddle. He tied up his moccasins and hung them around his neck. Itsepit stood there and handed him a cut of cold meat wrapped in a piece of cloth. She said nothing, but nodded to him when he took the reins of the gray and started to lead it away. He looked at her, saying good-bye with his eyes. "I'll leave my horse with you," he said. Itsepit nodded again. "We could be gone for some days." He had heard Swan Necklace tell Teeweeyownah that.

Seton turned away, letting Swan Necklace lead. They walked along the edge of the camp and found the other men of the scouting party on the west side, sitting with Lean Elk. Their saddled horses, including Swan Necklace's appaloosa, were behind them. Seton dropped the reins of the gray, and he and Swan Necklace sat down.

He had not yet seen Lean Elk up close. Lean Elk was a rather small man in his midforties, hair cut in mourning and streaked with white. He wore a fringed leather shirt and fringed leggings. The only embellishment was a small fluff of eagle down wrapped in a band of red cloth and tied to his hair above the left ear. The strength in his face made it clear he was a chief, a man of repute. Iron eyes, Seton thought when Lean Elk's brief gaze washed over him. Lean Elk seemed to repeat himself for the benefit of the two who had just arrived.

"When we are through the pass, we'll go south through the long valley," he said slowly. "Where the mountains end on the east side, we'll go northeast through the plain. There is a road from the Mormon land in the south. It goes to the mining towns in Montana Territory. There will be wagon trains on that road. We'll go on to Camas Meadows and Targhee Pass and through the mountains around the big lake where hot springs blow clouds into the air."

The young men sat in silence, thinking about it. Finally Tababo asked, "And from there?"

Lean Elk coughed. "To the Crow land and on, north to Grandmother's Land."

White Thunder nodded. "We'll stay behind you, cover your back." He got up, and the others in the party rose with him. Lean Elk looked up at them, his glance going from face to face. He raised his right hand. White Thunder did the same.

They mounted and rode west, up the sage- and grass-covered hills, through the quiet herds. First light cast its pale shimmer over the eastern horizon when they reached the height of the pass, the Continental Divide, and the border between Idaho and Montana territories. Below them lay the broad valley framed in the east by the mountain chain of the Lemhi Range of Idaho, its snow-packed peaks reaching over twelve thousand feet. They halted the horses for a brief rest and took in the spectacular view. Finally White Thunder made a clicking sound, and they started down the trail.

The trail went southeast for two miles to the heights above the head of Canyon Creek, then turned southwest, tracing the course of the creek on the mountain slopes above it. The men rode slowly, in single file. After another eight miles they were out of the Beaverhead Mountains and reached the bottom of the valley. The rosy melancholy of dawn spread over the sky as they turned northwest, riding half a mile east of the Lemhi River through flats blanketed with wheatgrass and sagebrush. Across the river, they saw the hamlet of Junction, a few wooden houses and cabins. Small herds of horses and cattle were bunched nearby. The men halted and looked. Seton thought he saw a barricade between two houses and movement on top of it.

"The suyapu have built a corral for themselves," Tababo said scornfully. "They knew we were coming." They rode another mile and forded the churning river to the west bank, the current reaching to their stirrups. The river ran north, blue gray and clear, fed by melting snow from the Beaverhead Mountains and the Lemhi Range. On the west bank the party came to a well-traveled road. Wagon ruts and horse and mule tracks were sunk into its soil. They halted.

"The road to the town of Salmon," Tababo said matter-of-factly. "The town is on the west bank of the Salmon River, across from where the Lemhi River runs into the Salmon."

He paused. "There is a big store in Salmon town. It supplies a mining town in the mountains west of Salmon, Leesburg. That is why many wagons use this road."

"How far is it to Salmon?" White Thunder asked.

"Forty miles, maybe more," Tababo said. "Leesburg is thirty miles past Salmon." He paused. "Maybe ten years ago, I was with my mother's band, Chief Tyhee's band, and we visited Leesburg." He laughed. "That was before I came to the numipu."

"How many suyapu in these places?" White Thunder asked.

"When I saw them, maybe eight hundred, maybe more. Now, I don't know." He laughed. "Not all of the white people were miners. There were women there, the kind who are paid to sleep with men."

The road lay empty under the rising sun. "This is the gold road," he continued. "Sometimes white bandits ambush wagons on this road."

"Where does the road come from?" Kowtoliks asked.

"From the Mormon land in the south," Tababo said. "Somewhere south of here it splits. One branch goes north to Bannack, one comes this way."

They moved on, following the road north. They went slowly, watching the country. They passed two ranches spaced miles apart. They saw grazing cattle but no people and no horses. At noon, before they reached the little town of Lemhi at the edge of the Shoshone reservation, Tababo pointed northeast toward a gap in the Beaverhead Mountains. "Lemhi Pass," he said. "It heads to Horse Prairie too. Bannocks and Shoshones used to go across to hunt buffalo at the three forks of the big river, the Missouri."

They sat their horses looking at Lemhi, another dusty hamlet made of a cluster of wooden boxes. This one also seemed to have been fortified with a stockade. "This was a Mormon place," Tababo said. "When I was two years old, Mormon missionaries came and built a fort. They dug irrigation ditches and planted wheat and potatoes. At first the Shoshones liked it, but then the missionaries tried to run their lives. When I was seven years old, Shoshones and Bannocks burned the fort and drove the Mormons away. No one lived there until the miners came to Leesburg."

They moved on and passed Lemhi a couple of hundred yards to the west. Heads appeared above the barricade—people silently watching them ride by. Now they had entered the Lemhi Shoshone reservation, and where McDevitt Creek runs into the river from Poison Peak, three miles below the government agency, they found an Indian man cutting willow branches by the river. They went down to the willows and dismounted and drank from the river and watered their horses. They sat while the horses grazed, and Tababo talked with the man. When he returned he looked vexed.

"The man is Shoshone. His name is Tesedemit. Tendoy is his chief. He said many weeks ago army officers asked Chief Tendoy for men to scout for Cut Arm. The chief said no."

He paused. "The officers went to the Fort Hall Reservation, south, and got themselves a bunch of Bannocks. They are with Cut Arm. They must be in the Big Hole by now. Their chief is Buffalo Horn. He has seventy warriors with him."

"How is it that we didn't see them?" White Thunder wondered.

"We didn't see Cut Arm's soldiers either," Tababo said. "But they are behind us somewhere." He made a gesture with his hand. "There is more. This man, Tesedemit, said that army officers are at Fort Hall right now, trying to get another bunch of Bannocks to scout for the soldiers. The chief scout is a white man named Fisher."

The men sat in silence. Finally Kowtoliks asked, "What will we do?"

"Nothing," White Thunder said. He thought for a moment. "We wait. We spend the night south of Bannock Pass and follow our people in the morning. By now they must have passed that place, Junction, and are on the way south. We will stay a day behind them and keep watch. Maybe Cut Arm comes this way."

"If he doesn't come over Bannock Pass, he may come over Monida Pass farther east," Tababo said.

White Thunder nodded. "Yes. I am certain Lean Elk knows that." They rested by the river for another hour, then rode back south. At the southernmost of the two ranches, Kowtoliks put a spring calf on a lariat and brought it along for the evening meal. They recrossed the river and rode past Junction and onto the wide and deep trail the bands and the herds had cut before them. In midafternoon they made camp by Hawley Creek in a draw, lined with firs and dogwood shrub and willows along the clear, cool waters. Here, they were two miles south of where the

Bannock trail comes into the valley and four miles southeast of Junction. From the rim of the draw they had a view of both locations and the wagon road. They butchered the calf and built a fire after dark so no smoke could be seen to reveal their presence. They talked and roasted choice pieces of meat. Later Seton sat for a long time on the rim of the draw, alone in the dark, thinking about where he was, wondering where he would be, wondering how all this would end.

They spent the next day in camp on Hawley Creek, keeping guard. They saw a few riders leave the hamlet going north, but the trail from the pass and the road lay quiet. They moved out before sunup on the following day, August 15, and rode south on the wide trail of their people in a drizzling rain. They passed the places where the bands had camped two nights before and the previous night. On Birch Creek, having ridden forty-two miles from Hawley Creek, they saw a thin swirl of smoke in the distance, coming from the road.

They crossed the creek and spread out over the road, holding rifles ready. They came on a site where a wagon train on the way north had been taken and sacked. Four wagons with merchandise had been plundered and set aflame many hours ago. The fires still smoldered. The rain stopped as the men dismounted and searched the ground. They found the tracks of unshod horses and prints of moccasins and knew that the warriors had done this. From the harnesses they saw that three of the wagons had been drawn by sixteen-mule teams, one wagon by eight horses. The animals had been unhitched and run off. Among the scattered debris around the wagons was a bashed-in whiskey barrel, its contents spilled over the ground. Two white men lay dead near the wagons, one more in the willows, another half submerged in the creek. Seton saw magpies circling a spot farther up the creek, and when he cautiously approached, found a fifth freighter's body near that of a dead mule. All had been shot with rifles.

The men gathered where their horses were standing. "This was not much of a fight," White Thunder said. After a pause, he added, "The place stinks of death and smoke and whiskey. Let's ride."

They recrossed the stream and continued on the trail, going around the southern spur of the Beaverhead Mountains and northeast into the open space of the Snake River plain. They saw bands of antelopes feeding on sagebrush. The men kept to the high ground and camped for the night along a trickle of creek with enough water for the horses and themselves. They knew that they were half a day's ride behind the bands. On the next day, twenty-five miles farther on, they passed the empty campground where the bands had stayed the previous night. A dozen appaloosas, sick or lame from the hard drive, stood forlorn among the cold fireplaces. They rode twenty miles more and came to another wagon road, much used but empty.

"This is the other part of the gold road," Tababo said. "Lean Elk talked about this part too. It goes north through Monida Pass. It could be that Cut Arm comes with his army over this pass. He certainly is not behind us."

"We will watch for him," White Thunder said grimly.

They continued on the road until they came to the Hole-in-the-Rock stage station where the stage road ran east through an opening in the deep, narrow canyon Beaver Creek had cut into the sagebrush plain. At this place the canyon walls receded, enabling horses and wagons to ford the stream. The bands and herds had gone through earlier, leaving the creek banks at the crossing place fouled and broken. In sight of the stage station, where armed white men stood looking on, the scouting party went through and continued on the stage road toward Camas Creek. They rode northeast for six more miles until White Thunder selected a campsite on Rattlesnake Creek where they could watch approaches from the west and northwest. Now they were in a beautiful high prairie grassland sheltered by the Centennial Mountains in the north.

They took their time in the morning, letting the horses graze and rest after the hard rides of the last days. Their people were moving toward the Camas Meadows, and they were content to be the eyes and ears that rode behind them. They saw nothing alarming. There was no traffic on either the stage road or on what they could see of the gold road. Around noon, they saddled up and rode seven miles, past another of the people's campsites, with dead fires and lame horses, to West Camas Creek, where they made camp below a high point that gave them a lookout to cover all approaches. When evening darkened, they built a small fire and ate jerky from their saddlebags.

The next day the men took turns as lookout. It was Kowtoliks who alerted the camp in the early afternoon. The others climbed up and looked west, hidden by a twisted fir. Seton saw dust rising in the distance, a thin cloud moving in the sagebrush plain. The men watched in silence. Slowly the yellow cloud came on, but it took a while until the horsemen who caused it could be made out.

"Tito'gan. Indians," White Thunder said. "They must be Cut Arm's Bannocks."

The men watched as the horsemen came into full view. Perhaps twenty Bannocks were fanned out in front, covering a stretch of five hundred yards between them. Behind was a tightly bunched band of Bannocks and, finally, the cavalry, a thin, long, dark file, barely visible in the whirling dust.

"There is Cut Arm," White Thunder said. He turned to Seton. "Ride and tell our people. We will stay back and watch." Seton nodded and slipped away. He went to his horse, already saddled, mounted, and rode to the trail plowed into the ground by thousands of hooves. He rode slowly at first, then urged the gray into a fast lope when he came into the grassy, lava-encrusted plain near East Camas Creek. On Spring Creek he came upon the Nez Perce rear guard.

They were about twenty-five men, heavily armed. They had seen him coming and halted, forming a half circle. Seton pulled his horse to a stop in front of them. Teeweeyownah and Short Bull of his wises were among them. The men waited quietly. Wottolen and Teeweeyownah seemed to be the leaders.

"What news do you bring us?" Teeweeyownah asked.

"Cut Arm and his army are coming up on your trail," Seton said, brushing sweaty hair from his forehead.

"How far away?" Wottolen asked.

"Fifteen miles from here, maybe," Seton said.

"How do you know this is Cut Arm?" Teeweeyownah asked. "Maybe this is a new army."

"There are Bannock scouts ahead of the army," Seton said. Then he explained what they had learned from Tesedemit on the Shoshone reservation. The men listened, their faces somber.

"Buffalo Horn," Teeweeyownah said. He scoffed. "Those Bannocks—they help Cut Arm because they expect to be paid in horses." He paused. "Our horses." There was an angry murmur among the men.

Wottolen looked at the sun dipping toward late afternoon. "I think Cut Arm is going to camp for the night somewhere near here," he said. He looked into Seton's eyes. "Ride and tell the chiefs."

Seton nodded and laid the reins against the left side of the gray's neck. He squeezed with his thighs and the horse turned to the right, and he rode around the half circle of horsemen and pushed the horse into a lope. He caught up with the bands twelve miles farther east, the long file of families with packhorses and extra horses and a few outriders. A cloud of dust hung in the air ahead of them where the herds were moving on. He rode along the column, and some people waved when he passed the Lamtama band. He expected to find Lean Elk at the point with the advance guard.

He passed the head of the column, came up behind the herds and went by their waves, and found Lean Elk and Ollokot a mile ahead of the Wallowa horses with their thirty warriors. He brought the gray to a walk beside the chiefs.

"Cut Arm has finally shown himself," Seton said. "He is behind us now, maybe thirty miles back. White Thunder sent me to tell you."

Lean Elk did not seem surprised. "Yes," he said. "You saw them?"

Seton nodded. "There are Bannock scouts with him. A chief by the name of Buffalo Horn."

Lean Elk nodded. He turned in the saddle to one of the men behind him. "Tell the chiefs to come. We must talk."

SEVENTEEN

LEAN ELK, OLLOKOT, AND SETON RODE A FEW hundred yards away from the trail and dismounted. Lean Elk had sent the advance guard ahead to reconnoiter a small lake two miles beyond Willow Creek. Two messengers were sent back to the bands to inform them that camp would be made on the east bank of Willow Creek, a little more than a mile away. The three men sat in silence, waiting for the chiefs.

Seton watched as the herds passed by in a solid stream nearly two miles long. The herders were now twelve- to fifteen-year-olds, a few girls among the boys. They were eager and serious in the performance of their duties. Atemis rode point for the Lamtama herd, carbine slung across his back. His eyes were concentrated on the drag of the Pekonan herd in front of him, so he did not notice Seton raising his arm. The chiefs arrived before the herds had gone by. First came Looking Glass,

accompanied by an Alpowai wi-ses chief, White Bull. Toohoolhoolzote and White Goose rode up together. Joseph and Naked Head were
last. They sat in a circle, Ollokot and Joseph together, Seton next to
Lean Elk.

Lean Elk pointed with his chin. "Seton was with White Thunder,
scouting in our rear. White Thunder sent him to tell us. Cut Arm is
coming behind us." He turned to Seton. "Tell them what you saw."

The chiefs' eyes on him, Seton spoke haltingly. He described
what they had observed. The chiefs listened intently. When he ended,
Ollokot asked the same question Teeweeyownah had asked earlier.
"How do you know this is Cut Arm and not another army?"

Seton once again told what they had found out on the Shoshone
reservation.

"So we have two bunches of Bannocks on our tracks," Ollokot
said. "The one with Buffalo Horn and another with that white man,
Fisher."

"How many soldiers does Cut Arm have with him?" Toohoolhoolzote asked.

"I don't know," Seton said. "We had seen only the first of the
horse soldiers when White Thunder sent me to tell you."

The long file of the bands began to pass them, the Alpowais still
in the lead.

"Where is White Thunder now?" Joseph asked of his nephew.

"He must still be back there, watching the army," Seton said.

"How many are in your party?" Joseph asked.

"Five," Seton said. "White Thunder, Tababo, Swan Necklace, and
Kowtoliks. And me."

Joseph nodded. "We'll hear from them soon."

"We have to stop Cut Arm," Ollokot said matter-of-factly. "We
have to stop him before we get to Targhee Pass."

There was a silence. "We send the horses and the families ahead
tomorrow and choose the place to fight," Looking Glass said. "We let
Cut Arm come to us and destroy him."

There were sounds of agreement.

A rider galloped along the column of the bands and came to a halt where the horses of the chiefs stood. He dismounted in a hurry and approached, calming himself. He looked along the faces of the chiefs, finally resting his eyes on White Goose, his band chief. "You know me," he said. "I am Swan Necklace." This introduction was meant for the other chiefs, not for White Goose. "White Thunder sent me. Cut Arm and his soldiers are making camp back there." He tossed his head. "On Camas Meadows, between two creeks that run south close together."

"How many men does Cut Arm have with him?" Toohoolhoolzote asked.

"We got close enough to count them," Swan Necklace said proudly. "There are about fifty foot soldiers. They ride in wagons. We think there are a hundred horse soldiers. Two big guns, we think. Bannocks, maybe fifty. And there are civilian volunteers with them, maybe thirty."

He paused. "They have a pack train with lots of mules and a bunch of suyapu packers."

"That is less than Cut Arm had in the fight by the Clearwater," Ollokot said. "We held him there for almost two days." He paused. "We could have wiped him out there if all the warriors had come with us." There was a note of anger in his voice.

"Yes," White Goose said in a conciliatory tone. After a brief pause, he added, "We must make plans tonight. Ollokot is right. We must stop the soldiers. We can't leave them at our backs."

One chief after another voiced agreement. Swan Necklace was asked more questions. While the talk continued, the last of the bands, Lamtama, went by. Behind them the rear guard had closed in. Teeweeyownah, Wottolen, and a dozen men rode over to the circle of chiefs and sat their horses behind them. "What are we going to do?" Teeweeyownah asked. "Do we fight?" He looked around, finally settling on Ollokot.

"We are going to fight," Ollokot said, looking into Teeweeyownah's unyielding eyes, knowing why a sardonic smile twisted his fellow warrior's lips. Teeweeyownah had called for an all-out assault on the general's confused troops in the Clearwater fight, to no avail. "We

all agree on that," he continued firmly. "I think we will fight Cut Arm
tomorrow."

Teeweeyownah nodded. Without a word he pulled the reins and
backed out of the half circle of horsemen. He turned and followed the
Lamtama band and the last of the disbanding rear guard. The meeting broke up. Seton and Swan Necklace left after the chiefs and looked
for their own wi-ses in the Lamtama part of the big camp on Willow
Creek.

Seton watered the gray in the creek and drank deeply also. He
found some of the women unloading packhorses, while others seemed
to have ridden away to get firewood. The men were coming in from
various guard positions. Teeweeyownah and Short Bull had been with
the rear guard; Allultakanin had ridden in the advance guard. The two
remaining men, Kywis and Thunder Eyes, had been outriders for the
Lamtama band. When on the march, women and children were on
their own, leading the wi-ses packhorses and extra saddle horses.

Teeweeyownah was sitting by his wife with Tsacope on his lap. Itsepit
and Talooth were unpacking food, tableware, and cooking utensils. They
saw Seton come and nodded as he passed. Itsepit smiled at him.

Seton noticed that Dawn seemed to have recovered from her injury. Between him and Itsepit's sister there had always been distance, the
shadow of an unspoken discord nursed by Dawn. Perhaps mistrust.
It was not based on any failure on Seton's part. Perhaps it was simply
because his father was a suyapu. The two had learned to avoid each
other when possible. The situation often made Seton uneasy, and his
uneasiness extended to Teeweeyownah, although the man gave no hint
that he shared his wife's feeling in the matter. Neither had anyone else
in the wi-ses or in the Lamtama band, as far as Seton knew. Hemene
had been more of a father to him than his real father. Everyone knew
this. Whatever discord had existed between Dawn and Seton, for whatever reason, was vanquished by Tsacope. The child was openly attached
to Seton, something her mother did not try to deter. On the contrary,
in an odd way Dawn seemed pleased about it.

"You appear well again," Seton said.

"Yes." Dawn looked up at him. Then she looked to Talooth and pointed with her chin. "She did it; she is my healer."

"Sit down," Teeweeyoenah said. "Tell us about your scout with White Thunder." Seton sat on the rocky ground next to Teeweeyownah and crossed his legs. Tsacope crawled from her father's lap to Seton's, hugging him. Her parents smiled. He put his arms around the girl's thin waist and told his story. With Dawn so close, and her eyes on him, he felt the old uneasiness as he began, but forgot it as he warmed to the telling of his story.

"We should have gone over that other pass—Monida Pass?" Teeweeyownah said slowly. "We took the long route; Cut Arm took the short route." He paused. "Tomorrow we will meet him one more time." There was a threat in his voice.

Short Bull called for Seton, and he got up and walked away, giving Tsacope, as she insisted, a ride on his shoulders. With the girl clamping her hands around his chin, he helped Short Bull and Kywis with the horses, finally putting Tsacope on the gray mare. After watering, a few of the saddle horses were hobbled close to the camp while the others and the pack animals were taken a little farther to forage.

They were a quiet group around the campfire during the evening meal. Their thoughts were still with the four from the wi-ses who had died because of the Big Hole massacre, empty places, never to be filled again. They also thought about the next day's fight. They did not think much of Cut Arm and his soldiers, but knew that some of their people would get hurt or killed. Some might have remembered what Teeweeyownah had said during the Clearwater fight as he tried to rally the laggards—that he would die soon. Did he really know, and how? Was this his time? No one spoke about it; it was not to be mentioned. But Seton thought about it. Could something be done? Could he, Seton, change something?

They ate mostly in silence. After the women cleaned the dishes, the men sat together for some time in the dark. All sought their sleeping places early. Under the starlit sky, Seton lay awake for a long time until the heavy hand of sleep closed his eyes.

Before first light, when the first sleepers began to stir, a muffled call went through the camps for all chiefs to gather in White Goose's wi-ses camp. Teeweeyownah went. He knew where to go. Other chiefs who did not were directed by low voices. After some commotion, quiet again descended upon the camps. The habitual sounds remained: the blowing, sneezing, and sighing of horses, the soft tapping of hooves, the occasional crackling of a fire, snoring, rustling of blankets, a baby crying. But by now most adults were awake. They knew what would soon happen.

Itsepit crept out of her robe and poked the embers in the fireplace and put some twigs on to restart the fire. She sat there until the first flames licked around the wood. She put three larger pieces crosswise on top. When she crawled back into her robe, she saw that Seton was watching. She blinked an eye and turned around.

It took almost an hour until Teeweeyownah returned. He walked in soundlessly. He stood by the fire that now burned brightly. He coughed. Men and women sat up, ready to listen. He stood looking at the ground, thinking. He stood like this for some time. Finally he spoke.

"Something wonderful happened," he said with a clear voice. "Black Hair, who was wounded in the Big Hole, had a powerful dream. His wéyekin came to him during the night, just a little while ago. His wéyekin is a spirit bird. It took him and flew him over Cut Arm's camp. It showed him everything from way up there. It said that Cut Arm is going to stay in this camp for another day and another night. Cut Arm is waiting for more soldiers. These soldiers are two days away."

He paused. "The wéyekin said he knows what is going to happen. He says we will attack Cut Arm's camp this next night and bring away the soldiers' horses. He said he saw us go back over the trail in the darkness. He said we will not lose a warrior, but that Cut Arm will lose many."

He paused again. "This is what Black Hair told us. If his wéyekin told him right, Cut Arm will still be camped on Camas Meadows today and the next night. If this is so, we will do as the spirit bird foretold.

We will attack his camp during the night and take his horses from him. Without them he can't follow us."

As foreseen, General Howard spent another day in his camp. Scouts White Thunder and Peopeo Tholekt confirmed it. They also reported the layout. The main camp was on the east bank of the easternmost of the two creeks. The wagons and big guns were protected by the tents with the infantry directly to the south, the company of civilians between the two streams to the west, and the tents with the cavalry troopers to the east and northeast. In the evening they hobbled the wagon horses to the wagons, tied the cavalry horses to picket ropes behind the cavalry tents, and held the mules between the cavalry horses and the creek. There were sentinels out, the scouts said. One picket post was established five hundred yards upstream on a rocky knoll near the creek. Two more were at different points south of the camp, one close to it, one farther away. The Bannock camp was downstream on the western creek, six hundred yards southwest of the main camp.

Bannock scouts had been seen spying on the Nez Perce camp and herds. It was assumed they had informed the general, though he had taken no action. Thus the Nez Perces also remained in place on Willow Creek. Their attack was scheduled for the following night of August 19. Most of the men, under Chiefs Joseph and White Goose, were left behind to protect the camp and the herds. Whether Cut Arm was asleep or waiting, there was no telling what the Bannocks might try to do. They were ancient enemies. The second bunch from Fort Hall had not made an appearance yet. It could be anywhere.

The raiding party consisted of twenty-eight men, including chiefs Ollokot, Toohoolhoolzote, and Looking Glass. They took the back trail before midnight, under a starry sky. They had sixteen miles to cover to the soldier camp. They rode slowly, making as little sound as possible. Of Hemene's wi-ses, Teeweeyownah, Allultakanin, and Seton went. Teeweeyownah had called on Seton to ride with him.

Before the raiding party left camp, Itsepit had taken Seton aside. "If you can, look out for my brother-in-law," she said. "We fear he no longer cares about his life." There was a quiet urgency in her voice. Seton looked into Itsepit's eyes. He was sad but not surprised. "I am not experienced in fighting," he said honestly. "He is. Still, I will try to look out for him." Itsepit nodded sadly and walked to where Dawn and the women were standing, watching silently as the warriors were swallowed by the night.

They rode fanned out, in three bands. One was led by Ollokot and Toohoolhoolzote. This was the largest one, twelve warriors beside the chiefs. It included a few men chosen to infiltrate the camp to the picket ropes of the cavalry. They would untie the horses and remove the bells from the bell mares of the pack train. The second band was led by Tee-weeyownah and Espowyes, the third by Looking Glass and White Bull, each a mere handful of men. Seton, riding beside Allultakanin, was thoughtful and observant. He had chosen the roan mare for this expedition, trusting his old companion in a tight spot more than the untried gray. The night rolled on as the warrior bands slowly traversed the distance. They halted about two miles from the general's camp.

They dismounted and tightened their saddle girths. They undressed to breechclouts, stuffing leggings and shirts into saddlebags. Objects with wéyekin power were brought out and put into place according to individual need: feathers and down feathers, necklaces with attachments, objects on strings, amulets, small pouches with sacred articles, war whistles, but no fancy headdresses or bonnets. Most men painted their faces. Some sang wéyekin songs with barely audible voices while they prepared themselves. Seton didn't paint himself but slipped the coyote claw necklace, which White Goose had made for him, and Hemene's war whistle over his head. He left Bear Shield's pouch with the red paint in his saddlebag. This was the first time he'd worn them, and he felt strange and somehow embarrassed, almost like an impostor. He looked around, but no one seemed to notice until he met Allultakanin's approving glance. He still felt odd. To hide his discomfort he unsheathed the Winchester and checked hammer and loading gate.

He tightened the cartridge belt around his waist by one notch. He was ready. He waited.

Twenty-eight men formed a circle, their horses behind them. Final decisions had to be made. There was silence until everyone was in place.

"We are close," Ollokot said. "How do we go in?"

"On horseback," Looking Glass said. "We wait until the men have cut the horses free. Some of us will run them off. The rest of us, we hit the camp." There was silence.

"This is not good," Two Moons said. "We remember how we took horses from enemy camps in the Plains—Lakotas, Blackfeet, Cheyennes. We walked into those camps and cut horses loose tied to tipis and walked away with them. Then we hit their herds."

He paused. "To ride in on horses is no good. This is the same as taking horses from enemy Indian camps, but it's less dangerous. These soldiers, they don't have ears as good as the Lakotas or Blackfeet. I say we walk in and leave the horses outside." There was a murmur of approval around the circle.

"I say we go among the soldiers on foot," Wottolen said. "We know their guns are stacked in front of their tents. We take many of their guns. We go in and kill the general and his officers."

He paused. "After that we whip the soldiers and drive off their horses and pack mules."

Once again there was a murmur of approval.

"Yes," Teeweeyownah said. "Wottolen is right. We go in afoot and take their guns and kill Cut Arm. We must finish this war with him. After tonight the soldiers are not going to put up a fight."

Seton listened as most of the men agreed. But Looking Glass was not swayed.

"No," he said. "We must have our horses. That is how we will charge through the soldier camp. We can capture all the horses after the young men go in and cut them loose and take off the bells."

He paused. "Warriors need their horses. It will spoil everything to go afoot."

There was silence. "No, it won't," Two Moons said. "We have done this many times."

"It would be good to kill Cut Arm and the officers," Espowyes said. "That's better than taking his horses. He won't be after us anymore." There was a long silence.

White Bull spoke in support of his chief. "We should listen to Looking Glass," he said. "He knows. He has fought battles with the Lakotas and Cheyennes. His name is known all over this country. There are many more soldiers than there are of us. It is better to have our horses. We can do everything from horseback."

Again there was silence.

"We could go in on horseback after the soldiers' horses and the pack animals have been cut loose," a warrior said. Seton didn't know who. "Maybe it's better that way."

"Looking Glass doesn't like plans that are not his own," Teeweeyownah said coldly. "I think we should do what Wottolen said we should do: go in on foot and kill Cut Arm and his headmen."

It was very dark, but Seton could see Looking Glass angrily shake his head. "You do what you want. I and the men with me will keep our horses."

There was a tense silence. Finally Ollokot mounted his war horse. "Morning is coming. Let's go." He backed his mount out of the circle and rode away. Teeweeyownah mounted, then Espowyes. One by one the men mounted. Seton and the other three of their little band moved up behind the two leaders. They rode cautiously, letting the horses find their way through the sagebrush and around blocks of lava.

Ollokot and Toohoolhoolzote and their band took the center of the raiding force, Teeweeyownah and Espowyes the left wing, Looking Glass and his people the right wing. As they neared the soldiers' camp the bands spread out. When they were closer still, the men of the left wing dismounted. It appeared to Seton that men in the center did the same. Leading the roan by the reins, Seton moved step by step through the darkness. Finally Seton saw something white nearby. A white blur. Another. Soldiers' tents.

Teeweeyownah nudged Seton. "Take the reins of our horses," he whispered. "Hold them, whatever happens. Do not move from here. Wait for us." Seton, holding five horses and the roan mare, stood peering forward, listening. Teeweeyownah and the other men had disappeared. The night was giving way to morning. The air was cold and dry, with a light wind out of the north. The horses stood quietly around Seton. Nothing happened for what seemed a long time. Then a picket called from the knoll north of the camp. His voice rang through the stillness of the night. "Who are you? Who goes there?"

His call was answered by a shot from where Looking Glass should be. It was followed by a flurry of shots and the tumultuous awakening of the camp. Shouts and screams from suyapu throats. More shots from Ollokot's and Looking Glass's bands, the screaming of war whistles, yells from Nez Perce throats. Teeweeyownah and the men with him came rushing back and mounted quickly. They raced toward the soldiers' tents, Seton at the tail, the mouthpiece of Hemene's bone whistle in his mouth, rifle butt pressed between elbow and ribs, finger on trigger. He didn't realize that he was blowing the whistle hard. They were among the tents, toppling a pyramid of stacked rifles as men in underwear tumbled free, dodging, crawling, running. Seton saw a shadow to his right and swung his arm and fired. He released the reins, guiding the roan with his thighs, and followed a rider in front of him. He levered another cartridge into the chamber and fired at another target, a white man ducking. The roan backed into a tent behind him. The tent half collapsed, and the roan kicked and bucked and almost threw Seton off. Men were running past him.

He fired again and again, and then, over the wild noise of shrieking bone whistles and cracking Nez Perce rifles, he heard the thunder of hooves to the north. The cavalry horses were being stampeded. Teeweeyownah's voice rose over the din and shouted they should go back, back, back. There was a wagon with rearing horses. Seton passed so close that the corner of the wagon wall almost knocked him off his horse. He turned and, after one more shot at an indistinct target, broke out and was in the open, the turmoil of the camp behind him.

He urged the roan to run and came up on Teeweeyownah and Allultakanin, who had slowed to wait for him. A trumpet blared from the soldiers' camp as they rode on together, the hoofbeats of the captured animals ahead of them. Only when they were half a mile away did the soldiers rally. First there were scattered shots, then more, slowly reaching a crescendo of fireworks. Too late to do any damage.

A few bullets whizzed by. "We were looking for Cut Arm's quarters," Teeweeyownah said. "We did not have enough time to find him." He looked Seton up and down, from the bone whistle and the claw necklace to the rifle in the boy's right hand. He seemed pleased but made no comment.

"We got the horses," Allultakanin said. "We got them. That's good."

They were no longer within the enemy's range. The trumpet called again, and the shooting ended. There was an ominous silence, the only sound the hoofbeats of the herd. With the first gray streak of morning, a night bird called as they came up on Espowyes and the rest of the band. They saw the bunch around Ollokot and Toohoolhoolzote and jogged their mounts to close with them. Everyone slowed to a walk to rest their horses.

"Where are the cavalry horses?" Espowyes asked.

"Back there." Toohoolhoolzote pointed with his thumb toward the soldiers' camp. His face was an ironic grimace. "We didn't get them. We got the mules, that's all."

"Where are they?" Teeweeyownah asked.

"Looking Glass is driving them," Toohoolhoolzote said, pointing forward with his chin. "It's his doing. He rode too close to a guard. The suyapu heard him and called. We got a few of their horses. We got all of the mules." He paused. "Then we had to get out quickly."

They rode in silence, glum, disappointed. Finally Teeweeyownah asked, "Anyone killed?"

"No," Toohoolhoolzote answered. "Not one of us was hurt."

They rode on. Five miles east of the camp, after they had crossed a timbered draw and a lava ridge, they heard hoofbeats behind. They moved a little faster and halted a thousand yards beyond the ridge. They waited.

In the gray light before sunrise a few horse soldiers appeared on the ridge and quickly pulled back when they saw the warriors waiting impassively on the sagebrush plain. Then heads appeared on the rim of the ridge. Soon after, a wide stretch of it came alive. Rifles barked. The warriors scattered. A few with .45-70 Springfields remained and dismounted. Standing by their horses they returned fire, but because of the long range they did not waste ammunition. Still they kept the soldiers where they were.

Three companies of dismounted cavalry maintained an earsplitting but inefficient salvo from the ridge until a few warriors outflanked them and closed in. Seton had followed Teeweeyownah, Espowyes, and another man as they slipped around the southern flank of the enemy. They tied their horses among junipers and crept up the ridge. The cavalry mounts were held by troopers in three different sections in the timber. When Seton got in position, he saw that the horse holders were coming under fire from the north. Teeweeyownah and Espowyes started firing, and then a bugler mounted and began to sound retreat. He was shot from the saddle.

The distance to the horses of the first company, partly hidden by junipers and brush, was about five hundred yards. Seton heard the rifles of his companions as they crawled closer to the soldiers. He fired a few shots when troopers began to leave the ridge. One company, then another, pulled away. When the men were mounting up in frenzied haste, Seton fired rapidly into the packed ranks before they got away. In the east the sun climbed over the mountain wall.

The third company, the one farthest north, did not run. It withdrew to the shelter of a small basin with timber around it. There the troopers built rifle pits from chunks of lava and dug in. Surrounded by Nez Perce marksmen, some were killed and wounded. Still they held on in a firefight lasting twenty minutes. Then, one by one, the warriors left. Two warriors, Wottolen and Peopeo Tholekt, were slightly wounded in the exchange. Seton did not see this fight from close by.

There was no celebration in the Nez Perce camp when the men returned. The sorrow over the losses from the Big Hole was still too great, too fresh. But there was happiness that everyone had come back, and satisfaction that Cut Arm had lost his pack train of over two hundred mules. Scouts reported that on this and the following day the general's camp remained where it was. In the afternoon following the skirmish, three wagons filled with dead and wounded left the camp on the road to Monida Pass. They were escorted by the company of civilians. Buffalo Horn and his Bannocks had quit the general's service and gone home. The Nez Perce stayed on Willow Creek for another day, moving out to Henrys Lake on August 22.

Seton had been in his second real fight, a boy among men who knew war. He didn't think he had done anything worthwhile, although his companions and the people of his wi-ses thought otherwise. During the night after the fight, he woke up when he heard wolves call from the high range to the north. They were either calling for someone, he thought, or Hemene was sending a greeting.

E I G H T E E N

THE NEZ PERCE COLUMN REACHED HENRYS LAKE
in late afternoon after a march of twenty miles. They camped on the
southwestern shore, and the herds spread out to the west, south, and
southeast. The lake, a blue jewel, lay in a small valley open to the south,
with grassy ridges and thick forests along the shores. On three sides
beyond rose the mountains of the Continental Divide, their peaks
reaching over ten thousand feet and revealing shiny snowfields when
clouds wandered elsewhere. The waters of the lake were dotted with
little green floating islands of dead trees and debris on which grew
plants and shrubs and small trees. They made good nesting places for
pelicans, trumpeter swans, cranes, geese, and ducks. These hosts rose
and swirled and circled above the lake and dropped to the surface again,
filling the sky with color, the sounds of countless wings, and discor-
dant voices. Soon the birds would be leaving for the south. Nights

had become freezing cold in late August, and ice was gathering among rocks on the shoreline.

A rough wagon road led from the valley east to Targhee Pass, an opening in the mountains 7,072 feet high, and into Yellowstone Park beyond. The road had been started by miners in the 1860s but had fallen into disuse. After 1872, when Yellowstone was declared a national park, it became an access route for the first tourists to visit geyserland from Montana and Idaho.

As much as the Nez Perces wished to linger at Henrys Lake, they knew they had to move on. At first light, Lean Elk sent a crier through the camps to make the people ready. When the advance guard ahead of the herds took the wagon road to Targhee Pass, White Thunder's scouting party was already miles away.

They were the same five who had reconnoitered the Lemhi Valley and discovered General Howard's command closing in. A northern branch of the road ran south from Montana. At the spot where the two branches met and the slow climb to the pass began, the scouting party found the tracks of two wagons and hoofprints of a dozen horses, going up.

White Thunder dismounted and walked along the tracks. The others sat their horses. White Thunder knelt and felt the tracks with his fingers, probing the earth around the depressions cut by horseshoes. The earth was loose and crumbled between his fingers.

"Soldiers?" Kowtoliks asked.

White Thunder shook his head. "I don't think so. Maybe civilians come to see the clouds thrown up by the hot springs."

"They came from Montana Territory," Tababo said. "Whoever they are." He looked at White Thunder. "How long ago?"

"Ten suns, maybe more."

"How many people?" Seton asked.

"One buggy—see the narrow wheels? One wagon. Maybe seven or eight horses ridden." He stood, head bent, thinking. "Ten to twelve people. Maybe a few more." He mounted and they rode on, following the tracks in single file. They came into a mixed forest of yellowing aspens and ponderosa pines. Tall grasses on open glades and along the trail showed the hues of fall, red through brown to yellow. Spider webs hung between tree branches, their threads spun silver in the early sunlight. On exposed wet stretches of dark soil, partly covered by the recent wagon ruts and horse tracks, and superimposed over them, were prints of deer and elk and wolf and bear. They rode on in silence, watching, and crossed the Continental Divide a third time since leaving Weippe Prairie. The road, a narrow trail, was overgrown with grasses and herbs and low shrubs. In places the unknown travelers had cleared it of fallen trees and dead branches to get the wagons through. Behind the summit the road went down, hugging the side of the mountain, and then spiraled up again into a tumble of hills.

About twenty-five miles east of Henrys Lake, they came across a campsite where the strangers had spent a night. They saw where the horses had been tied up on a meadow and where the buggy and wagon had been parked under the pines. There was one fireplace and a spot where a tent had sat. From slight depressions still visible in the grass, White Thunder confirmed that the party consisted of about ten people. Walking the site, he found an earring in the grass next to where a tent wall had been. He bounced the earring in his hand, a tiny golden clasp with a blue stone pendant. He held it up for all to see.

"There must be a woman with this outfit," he said.

"They aren't soldiers then," Tababo said.

They mounted again and rode on. A few more miles and they came into the valley of the Madison River. This was in early afternoon. They rested by the river, ate dry food, and let the horses graze. They had seen elk and deer but of humans only the empty tracks they were following. After an hour they saddled up again and went on, following the river upstream toward Madison Junction where the Firehole River, coming from the south, ran into the Madison.

For Seton, it was his first time in the park. On 1870s journeys to the Plains, Lamtama and Pekonan bands had preferred a more northern route. The last time he and his mother had been in the northern Plains with a joint Lamtama-Pekonan camp was from 1872 until 1874. Of the five men in their party, only White Thunder and Tababo had traveled through the park before. As on the ride through the Lemhi and Birch Creek valleys, Seton's gaze swept all around, trying to see everything, trying to make himself remember it.

As they neared Madison Junction, they saw buffalo, a herd of about two hundred animals, grazing on a fine prairie behind the east bank of the Firehole River with its edge of dark, serious-looking Douglas firs. The wagon tracks crossed the river near its mouth and turned south. The buffalo herd was unimpressed, barely taking notice of the intruders as the party forded the river and took the rough trail through dense timber on high ground east of Firehole Canyon. The warriors came down to the edge of the Lower Geyser Basin where Nez Perce Creek comes in from the east. The tracks they followed had passed through the creek and continued into the basin. The warriors halted to watch a male grizzly walk unhurriedly through the upper part of the basin toward Buffalo Spring. The sinking sun laid a golden glow over the steam columns rising from the many geysers dotting an area three miles in length and width.

"We camp here for the night," White Thunder said. "Tomorrow we follow the suyapu trail." They watered the horses and made camp in a bend of the creek. They staked their horses. Only after dark did they see what the geysers had concealed from them: a distant tiny, glimmering dot in the quiet dark. White Thunder saw it first.

"Look." he said. "Look that way."

"A fire burning," Seton said.

"Yes," White Thunder said. "It may be the suyapu we are after. Or soldiers. We will go to see who they are."

"We better not go now," Tababo said. "It is a swampy place. Our horses might get mired down. It's too late now. We cannot see."

White Thunder thought for a moment. "Yes. We will stay here till morning. Then we will have a fight with them." Everyone agreed. They spent a cold night wrapped in robes and blankets. At first light White Thunder woke everyone. The men washed themselves in the creek, watered the horses, and saddled up. They stripped for battle. White

Thunder and Tababo painted their faces. White Thunder and Seton slipped war whistles over their heads. The two had been in the Camas Meadows raid; the other three had not. They rode off with rifles held in their right hands, butts resting on their thighs.

They rode slowly, concerned not to make much sound. They had marked the location where the fire had burned and found the campsite. First they saw the horses grazing among trees, then a buggy and the wagon, and finally a white, rectangular tent. The fire had died. Four white men lay close to the ashes, covered with blankets, still asleep. Three more slept a dozen feet away under the low branches of a fir. A small white tent stood on the east side with a closed door flap. The men of the scouting party stopped yards from the camp.

"What do we do with them?" Kowtoliks whispered.

"We kill them," White Thunder said. "They are not soldiers, but they are our enemies. If we let them live, they will tell the soldiers about us."

"We should capture them and take them to the chiefs," Tababo whispered. "Let the chiefs say what will be done." White Thunder thought for a moment. "If they put up a fight, we kill them. If they don't—let's see."

He edged his horse forward. Behind him the others fanned out. Seton was on the left, Swan Necklace on the right. Tababo and Kowtoliks stayed behind the leader. They rode up to the camp and paused. White Thunder and Tababo dismounted. They walked to the fireplace. One of the white men awoke and sat up. It took him a moment to become aware of the two warriors in front of him, their painted faces, pointed rifles. He made a low sound, surprise, fear. One by one the other white men woke and realized that something was wrong. They tossed their blankets aside and stared at the warriors. Some glanced at their weapons lying close by. But they saw Seton's and Swan Necklace's rifles trained on them and did not move. One of them got up slowly and walked toward White Thunder and Tababo. "Who is your leader?" he asked.

Tababo pointed with his chin to White Thunder. The man reached out with his right hand. White Thunder took it and shook hands with him. The man shook hands with Tababo also. He looked at White Thunder. "Why have you come here?"

Tababo translated. He looked to Seton, who only shook his head. He did not want to talk with the suyapu.

"Numipu," White Thunder said. It was the whole explanation.

"I heard something about you," the man said. "Are the Nez Perces coming through here?"

White Thunder waited for Tababo to translate. He nodded as an answer and glared into the white man's eyes.

"Will you kill us?"

"Many of the warriors are angry," Tababo translated for White Thunder.

"Can we see Chief Joseph? Will you take us to him?" The man was clearly troubled.

"Yes," White Thunder said. "But some warriors are bad. They might kill you."

The man inhaled deeply. He looked toward the other men who sat silently on the ground. "Will the chiefs do anything to us?" he asked finally.

"I think not," White Thunder said.

"All right," the man said. "We want to see Chief Joseph. We will go."

Kowtoliks dismounted and went with Tababo to collect the white men's rifles and side arms. With Seton's and Swan Necklace's rifles still covering them, the men got up slowly. White Thunder went to the tent and threw the door flap open. A tall white man stood there, pale as a bone. The warrior pointed with the muzzle of the gun and the man stepped out and joined the other prisoners. The one who had shaken hands with the two warriors seemed to be the leader of the tourists. He called out to break camp, saddle the horses, and harness the horse teams. Some disparaging remarks were made by the whites under their breaths. Seton caught them but said nothing. The white man called toward the brush behind the tent until a young woman and a teenage girl, both in long dresses, came out of hiding. Their faces were ashen, but they did not cry. White Thunder nodded to them, trying to make his face friendly. But they saw only the paint, the rifle, and the body naked to the breechclout. He pointed toward the wagons, and they walked there quickly.

The whites took the tent down and piled bedrolls and equipment into the wagon. Kowtoliks and Tababo put the captured weapons in the buggy, a light, one-horse carriage with four wheels. Tababo tied his horse to the rear board of the buggy and took the driver's seat. The two women and one of the men sat on the wagon seat; the other seven prisoners rode horseback. Tababo called to the horse pulling the buggy and slapped the reins on its back, and they started on the trail back. White Thunder rode next to the buggy. Behind came the wagon, drawn by two draft horses, and the mounted prisoners. Seton, Swan Necklace, and Kowtoliks brought up the rear, rifle butts sitting on their thighs.

The first slanted rays of the sun fell on the basin when their little caravan passed the steamy Fountain Geyser and the Fountain Paintpot. They went by a small lake, and, when they neared the splendor of the Morning Mist Springs, they saw the advance guard of their people and the herds streaming out of the dense timber east of the Firehole and dropping into the valley of Nez Perce Creek. White Thunder signaled a halt. Wide-eyed, the prisoners stared at two miles of horseflesh. When White Thunder rode on, everyone followed, and by the creek the warriors around Lean Elk splashed through the water and surrounded the scouts and their prisoners. White Thunder searched for Lean Elk. "We brought these suyapu," he said. "They are scared. They want to see Chief Joseph." He shrugged. "We didn't know what to do with them."

Lean Elk saw some of the warriors fondle the prisoners' weapons in the buggy. "Leave them," he called. "The chiefs will give them away." He turned to White Thunder. "It is good you caught them!" He touched the scout leader's shoulder and paused.

"We are going up the trail to Mary Lake and into the valley by the big river. We camp tonight in that round basin by Mud Volcano."

He paused again. "I want you to go ahead and scout the trail for us."

White Thunder nodded. He backed his horse out of the throng
of warriors and signaled to the other men of his party. Tababo climbed
out of the buggy, untied his horse, and mounted. They bunched up and
rode off, taking the Mary Mountain trail up to the Central Plateau.

When they were half a mile away they heard a couple of shots
behind them. "They are killing the prisoners," Seton said to Swan
Necklace. His friend shrugged. They crossed the Central Plateau with-
out seeing any evidence of people. In early afternoon, they came into
Hayden Valley and the basin near the Yellowstone River, the place
Lean Elk had designated as the camping place.

Three hours later the bands and the herds arrived. Only three of
the tourists were still with them, under the protection of Lone Elk and
women of the Wallowa band. They were the woman, her teenage sister, and their brother. They called themselves by the name Carpenter.

Seton had one more night with his family. They enjoyed the meat of
buffaloes killed the evening before when the bands had camped at Madison Junction. He was asked how they had captured the tourists and
told the story. Next morning the bands crossed the Yellowstone River
at the Buffalo Ford. It was a crossing made easy by three islands in the
stream.

While the herds were fording the river, three scouting parties left
the camp. They were led by Kosooyeen, Lakochets Kunnin, and White
Thunder. Kosooyeen's party went downstream on the west bank of the
Yellowstone. Lakochets Kunnin's party went over the back trail. White
Thunder and the four with him were to explore the Wabash Range and
the upper Gibbon and Gardiner rivers toward Mammoth Hot Springs
and the northern entrance to the park. The three parties had been
informed by Lean Elk that the bands would march up Pelican Creek to
the Lamar River, follow it to Cache Creek, move up Cache Creek to
the watershed in the Absaroka Mountains, and cross into Clarks Canyon. The three scouting groups were to join the bands on the route to

Clarks Fork if there was no reason to come in earlier.

White Thunder and the companions aimed northwest toward Trout Creek, a beautiful little stream meandering through green meadows below a low bench. They rode at a walk in a loose group, preserving the horses' strength. Seton had taken the gray mare for this journey. They crossed the creek and rode on through the vast prairie of Hayden Valley, crowned on higher elevations with dark spruce-fir forests and stands of yellow-leafed aspens. As they neared Atum Creek they heard gun reports from the direction of Sulphur Mountain to the northeast. They knew that a white man had been captured the day before and had said that a tourist party from Helena, ten men including a black cook, were camped by the Sulphur Springs. The men around White Thunder halted and listened. There were no more shots.

"Kosooyeen found the suyapu we heard about," White Thunder said. They rode on and crossed Atum Creek and once more climbed to the Central Plateau. They moved on game trails through the dense forest, saw some elk and other animals but nothing else. They shot an elk cow for food and built a good fire in a mountain grove in the evening. During the night they heard the familiar calls of a wolf pack to the west, and before morning it started to rain. It rained almost all day, but stopped when they made their second night camp not far from the Virginia Cascade on the Gibbon River. On the third day they found two cabins in the Norris Geyser Basin, both empty. In hopes of deceiving possible watchers, to lead them on the wrong track, they burned them, making sure that smoke rolled thick and black so it could be seen a long way.

That night they camped by Whiterock Springs, while moose fed in the marsh to the south and a buffalo herd on grassy slopes to the east. While they were getting ready in the morning of the fourth day, a grizzly mother with two spring cubs walked by the camp. The bears took a short look standing upright, then loped off, the youngsters tumbling after their mother.

The men saw nothing but sky and grass and mountains and forests of green and flaming aspens, and an occasional herd of elk or antelope on this day and the next. They went by Obsidian Cliff, the hill of black glass, and into the valley of the Gardiner River, where they burned another cabin and a pole corral. They went past Sheepeater Cliffs and Osprey Falls and finally, on September 1, they came upon a site where they found a white man. This was at the rough-and-tumble log hotel near Liberty Cap at Mammoth Springs. A single white man stood in the open door of the hotel, looking out at the approaching scouting party. Two more white men had already run and hidden themselves in the brush behind the hotel, though the scouts didn't know it.

They rode up and sat their horses in a line. The white man didn't move. Swan Necklace said to the others, "My two cousins and my younger sister were killed in the Big Hole by men like this one." He pointed with his chin at the unsuspecting young man standing in the door. "It is just like this man killed my cousins and my sister. He is a killer who will become a soldier sometime. I am going to shoot him. When I fire, you shoot after me."

He quickly brought up his Winchester and fired. The bullet clipped the man's arm and, as he turned to step back, Kowtoliks shot him through the belly. The man collapsed to the ground, groaning, and White Thunder rode close and shot him again. The man jerked once and lay still. They rode north from there, for four miles until they came to the Yellowstone River and made camp as the sun was going down.

On the next day they followed the Yellowstone out of the park through the north entrance and, after a ten-mile ride, came to Henderson's ranch. White Thunder had seen it on an earlier visit. While Seton and Swan Necklace covered the cabin with their rifles, White Thunder and Tababo went in. It was empty. It seemed that the people who lived there had left in a hurry. The warriors set fire to the cabin and went to the pole corral behind it. Tababo swung the gate open, and Kowtoliks rode in and drove out nineteen horses. Kowtoliks rode drag when Seton and Swan Necklace took the point. It seemed like old times. The others fell in behind, and they rode upstream on the trail back to Yellowstone Park while the cabin threw billowing smoke into the sky.

They had ridden about a mile when they saw horsemen on a little hill to the right, partly covered by gold-flecked aspens. They went on, urging their horses and the herd into a gallop when they saw the horsemen rode appaloosas. The horsemen came down the hill in a clatter of hooves. They yipped and held their rifles high as they circled White Thunder's party and the captured horses. They were Kosooyeen's group of seven warriors who had ridden north along the Yellowstone. They were still going through their noisy greetings when one of Kosooyeen's men shouted, "Soldiers!"

Both parties milled their horses and looked. A troop of cavalry appeared on the back trail and brought their mounts to a halt, startled to find Nez Perces so unexpectedly close. Kosooyeen shouted, and the warriors with him charged. The cavalry turned and galloped away. Seton and the others of White Thunder's party watched. One of the warriors, Watyahtsakon, closed with a soldier. Both drew their rifles and fired at the same time. The soldier missed, but the warrior did not. The soldier fell from his horse, dead. Watyahtsakon dismounted and took his rifle and ammunition belt. The man's horse raced away. They chased the soldiers into a timbered ravine before giving up.

Later, Kosooyeen's party hung back, covering the back trail while White Thunder and his group, driving the captured horses, went southeast in the direction of the Lamar River. There was no further incident, and both parties spent the night in a marshy basin at the head of Geode Creek. On the following day, Kosooyeen's group took the lead, and they crossed Baronett's toll bridge across the roaring torrent of the Yellowstone. Here, above the mouth of the Lamar, the river ran through a narrow, rocky defile. The wooden bridge, a wagon-width wide, fifty feet above the boiling waters, had only one intermediary support, a pier made with crossed logs. When they had passed over it, Kosooyeen's men set the bridge on fire to make it useless for pursuers.

Now they came into the broad valley of the Lamar River, with long, swinging slopes covered with grasses and shrub and sage, and with pines in draws and ravines. Toward the crests of mountains and on both sides stood white-trunked aspens with golden plumage among dark green pines and spruces. In the center of the valley the river ran blue and swift over its rocky bed. They rode upstream near the river and made camp for the night across from the mouth of Soda Butte Creek. There was a brief scare that evening when a big male grizzly came too close to where the horses were staked out near the river. The horses were beginning to panic when two men went out and shooed the bear away, careful to keep a respectful distance. They did not want to provoke him into a charge and be forced to kill him. Grizzly was not the game they were after.

On the next day they continued upstream on the Lamar to the mouth of Cache Creek and went in and up on the trail the bands and the herds had cut three days before them. Finally they were getting back to their people. The trail was narrow along the winding creek, steep slopes on both sides reaching to the nine-thousand-foot level. Now they were climbing toward the watershed, the divide of the Absaroka Range. They made poor time, mostly walking the horses along the face of mountains on the same trail on which the youthful herders of their bands had driven thousands of horses ahead of them. Two of the captured horses fell and died on the rocks below. There were other horse carcasses down there. They made night camp in a glade by the creek below the Thunderer, a mountain peak over ten thousand feet high and three miles long, southwest to northeast, capped with snow.

In the afternoon of the following day, at the end of a rain shower mixed with snow, they came up on the camps of their bands on the divide.

NINETEEN

THE CAMPS WERE SPREAD NEAR THE TOP OF THE divide of the Absaroka Range, a ridge a quarter of a mile wide. The ridge itself trended generally from north to south, in height ranging from 9,800 to 10,200 feet. Stretches of the ridge not covered with snow were blanketed with mountain meadows of grasses and lichens, with dwarf whitebark pines and rustling stands of aspens. On the western flank of the divide originated the headwaters of all creeks that ran into the Yellowstone Basin and the river—Soda Butte, Cache, and Miller creeks, and the Little Lamar River.

On the eastern flank of the divide lay the headwaters of all creeks that ran into Clarks Fork of the Yellowstone. These were, from north to south, Republic, Pilot, Crandall, Hoodo, and Sunlight creeks. South of these lay the headwaters of the North Fork of the Shoshone River, called the Stinking Water by Indian travelers. There were two trails leading from the divide east into the Plains, the Clarks Fork trail and the Stinking Water trail. The first of these angled northeast and reached the Yellowstone River after eighty-five miles. The second angled east toward the Bighorn River and the Bighorn Mountains.

The Nez Perce camps and the herds were located above the headwaters of Cache Creek, with access to Clarks Fork through the narrow gap of Pilot Creek. In this location they were six miles away from Clarks Fork as the raven flies. From there, and after passing a forbidding canyon, they could travel on an easy route toward the Yellowstone and the northern Plains.

Seton halted the gray when they neared the camps. He let the captured horses and Kowtoliks ride by and spoke to White Thunder as he passed. "I don't want any of the horses. Do with them as you want." White Thunder nodded and raised his right hand. Seton went to look for his wi-ses. He rode through a segment of the herds, the horses feeding on the thin grass between rocks and snowfields and wind-bent evergreens or standing still, with heads drooping. There was no good water on the ridge but for some puddles and the snow. It was enough for the people and the horses. A wind gusted from the west and campfires burned below the crest on the east side. The sparse firewood, wet from rains, caused much smoke that was blown around by the wind as it swept over the ridge. These fires were unpleasant, and most camps gave up on them.

The first person of the wi-ses Seton saw was Atemis. He stood on the ridge, looking at the sweep of land to the east, the backs of mountains upon mountains gradually sinking away to the High Plains. The eyes could lose themselves in the view from this aerie. He turned slowly when Seton dismounted behind him, his eyes still filled with the vision of the horizon. It took a moment for him to recognize Seton. Slowly a broad grin stole over his face. "You are back," he said.

The two slapped each other on the shoulder. Atemis looked older than his sixteen years. His face showed a few hard lines Seton had not known before. His hair, cut short after the deaths in the wi-ses, was matted and disheveled. With the responsibility for the Lamtama herd thrust upon him, the task of overseeing drovers younger than himself showed on him. His eyes had become hard, but now they smiled.

"You look different from when I saw you last," he said, glancing over Seton's trim body and serious face. Seton's coyote claw necklace hung below his throat. His braids were tussled and his moccasins barely held together. His leggings and leather shirt showed intense wear from a long ride. "So do you," Seton said, his face breaking into a smile.

Atemis shrugged. "Come. Let's see what they have made for food." They walked through about thirty wi-ses saddle and packhorses tethered on the ridge. Seton slung the reins of the gray around the branch of a stunted fir. He noticed that his roan mare was among the horses. Below them was a fireplace, partly sheltered by a clump of crippled pines. Its smoke was shredded by the wind. "Why have fires?" Seton asked incredulously. "This smoke can be seen a long way. Why tell everyone where we are?"

"They already know where we are," Atemis said. "We are still here because two armies of horse soldiers are down there, waiting for us."

Seton grunted angrily. "Where did they come from? It can't be Cut Arm. He is way back there." He pointed west.

"I don't know," Atemis said. "Ask my uncle. He knows." Seton understood that he meant Teeweeyownah.

Talooth was working on the fireplace, trying to keep the fire going. Itsepit and Tannish roasted elk meat on wooden spits. The remaining people of the wi-ses were huddled a little higher up, away from the smoke. Seton was greeted with nods and raised hands. Teeweeyownah, who sat with his brother and Dawn, pointed to the place next to him. Allultakanin moved a little, and Seton sat down between the brothers. He looked around. The adults of the wi-ses and four children, one to three years old, were present but not the older ones. When he looked to Dawn, she seemed to know whom he was searching for. "Tsacope and Ilsoo are in that camp over there, playing," she said, pointing with her chin.

For the first time Seton noticed that the appearance of the people had changed. They had changed as much as he had himself. They were marked by the distress of losing their homelands, deaths, constant danger, worry about the future, and the demands of ceaseless traveling—often through the most difficult terrain. Their spirit had not died, but many faces looked weary, haggard, grim. Hardship had always been part of numipu life, but the hardships of this journey into the unknown were beyond the memory of numipu oral tradition. Their clothing was ragged. There were not enough hides to replace torn or frayed clothing. There were just enough for moccasins so people did not have to go barefoot.

Teeweeyownah touched his arm, and when Seton turned to him, he counted fourteen .44-40 Winchester cartridges into his hand. "Your share of the ammunition we took from those tourists your party captured," he said. When Seton put them into a pouch attached to his cartridge belt, Teeweeyownah said, "Now tell us what you learned on your scout with White Thunder."

Seton began to speak, but Tamonmo called out, with Magpie, her baby, on her arm. "Louder, we can't hear."

Seton did as she asked. Their faces were on him. They listened intently. A few times he was interrupted for more details. There was a murmur of satisfaction when he ended. Even a flicker of joy that the men had all come back unscathed. There was a pause, and then Seton asked, "What is happening here?

Teeweeyownah shook his head. "Nothing good," he said curtly. After a pause he explained.

"Horse soldiers are waiting for us on both trails. Bad Grizzly Bear Boy and his brother, Tepsus, scouted the Stinking Water trail. They saw a soldier camp. They killed three of the soldiers' scouts, two suyapu and a Crow. One of the suyapu said, before he died, that the chief of the soldiers was a Colonel Merritt." He paused.

"Seeyakoon Ilppilp went over the other trail. He saw a soldier camp at the opening of the canyon on Clarks Fork. He did not get close. He saw it from a distance. He saw it through the spyglasses he took from that suyapu scout he killed close to our camp on aipadass."

Seton remembered the incident. On the morning after the bands had crossed the Salmon, Seeyakoon had ridden into camp singing the victory song of a warrior who had just killed an enemy.

"He saw Crow scouts in the soldier camp," Teeweeyownah said. There was a pause. "What are we going to do?" Seton asked.

"We wait. But we can't wait long."

"Where are the most soldiers?" Seton asked. "On the Stinking Water or by the canyon?"

"By the canyon," Teeweeyownah said. "I know what you are thinking. We can beat those soldiers on the Stinking Water, but we don't want to take that trail. It goes too far east."

Allultakanin joined in. "Bad Grizzly Bear Boy told us there is a new soldier fort on the Yellowstone by the Tongue River. They built it last year, after the Lakotas wiped out that general and most of his horse soldiers. Custer, the one with the baby hair. Bad Grizzly Bear Boy and Tepsus were scouts for the new general who lives at that fort. It is called Keogh. The general's name is Miles." He laughed. "The Lakotas and Cheyennes call him Bear Coat. He is a dresser they say."

He paused. "The Stinking Water trail brings us too close to Fort Keogh."

There was a silence. Seton glanced at the faces before him. They were somber, bitter, but unyielding. They sat for a while, no one speaking. Then Itsepit and Tannish brought food from the fireplace and they all ate. They did not pay much attention to the elk meat. They were still thinking about the enemies waiting below.

They let the fire die. Once Seton asked Atemis about the Lamtama herd, how the horses were taking the misery of the trail. "We lost quite a few," Atemis said morosely. "We hurry them too much." Everyone agreed, but nothing could be done about it. The camps spent another freezing night on the divide. At least the rain and snow slurry had ended.

For three day the camps remained where they were, uncertain what they should do. Then Bad Grizzly Bear Boy and Tepsus brought miraculous news: the horse soldiers on the Stinking Water were gone. Perhaps they had waited for too long. In vain. Perhaps the loss of their scouts severed their communication with the other command on Clarks Fork.

Perhaps they had exhausted their supplies and were in the dark about where their prey was. Whatever, their chief had called off the operation. All these things might have played a role, but there had also been something from the spirits. Tiwét in the camps had gone through a ritual asking wéyekin spirit powers to drive the soldiers on the Stinking Water away. The soldiers were gone.

The bands sprang into action. Their plan was to draw the soldiers on Clarks Fork away from there to the open Stinking Water trail. Bands and herds were started south along the divide toward the Stinking Water. The going was rough and slow, passing over rock-strewn, snow-covered heights and through thick, pathless timber. They were not hiding their move. They let it be seen. Outlined against the sky above the summit, their seemingly endless column could be spotted from far away. While they went slowly, sparing the horses and themselves, Seeyakoon reported that the army, identified as the Seventh Cavalry, had broken camp and was making its way to the Stinking Water, a detour of ninety miles. The ruse had worked. Lean Elk and the chiefs waited until September 9, when the six companies of the Seventh were committed to the Stinking Water trail and had camped only fifteen miles below the Nez Perces.

At first light the next morning the bands covered their trail by milling the horses back and forth over it. Then they doubled back to the north and, after five miles, turned east toward Dead Indian Peak, 12,253 feet high. They had ten more miles of extreme terrain, which carried them close to the peak of the mountain, then they descended into Dead Indian Creek and from there down to Dead Indian Pass and Clarks Fork Canyon. But the only dead Indian claimed by the Nez Perce trek through the Absaroka Range was the Crow scout killed by Bad Grizzly Bear Boy and Tepsus.

The bands spent a rough night on the trail between Dead Indian Creek and Dead Indian Pass. There was water in the creek but hardly any fodder for the horses. The descent into the canyon started at sunrise on the following morning. Seeyakoon, who had been over the trail three times during the past days, went first with a scouting party to explore the valley of Clarks Fork beyond the canyon to the Yellowstone. Behind came the advance guard led by Lean Elk and Ollokot. The band chiefs, Joseph, White Goose, Toohoolhoolzote, Looking Glass, and Naked Head, went with the families. They left before the herds. The leaders of the rear guard were Teeweeyownah and Wottolen.

White Thunder and the companions stayed behind to watch over the back trail. They left before the last of the herds and the rear guard disappeared into the canyon. They went back over the trail for about five miles to a point on the high shoulder of Dead Indian Peak, just below the snowline. From there they could watch the spot on the divide where the bands had turned toward Clarks Fork a day before. If the soldiers were following, they would become visible there first.

The view from the peak under a clear sky was tremendous in all directions but west. They could see Heart Mountain to the southeast, already in the Plains, yellow in fall grass. To the north lay the snow-covered summits of the Beartooth Mountains and the Granite Range, nearly thirteen thousand feet high. To the northeast lay the Pryor Mountains, surrounded by grasslands that touched the horizon. Almost straight north, the valley of Clarks Fork meandered toward its meeting with the Yellowstone, the river a shiny ribbon between yellow-leafed cottonwoods and low hills decked out in yellow grass. For a long time Seton stared into the blue vision of the Plains.

They sat in a half circle facing the divide while the horses behind them nibbled on sparse, wet grass between the rocks. They talked and fell silent and talked a little more. It was midafternoon when Kowto-liks got up and pointed with his arm. "There! They are coming." They stood and looked. Five miles away they saw a trickle of movement in pale colors spilling over the divide, horses brown and soldiers blue. "It took them a long time to get there," White Thunder said with contempt in his voice. "Let's ride."

They mounted and took the trail east. They reached Dead Indian Creek and the pass and went down into the canyon. The top of the pass was on the eight-thousand-foot level, the bottom of the canyon four

thousand feet lower. The trail was a little more than a mile long, dropping close to a thousand feet in a quarter mile. For some distance the
trail hugged sheer cliffs and was so narrow that horses could walk only
in single file. A fall meant certain death on rocks a thousand feet or more
below. Over this perilous pathway the bands, with young and old and
packhorses and the herds, had gone. A few times Seton saw horses' shattered bodies far below. Progress was slow. It took the men some time
before they reached the canyon floor. Blue and fast the river snaked
through sandbars and rocky outcrops and low, yellow slopes below the
curving, towering canyon walls dotted with green stunted pines.

After the restriction and the menace of the trail, the horses ran
eagerly. The men let them. They felt the same. They ran down eight
miles of canyon floor, splashing a couple of times through the river to
shorten the distance, until they came to where the canyon walls converged. At its mouth the nearly perpendicular walls were not more than
twenty feet apart, a veritable slit in the rock. The egress had been made
by the river. Plunging for eons over a waterfall, the river had worn
away the precipice. In this tight space the floor was filled with a jumble
of rocks. They went through carefully, avoiding injury to their horses'
hooves, pasterns, and cannons, and came out into sunlight and the broad
river valley. Seton looked back, trying to remember everything.

They rode north through the flats along the river and came upon
their camp a dozen miles beyond the canyon's mouth. A few miles
before they reached it, they saw the bodies of four white men. They had
been shot because they were suspected of being scouts for one army or
another. Horses and weapons had been taken, but the dead were neither
scalped nor stripped. Numipu did not believe in scalping. From prisoners they learned later that General Howard's Bannock Indians and some
of the white civilian volunteers dug up numipu burials in the Big Hole
and on the trail and scalped the bodies of men, women, and children.

The chiefs were not surprised when White Thunder and the men
reported. "I'm glad those soldiers are behind us and not in front of
us," Lean Elk said. He sat on a rock by the river, upper torso naked,
leather shirt on his knees. A woman of his band was dressing a partly healed entrance wound in his right chest and a larger, jagged exit

wound in his back. She had rubbed a salve into both wounds. Seton
had not seen them before, though Lean Elk was shot during the Big
Hole fighting. Hemene had died from such wounds. Chiefs Ollokot
and Joseph sat with Lean Elk, who nodded to the woman and waved
her off. He slipped the shirt over his head. "They're not going into the
canyon today," he said. "Maybe they won't at all. Maybe they will try
to get around it." He grinned.

"We have to move fast," Joseph said. "It is going to be hard on the
people and the horses. They have suffered a lot." There was a pause.

"We don't have to hurry too much," Ollokot said. "These soldiers—they are no danger to us. We'll keep them away if they get too
close."

He nodded to the scouts. "You watch out for us. Keep track of
those horse soldiers." His dark eyes went from face to face. Ollokot
was still a young man, but Seton felt the power in his eyes and in his
bearing, quiet, indomitable. Joseph's eyes were on the companions, too,
dark as his brother's, shaded, perhaps worried, but also unwavering.
After all, they came from the same father, and though they had accepted different obligations, they saw things the same.

The scouts rode off, and Seton went thoughtfully to his wi-ses
camp. He had to tell them about the bluecoats. One of the packhorses
had fallen to its death, but nothing bad had happened to the people.
He looked at Itsepit and Tsacope and his heart filled. He would defend
them if it cost his life.

The demands of the evening camp were more mundane. Horses
had to be watered and fed, equipment had to be repaired, rifles cleaned.
They talked around the fire until the moon came up, happy that they
had cleared the canyon and left the cavalry behind. They spent a still
night by the whispering river, and by first light the camps packed up
and moved on. The people and the horses made a column three miles
long. They carried with them their memories, their sorrow, and a love
for what they had left behind in the mountains—*alayntsix,* their land,
the land Old Man Coyote had given to them in the misty past.

White Thunder's party stayed behind. About a dozen lame horses
were left on the campground, sad and forlorn. When the bands and

the herds had disappeared, the scouts saddled up and followed slowly. They kept about fifteen miles back, taking their time. The valley was an open grassland of mixed wheatgrass and bluegrass, sprinkled with sagebrush and an occasional dwarf shrub. Mighty golden-leafed cottonwoods were strung along the riverbanks. Bluffs on both sides were cut by ravines and coulees. The creeks that ran down from them had dried except for a few alkaline puddles. Stagnant rainwater had collected in some buffalo wallows. The scouts passed a couple of prairie dog towns and saw antelopes but no buffaloes. It was an uneventful day, and they made a cold camp in a draw by the river in the shelter of ancient cottonwoods.

At first light in the morning, White Thunder, Tababo, Seton, and Swan Necklace took a bath in the river. They were splashing in the icy water when Kowtoliks, who had stayed with the horses, called softly. He made urgent signs, and when the men rushed to him, they saw it. A tiny red dot in the south. A fire. They dressed and made the horses ready in a hurry. They rode off and fanned out, rifles ready. They rode at a walk. The fire was a little less than a mile away, a thin curl of smoke rising in the dime light. Two horses were tethered behind a small fire, already saddled. When the companions were two hundred yards away, two men by the fireplace saw them and ran for the horses. A tall white man in buckskin pulled the reins up and jumped into the saddle. Behind him came a small white man wearing a soldier's blue jacket.

The companions urged their horses into a gallop and closed quickly. Shots rang out. Seton and Tababo had fired at the tall man, and he fell to the ground as his horse ran on. White Thunder was a horse-length behind when the small white man jumped to the ground. The horse knocked him over. White Thunder passed, pulled his horse up, and slid from the saddle as the man regained his feet. Both raised their rifles and fired at the same time. White Thunder seemed to have missed. The white man's bullet grazed White Thunder's head on the right side and knocked him to his knees. The white man feverishly worked the lever of his rifle until Swan Necklace rode up and killed him. Then they saw why the man's gun wouldn't work. White Thunder's bullet had knocked the hammer off.

White Thunder got up slowly, the hair behind his right temple dripping with blood. "It's nothing," he said, as the men dismounted and stood around him. "A good scar." He was dazed but managed a dismissive grin.

They stood and looked at the small white man, the one who had put up a fight. Swan Necklace's bullet had gone through his throat. "This one is alive," Tababo called. The men walked back to where the man in buckskin lay in the grass. He was on his stomach, groaning. A trickle of blood ran from his lips. He had two bullet wounds, one in his left hip, one in his back high up on the right side.

Seton bent and turned him over. He was in his midforties with a tanned face and the stubble of a beard. One of the bullets had been Seton's, the high one. There were two bad exit wounds in front. Blood seeped through holes in the buckskin. He could almost be my father, Seton thought. The man looked at the dark faces above him with wide, fearful eyes. Perhaps he expected to be tortured, that unspeakable things would be done to him. Seton thought he knew what the man feared. He slowly shook his head.

"Let's kill him," Kowtoliks said.

"No," Seton said. "He'll die anyway." White Thunder nodded. He pressed his right hand against the bloody furrow on the side of his head. "He knows things we don't," Seton said. He went to the dead man's horse, untied the cinch, and plucked the saddle off. He carried it to the wounded man and raised his head and placed the saddle under it. The man's eyes followed him when he stepped back.

"You are a scout?" Seton asked in English.

The man nodded.

"For whom, what officer?"

"Colonel Sturgis."

"What post is he from?"

"Fort Keogh."

"How many men are with him?"

The man coughed. More blood oozed from the corner of his mouth. "He has six companies of the Seventh and two companies of the First Cavalry." He spoke with difficulty. "He has two mountain howitzers on pack mules." He coughed again, wiping his mouth with his right hand. "He has a mule train."

Seton translated for his companions. They stood and listened. "How far away are they?" White Thunder asked.

Seton translated the question. "They will try to get through the canyon today," the man said.

The warriors looked at each other. "They won't catch the camp," Tababo said. "By the time the soldiers come to this place our people will be across the Yellowstone." They carried the wounded man to the river and bedded him down in a hollow close to the water. They put his head on the dead man's saddle and set his bedroll next to him. They checked the saddlebags and took ammunition and a knife from it, then tethered the dead man's horse close to him and to water. They took his Winchester and his and the dead man's ammunition belts. When they mounted, Seton went to look at him one more time. "Your people will come through here tomorrow. They'll find you." The man nodded. His eyes filled with tears. His lips moved, whispering something. But Seton did not hear it. He joined the others, and they rode off. The dead man lay where he'd fallen, his head in a pool of blood.

They saw antelopes in the flats, and once they saw wolves chase the antelopes. They saw deer in the brush under the cottonwoods and twice saw grizzlies feeding in berry patches on the hillsides. White Thunder's head wound stopped bleeding. They went in a cold rain and saw wolves feeding on one of the lame horses left by the bands. Wet to the bones, they paused to rest under huge cottonwoods by the river. There was good grass for the horses, but the men, sitting with their backs against the knotty bark of the tree trunks felt miserable in the deluge. After some time they moved on and made their night camp eighteen miles below the mouth of Clarks Fork. Once the rains had stopped, they built a fire in a draw after dark to dry themselves.

They awoke to a brilliant clear day, the sun rising as a golden disk into the sky. It was the 13th of September. They awoke to the rasping cries of sandhill cranes as formations flew overhead going south, wave after wave of gray, black-tipped wings. And then came formations of whooping cranes, white and black, filling the sky with trumpet calls. There were also flocks of yellowlegs, of plovers, and waves of geese and ducks. Then, farther east the sky darkened with the packed masses of passenger pigeons, the living wind. It seemed all the world had taken wing.

The men watched silently, awed. "It is a good sign," White Thunder said finally. "It is a happy sign." They saddled up and rode on. Behind them nothing threatened. The evil was far away. Before they came to the Yellowstone River they saw smoke billowing from upstream, where raiding parties had torched two ranches, and from downstream, where they burned the hamlet of Coulson. They rode on and, in early afternoon, came to the river between the bluffs around the mouth of Clarks Fork. Their people had crossed. The tail end of the herds was moving downstream on the north bank. The bands and the bulk of the herds were already gone into the valley of Canyon Creek.

The companions lingered while the last of the herds and the rear guard pulled away into the bluffs. They watched as the overhead flights continued, noisy flocks of white-fronted and Canada geese. Those went by and others came, and once again the V formations of cranes passed, filling the sky with their calls. The men watched until White Thunder kneed his horse forward, and they went down into a dead streambed with pools of stagnant water and went through and over the wet trail the herds had made and to the main channel of the river.

The river was low at that time of year. The water reached only to the forearms of the horses until they came to two depressions where the horses had to swim. The men held on to their necks, swimming alongside, holding their rifles aloft so they did not get wet. They made the north bank, climbed out of the river, and held the horses to tighten cinches. The animals were skittish from swimming with the current and stepped gingerly, but the men laughed and made them move. Instead of following the broad trail along the river, they rode up the bluffs, thinking to cut the distance and join the column in the valley beyond.

It was a lucky decision. Looking back from the top of the bluff, they saw the estuary of Clarks Fork come alive with enemies. Horse

soldiers and Indians poured out of the bluffs and rushed toward the crossing place. The scouts sat their horses, staring in disbelief. "Eeh, Crows
have joined the suyapu," White Thunder said angrily. "Our friends,
the Crows. Looking Glass's friends." They watched as the Crows broke
away and rode upstream to cross farther west.

"How many Crows?" Tababo asked. "Two hundred? Maybe
more?"

"Yes, more," White Thunder said.

"How many soldiers?" Swan Necklace asked.

"Four hundred or more," Seton said. "The white scout we shot
didn't lie about their numbers, but maybe they were closer than he
admitted."

They watched as the first company of cavalry plunged through the
dead streamed and made for the main river channel. Other companies
moved up behind. A mule train came into view. White Thunder turned
to Seton, "Go tell the warriors. Tell Teeweeyownah, Wottolen."

Seton nodded. He backed the gray out of the half circle and moved
it to the side and rode over the crest of the bluff. He rode three miles at a
fast lope until he came to the downward slope and saw the valley below.
The bands and the herds were moving leisurely northwest toward the
canyon through which the creek ran down from the uplands beyond.
The creek bed curved through a slight depression in the valley and was
empty but for a few alkaline pools. Along the creek stood a handful of
weatherworn spruce trees. The valley floor was covered with sage and
short reddish grass. The valley, flat and broad toward its mouth, was
encircled by rimrock cliffs toward the canyon at the northwestern end.

Seton noticed that the bands and the herds were moving side by
side, a column two miles long, and that the head of the column had
entered the canyon. He saw the rear guard to his right, about thirty
warriors, riding in a group a few hundred yards behind the drag riders
of the horse herd. He yelled and galloped down the slope, waving his
rifle over his head to catch their attention. The men halted and formed
a loose half circle when he pulled his horse up before them. He looked
for Teeweeyownah and Wottolen, and they were there.

"Suyapu," he said hastily, pointing behind him. "Horse soldiers. They are now crossing the river."

Teeweeyownah nodded. "Yes," he said. "Yes. Speak clearly. How many?"

Seton brushed sweat from his forehead. "About four hundred. They have two cannons with them."

"Two cannons," one man said with a laugh. "Cut Arm had cannons everywhere he went. This is not Cut Arm, is it?"

"No," Seton said. "The chief of the horse soldiers is a Colonel Sturgis. He came from Fort Keogh." He explained what they had learned from the wounded scout. The men listened in silence. Seton ended by saying, "There are Crows with the soldiers. We thought about two hundred."

"Crows." Wottolen smirked. "Every dog around sides with the suyapu."

"They are crossing the river upstream from the soldiers," Seton said. "We think they might attack from the west while the soldiers attack from the south." Teeweeyownah nodded. He called to one of the men to ride and inform the chiefs, make the bands hurry, drive the horses fast. "Where is White Thunder?" he asked.

Seton pointed behind him. "Up on the bluff. He is watching to find out what the soldiers do."

Teeweeyownah sent a second man after the first to urge the children driving the horses to push them hard toward the canyon. Then he looked to Wottolen and the men around him. "Let's get ready," he said quietly. To Seton he said, "Stay with me." The men spread out and stripped down and prepared for battle. Seton had seen this before the Camas Meadows fight. Most painted their faces, took bone whistles and kopluts from their saddlebags, slipped charms on. Some fastened feathers to their hair. Seton only took the bone whistle out and put it over his head. He checked his rifle. The men fanned out and, widely spaced, formed a skirmish line across the center of the valley. They sat their horses facing southeast, toward the wide mouth of the valley. Seton noticed that behind them the bands and the horses had begun to move faster. There were yells and yipping as the young drovers hurried the stream of horses.

Seton sat his gray on Teeweeyownah's left, about twenty yards distant. They waited. Behind them people and horses drew farther away. They heard a clatter of hooves from the bluff to the south. White Thunder and the companions rode down the slope at a gallop and brought their horses to a halt.

White Thunder raised his right arm. "They are coming," he said. "The soldiers have split into two groups. One circled west. I think they will attack the families from that side. The other went east along the river. They will come in from that side," he pointed to the mouth of the valley." He paused. "That group is the biggest bunch."

Teeweeyownah looked back to where the bands and the horses were. Only about a third of the column had disappeared into the canyon. Its narrow mouth prevented a faster passage.

"The Crows," Wottolen said. "Where did they go?"

White Thunder shrugged. "West where we could not see them anymore. Maybe they're trying to go around to come in from up there." He pointed with his chin north. "If they can get up enough courage." He nodded with a grim smile.

Teeweeyownah agreed. "Yes," he said. He looked into White Thunder's eyes. "I want you and your party to ride up to that hill on the west side of the canyon. Get into the rocks. Wait there. If soldiers come from that side, throw them back."

He paused. "Can you do that?"

White Thunder nodded. "Ride then," Teeweeyownah said. "Stay there until we are coming through."

White Thunder and the companions raised their right hands and turned. Swan Necklace cast a glance at Seton. Seton waved to him, and he waved back. They rode off at a fast lope.

A clatter of horses rose from the southeast. Into the mouth of Canyon Creek valley rambled a yellow stage coach drawn by four horses. The warriors watched in wonder as it approached. On the roadless plain the coach bounced over the uneven ground. As it came closer Seton saw that one man sat on the driver's box while others squatted on the roof, holding on for dear life. Horses were hitched behind the coach. They came on at high speed, and Seton saw that the driver on the box was a Nez Perce. The men on the roof were warriors of a raiding party. The rear guard bellowed with laughter as the coach came to a stop in front of their line in a cloud of dust. The man who climbed down from the box was Wettes Kunnin, whom Seton remembered from the Camas Meadows raid. Five warriors jumped down from the roof. They untied their horses and stood for a moment in a group, laughing and joking.

"Where did you get this?" Wottolen asked.

"Upstream near the river," Wettes Kunnin said. "We came to the stagecoach station as it arrived. The people who were in it scattered like quail."

"Did you see the horse soldiers?" Wottolen asked.

Wettes Kunnin nodded. "Yes. They are right behind us." He pointed.

"Help us," Teeweeyownah said. "Go with your men to the hill next to the canyon, on the west side. White Thunder and a few men are there. Stay there. We expect an attack from that side." He paused, looking hard at Wettes. "We need you there. Protect our families! Hurry!" The six men rode off. Finally the horse soldiers showed. Horses and blue uniforms were four miles away, weapons and metal glinting in the sun. Cavalry coming fast, eager for a fight.

Seton looked along the Nez Perce skirmish line. Warriors stoically sat their horses, cradling their rifles, watching the bluecoats. Oddly, when the cavalry was less than a mile away, it dismounted, formed a skirmish line, and advanced on foot. Horse holders stood back with the mounts. Moving forward in a broad line the bluecoats began a ragged, long-range rifle fire. Their approach made a tremendous noise among the bluffs but was ineffective because of the distance.

Those warriors with Springfields made a few answering shots, but there was no reason to waste ammunition. Perhaps Colonel Sturgis intended to draw mounted warriors into a charge, but the rear guard's only concern was the escape of their families and the horses. The warriors were pleased that the horse soldiers preferred to fight on foot. They blew their eagle bone whistles, the shrieking sounds of the hunting raptor rising clearly above the rattle of the guns.

Seton used his whistle too, seeking protection from bullets that whizzed by. Most shots fell short, throwing up small flags of dust. Some went wide, some ricocheted wildly, and some whipped through the Nez Perce line. Seton did not fire. The distance was too far for his .44-40. The thin line of horsemen held its ground until the troopers were about seven hundred yards away and the bullets fell more closely. Then the warriors began a slow retreat, keeping a constant distance from the advancing enemy. Seton looked back a couple of times and saw that most of the family train had gained the canyon but half a thousand horses were still moving toward it.

Then gunfire erupted in the northwest. The second bunch of horse soldiers made its appearance. Seton looked in that direction and saw about a hundred cavalry charge toward the canyon mouth. Withering fire from the rimrock cliff drove them back. Seton watched. There was nothing in front worth his attention. The cavalry charged a second time and was driven back again. It was White Thunder and Swan Necklace and the others, he knew.

In front of them the noisy game continued. The cavalry playing infantry advanced, and the warriors retreated. The warriors remained under long-range fire, but no one was hurt on either side. This went on for almost three miles until the families and the herds were safely inside the canyon. Then Teeweeyownah called, and the warriors wheeled around and galloped away. There was no pursuit. The cavalry horse holders had not followed the firing line.

Near the canyon mouth Seton saw sixty to eighty dead or crippled appaloosas, the result of the cavalry charge. Farther west were a dozen dead cavalry horses and a few dead bluecoats in the grass. When they came into the canyon mouth, two dozen warriors rose from behind the rocks on the steep hillside, waved their rifles, and scrambled to where their horses were hidden.

The sun was resting on the mountaintops to the west. Seton halted when the men of the rear guard rode into the canyon. The men who had defended the families against the cavalry assault rode up after a while and went in too. Three were lightly injured, two with flesh wounds, one with a bullet through the left thigh. With a wave Seton let White Thunder and the others pass by. He waited for Swan Necklace. When he came up, they rode into the canyon together. About twenty yards inside they saw a single warrior lying in cover behind a large rock. He waved them on, but they dismounted behind a scree in a turn of the canyon, where his horse was tied up, and walked back. They knew him. He was Teeto Hoonnod of the Wallowa band.

He shook his head when they crawled up behind him. "Go on," he said. They only smiled. Teeto had a Sharps buffalo gun before him and next to it a belt holding the Sharps long cartridges in its loops. Seton took cover higher up and behind Teeto, and Swan Necklace lay below him. From where they were they could see through the mouth of the canyon into the plain.

It didn't take long for the frustrated bluecoats to attempt pursuit. The front of their line was about four hundred yards away when the Sharps boomed. Seton saw the cavalry halt. The gun boomed again, and this time a horse reared up and threw its rider. Teeto fired, loaded, fired. A few horses among the cavalry fell. There were two bluecoats on the ground when the cavalry fell back. Teeto fired a few more rounds into the backs of the retreating horsemen before they got out of his range.

He lifted the rifle and stood up. He nodded to the two young men. He grinned. "We go now." They went to their horses and rode up between the canyon walls. A little farther in they came to a place where the walls came close together. The men of the rear guard waited there. After the three riders passed, the warriors blocked the trail with dead trees, brush, and rocks tumbled down from higher up. With the dark coming on, the bluecoats would not be able to come through until the morning. In their language, the bands called the place of the fight *tepahlewam wakuspah,* Place Similar to the Split Rocks, referring to the Tolo Lake area in Idaho. They remembered it from their long history of journeys into the buffalo plains.

SETON AND SWAN NECKLACE REACHED CAMP AT DUSK. The bands were crowded closely together, and small groups of warriors guarded the herds. The horse soldiers were no longer a concern, but the Crows had not yet shown themselves. Nez Perces knew Crows well. Enemies in the past, they had become allies, even friends to some like Looking Glass. They were clever horse thieves. Some believed that those who joined the soldiers were after Nez Perce horses.

Arriving at the camp, the two companions separated, each seeking his own wi-ses. Seton found his people among packs and saddles and horses, sitting around a small fire made from buffalo chips. Of the men, only Kywis was present. Petolwe was feeding him with cooked strips of elk meat. Since his wife and little boy had been killed in the Big Hole, his sister-in-law, Petolwe, who had lost her husband there, cooked for Kywis and made his moccasins. The women, robed and listless, sat staring into the fire. The children were bundled up, asleep. Seton dismounted and stood behind the women, silent until one recognized him. It was Dawn, and there was a question in her eyes.

Seton looked at her and understood. He made the sign "good" with his right hand. "Your husband will be here soon," he said. "He and the men are plugging the canyon so no one can get through in the dark." Dawn nodded. She was relieved. Itsepit looked up at him. "You want to eat?"

Seton nodded. He had eaten nothing since early morning but felt no hunger. Itsepit got up slowly and went to a pack to get one of the enamel plates Seton had bought for them in the Buck Brothers' store in Stevensville. With her belt knife she removed two strips of meat from wooden spits stuck around the fireplace and handed him the plate. "There is no more," she said with a serious face. Seton nodded. He looked down at the plate and remembered the Bitterroot Valley. It seemed a long time ago. It had been a happier time then.

He stood, stretching. He was stiff from the long day in the saddle. The gray mare still stood where he had dropped her reins, hanging her head. Seton handed his plate back to Itsepit and walked to his horse. He stroked her neck and spoke softly into her nostrils. She slowly lifted her head and relaxed with pricked ears. Next Seton walked around her and undid the cinch and slipped off blanket, saddle, saddlebags, and rifle scabbard. He took the end of the double reins, the war bridle, out of the gray's mouth where it had been looped around the lower jaw, and put it over her neck as a halter. He led her away to the creek west of the camp through dozens of horses and let her drink. Afterward he did the best he could to rub her dry with grass. He took the halter off and rolled it up in his hand. He left her with the other horses of the wi-ses to graze. He would give the gray a rest and take the roan mare next. He walked back to the fireplace, through the warm bodies of horses shuffling in the dark, and sat down. Itsepit passed him the plate. The meat was cold and he chewed it without taste, thinking of things other than food.

There was not much talking. The day had been hard for everyone. Once Seton asked about the other men and was told that they were out

on guard somewhere. He found a corner where he dropped his things
and tried to sleep. Above, through the starlit sky, flocks of geese hurried south. He listened for a while to their honking calls. Wings, he
mused with envy, made them partisans of the limitless sky, unbound to
the clods of surface dwellers. They were free to travel from horizon to
horizon, to Grandmother's Land or anywhere in a boundless world. He
finally fell asleep to the sound of a tiwét drum calling on the spirits.

He was crossing a swift river, swimming on the side of the gray
mare. He swam on her left side and had his right arm around her neck.
His rifle was in his left fist, and his left arm was stretched high. The current had caught them and was pushing them downstream. It was dark
and something hit his left shoulder, perhaps a piece of driftwood. He
heard his name called, but there was nothing he could do. The current
was too strong. He heard his name again. Once more something hit his
left shoulder. And again. He awoke startled. It was dark, and someone
was bent over him, speaking. His eyes snapped open, but he saw only
darkness. Someone spoke, close to his face. He recognized Thunder
Eyes's voice, repeating, "Come! Get up! Get up!"

Seton grunted and rolled out of the robe. He stood up slowly.
"We need you out there," Thunder Eyes said. He pointed, but Seton
did not see it in the dark. "Where?" he asked.

"On the east side, around the horses," the man said.

Seton looked across the fireplace. The fire had burned out, and
he saw only dark bundles that did not reveal who the sleepers were.
"Where are the other men?"

"I just came back," Thunder Eyes said. "Kywis and Allultakanin
are out there; the others came in late and are sleeping."

"Yes," Seton said. "I will go." He quickly dressed and took the
double rein bridle and went to look for his roan mare. He walked slowly through the wi-ses horses, talking softly, sliding his right hand along
their bodies in passing. They knew his voice and his smell and were
relaxed. He found the roan and took her head in his hands and talked to
her. She pricked her ears, listening. He stroked her neck and slipped the
reins over. He clucked to her and talked her gently out of the bunch.

The mare stood still when he slipped the war bridle in place. The lariat was carried back of the mare's ears, crossed in her mouth, one end going clear around the lower jaw, passing under the other end on the right-hand side, and coming back through the mouth again. He let the loose ends of the double reins drop to the ground and went for his gear.

The mare was trained not to step on the reins or walk away. He juggled blanket and saddle into place and tied the cinch. He added bedroll, rifle scabbard, and saddlebags and led the mare away from the camp. He mounted and made a wide circle around the camp and the tail end of the herds and rode slowly up the east side. He passed two of the herders, girls thirteen or fourteen years old. They pointed east, and he rode in that direction and after half a mile came upon three men sitting on the ground, their horses behind them. Looking at the stars, he guessed that it was three hours before first light.

Two of the men were Pekonan, one Lamtama. They knew each other. One of the Pekonan had been in the Camas Meadows raid with Toohoolhoolzote. When Seton sat with them, one said, "The Crows won't come tonight. It's too dark. They'll attack when we are on the march." The others grunted in agreement. There was some small talk. The cold night turned toward morning, but before the gray haze of first light crept over the eastern horizon they heard the strong voice of the crier call through the camps. "Lean Elk wants us to move," one of the men said. "He is right. We should move on."

They waited as behind them the camps slowly stirred and went into action. The bustle carried over to the dark mass of horses. They became restless, but the herders held them. Slowly the dark retreated, and Seton began to distinguish features in the distance: a shrub, a broken cottonwood, the wide sweep of the Plains. "This is a good time for the Crows," one man said. But there was no sign of them. Behind them they heard rolling hoofbeats as the bands started out, and then the herds were set in motion with the sound of dull thunder, the herders yipping in their high voices.

The men mounted. The three rode north, but Seton went west toward the tail end of the column where the rear guard was forming.

There was Wottolen, and of his wi-ses there were Teeweeyownah and Short Bull. With two dozen warriors, they were keeping only three hundred yards behind the nearest families and the pack train. Seton noticed that the band column and the herds went side by side. The herds were held to between ten to fifteen animals abreast, but even so their formation was three-quarters of a mile long, longer than the family train with its packhorses and extra horses. Seton also saw that there were small bunches of outriders on both sides of the march. Seton stayed with the rear guard until White Thunder, Tababo, Kowtoliks, and Swan Necklace came up. Seton wanted to talk with Teeweeyownah first, but Teeweeyownah waved him on when his companions rode out to cover the back trail.

They rode south in a gray haze, moving at a walk while the columns marched north into the Lake Basin. This was High Plains country, where the eye could be tempted to think it could see to the end of the world. It was flat and treeless, covered with short grasses, such as blue grama, wheatgrass, and needle-and-thread grass. But the land's sweep was broken by draws and gullies and coulees, and by ridges so low they did not seem to interfere with the contour of the horizon. They rode for four miles and, when the sun was about to peek over the rim of the world, they saw the Crows.

They all saw them at the same moment. Tababo was the most excited. "There," he exclaimed, "there. They come." The Crows came around the shoulder of Antelope Point, up from the draw of the South Fork of Alkali Creek, due west of the scouts and four miles away. Even from that distance they could see that the Crows had dressed for battle and were making for the northeast, following the bands.

"That's the bunch we saw with the soldiers on the river," White Thunder said. "The horse soldiers are whipped. They send the Crows to do their work." The Crows rode at an easy lope, saving their horses for the chase. The scouts turned and rode back at a gallop. The bands were a dark blot on the Plains ahead of them, perhaps eight miles away. When they raced north, the Crows speeded up too. The scouts tried to stay on high ground but had to cross through dips in the land. The sun came up golden and shining as the race continued. After they covered a few miles, White Thunder unsheathed his Winchester and fired three shots in quick succession. If the rear guard had not yet seen the Crows, they would now.

The bands and herds moved on without changing speed, but the rear guard formed a skirmish line behind them after closing up. The scouts arrived before the Crows. Yelling and waving lances and staffs and bows and some rifles, the Crow force split into two bands, one racing up the western edge of the column, the other taking the east side. In a cloud of dust, under accurate fire from the rear guard and outriders along the flanks of the column, the Crows suffered. They left three bodies and a dozen horses on the ground. But their waves lapped on until they neared the advance guard in front of the march. Rifle fire threw the heads of the two attacking prongs back, and the Crow warriors turned away and ran out of rifle range.

Seton had emptied his Winchester. He thought that one bullet had struck home. He fed new shells through the loading gate, and rode on with everyone else, watching the Crows reassemble behind the column. War whoops and the crashing of rifle fire had made the herds nervous, but the enemies had not gotten close enough to stampede them. "They'll come again," Teeweeyownah said. "Shoot at their horses."

The Crows returned in one body, but split again at the rear of the column and flooded along its sides, trying to get close to both the family train and the herds. Heavy fire from Nez Perce rifles kept them at a distance. One warrior who made a suicidal rush to get into the moving column was brought down.

Once again the Crows withdrew and reassembled. This time they stayed back for a while. The Nez Perce column moved on steadily. Eventually the enemy split into two bands, each shadowing the flanks of the column but staying beyond the range of Nez Perce rifles.

For a few hours the Crows kept their distance. But they remained in sight, a threat. The time passed for the camps and the horses to pause to rest and eat. Lean Elk, and Ollokot, who was with him at the head of the column, had decided to go on. Again the Crows charged. This

time they tried to force their way into the column, to split it apart.
They massed on both sides, and with wild whoops tried to go straight
in. The Nez Perce had seen this coming. Men had been pulled away
from the guards in front and back and concentrated along the sides. It
was an unequal duel. The Crow outnumbered the Nez Perce, but Nez
Perce rifles and marksmanship won out. The Crows were thrown back
with heavy losses.

Seton had ridden next to Teeweeyownah and Short Bull and Allultakanin and had the satisfaction of knowing some of his shots hit. The
families and the horses were safe. This time the Crows did not come
back. They rode off to the east. "Our friends," Teeweeyownah said,
staring after them. "Looking Glass's friends. The ones he said would
help us. The ones we came so far for."

"They won't come back," Allultakanin said, hopefully.

Despite the running fight, the bands had traveled nineteen miles
that day. They made camp for the night by a little lake near one of
the upper forks of Cedar Creek under covering cottonwoods. Again
during the night they placed guards out all around the camps and the
herds. During the night the honking of geese mixed with the sound of
a tiwét drum. The moon came and first light came and nothing happened. But the people were wearing down.

On this morning the crier called to break camp just before sunrise.
Horses were watered and made ready. The women filled skin bags with
water for the day. Every woman led from two to four horses—packhorses and extra saddle horses. Some men beyond warrior age, and
youngsters not serving as drovers, did the same. Women carried their
babies in cradleboards on their backs or attached to the horn of their
saddle. Itsepit, who usually had Tsacope riding with her, led three saddle horses: one for herself, her father's war horse, and Seton's gray mare.
Dawn led five animals: two packhorses and three saddle horses, one
horse hers and two her husband's. Among them was the untried racer

Teeweeyownah had chosen from the herd captured on Horse Prairie. At sunrise the column of women and children and old people moved out, the herds driven along on the eastern flank. Scouts went ahead of the advance guard. A thin screen of warriors guarded both flanks.

The Crows appeared to the east when the Nez Perces broke camp. They kept out of rifle range but shadowed the herds. The march left the little valley of Cedar Creek, its yellow-leafed cottonwoods and red-leafed maples burning bright in the morning sun, and went up a low slope covered with yellow grass. The column moved warily, anticipating another attack. Teeweeyownah, riding with his brother, with Seton and Short Bull, explained what experienced warriors were thinking. "The Crows are back because they have nothing to show for their losses. They'll fight to get something from us they can boast about."

Seven miles after leaving the headwaters of Cedar Creek, the point of the column went up to the broad ridge from which one could spy the valley of the Musselshell River, fourteen miles to the north. They crossed the ridge, and when the bands and the herds went down toward Big Coulee Creek, the Crows struck. This time, whooping, in a wild, massed charge, their whole force made for the Nez Perce herds. Nez Perce warriors managed to form a line in front of the herds, and their rifle fire once again split the oncoming surge, directing it to the left and right. Teeweeyownah, Wottolen, Ollokot, and Toohoolhoolzote called for the warriors to stand firm and shoot straight, and they did.

Seton, holding the spot next to Teeweeyownah, did what was expected. He did not shoot into the maze of figures and forms but selected individual targets. He tried to hit horses and men, and perhaps he did. Once he thought it was his bullet that hit a Crow who, above the dust and the screaming, waved a long, curved staff over his head. He saw the man clutch his chest and fall forward, holding on to his horse's mane as the horse swerved with the others and, in the rising dust, passed south along the firing line. Like his companions, Seton did not feel or think of fear. The crashing of rifles, operating the mechanism of his Winchester, the trivial things one must do when shooting, did not allow it. Fear might haunt him later, like a ghost, but by then it would not matter and no one would see it. And, even if they did see it, it would not matter.

In passing, Crow warriors, hanging on the off side of their horses, shot with rifles and bows at the Nez Perce warriors from under their horses' necks. Arrows fell short of the herds, but some of the bullets hit among the horses, creating serious confusion. Already frightened by the noise of battle, the smell of blood and the jumping and kicking and screaming of stricken horses threw others into panic. The Crows almost succeeded in breaking up the herds and causing a stampede. Herders and warriors rushed to contain the animals. After a desperate time they managed to do it. It was good that the herds were kept in motion, moving along beside the bands. The Crow attack had not slowed the march but had almost broken it.

The Crows had killed or injured about four dozen horses but without doing injury to either the warriors or the people in the family train. The families had been on the off side of the charge, behind the herds. While the Crows reassembled in the distance, another enemy entered the plain.

About seventy warriors suddenly appeared on the western side of the trek. They rode in a tight, fast bunch until they were parallel to the moving families. All carried rifles, and when they got closer it could be seen that these were Springfields. These men did not carry the traditional Plains paraphernalia of coup sticks, feathers and headdresses, painted horses, lances, and eagle feather flags. Instead they wore colorless white men's clothes mixed with leather. They all wore white plumes in their hair. They were not Crows. But who were they?

"Bannocks," Tababo said in disbelief. "Bannocks!"

The men looked at them coldly, trying to decide how much trouble they might be. "They must be the Bannocks Cut Arm got from Fort Hall," White Thunder said. "I don't see the suyapu scout chief."

"Fisher," Tababo said. "He is not with them." Tababo led his horse out of the loosely spaced group of warriors and kneed it into a gallop. Swinging his rifle in his fist he raced toward the Bannocks, shouting in their language, Paiute, at the top of his voice. The Bannocks did not let him get close. They wheeled and ran their horses northwest into the valley of Big Coulee Creek. Tababo followed them a short way and brought his horse to a halt. Standing in the stirrups, he called after them. He turned the horse and slowly rode back.

"What did you yell at them?" Wottolen asked.

"I told them to go home—we have no war with them," Tababo said angrily. "When they ran I called them the suyapu's dogs and said that we will kill them all if they bother us."

At the bottom of the valley the Bannocks crossed the creek and rode slowly up the opposite slope. To the east, the Crows also headed for the creek. When the Nez Perce column reached the water course, the advance guard halted for a moment, uncertain what to do. Then they went through the broad creek bed with the thin trickle of water sliding around sand and gravel bars. The advance guard fanned out on the slope beyond, and the men of the rear guard moved up on both sides of the column as the Crows crossed the creek three-quarters of a mile away. The head of the column reached the creek, and the bands spread out to let the horses drink. There was no way to hold them back. The herds were moved forward slowly, but then, in a rush, stampeded to water. The herders could not hold them. The thirsty animals massed in the creek bed, spreading out, standing head to head.

The Crows saw the opportunity and charged. Desperately, a handful of warriors raced to keep the enemy from the horses. Rifle fire from the advance guard and the few who arrived at the last moment made the Crows turn away yet again. Seton stayed at Teeweeyownah's side during the wild scramble. As they watched the Crows trot off, there were suddenly shouts from the women by the creek and wild yelling from the other side. Quickly the men around Teeweeyownah made their way through the nervous herd and the family train. The Bannocks were charging women and children and camp horses by the creek.

The men of the advance guard raced to that side and opened up on the Bannocks as they got close to the creek. Their sudden arrival made the Bannocks swerve and go back through the creek and up the southern slope. Teeweeyownah went after them and the men around him followed. They yelled and whooped and drove the Bannocks for half a mile until Teeweeyownah stopped.

"They'll come back," he said. "The Crows will come back too. I need a fresh horse."

They rode back at a fast lope, listening for another Crow charge. None came. The men looked for their families and the women who held the extra horses. Seton exchanged the roan for the gray mare, and Teeweeyownah took the chestnut stallion from the Horse Prairie raid, for speed. He and Seton and Short Bull mounted and waved to the women, trying to give them courage. Worried faces looked up at them. They returned to the east side, to the Crow side. They were the more numerous enemy.

On the creek the herds pushed and shifted, and slowly the heads of the band column and the herd pulled away and went up the north slope of the valley. It took another hour until the rest of the herds was watered and brought under control and the whole mass was moving again. Looking back, Seton saw that the Bannocks had moved to the creek again and shadowed the march on the left, while the Crows shadowed it on the right. Before the advance guard reached a breach in the rimrock cliffs that fenced the Big Coulee Valley in the north, the Crows struck again.

This time they made a feint toward the northern part, and when the warriors once again threw themselves in their path, the Crows went around and hit the tail end of the herds and drove away half a thousand horses. Two old men who had tried to help the herders were shot by the Crows as they passed. In the confusion, the rear guard was almost run over by the stampede.

As the Crows departed with their trophies, women again called from the west side. Teeweeyownah and the men of the rear guard let the Crows go and raced to meet the new danger. Getting around the tail end of the family train they discovered that the Bannocks were dangerously close to the women and children. Yelling and firing their rifles on the run, the defenders galloped toward the enemy. The Bannocks broke and raced for safety. The warriors tried to intercept them and, after a hard race, caught up with about a dozen stragglers. Teeweeyownah on his fleet stallion was a few hundred yards ahead of the others. He went on when the companions stopped where the stragglers had dismounted and run into a narrow gulch, leaving their horses behind. They shot three of the Bannocks before they reached the gulch.

The men did not bother about the fugitive Bannocks. They gathered rifles and ammunition belts from the dead and rounded up their horses and drove them back toward the column. They had not gone far when they heard shots to the west. Looking there, they saw a group of horsemen, Bannocks, sitting their horses around something on the ground. They also saw Teeweeyownah's stallion running wildly up the valley.

"Teeweeyownah!" Seton shouted. He turned his horse and galloped toward the distant group of men. White Thunder and Short Bull followed him. The Bannocks saw them coming and rode away, gaining speed as they went. Seton and the other two arrived to find Teeweeyownah dead. He had three bullet wounds in his chest and one in his abdomen. He lay on his back, eyes open, filming over. He had been scalped and both his arms had been hacked off and taken. Blood ran freely from his wounds, forming a pool around him. The Bannock's knife had taken part of the skin of his forehead with the scalp. Teeweeyownah's face was blood-soaked but peaceful.

Seton knelt and closed the warrior's eyes. The fearless man who had taken him under his wing was dead. The man he had been asked to protect was dead. The man who had known that he would die soon had died. Seton touched Teeweeyownah's bloody face. Never had he felt as close to him as in that moment when he was gone. He tried to speak a prayer, but no words came. In the distance the Bannocks were gathering. "Come," White Thunder said gently. "This man has gone into the spirit world. He does not need us anymore."

Seton stood. They mounted and rode away. The bands made eight more miles to the Musselshell River by late afternoon and camped for the night above the south bank under golden cottonwoods.

The river, a stone's throw wide, waters blue and swift, ran west to east through meadows thick with grass and flowers in fall colors. The camps were lined up along it in the shelter of the big trees. The herds were spread between the camps and the river, over an area almost a mile long. There were still about two thousand horses, and they needed rest, water, and grass. The people needed a rest too. In the camps people sat around, tired and perturbed, few doing chores. Silent camps they were, with even the children quiet. Somewhere a baby cried as Seton and Short Bull searched for their wi-ses.

Itsepit stood there waiting for them. "You are the last to come in," she said. Her face looked weary, but her eyes were keen. "Where is my brother-in-law?"

Seton and Short Bull dismounted slowly. They had dreaded this moment. They stood dejected in front of their horses. Itsepit searched their sallow faces. She knew in an instant. "He is gone," Seton said. He looked sadly into Itsepit's eyes.

"How?" Itsepit asked, her face taut.

"The Bannocks killed him," Short Bull said.

"You saw him die?" Itsepit asked.

"Yes," Short Bull said. "We saw him. Seton touched him."

Itsepit looked at Seton. "Why didn't you bring him?" She paused. "We should bury him here."

Seton shook his head. "We didn't want Dawn and Tsacope to see him that way."

"The Bannocks scalped him," Short Bull stuttered. "They chopped his arms off. They took his scalp and his arms."

She was silent.

"He was dead when they did this to him," Seton said. "We went after him, but we didn't get there in time." He paused. "It was that stallion. That stallion went wild. Teeweeyownah could not hold him."

Itsepit nodded. She turned and walked toward the wi-ses camp,

Seton and Short Bull following her, leading their horses. The people were sitting among packs and horses. They looked up when Itsepit and the two men drew close. They looked at their faces and knew. Dawn's eyes widened, disbelieving, believing. Itsepit looked at her and nodded, making a gesture of helplessness with her hands.

Dawn bent forward and closed her eyes. She began rocking back and forth. From deep within her came a moan, then a long-drawn whining sound. The keening issued from between her half-closed lips. Tsacope, next to her, started to cry, and the other children fell in, frightened as the women joined Dawn in the lament. Seton and Short Bull stood motionless, looking at their feet. The men who were sitting stared at the ground in front of them. Itsepit went over to her sister and sat down, her arm around her. Tsacope climbed between them, crying softly.

Silence had spread up and down the camps. People were listening in sorrow. Even the horses sensed that something was amiss and stood quietly. Two laments had been cried earlier in other camps, before Seton and Short Bull came back, for the two old men who were killed by the Crows when they stole part of the herds.

The keening went on for a time, then came to an abrupt end. Dawn ended it. She wiped the tears off her face and straightened up. The other women also fell silent. They dried their eyes and slowly seemed to come back to themselves.

"I knew this would happen," Dawn said. "I waited for it. I was afraid of it." She looked down at Tsacope and hugged her. Then she looked at Seton and Short Bull. "You saw it?" Both men nodded.

"How did it happen?"

"We went after the Bannocks," Short Bull said. "The Bannocks ran away." He paused. "Teeweeyownah was ahead of us. I and Seton and White Thunder stopped where some Bannocks tried to hide. We took their horses and killed three of them. We thought your husband was coming back. But he wasn't. That new stallion of his was a racer, not trained for battle. It ran away with him. It ran him into a bunch of Bannocks."

He paused. "That happened too far away for us to help him. We tried to, but it was too late." He did not say what the Bannocks had done to Teeweeyownah.

"Couldn't you bring him back to us for burial?" Dawn asked.

Short Bull shook his head. "No. We couldn't." Dawn looked at Seton. He also shook his head. It was a lie, but it was better for Dawn and the little one to remember Teeweeyownah as he had been, a strong man, proud, brave, not the butchered corpse the Bannocks had left behind. There was a long silence. Looking over the downcast people around her, Talooth spoke the final words.

"I am the oldest left in this wi-ses," she said. "I must say something. We have lost Teeweeyownah. He was close to our hearts. We will remember him. We lost Hemene, my brother-in-law. We lost Ayokka, my son. We lost Elk Blanket, who was like a daughter to me. We lost her little one, Tasshea, my grandson. We remember them. They were all close to our hearts.

"They are safe now. They have gone into the spirit world, ahkunkeneko. They have gone ahead of us. We all die. Nasawaylu has made it this way. Perhaps we will die soon. I am longing to see those who have gone before me. I am lonely for them. Only our body belongs to this world. Our spirit belongs to ahkunkeneko. Our spirit lives on. Our body is grass.

"This is what I have to say."

Later, word having gone around the camps, some of Teeweeyownah's warmates visited with Dawn. Ollokot came, Toohoolhoolzote, a bear of a man, Lean Elk, Wottolen, Espowyes, Yellow Bull, and others. White Goose and Bear Shield came; they stayed the longest. Ollokot also spoke for his brother, Joseph. Looking Glass stayed away.

TWENTY-ONE

THE BANDS CROSSED THE MUSSELSHELL AT SUNRISE just west of the mouth of Careless Creek. The river was so low it only wetted their stirrups. The crossing was accomplished in a short time, and while the rear guard lingered on the north bank, White Thunder and the companions, in a somber mood, rode south over the back trail. White Thunder waved once, Wottolen waved back, and then the scouts rode into the vastness of grass and sky.

Seton had talked with Itsepit, offering to ride with the families for a day or two. She had not thought it would help. "Ride with White Thunder," she said. "Keep us safe, but come back to us." She had looked at him with deep concern in her dark eyes.

"Yes," he said. "I will come back. I was told I am protected." Itsepit nodded sadly, unconvinced.

They rode south toward the high ridge above Big Coulee Creek, four miles away. They paused below the crest so they would not be outlined against the sky. White Thunder dismounted and went up. He crouched and looked across the valley. He came down, making the gesture that said, "nothing." He mounted, and they rode over the crest and into the valley on the broad trail their people had made the day before. They halted once when they saw a mass of dark dots to the southwest, about ten miles away. Buffaloes. They looked at them hungrily.

"Farther that way, on the Sweet Grass, that's where we camped four years ago," Seton said. "It was a good camp. Plenty of buffaloes, antelope, even elk. I remember a fight with Bannocks and Shoshones. I saw it from a distance." He snickered. "They had come to steal horses. They didn't get any. The warriors killed a dozen of them. Eagle from the Light was with us. White Goose, Toohoolhoolzote, Cloud Chief." He paused. "Swan Necklace and Kowtoliks were there too."

White Thunder looked at him curiously. "I heard about that," he said. "Was Looking Glass in that camp too?"

Seton shook his head. "No. We heard the Alpowais were with the Crows on the Yellowstone." They rode on and crossed the creek and went up the long slope to the next ridge that sheltered the valley of Painted Robe Creek. When they neared the crest, White Thunder again went up to search the valley below. He made the gesture of "nothing" once again when he came down. "We wait here," he said. The men dismounted, hobbled the horses, and climbed to the top of the ridge, where they sat in the cover of a stunted pine. From there they could see for miles to the east and west, to the opposite ridge, six miles away, and to the southwest as far as the high hills above Sweet Grass Creek, thirty miles distant.

Before them only the tall grass moved, swirled by the wind. Antelope fed their way west, a red-tailed hawk grabbed a jackrabbit, the sun moved, and the buffaloes grazed away out of sight. There was no sign of either the Bannocks or the Crows. It was midafternoon when the cavalry appeared, dark dots coming over the opposite ridge.

"No scouts," Tababo said. The head of the soldier column moved slowly down the slope to the creek, troopers walking beside their mounts. A group of officers was in the lead, a swallowtail guidon of the Seventh Cavalry fluttering behind them. "They are tired," Swan Necklace said. "They'll never catch up with our people."

The scouts watched as the cavalry halted by the creek. The officer walked to the side, and a trumpet blared stable call. The column broke up. Troopers unbridled the horses, removed saddles, and, by companies, took the mounts to water. It seemed the companies were preparing to form a camp in the shape of an open square on the north bank, the open side facing the creek. Finally, the mule train came down the slope.

The scouts had seen enough. "They will camp there for the night," White Thunder said. "This is pretty early to make camp. They must be too tired to go on." The scouts slithered off the crest and went to their horses, removed the hobbles, mounted, and rode the eleven miles back to the Musselshell. They crossed the river and rode up Careless Creek for two miles on the trail of the bands. They selected a safe place to camp and let the horses graze. Tababo and Kowtoliks went out and killed a young mule deer buck. A fire was built in a draw after dark, where it could not be seen, and the men had the rare chance to eat all they wanted. They roasted most of the meat for supplies, and, when they were done, covered the fireplace with sand.

They slept two hundred paces away in case a searcher with an exceptionally fine nose was drawn by the scent of smoke and came to investigate. They would hear him before he became aware of them. Coyotes, who had such noses, visited the dead fireplace during the night. The men listened as the pack went away with deer bones, entrails, and the scraps left for them.

In late morning of the following day, the scouts watched the cavalry arrive on the Musselshell and establish a permanent-looking camp above the south bank. Details of troopers armed with axes went out to chop firewood and mounted parties to hunt for game. Looking over the square of white tents upriver from the ford, White Thunder said, "I think these bluecoats have had enough. Let's ride after our people."

They rode on the broad trail along Careless Creek northwest toward the Judith Gap, the north-south corridor between the Big Snowy Mountains in the east and the Little Belt Mountains in the west. Their peaks, towering over thick, dark pine forests, gleamed with fresh snow. The scouts spent the night near the bands' first night camp after the Musselshell, at the mouth of Blake Creek. During the day they had seen buffaloes and antelope in the low, yellow hills, and a few times grizzlies gorging themselves on buffalo berries. In early morning they awoke to the calling of wolves.

On this day they rode into the Judith Gap under a cold rain. It ended around noon with the most beautiful rainbow Seton had ever seen. Sometimes they saw game, sometimes none at all. They made camp for the night on the Ross Fork of the Judith River in a peaceful grove of colorful cottonwoods. They had seen no trace of humans except for the deep trail cut by Nez Perce horses that they faithfully followed.

On the next day they rode around the western shoulder of the Big Snowy Mountains, and on Beaver Creek, which ran north into Big Spring Creek, they came on a site where a fight had taken place. They sat their horses on a low ridge and looked down into a partly timbered flat by the creek. The creek formed an oxbow there, and inside the oxbow stood six large tipi pole frames, two smaller ones, and two willow arbors. There were a few places where tipi frames had been disassembled. Hide covers were gone. Stone rings that had held down tipi covers showed fourteen tipis had stood in this village.

There was an eerie silence. No dogs barked. There were no people and no horses. Drying racks stood empty. This tipi village had been deserted, but not without a fight. On the grassy slope below the oxbow stood three new burial scaffolds, each made of four lodge poles, with a platform on top holding a body wrapped in buffalo robes. These were dead warriors, as was indicated by the items suspended from a fifth pole jutting from each scaffold—shields, medicine bundles, bow-and-arrow cases, a lance, horse tails. "A Crow village," White Thunder said in surprise.

The scouts rode down slowly, checking the ground. They made a wide circle around the burial site. They rode through the creek and over the adjacent slope. There were horse tracks there, cuts made by poles dragged over the ground, moccasin prints of adults and children, dog tracks. The scouts dismounted and walked along the tracks.

"Maybe twenty horses," White Thunder said. "Maybe more. Most or all dragging lodge poles with loads. Maybe seventy people, most of them walking. They don't have enough horses to ride." He paused. "Why are they going northeast?"

"There is a trading post there," Seton said. "It has cabins and a stockade. The Reed and Bowles Trading Post. We traded for ammunition and dry goods there four years ago." He paused. "Maybe the Crow have gone there for help."

White Thunder nodded. They walked on. Horse tracks crisscrossed the creek and the slopes. And then they saw the deep trail where many horses had been driven away to the west.

"I think our warriors took their horse herd," Tababo said. "Quite a few horses."

"What about the burials?" Swan Necklace asked.

"Some Crow warriors put up a fight," White Thunder said. "Three were killed."

"You think *our* warriors did this?" Seton asked.

"Yes," White Thunder said. "They took the horses and let the people go. Probably Ollokot and Lean Elk and those warriors who ride ahead. If those Crow warriors had let them have the horses, they would be alive." There was a silence.

"You sure they are Crows?" Kowtoliks asked.

"Look at the shields," White Thunder said. "Crow. Our men let them walk away with the horses they had around the tipis." He paused. "Our men took revenge for what Crows did back there." He pointed south. "They killed two of our old men, not warriors, Tookleiks and Wetyetmas Hapima. They were unarmed, but the Crows killed them."

The men stood in silence. White Thunder mounted, and the others followed. They rode through the creek and into the oxbow. The usual camp debris lay around lodges and inside tipi rings. There was also a kitchen midden with layers of heavy bones, buffalo skulls, and other parts the camp dogs could not consume. But everywhere there were objects that had been left behind: bundles of buffalo robes, stacks of green buffalo and antelope hides, a few parfleches, bone tools, rawhide ropes, a single leather doll, many things. The scouts rode slowly through the village, not touching anything. These things might have belonged to dead persons, and they did not feel safe handling them. Finally White Thunder said, "Let's leave. The dead are watching us."

They rode away from the village and back to the trail and made camp later on Cottonwood Creek. Six miles straight east was the Reed and Bowles Trading Post, the only suyapu dwelling and business place in all of central Montana Territory. They had no reason to visit it and passed from a distance on the following day.

On that day they rode northeast toward Big Spring Creek and crossed and went through the gap between the Judith Mountains in the east and the South Moccasin Mountains in the west and up toward Warm Spring Creek where, after nineteen miles, they stopped for the night. They had kept their eyes and ears open but had seen only the yellow hills with their yellow sea of grass, where antelope and wolves roamed. From passing the campsites of their people, they knew that they were one and a half days behind them.

The next day they rode faster to catch up before the bands crossed the Missouri River. They followed the trail downstream on Dog Creek to where it turned east, on Rose Creek.

"Where are the bands going?" Tababo wondered. "Why are they switching to the east?"

"They are looking for a place to cross the big river, I think," White Thunder said slowly. "Lean Elk knows where he is taking them." There was a silence.

"I heard about a place," Seton said. "Hemene told me about it. It is called attish pah, the Cave of Red Paint. I know nothing about the cave. The suyapu call it Cow Island. There is an island in the river. Hemene said it is the only crossing place where one does not need hide boats. He said it is the farthest place where steamboats can go in the summer when the river is low."

"You mean we might catch a steamboat?" Kowtoliks laughed.

Seton shrugged. "Maybe." He paused. "I have never seen that place. But Hemene knew. He had been there. He had been all over this country."

The scouts camped for the night on Rose Creek and left at sunrise. They had not seen buffaloes for two days. In early afternoon on the next day, September 22, they reached the bands and the herds where they were resting on the headwaters of Two Calf Creek, nine miles southwest of Cow Island and the Missouri Breaks.

The scouts took in the sight with a feeling of coming home again. Horses everywhere, smoke spiraling up from many campfires, golden cottonwoods. A few warriors sitting on a low knoll half a mile west of the camp waved them through as they rode up. They slowly made their way through the herds and came up on the first wi-ses camp. A woman stood and pointed north. They followed the direction of her arm and came upon a flat span of prairie. About eighty warriors sat in the grass in three rows of a tight half circle, facing the chiefs who sat side by side in front of them.

Ollokot and Joseph sat next to each other. There were White Goose, Toohoolhoolzote, Looking Glass, and Naked Head. The scouts dismounted behind the warriors and stood. Ollokot and Lean Elk waved for them to come in. Tababo shook his head and gave White Thunder a gentle push. White Thunder squeezed himself through the packed ranks of warriors. Tababo, Seton, Swan Necklace, and Kowtoliks sat behind the last row. The men sat so close that every word could be heard by all.

There was talk among the warriors, and Lean Elk asked White Thunder twice to silence it. When the crowd grew quiet, Lean Elk asked a third time. "You went over our back trail. What did you find? Where are the horse soldiers?"

White Thunder stood tall between the chiefs and the first row of warriors, a strong and courageous man, but a shy man. His face, his leather clothing, his tousled hair showed fatigue from the long ride. "We saw them," he said simply. "The bluecoats who attacked us at tepahlewam wakuspah." He paused. "They made camp on the Musselshell two days after you left. They were tired. Their horses could barely walk."

There was a silence. "Are they coming after us?" Lean Elk asked.

"No," White Thunder said. "We watched them. The camp they made, it looked to us like they would stay there for some time."

"Why?" Looking Glass asked.

"Parties of soldiers went to hunt. Other parties cut firewood. We thought they were starving. They set up a town of white tents." White Thunder smiled.

"What about the Crows, Bannocks?" Lean Elk asked.

"We watched. We didn't see any," White Thunder said. "These, they are not following us. We saw nothing of them." He paused. "We saw the Crow camp you attacked." There was some laughter among the warriors. "We saw three burials on tipi poles," White Thunder continued. "The Crows of that camp walked out."

"Where to?" Looking Glass asked.

"Northeast. Seton said there is a trading post there. We think this is where they went." There was a silence.

Looking Glass cleared his throat. He looked sharply at White Thunder. "You say there is no one following us, no bluecoats, no one else?"

White Thunder shrugged. "We watched. We traveled slowly. We stayed almost two suns behind you. We saw nothing."

Looking Glass turned to Lean Elk. "If there is no one following us, why do we hurry so much?" He paused.

"Our horses are worn out. We left many on the trail. Our women and children are worn out. Our old people are worn out. Why do we hurry? Why do we ride so hard? After we cross the big river we are close enough to Grandmother's Land." He paused.

Seton looked at the chief. He did not like the man's arrogance, his brusque, challenging attitude.

"Why don't we slow down?" Looking Glass said. "Give our people a rest. Give our horses a rest." There was some agreement among the warriors.

"We need to be rested when we get to Grandmother's country," he continued. "Winter is coming. It is going to be hard up there."

There was a silence. Finally Lean Elk spoke. "From attish pah, where we cross the river, to the border of Canada, it is four suns riding the way we have ridden since the Big Hole." All present knew that this was a jab at Looking Glass. Under his leadership the camp had suffered a devastating surprise attack. "We can take four more suns of riding. The women and children and old people can take four more suns. The horses can take four more suns . . ." He paused. "Four more suns and we are safe. Then we can rest."

"We are already safe," Looking Glass said. He pointed with his mouth to White Thunder. "Our scouts have seen no enemy behind us. I say we slow down. Make it six or seven suns. Make winter supplies when we find buffaloes." He paused. "We don't need the Lakotas to feed us. We will bring our own food."

Again there was a murmur of agreement among the warriors. "We will never be safe in this country," Lean Elk said quietly. "Don't you remember? The suyapu have come against us from all sides, soldiers and civilians. Even the merchants who sold us all they had in their stores. Those whom we regarded as friendly. Even the Crows came against us." To mention the Crows was another jab at Looking Glass.

Looking Glass was angry, but tried to hide it. He sensed that many of the warriors agreed with him, that it was safe to slow the march, let people and horses have a reprieve from the grueling trek and the strain of the past weeks.

"Don't talk that way," he said. "We could not know that everyone would betray us. We could not know that." He paused.

"You have been the leader long enough. You are no chief. I am chief of the Alpowais. I have been a leader in war. I am going to be the leader on the trail to Grandmother's Land after we cross that river there." He pointed with his head to the northeast.

He looked along the faces of the chiefs next to him. Seton watched. It was impossible to know what the other chiefs felt. They looked at the ground between their knees or straight ahead. White Goose's face was covered by the eagle wing fan. Conflict within their ranks was the last thing they wanted. No one spoke. None of the warriors spoke either. Seton knew that many disliked Looking Glass and held him responsible for lives lost in the Big Hole and later, also for bad things that had happened since. But no one objected to Looking Glass's conceited assumption of leadership.

It was Lean Elk who decided the issue. He was too proud to remind Looking Glass that he was a chief himself. With a cold voice, a mocking undertone, he said, "Yes, Looking Glass. You can lead. I see nothing good to come from it. I was trying to save the people, doing my best to get into Grandmother's Land before the soldiers find us. We do not know yet where they are, but they will try to prevent us from leaving this country! They won't give up. They'll try to catch us and put us in their prisons."

He stared at Looking Glass, his face solemn, his eyes burning. "You can take command, but I think we will be caught and killed."

So it was decided. Everyone had heard; no one had stepped in or raised a voice. No one knew whether it was better to keep hurrying or if it was safe to give everyone a rest. The meeting broke up. The men got to their feet and stretched their legs. Seton saw Allultakanin and wormed his way through the dispersing crowd. "What was the meeting for?" he asked. "What was discussed before we came in?"

Allultakanin nodded. "There is a soldier camp on the other side of the river. Not many soldiers. It is at the place where we must cross. It has been decided that we cross at sunrise. Twenty warriors go first. There may be fighting. Ollokot and Toohoolhoolzote and Wottolen are the leaders. They picked the men to go with them."

"You?" Seton asked.

"Yes." He scowled at Looking Glass as the chief passed by them.

"This man," he said, not bothering to lower his voice, "this man has brought us only misery and death. He has a strong mouth but he doesn't show where bullets fly." He shook his head. "This is not good."

The camp crier, under Looking Glass's direction, did not call at first light. It was at sunrise. The families broke camp, and in a short time the bands and the herds were on the move. The twenty warriors of the first wave to cross the river, with Toohoolhoolzote, Ollokot, and Wottolen in the lead, rode ahead. They were painted and dressed for battle. The column went due north on the high, grassy plateau and into the Missouri Breaks, a wild jumble of rust-colored hills banded horizontally with alternating layers in whitish gray, dark red, and pale red. These hills had been sculpted by eons of wind and water erosion into labyrinths of triangular ridges, which, in their lavish colors and striking forms, resembled the so-called badlands in the Lakota country of the Dakotas. They extended for many miles on either side of the river between the White Cliffs and the mouth of the Musselshell.

Three miles north of their campsite the column went down into the Woodhawk Creek hollow and up over a series of red ridges into a winding canyon. After two miles, that brought them down into the narrow sage- and grass-covered flats along the south shore of the river. The advance party held for a long moment, taking in the view of the light blue band of the stream, the silvery flats, and the multicolored phantom hills surrounding both. This was the last major river to cross before they reached the Canadian border. The Milk River below the border was not a serious obstacle. They yelled and urged their mounts to a fast lope. The bands with the packhorses followed more slowly, and the herds, still numbering over two thousand horses, burst like a spring flood from the canyon and spread out along the shore.

The advance party turned east and rode downstream to where Cow Island sat in the river, two and a half miles away. The island was a third of a mile long and two hundred yards wide. Shallows in the stream connected its western end with the north shore, and shallows on its eastern end connected it with the south shore. These shallows around Cow Island prohibited steamboat travel farther upstream at periods of low water.

To the northeast of the island, on the north shore, great stacks of freight were stored beside a bluff in an open-air depot. From this depot, bull trains carried freight to Fort Benton, 90 miles west as the raven flies, but 130 miles by bull train. Guarding the freight depot on September 23 were four civilians and twelve soldiers.

Passing along the island on the south shore, the advance party saw the stockpiles of canvas-covered freight across the river, some stacks as high as houses. Just east of the depot stood the white tents of the soldiers' camp. When the advance party crossed to the island through the shallows on the eastern tip, another bunch of warriors, including Seton, rode on and took up a position on the south bank across from the soldiers, ready to pin them down in case they tried to interfere. But no shot was fired. The advance party rode the length of the island and into the shallows on its western tip and reached the north shore. From there, the men rode past the depot and encircled the soldiers' camp within rifle range. They sat their horses, making no effort to move closer, while the soldiers frantically put up breastworks.

Now the bands began to cross, and when the families had gained the north bank, the herds followed. When they were through, in early afternoon, the remaining warriors closed up behind. The bands moved over the broad flats north of the depot toward the mouth of Cow Creek. Two miles upstream, in a valley with good grass for the horses, with wild rose bushes and rustling cottonwoods, Looking Glass decided to make camp.

Most of the warriors of the advance guard departed for camp. Wottolen cut across the flats to where the rearguard warriors rode up. He waved to Seton, and when Seton rode over, he said, "I need you to translate for me."

They rode side by side around the freight stockpiles and stopped a hundred paces from the soldiers' breastworks. A civilian, apparently a shipping clerk, came out and walked cautiously toward them.

"Tell him I want to talk with the chief of the soldiers," Wottolen said in numipu. Seton translated and the man went back. Shortly afterward a soldier stepped over the barricade and came to stand before the two riders. Three golden chevrons with a diamond on the sleeves of his blue, five-button, yellow-piped tunic identified him as a first sergeant. The face under the flat infantry cap seemed unruffled. Perhaps he pretended. He saluted. "Sergeant Wilhelm Moelchert," he said. "Company B, Seventh Infantry." He stood at ease.

Seton pointed with his chin to Wottolen. "Wottolen. He is a warrior chief. My name is Seton."

"You are the chief of the soldiers?" Wottolen asked. Seton translated.

"Yes," the sergeant said.

Wottolen spoke and Seton translated into English. "You have seen our people ride by. We are many and we need supplies. We want no fight. We want some supplies. Then we move on."

The sergeant listened carefully. He shook his head. "I have been ordered to protect this depot. I cannot let you have anything."

Seton translated into numipu. Wottolen thought for a moment. "Tell him we will pay for what we want. We have money."

The sergeant looked at the two men in front of him. Both rode speckled horses; both carried sheathed rifles below their saddles. They wore ammunition belts around their hips and bandoliers with webbed loops across their chests. The older of the two, a mature warrior, was dressed only in plain moccasins and breechclout. His face was painted with a white line across his cheekbones and the bridge of his sharp nose. He wore a single eagle feather fastened horizontally to the hair on the back of his head. A medicine pouch hung down over his chest. There was power in his face and dark eyes. The man would be authoritative, fierce even without the facial paint, the sergeant thought.

The young man beside him sat easy in the presence of the warrior leader. His sweaty hair was cut short in mourning. He was dressed in leggings and a fringed leather shirt, with moccasins that had a beaded design on top. He wore a claw necklace under his throat. His face was open, quizzical, perhaps mocking. He appeared calm and resolute. His eyes went from the sergeant's face to his body, as if spotting a target. The sergeant felt extremely uncomfortable. These were tough men to have as enemies. He was in big trouble if the other Nez Perces were like them. But he had orders from his superior officer. "I cannot let you have anything," he said meekly. "I have regrets, but I have orders."

Seton had caught an accent in the man's English. "Tell me, what kind of white man are you?"

The sergeant hesitated. "German," he said finally. He shrugged. He looked into Seton's face, perhaps wondering where this man's gray eyes came from, and why this Nez Perce's English, a foreign language to both, was better than his.

Seton nodded. "We have no war with German white men," he said matter-of-factly. He thought about it. "Are there German white men in your command?"

The sergeant nodded, it seemed reluctantly.

"Tell them we have no war with them," Seton said.

The sergeant looked uncomfortable. German or not, he could not give them what they wanted. If they took it by force, he could not stop them. He was not sure if he wanted to try. If he could keep his men alive, he thought he would have done a good job.

Wottolen brusquely pulled his horse back. "Enough talk," he said in numipu. Seton once more glanced over the sergeant as they rode off. The man stood stiffly, almost at attention, perhaps concerned by the way the discourse had ended. Riding on, Seton saw that three warriors remained a distance from the breastworks to keep an eye on the bluecoats. At the camp Wottolen nodded to Seton and went on to inform the chiefs. Seton searched for his wi-ses.

Soon a crier went through the camp calling for the people to make packhorses ready. Warriors would fight the soldiers, and each wi-ses should take from the suyapu stores what it needed. He called out that there was a coulee running by the pile of goods out of sight of the soldiers. A little later, gunfire erupted. While the soldiers were pinned down, women and a few men removed stocks from the off side and took them through the coulee on horseback to the camp.

Seton went with Itsepit, Talooth, and Short Bull. They brought two packhorses and took a sack each of beans, flour, rice, and several bags of coffee, sugar, hardtack, two sides of bacon, some cooking pots, pans, cups, and buckets. They also took some of the canvas covers. By sundown the wi-ses foragers had withdrawn, and the remaining stockpiles, about fifty tons of supplies, were set on fire.

A few warriors kept the soldiers awake during the night with sporadic sniper fire. The breastworks were lit by the huge bonfire for a long time. One warrior, Husis Owyeen, received a light head wound from a piece of bullet-splintered wood. The small force of soldiers went unharmed. In camp the fires burned bright and the feasting lasted until midnight.

TWENTY-TWO

AT SUNRISE THE BANDS BROKE CAMP AND MADE
ready to continue north along Cow Creek toward the gap between
the low, almost treeless Bear Paw Mountains to the west and a smaller,
similar range, dubbed the Little Rocky Mountains, to the east. White
Thunder and the companions left to cover the back trail. They rode the
short way south to the edge of the Breaks. Leaving the horses below,
out of sight, they climbed halfway up one of the bizarre red-painted
hills. From there, well hidden, they had a clear view of the flats by
the river and the soldiers' camp, half a mile away. The stockpiles had
turned to ashes, but some parts were still smoldering. There was no
movement within the breastworks or around the white tents.

The sun had walked slowly to midmorning when Kowtoliks said,
"Look." The others saw them at the same time. About forty horsemen
were coming on the north bank of the river from the west. The scouts

watched for a while, then Swan Necklace said, "They must have crossed over the island as we did. Where did they come from?"

"We didn't see them come from the south," White Thunder said. "They must have come from the west." He paused, wondering. "What is west of here? A soldier fort? A town?"

They thought about it. Finally Seton said, "I believe Fort Benton is there."

"Only two are bluecoats," White Thunder said. "The others are suyapu civilians." They watched. "Perhaps they are scouts for someone," he continued. "Maybe for Cut Arm? Is he still behind us?"

They had no answer to this question. They watched as the riders passed the burned-out depot and dismounted in front of the breastworks. The suyapu stepped over the low barricade and gathered with the soldiers among the tents. After some time, they went back to their horses, mounted, and came at a brisk lope over the Nez Perce trail.

"They are coming after us," Tababo said, surprised. "They're either good or they're dumb."

The companions went down to their horses, mounted, and rode back to the creek and turned north under the cottonwoods. Farther up, at a bend in the valley, they waited and watched for the suyapu. The whites had slowed down. Perhaps they feared an ambush. If they could read tracks, they would know that a few horses were just a little ways ahead of them. The scouts pressed on and stayed out of sight.

They had covered about five miles when they heard a flurry of shots from a distance ahead of them. Then silence. They halted and listened. No more shots came. "What was that?" Swan Necklace wondered.

"I don't know," White Thunder said.

They kept listening. "Must be our men." White Thunder kneed his horse into an easy lope. "They shot at something, somebody." They rode on but kept sharp eyes on the back trail. The suyapu riders still came on but even more slowly than before. Another four miles and the companions came upon an unexpected scene.

Before them, along the creek, stood a bull train, a long line of ox teams and covered wagons facing north. They rode slowly up to it and passed on both sides. They saw three bullwhackers shot dead on the ground, stripped of weapons but otherwise untouched. The canvas covers had been ripped from the wagons. They counted nine wagons, each pulled by eight to ten pairs of oxen. The oxen stood quietly, unperturbed; none had been hurt. The wagons, however, had been ransacked. Goods and supplies were spilled over the ground around the wagons. The companions came together at the head of the train.

"These men behind us," Seton said, "they are not after us. They are looking for this wagon train."

"Yes," White Thunder said. He rubbed his chin. "There are nine wagons here but only three dead suyapu. There must be more. Either they got away, or our people took them prisoner." He thought for a moment. "Let's hurry back and hit these others before they get here."

They rode back along the trail, and in less than half a mile they prepared an ambush at a place where a dry creek bed ran into Cow Creek from the northwest. White Thunder and Tababo took up positions among rocks above the fork. Swan Necklace, Seton, and Kowtoliks hid on a tongue of land that dropped into the east bank of Cow Creek to give a flanking fire. Their horses were safe. They waited.

The riders had to come along the west bank of the creek, on the ruts of the bull train and the deep Nez Perce trail. After a while the companions heard the thudding of hooves on soft ground. Seton looked at Swan Necklace who lay beside him. Kowtoliks crouched behind a rock a few yards to the right. Behind the broken screen of cottonwoods a rider appeared, then more riders. A man in blue uniform was in the lead. They rode in a compact group, holding their rifles close, looking around them.

Seton watched a black-billed magpie that had alighted on the ground below them. The light played on the iridescent turquoise colors of the bird's long tail feathers and upper wings, the gleaming black, inquisitive eyes. Suddenly the magpie cried out, two loud and harsh notes, and threw itself into the air. Kowtoliks's Springfield crashed. Seton shifted his sight to the riders, about two hundred yards away, took aim at one a little farther behind, and pulled the trigger. His ear rang from Swan Necklace's rifle exploding beside him. The man he had aimed at clutched his arm. When Seton pulled the trigger again he heard the rifles of White Thunder and Tababo bark from across the creek. Once. Only then the shooting stopped.

The small column of horsemen had broken up, men circling desperately to get away. They left one man and two horses dead on the ground. Some men, wounded, held on to their saddles as they raced away. It was over. The scouts stood up. If Kowtoliks had not fired too early they would have gotten more of the suyapu. But no one said anything. They went to their horses and rode over to the dead man. He lay on his face, a well-built man in his thirties. They took his .44-40 Winchester rifle, ammunition belt, and his belt knife. They checked the saddlebags of the dead horses and found three boxes with .44-40 cartridges. They distributed these, and the ones from the dead man's belt, evenly among those who used them in their rifles. Seton put one cartridge box into his saddlebag and thirty-two new cartridges into empty loops in his bandolier.

They looked down the trail where the suyapu had fled. These men would come back, perhaps in another day, because of the bull train. But not until another day, and then they were no danger to the bands. The companions turned their horses and rode north past the wagons and the patient oxen. The wind had shifted. It came cold from the north. They had ridden three miles when they saw the herds grazing in the valley and on the adjacent slopes. It was only early afternoon; Looking Glass had called another early camp. The wi-ses were spread out under cottonwoods in a bend of Cow Creek, upstream from the herds. The party broke up. White Thunder went to tell Ollokot and Looking Glass. When Seton found his people, the women had just started a good fire and begun to prepare food. Dawn still looked disconsolate. Short Bull and Thunder Eyes were putting up a simple shelter with canvas taken from the Cow Island depot, a flimsy protection from the chilly wind. Atemis was there too. He usually stayed with the Lamtama horses, and his mother, Oyipee, took food there for him. He waved as Seton strolled in, leading his horse. Seton took care of the horse first.

Then he stashed saddle, saddle blanket, saddlebags, and rifle scabbard at the edge of the canvas shelter.

Before he could sit down, Tsacope flung herself at him. He picked her up and held her in his arms. She pressed against his chest. Pulling back a little, she looked into his gray eyes with her dark ones. "Don't leave us," she said seriously, yet with a slight smile. She was happy to see him. "I missed you," she said.

Seton nodded. He hugged her. Her body was light, a feather. "I always think about you," he said. "I worry about you. I want you to be safe. That's why I am away so much."

Tsacope pressed herself against him again. "I know," she whispered.

"We heard some shots," Allultakanin said. "Was that you?"

Itsepit called to Tsacope. The girl wriggled in Seton's arms, and he put her down slowly. She ran to her aunt. "Yes," Seton said.

"There was danger?"

Seton shook his head. "They were suyapu civilians. One bluecoat officer was with them. There were about forty of them. We think they were looking for the wagon train. They ran. We killed one." He tapped the bandolier across his chest. "We got some ammunition from them."

Allultakanin nodded. "We got ammunition from the wagons. Quite a few boxes. Mostly for guns like yours and for the little guns, six-shooters. Some for Henrys. Nothing for the soldier rifles." He paused. "The chiefs are going to divide the ammunition. There were two big boxes with rifles too. Twelve rifles in all. Rifles like yours."

The talk ebbed away. No one was interested in small talk. The men rested while the women cooked. Slices of bacon roasted on spits, and a thick bean stew boiled in two of the pots taken from the depot. It took well over an hour until the meal was ready. No one was in a hurry. Before they ate, Talooth took some food and walked away to feed the spirits, depositing the food under a rose bush beyond the camp. She stood there for some time, praying quietly.

After they finished, Itsepit, Talooth, and Tannish took the cooking pots and dishes to the creek to clean them. Seton accompanied Itsepit. "Your sister," he said. "She doesn't speak anymore."

Itsepit nodded sadly. "Yes," she said. "It is hard. Husband and father gone." She made a forlorn gesture with her hand. "She is tired of everything. We all are." Later, in the dark, Talooth made coffee, a thick, black brew with much sugar, a treat the adults had not had for a long time. Seton took only half a cup, mostly for the sweetness. He had never cared much for coffee. Rolled in his blankets, he lay awake for a long time, listening to the wind rattling the dry bronze leaves of the cottonwoods.

For the next three days the bands marched slowly, traveling no more than eleven miles a day, making camp early, resting the horses and the people. At the place where Cow Creek runs down from the northwest, they turned east at the mouth of Suction Creek and followed its wide curve north, passing the eastern shoulder of the Bear Paws around Miles Butte. On September 28, two scouts who had gone ahead, Seeyakoon Ilppilp and Espowyes, discovered an Assiniboine buffalo hunting camp on Peoples Creek north of the mountains. They led the bands there.

White Thunder and the scouts held back on the trail as they had done so often. They saw great herds of buffalo and herds of elk grazing undisturbed, but no trace of an enemy. When they reached a low hill above Peoples Creek in early afternoon, they saw the Nez Perce herds dispersed over flat and rolling country and their camp settled by the creek. There were no trees but a few scattered bushes, dwarf willows, along the creek. Toward the north, in the direction of Milk River and the Canadian border, the grass country rolled on, dipping and rising in a treeless, shadowless plain under an infinite sky. To the west of their camp they saw another camp. It was a village of about forty buffalo-hide tipis in colors from cream to light brown, dark at the tops around the smoke holes. Thin smoke rose from both camps.

The scouts halted. It had been a long time since they had seen an intact tipi village. It brought back memories of times past, from before the suyapu war. They looked with experienced eyes, remembering. Around the tipis they saw drying racks hung with slabs and chunks of buffalo meat, spots where green hides had been pegged out. Two tipis were painted. A few buffalo horses were tied up near tipis. Large dogs, wolflike animals, stood guard like bluecoat sentries around a suyapu fort. A small horse herd was under guard farther west. This looked like a well-organized camp.

"Dogs," Kowtoliks said ruefully. "They have dogs." Their own dogs had fallen away on the long march, the last, hardiest ones, after the Big Hole.

"Who are they?" Swan Necklace pointed with his index finger.

"Probably Walk-around Sioux," Tababo volunteered. "One time I heard them called Assiniboine."

"Are they friendly?" Swan Necklace asked.

They sat their horses, thinking. "They have to be," White Thunder said at last. "They are afraid of us. They will at least pretend to be friendly."

"Are they like Sitting Bull's Lakota people?" Swan Necklace asked.

White Thunder shook his head. "No. If they are Walk-around Sioux, they are a different people. Sitting Bull and his people are up north, in Grandmother's Land. They went there last year after their war with suyapu. Bad Grizzly Bear Boy told us. These people here have no trouble with the suyapu."

He clicked his tongue, and his horse started walking. The others fell in, and they rode slowly down to their camp. Theirs was a poor camp compared to the tipi village—packs lying in the open, strips of canvas and blankets raised as the only protection from the north wind.

At Seton's wi-ses a slow fire was burning. It was made from buffalo chips that were odorless and made a hot fire with more glow than flame. When he sat down he noticed that Tsacope and her little friends, Ilsoo and Red Walker, were not there. They were playing with other children by the creek, he was told. Of the adults, only Allultakanin and Oyipee were missing. He did not ask where they were. The women sat around Dawn, talking quietly among themselves. It seemed they

were waiting. He discovered what they were waiting for when Oyipee
and her husband rode in. They dismounted with a bulky bundle and a
smaller one. The big bundle consisted of two treated cow buffalo hides
in prime winter fur. The smaller bundle, opened by Oyipee, contained
a buffalo liver, kidneys, tongue, and the ribs of one side of a buffalo
with meat attached. She exposed the meat with a smile.

"We traded a six-shooter and ammunition from the Big Hole,"
Allultakanin said. The leadership of the wi-ses had fallen to him after
his brother's death. He felt uneasy about the obligations that came with
it, but he was forced to accept them. "Whoever wants a hide can take
one," he said. Tamonmo and Tannish got up and each took one, mainly
as bedding for their toddlers.

Talooth took the kidneys to the creek for washing. Itsepit and
Petolwe began working on the meat with belt knives, slicing liver and
tongue into cubes they impaled on wooden spits. The spits they lodged
in the ground, angled over the fire. When Talooth came back, they prepared the kidneys the same way. The fire was fed with more chips. The
adults lounged around the fireplace, watching the meat cook. Again
Talooth took tiny pieces of the different kinds of meat to feed the spirits, one each from kidneys, tongue, liver, and rib. She took the gift outside the camp. When she returned, the men were fed first, each nibbling
a small piece or two, leaving most of the meat to the women and children, who ate next. Liver and tongue were eaten half raw, but the kidneys were roasted more thoroughly. After the spits had been emptied,
the ribs were cut lengthwise along the bones and propped over the fire.
It would take a while until they would be ready to eat, but everyone
waited patiently, sometimes talking.

"Who are these people next to us?" Seton asked. "Are they Walk-
around Sioux?"

Allultakanin nodded. "Yes. This is their country I guess."

"The Sitting Bull Lakotas . . ." Seton said, "are they related to these
Walk-around Sioux?"

"I don't know," Allultakanin said. "I think not. Bad Grizzly Bear
Boy told us that they speak languages that are related. But that is all.

He said they are enemies of each other." He paused. "He also said that these Walk-around Sioux did not like the Sitting Bull people fighting with the suyapu. They took the suyapu side. We have to watch our backs. They don't like us coming through here."

The men listened. "Did they say how far it is from here to the border of Grandmother's Land?" Short Bull asked.

"Fifty miles," Allultakanin said. "We could be there in three days and would not have to hurry." He paused. "But Looking Glass wants us to go slow. I have a bad feeling about that. Some others do too."

There was a silence. "How far into Grandmother's Land are the Sitting Bull Lakotas? How far north of the border?" Seton asked.

"They are living in the Cypress Hills, the Walk-around Sioux said. These hills are forty miles north of the border, perhaps less."

"What about soldiers? Are there soldiers on the border?" Short Bull wanted to know.

"No, these Sioux here said there aren't any." Again there was silence.

Seton had another question. "Are we at peace with the Sitting Bull Lakotas? Will they be friendly when we meet them?"

Allultakanin nodded. "We made peace with them two years ago, I think. I wasn't there, but I heard about it. Our chiefs smoked the pipe with them, White Goose, Toohoolhoolzote, Looking Glass, Eagle from the Light. The Wallowa people were not there that time. That is what I know."

After the meat from the ribs had been eaten, the children were bedded down for the night. The adults sat around the glowing fire, wrapped in blankets or robes. Dark had settled, and the stars were out. The camp was quiet, but there was the swishing sound of horse tails and the soft tapping of hooves as horses moved in the dark.

There was some talk, but men and women sat mostly quiet, thinking about what they had learned, thinking back over what had happened, about the unknown country they were going to and what might await them there. When would they get back to their own country, far away to the west behind the mountains?

Suddenly there was a new sound in the air, a muffled swish, a low whistling. They all heard it. They straightened up, listening. "Look," Thunder Eyes said in awe. He stood up, pointing north. They all scrambled to their feet. There were shouts from another camp.

A hushed silence fell over the people, a nervous shuffling of hooves as the horses moved around, snorting, neighing. Across the northern sky, filling the space from earth to zenith, hung a curtain in crimson light, transparent and delicate. The curtain unfurled in lateral movements and swung back again in graceful motion. Overwhelming in size, the curtain undulated in a horizontal direction and furled back on itself in huge S-curves and unfurled again. This dazzling display emitted a swish or whistling sound. Then the colors shifted. The bottom of the weightless curtain remained in crimson red, but upward it turned pinkish rose, with a tinting of whitish green at its upper end, directly above the watchers, it seemed.

They stood speechless, deeply moved, experiencing something wholly spiritual. Seton felt that the spirit world was putting in an appearance, unveiling itself in a wondrous display for all to see. Was this what ahkunkeneko was, the world of the dead? The aurora trembled and shifted and swung before them, drawing every viewer out of himself. It seemed to go on for a long time. Then the ghostly fire paled and receded, and the curtain flapped and waved and disappeared.

There was a piercing cry from among them. Dawn, wailing alone, inconsolable. The others stood like statues of stone. Dawn's grief burst open with an explosion. She cried and cried, then suddenly fell silent. Finally the others stirred. Itsepit held her sister around the shoulders and led her away, talking to her as to a small child.

They had never seen the northern lights before. They wondered if there was meaning to it. No one knew the answer. Later, there occurred something on the human scale. Two tiwét drums sounded across the camps, sounds of devotion, of memory, of gratitude.

TWENTY-THREE

AT SUNRISE, WHITE THUNDER, SETON, AND SWAN Necklace rode south from the camp over the back trail. Tababo and Kowtoliks were not with them. Kowtoliks hadn't felt like going that morning, and Tababo stayed with the Wallowa train and his wife, who had become sick. Looking Glass had decided that the bands would travel northwest for less than ten miles that day and camp on Snake Creek, at *tsanim alikos pah,* Place of Buffalo Chip Fire—one of a number of campsites in the treeless plains the Nez Perces called by that name. Scouts had gone north ahead of the bands, and small groups of hunters went to kill some buffaloes for meat and hides.

White Thunder and the two companions rode slowly over the wide and deeply furrowed trail. They had chosen fresh horses that morning; Seton was riding the gray. A cold wind was at their backs, blowing from the north. The leaden sky carried a suggestion of snow. Their camp, where people were getting ready to march out, and the Assiniboine camp disappeared behind them. After five miles they reached Miles Butte. They rode up on the butte and chose a place behind its southeast shoulder, away from the wind. The horses were hobbled two stone's throws below on a saddle with good grass. There were no trees, so the men wrapped themselves in robes and blankets and kept watch.

From where they sat they could see for many miles over low, rolling grasslands in all directions but west and southwest. There, the sweep of the Bear Paws with its conical, barren peaks obstructed the view. Compared to the mountains the Nez Perces had known, the Bear Paws appeared as a sprinkle of high hills, its peaks reaching only the five-thousand-foot level. Because no enemy could be expected from the north, where the Canadian border ran invisibly through a suyapu no-man's-land, an enemy, if there was one, could come only from the southeast or east, and from a long way off. The military had begun penetrating the edge of the northern part of Lakota country only in the previous summer, after the defeat of the Seventh Cavalry on the Little Bighorn. Most of the Lakotas had withdrawn to Canada after that. Bad Grizzly Bear Boy, who had been a scout for Bearcoat (Colonel) Miles after the Little Bighorn, had informed the bands about the situation. So the watchers kept their eyes on the southeast and east.

They did not talk much. But the spectacle of the northern lights was very much on their minds. Finally Swan Necklace burst out with the question everybody was asking himself: "These lights . . . these lights we saw, what were they?" They sat in silence, mystified.

"I don't know," Seton said. "Maybe Bear Shield knows. He is tiwét. Or White Goose. He is tiwét too. Perhaps it means something . . ." He stopped. There was silence again.

"Perhaps we were shown something for a purpose," White Thunder said. "The spirits may have been trying to tell us something."

"They made a sound," Swan Necklace said. "The lights made a sound. Something like a whistle, a war whistle, but softer."

Seton nodded. He had not thought about the sound.

"I don't know," White Thunder said. He fell silent, thinking. Then, "You are right. It sounded like a whistle." He paused again. "If it was kind of a war whistle, maybe that's what it means." That was a sobering thought, so they did not speak of it. Then Seton said, "If it is important, the tiwét should tell us, tell the chiefs. And most important, tell Looking Glass who is leading us now."

White Thunder nodded. They left it at that, each with his own thoughts.

The hours went by slowly. Herds of buffalo, elk, and antelope were southeast and east, grazing quietly under gray, low-hanging clouds and moving slowly north. In late afternoon the scouts spied riders a few miles to the northeast. There was some movement among the buffaloes there, but not a stampede. Assiniboine, Nez Perce hunters, or someone else? Then, despite the distance, their sharp eyes observed the striped blankets behind and under the saddles.

"Those are our men," White Thunder said. "Let's ride. We are not needed here anymore."

The scouts went down to their horses, mounted, and rode northwest over the trail. They crossed Peoples Creek near the Assiniboine village and rode another eight miles to where the bands were camped on Snake Creek.

This tsanim alikos pah campsite was on flat, grassy ground along the meandering creek. It was in a pocket surrounded on three sides, west, south, and east, by bluffs up to fifty feet high. To the north the pocket was open, with a few low rising benches. Across the pocket the distance from the western bluffs to the eastern ones was almost half a mile. There were no trees in the pocket, but there were dwarf willows around the creek. Plenty of buffalo chips, too, and when the scouts rode into the camp through a break in the bluffs on the southeast side, they saw many fires.

The bands were camped in the pocket along the creek in an arrangement resembling an inverted L and J. Inside the long arm of the J, pointing north, the Wallowa band was settled on the lower half of the arm, the Alpowais above them, and the Palooses above the Alpowais, in the northernmost position. Above the short arm of the J, pointing west, the Lamtamas were camped in the eastern half, neighbors to the Wallowas, while the Pekonans were in place west of the Lamtamas, in the westernmost position. In these locations crude shelters had been built with canvas and blankets, using willows as support where possible. The herds were grazing to the north and northwest of the band camps, although quite a few packhorses and saddle horses were held closer, in the vertex of the J.

Seton found his wi-ses camp near the western edge of the Lamtama encampment, close to that of the Pekonan. Short Bull and Thunder Eyes had been with a hunting party and brought in a packhorse loaded with buffalo meat. They ate well that evening. The women kept cooking, making supplies until nightfall. The children dealt with the gray and cold weather and the bleak camping places as best they could.

Around midnight, a driving rainstorm hit the camp and turned the ground into a quagmire. Flimsy shelters collapsed or were ripped away by the storm. The people huddled under blankets and buffalo robes, wet to the skin and crouching on wet ground. There was no protection. It had to be endured. Here and there a child cried, wet and cold and frightened, and the rain pounded on and on. This lasted for more than an hour. When the storm relented, it turned into a drizzle that lasted for another two hours, followed by a fine mist, then fog. First light came gray and feeble and barely lit a wretched-looking landscape, the world soaking wet. The horses stood miserably, listlessly, waiting for a warming sun, but none came. Slowly the people began moving around, shaking out covers and clothing. A few fires were started. Even when wet from rain or snow, buffalo chips remained dry in the center and could be made to burn. The first men went out to bring in horses.

A man walked through the camp wrapped in a blanket. It was Wottolen. "My people," he called for all to hear. "I have been delayed by this, my dream. In lahmotta, when I joined in the war, I knew I was directed by a vision. Listen to my words! I dreamed last night! I dreamed. And when I woke up, here, this ground where we are camped, is the very ground I saw in my vision."

He paused. "Above was the thick smoke of battle. On the stream from which we drink was the blood of numipu and suyapu soldiers." He paused again.

"Very soon now, we will be attacked. I slept again and the same dream came to me. I heard the voice of my power saying to me: Open your eyes.

"Hearing, I opened my eyes. I saw falling from trees frost-yellowed leaves, mingling with withered flowers and grass. In my own country, before each snow I have seen this. I know it is the end. Those leaves are dead, those flowers are dead. This predicts the end of our fight. Soon we will be attacked for the last time. Guns will be laid down."

Wottolen ended. People stood in groups, listening. The man was a great warrior. He had been prominent in every fight. He was respected. But then one man shouted, "There are no soldiers to attack us. Scouts have seen no soldiers. They have looked everywhere."

Another man said, "Your vision was true for the Big Hole. But there are no soldiers here."

There was a murmur of agreement among some of the people. Warriors who had fought side by side with Wottolen stood motionless, staring at the ground. Seton wondered why none of the chiefs spoke up or came forward. Slowly the people drifted away.

"We should listen to Wottolen," Allultakanin said darkly.

"Why don't the chiefs speak?" Seton asked.

"Because of Looking Glass," Allultakanin said. "The chiefs let him lead on this march after Lean Elk. Looking Glass thinks he is a great man. He doesn't want anyone to question him." He spat and walked away.

Seton watched Wottolen walk back to his wi-ses camp. Seton had been with him and Teeweeyownah in the fight with the Crows and in the Camas Meadows fight. He had seen the man's courage and level-headed leadership, his staunch composure in difficult moments. If his power had spoken to him, it could not be denied. Why was no one pay-ing attention? The strange lights in the sky, Wottolen's dream—was there a connection? Seton told himself that he would accept what Wottolen had said and watch and follow the man's lead.

Slowly the camps overcame the thrashing they received from the storm. Morning activities returned to almost normal. Drenched pieces of clothing, bedding, and equipment were laid out to dry. White Thunder and Swan Necklace did not appear. There would be no scouting over the back trail that morning. Instead, Seton rode with Allultakanin, Atemis, and Short Bull into the Lamtama herd to select fresh horses for the day. Atemis had spent the night in camp and returned to his duties with the horses. They cut out the required number of animals and hazed them to camp.

A cry came from the southeastern corner of the encampment. Two boys galloped their horses through the break in the bluffs, one shouting at the top of his lungs, "Stampeding buffaloes! Soldiers! Soldiers!" They ran the horses through the opening between the Lamtama and Wallowa camps and raced along on the inside. One of the boys, Whistool, kept shouting the same over and over, "Soldiers! Soldiers!"

People ran together, standing, looking. "Where?" shouted one man.

Another, "Soldiers? Where?"

The boys pointed with their arms. "South! South! Down there!"

Looking Glass rode into the excitement on a blanket pattern appaloosa, white quarters and loins on a dark coat. He sat easy on the unsaddled mount, sporting his plumed hat, his face relaxed. "No hurry!" he called. "No soldiers! It's a mistake! Take your time!" He rode along the camps waving to people. "Plenty of time! There are no soldiers near! Let the children eat all they want!"

"We better get ready," Allultakanin said. He looked at Seton. "You didn't see anything down south?"

Seton shrugged. "No. Nothing."

Allultakanin said, "Let's get ready anyway."

They got the packhorses finished and the riding horses saddled. In some of the camps people were still cooking and eating the first meal.

Seton wondered if he was being too hasty. The crier had made no call to tell the people to prepare to march. Some said Whis-tool and the other boy had spent the night in the Assiniboine camp. They had seen the buffalo stampede when they left.

Some time later, a rider appeared on the bluff above the Lamtama camp, one of the buffalo runners who had gone out earlier. He gave the blanket signal, riding his horse in a tight circle, waving the blanket in the air. The signal meant, "The enemy is upon us. Soon, an attack."

Panic struck. People were shouting, running aimlessly. Above the noise Chief Joseph's call could be heard plainly, "The horses! The horses! Save the horses!"

About two dozen warriors complied. Running on foot, or riding any horse they could catch, they made a dash to save the herds north and northeast of the camps. Chief Joseph was among them, unarmed. In the urgency of the moment he had forgotten his rifle. In the camps, some men hastened to get ready to meet the coming assault. Others tried to secure horses to get away. Women struggled to gather their children. There were not nearly enough horses in the camps to mount everyone. Children cried. Horses spooked at the turmoil, a few rearing, neighing with fear. Some got loose and galloped away.

In the midst of this confusion a distant rumble came from the south, a sound like a buffalo stampede. It grew louder as it neared. It turned into a rolling thunder. Cavalry raced up at full speed for the charge.

Some of the people of Seton's wi-ses attempted to get away. Two of the warriors, Thunder Eyes and Short Bull, managed to mount. Their horses turned round and round, rearing to break away. The men held the reins for their wives' horses, but Tamonmo was thrown by her horse and Tannish had trouble staying on hers. Thunder Eyes held one of their toddlers close to his body. Allultakanin picked up the other child. He had been in a shawl on his mother's back when she fell. Little

Magpie was unhurt but screamed in terror. Allultakanin held the boy until Tamonmo was able to pull the horse around and get into the saddle. He lifted the child into her arms and hit the horse on the rump with the flat of his hand. "Ride!" he shouted. "Save your children." Thunder Eyes managed to pull along one of the packhorses as they made off.

Allultakanin turned to Short Bull and Tannish. The woman, with her baby in a cradleboard on her back, finally succeeded in bringing her mount under control. "Ride!" he told them. "Ride!" They galloped off behind the other two.

His wife, Oyipee, was mounted, with their eight-year-old boy behind her. "Ride!" Allultakanin bellowed, "Hurry!" But the woman shook her head. "Not without you."

"Ride!" he demanded, falling into his wife's reins, trying to push the horse back. The appaloosa rolled its eyes, throwing its head up. His wife only shook her head. Talooth and Itsepit sat their fidgeting mounts beside Oyipee. Itsepit held Tsacope in front of her. Seton had struggled with their horses but was now helping Dawn, who had been thrown by a bucking mare. He caught the trailing reins and pulled the horse around, but Dawn was unable to climb into the saddle. Near them, Kywis worked desperately to hold a panicked animal for Petolwe and her daughter. It broke loose and bolted. Two packhorses galloped after it. The man stood there, hands hanging down, defeated.

The wings of the cavalry charge began to flow along the outside of the bluffs to the east and west of the pocket. Nearly a hundred people, some with packhorses, escaped ahead of the cavalry. Now the shouts of the chiefs sounded over the din, "Warriors to the bluffs! Warriors to the bluffs! Defend the camp!" White Goose and Wottolen called to the Lamtama, Toohoolhoolzote to the Pekonan warriors from their camp west of the Lamtama. Heavy gunfire erupted in the northwest where one wing of the cavalry surged toward the herds.

Dawn took the reins from Seton's hand. "Go and fight," she said. "We'll stay." He had no time to care for his own horse, the roan. He stripped his leather shirt off. When he started for the bluff, running

with Allultakanin and Kywis, he saw that Itsepit and Tsacope had dismounted and were rushing to a depression in the valley floor by the
creek, pulling horses with them.

Now heavy gunfire came from the east. Halting for a moment
and looking that way, Seton saw a cavalry battalion appear on the bluff
above the Wallowa, Alpowai, and Paloos camps. The bluecoats were
in disarray from their forward rush, but a trumpet blew and the companies began to wheel into a long line of horses and men. They were
already under fire from the camps below as they formed up to charge.
A battalion flag wafted in the center of the line. Another bugle call.
Seton saw a handful of warriors emerge and scurry to the ground in
front of the camps, standing in the open on the barren, grassy slope.
They fired into the cavalry as it came down.

"Down! Down!" Toohoolhoolzote called from Seton's right. Suddenly, on the bluff before them, a long line of blue-clad soldiers came
into view. About three hundred men hurried to the round top of the
bluff, leaving Indian ponies, their mounts, on lariats behind. The four
companies of the battalion advanced and, on command, knelt in line
and brought their Springfield rifles up.

Seton stood numbed, staring. It was as if a bad dream was playing
itself out before his eyes, a strange dance, something unreal. The yellow grass on the bluff, the line of faces above the blue coats, the gray
tent of the sky above them. So many faces. White faces. Faces like his
father's.

And then the rifles crashed, earsplitting, a noise from so close by.
Seton looked into the muzzles. A ripping splash of heavy bullets struck
all around. White powder puffs merged into a white cloud on the bluff.
Behind him, in the camp, women screamed, horses squealed.

A harsh voice came from the left. Allultakanin. "Seton! Lie down.
You will be killed." The men on the bluff were reloading their long-
barreled, single-shot rifles. Seton saw a gully and dove in. Two warriors
were there. He heard their rifles crack.

Images of the Big Hole flashed through his mind, the killing of
women and children and old people, of horses and dogs. On that day,

he had gotten to the camp too late, after the innocents lay dead. Now he was in front of them. There was no one behind him but terrified women and children and the old.

A deep anger seized him. He took careful aim at a soldier with golden chevrons on the sleeves of his coat. When the rifle bucked against his shoulder, he saw the man fall facedown. Other soldiers fell, too. He aimed at an officer standing directly behind the firing line and pulled the trigger again. The man dropped. Seton kept shooting, emptying the tube of the Winchester. He sat, to thumb new cartridges into the loading gate. He levered a shell into the chamber and half raised himself. Rifles fired at the soldiers from the right, from the bluff to the west. Toohoolhoolzote and a handful of Pekonan marksmen hit the bluecoats with flanking fire from there. Before Seton could take aim again, the line of soldiers disappeared.

"Up! Up! To the bluff!" Wottolen called and ran forward. Behind him the Lamtama warriors scurried up the north face of the bluff, a pitifully small bunch of thirty men. On top of the bluff lay a few dead soldiers, the area behind them littered with dead horses. Pekonan marksmen had found their targets. The bluecoats had dragged their wounded with them and were flat on the ground, digging rifle pits, about four hundred yards away. Their line was long and fronted the whole of the southern part of the pocket. Shots were exchanged. The opposing lines remained where they were.

Then suddenly the battlefield lay quiet. Seton looked to the northeast, where the cavalry had charged the Wallowa, Alpowai, and Paloos camps. As on this side, the horse soldiers had not made it into the camps. They had been stopped on the slope and driven back. Their bodies and the bodies of horses cluttered the slope. The warriors had taken the height of the bluff and made it their defensive line.

Sporadic gunfire could be heard far to the north, and then Seton saw that Indian scouts with the cavalry were driving a dark mass of Nez Perce horses away to the southwest. There were twenty or thirty of these Indians, naked brown bodies, black hair and feathers floating as they rode. One of them wore a war bonnet.

"They have taken our horses," Seton said in desperation.

Wottolen lay nearby on his back below the crest of the bluff, watching the enemy Indians. He had foretold what was happening. The chiefs hadn't listened to him. Now, there was nothing to say. Because of Looking Glass, they had been trapped. Without the horses they could not get out.

"They took our horses," Seton repeated.

"It can't be all of them," Wottolen said. "Our people must have saved some." But there was little hope in his voice.

Seton thought of Atemis and the youngsters, boys and girls, who had herded the horses to this place, guarded them. Where were they now? Had the Wallowa chief and the men with him reached them before the enemy struck? "Who are these Indians?" Seton asked angrily.

"I think they are chatehteh [Cheyennes]," Wottolen said. He paused. "Another tribe helping the suyapu against us."

Seton became aware of the keening, female voices coming from the camps, desperate. His eyes searched for the location where the women of the wi-ses had sought shelter. He located the spot. He saw no people, but the packhorses and saddle horses they had dragged with them lay dead, his roan mare among them.

He stared, overcome by a feeling of emptiness. Dead, he thought. All dead. Everything they had fought for was gone. He stood. He no longer cared about himself. He aimed his rifle at the distant troopers and fired shot after shot. He saw flashes from the muzzles of the soldiers' guns and felt the air around him brushed by their bullets.

"Get down, Seton!" Wottolen barked. "Down!" But he did not. He emptied his rifle until finally someone grabbed him from behind and pulled him down. "Don't get yourself killed," Wottolen said harshly. "This isn't the time to throw your life away."

TWENTY-FOUR

SETON HUNCHED LOW. HE LOOKED BACK OVER the flat by the creek with empty eyes and saw women and children emerge from cover. Finally, he saw the women of the wi-ses come from behind the dead horses. Talooth and Itsepit had Dawn between them. Dawn had trouble walking. She had been wounded again. Oyipee and Petolwe came out with the children. Only Dawn was hurt. The women spread robes on the ground and laid Dawn on them. Talooth bent over Dawn, applying her medicines. That was all Seton could see. But at least he knew the people he cared for most were alive. Looking over the Lamtama and Pekonan camps, he saw that a few wounded were laid out and surrounded by crying relatives. The dead and wounded warriors were still on the bluffs.

"We dig shooting pits now," Wottolen called. He gestured to the warriors to spread out along the bluff just below the crest. He started to remove sod with his hunting knife. Seton followed his example. So did the others. A few used broad-bladed trowel bayonets taken from soldiers at the Big Hole. Seton looked for Allultakanin and Kywis. They were farther down the line toward the Pekonan warriors. So was Swan Necklace, whom Seton had not seen before, though he had been with the thirty who drove the soldiers back.

Word came that two of the Lamtama warriors had died. Three were wounded, one badly. Women walked up and carried the dead and seriously wounded down on blankets, crying. They bedded them in the open, between ripped packs and dead horses. The warriors on the bluff watched with heavy hearts. These were relations, friends, people they had known all their lives, swept away like leaves before a storm.

They worked on their pits with grim resolve. As long as they held the buttes around the pocket, the camps were safe from the enemy's rifles. Occasionally, a flurry of shots rang out, but the soldiers did not attempt another frontal attack.

Word came that Toohoolhoolzote had been killed. Seton sat down, letting the knife slip from his hand. Toohoolhoolzote gone? Images of the chief went through his mind: speaker at the Fort Lapwai meeting, warrior leader in all of the fights since Iahmotta, his voice breaking through and calling above the roar of guns. Bear of a man, he-bear, strong as a grizzly, fearless protector. Gone.

Seton dug again, stabbing and cutting into the earth as if he were stabbing an enemy. After he had excavated a shallow pit, he watched what Wottolen did and copied him. At the head of the pit facing the soldiers, he built a pile of rocks with a slit in the center to shoot through. Lying in his pit on the cold wet ground, dressed only in breechclout and soaked moccasins, he suddenly felt the cold, felt the icy wind from the north. Clouds hung low and dark, moving slowly. There would be snow soon.

Near noon, Wottolen went down to talk with the chiefs. When he returned, the warriors gathered around him below the north face of the bluff, leaving one man as lookout. Wottolen's face was grave. Absently he fingered the bandolier across his chest.

"We had a talk," he said. "It is not good." He paused.

"Ollokot was killed. Joseph is leading the Wallowa warriors now." He paused again. A hush had fallen over the men. Seton saw Allultakanin's eyes stare vacantly at the side of the bluff. No one spoke.

"Lean Elk was killed too. We lost fourteen warriors killed from all the bands, more wounded. A few women and children in our band and the Pekonan band were wounded."

There was a silence. "The Cheyennes got a third of our horses, about seven hundred. The others were driven north. We don't know where they are. A hundred of our people are with them. They pushed the soldiers and the Cheyennes back." Seton thought about Short Bull and Thunder Eyes.

The warriors squatted in silence, thinking. "White Goose and Looking Glass sent six scouts north to find Sitting Bull and the Lakotas. To ask them to come and help us. Seeyakoon Ilppilp and Teeto Hoonnod are two of them. They know what to do. They'll find them."

There was a dull boom about a mile to the south. An artillery shell wobbled overhead and exploded into shrapnel near the center of the pocket. The warriors got up and stood motionless, listening. There was no sound but the wind. Then another boom, and a shell exploded as a flashing white puff over the creek.

The warriors saw that from the camps on the east side women and children and old people were drifting toward some gullies below the bluffs. There, they started digging shelter pits. Women standing in the open held buffalo robes over their heads as protection from shell fragments. Below, White Goose was urging the Lamtama noncombatants toward the slope where the warriors stood. Seton saw Itsepit and Talooth walking slowly with Dawn between them. There were others, including two children, carried on blankets. A stone's throw away to the right, White Goose chose a slough to excavate a shelter trench. Women dug with knives, trowel bayonets, and camas hooks. More shrapnel burst over the center of the pockets, a few times over the abandoned Wallowa and Alpowai and Paloos camps. No shells were directed toward the bluffs and the rifle pits of the warriors.

As their families worked near them, some of the warriors started to leave to help. Wottolen held them back. "We have to stay and protect them," he said. "They are safe from the suyapu cannon now. If the soldiers overrun us, they will die."

"How long can we hold out?" Allultakanin mused in a low voice, asking himself more than anyone else. There was a silence. Kywis nodded. Swan Necklace nodded, his young face tired.

"We have to fight until the Lakotas come," Wottolen said "And they will come."

Seton looked at the faces around him. They were haggard, weary. He felt the same. But he knew, with their people at their back, they would fight to the end.

The big soldier gun fell silent, but the excavations continued. "Go back to your shooting places," Wottolen said. The men went. Seton's world had shrunk to a rifle pit where his freezing body was committed to the cold earth, a rifle, and the slit in the rocks. Once in a while he checked on the soldiers. At long intervals, he fired at gun flashes on the other side. The soldiers fired often. Their ammunition supply seemed inexhaustible. The warriors saved their ammunition to fight off a charge that did not come. Snow came instead.

At dusk, it began falling out of the darkening sky in large, watery flakes. Soon it covered the country with a white blanket, the flat around the creek, the empty camps, and the bluffs and benches where the warriors and the soldiers had gone to ground. Everyone suffered from the snow and the cold, the half-naked warriors and soldiers in thick winter coats. The snow lay five inches deep when, one by one, the warriors went to visit the trenches where their families and relations were hiding. They got their first food of the day, jerked buffalo meat and hardtack, taken from the Cow Island depot. They took robes and blankets back to their vigil on the bluff. The snow kept falling. It covered the graves and the dead horses, falling equally on the dead and the living.

Seton went to look for his horse. Under the dark sky, the whiteness of the snow let him see a little. There were footprints in the snow ahead of him when he searched for the wi-ses camp by the creek. The creek ran black and sluggish. Seton stopped for a moment to dip water into his cupped hands and take a drink. There were more footprints where women had scavenged the packs of dead horses or those that were strewn on the ground. Swirling snow danced before his eyes and settled in his hair. He brushed it off and finally found the camp.

Six dead horses lay close together, their bodies looking like humps of snow. Three had been partly cleared. Seton found his mare off to the side. He brushed the snow from her head and ran his hand along her body. She lay on her left side. A bullet had smashed through her neck. The cannon bone of her left leg had been shattered by another bullet. Her nearly severed foot hung loose, white tendons showing.

Seton squatted in the snow beside her head. The one eye he could see was open, glassy, staring forward. He thought she might have suffered. He wiped the snow off her muzzle and touched it. She had brought him here on the long trail. Now she was dead. He tried to talk to her, to explain, but what? He had no words to express his grief over her death, all the other deaths.

He sat a while, honoring her spirit. He got up and went to her back and wiped the snow off his saddle and saddlebags. He left the saddle but took a robe and his saddlebags. He had to pull hard to get them off from under the heavy, stiffened body. His rifle scabbard was below the saddle on the mare's left side. He could not get to it. He could not move her. In one of the saddlebags was a box of .44-40 shells, in the other Hemene's war whistle and his kopluts, the stone-headed club for hand-to-hand combat. And there was the paint bag Bear Shield had given him. He touched the coyote necklace under his throat, White Goose's gift. He now thought he needed these four items. He unfurled the robe and wrapped himself in it. He looked once more at his horse and walked away.

He went toward the shelter pits and met a few women out in the cold. In the dark they felt with their bare feet for buffalo chips under the snow. They had found a few. One woman had a stack of three in her hand. He asked for Dawn and Itsepit. "Over there," the woman said. She pointed with her arm, but her arm was hard to see in the dark. He almost fell into the first trench he came to. Buffalo hides and canvas had been stretched over it and pegged to the ground on both sides. The snow-filled covers blended with surfaces around them. He stopped and called softly. "Itsepit."

A woman's voice answered, as if from deep in the earth. "Not here," the voice said. "Farther down."

He walked on. A tiwét sang, muffled by distance. At another section of trench, he called again. "Itsepit. Talooth."

"No," someone answered. "East."

He walked toward the singing. After two more tries he found Itsepit. She lifted the cover a little, looking up at him from out of the dark. He could barely see her face in the driving snow.

"Are you well?" she asked.

He nodded. "Yes. How is Dawn?"

"Not good. A bullet through the left side. Talooth worked on her."

"What is the singing?" he asked.

"Bear Shield. He is singing medicine songs. He is with Bobtail Horse." Bobtail Horse was the young warrior badly wounded on the bluff. "He has a stomach wound."

She shook her head and looked away. Then, "Let me give you some food." She disappeared under the white cover. He stood looking at it until she lifted it again. He held his hand out and she put a few strips of jerked meat and four little cakes of hardtack in it.

"How is Tsacope? The others?"

"The children are asleep. Talooth and I are sitting with Dawn. Dawn is asleep now."

He nodded. "I have to go now."

Itsepit nodded and followed him with her eyes. For a moment he was there, bent away from the wind, a dark robe walking. She wanted to call him back. Another moment and he was gone, swallowed by the whirling whiteness.

Seton plodded by three rifle pits. The warriors in them lay flush with the ground, covered with a blanket of white, indistinguishable from their surroundings. His own pit had half filled with snow. He knelt and cleaned it out as much as the frozen ground allowed. He placed the saddlebags on the left side below the shooting slit, drew the robe around him, and lay down. He rested the rifle at his side, next to his skin. He stripped his wet moccasins off and rubbed his feet, numb from the moisture and the cold. He pulled his knees up and folded the robe at the lower end to include his feet in his little tent of buffalo hide.

He did one more thing. He scratched the shooting slit free of snow and peeked through toward the soldier line. He could see only two stone's throws in the dark and wild deluge. How easily the soldiers could overwhelm them with their great numbers now! He watched for some time but saw nothing but the dancing flakes. Finally he lay back, resting the side of his head on the saddlebags. He felt the hard round ball of the kopluts on the side of his face, reassuring in this lonely place. His head was covered with the robe, but the upper part of his face was free, turned toward the firing slit. He twisted off a piece of jerky and chewed slowly. It was his first food of the day.

The bluecoats' rifles were silent, but once in a while a Nez Perce gun barked to let the enemy know they were still there. The night passed slowly. Seton lay awake most of the time. Snow gathered a few inches deep on his robe and filled the pit around him. Toward morning the snow stopped, but the north wind did not let up. The world seemed to have turned to ice. There was no sunrise. Somewhere above the clouds the sun walked his course, hiding from hungry eyes, perhaps ashamed of the cruelty enacted below him on the ground.

When there was enough light to shoot by, the bluecoats opened up again. Gun flashes ran along their lines, divulging how extensive and complete their encirclement was. Perhaps this was what they wanted to demonstrate. But rifle fire did not reach the shelter pits below the off-side slopes, and the warriors in their rifle pits were unaffected by the hail of bullets. Only warriors with captured Springfield rifles, for which there was plenty of ammunition, fired occasionally in response.

The opposing lines remained where they were. Later in the morning, the twelve-pound cannon again blasted the area around Snake Creek with shrapnel. The shells were wasted on dead and empty ground. Perhaps the bombardment was intended to break the morale of the defenders, but in this too it failed.

At noon a white flag was hoisted above the soldiers' line on the east side. The firing ended. Warriors called from pit to pit and watched in surprise as the bluecoats came out of their trenches and marched off.

"What does this mean?" Seton asked. "Are they giving up?"

Wottolen, in the pit to his left, looked around in disbelief. Everywhere, bluecoats were leaving their positions. "I don't know," he said. "Perhaps the Lakotas are coming. Maybe the suyapu have scouts north who told them." He paused. "Or maybe it is a trick. Maybe they'll get to their horses and make another attack."

Seton stepped out of his pit, shaking his robe to get the snow off. All along the line warriors were doing the same. The warrior on Seton's right had overheard Wottolen's comment. "It can't be the Lakotas," he said. "It's too soon. They are on the other side of the border."

"Lakotas could be hunting buffalo on this side of the border," Wottolen said. "In this weather they might come south." They left it there. Seton worked on his pit, brushing the snow away and clearing the shooting slit. Later a dozen men sat in the snow around Wottolen, talking. "If we had our horses, we could mix the suyapu up good," one man said.

"We can still do that," another said. "Fight it out. If we beat them, we are free. If not, we will all die. No more trouble." It was Kywis, who had lost his wife and child in the Big Hole.

"No," a warrior next to Seton said. "If we are killed, we leave our women and children, old people and wounded. I have never heard of suyapu making wounded Indians healthy again."

"Look!" a warrior said. The soldiers were marching back and taking up their positions again.

"That flag is a lie," a warrior said. "It does not count for peace."

"They quit the fight to eat," Allultakanin said. "They can't stand hunger." Seton looked to the east. Behind the bluff held by the Wallowa and Alpowai warriors it was the same. Soldiers were marching up from their camp to their trenches. The white flag came down.

The warriors took to their shooting places, and the rifle fire started anew. Again the cannon boomed and threw shrapnel over the creek and the camps. This lasted for some time, then died away, was repeated and died again, and finally ended in the evening.

Allultakanin returned from a visit to the family shelters and squatted at Seton's hole. He handed him strips of jerky and hardtack. "Dawn is in a bad way," he said. "She has lost much blood. The bullet missed her heart by only a little." He stared at the snow between his knees, then looked into Seton's eyes. "Talooth does not know if she will live."

Seton said nothing. Allultakanin got up and went away.

A great surprise came a little later when the women sent a message for the men to come and get some clothing. From what? They went one by one. Itsepit stood there, waiting for Seton. She held out a pair of leggings, a shirt, and a pair of moccasins. The leather of leggings and shirt was smooth and darkened from smoke. The moccasins had been cut from a robe and sewed with the fur side in. Seton looked at them.

"The stitching is poor, I know," Itsepit said. "I couldn't do any better here.

"No," Seton said. "'That's not it. They will be so warm." He looked into her eyes. "Thank you. How did this happen?"

"We cut up the tipi covers," Itsepit said. "We don't need them anymore. This way we won't freeze to death." She lifted her long leather dress a little and Seton saw that she was wearing leggings under the dress. "See?" she said.

Seton cracked a rare smile. "Who thought of it?"

"We thought of you men up there in the snow. Then Oyipee said we should cut the tipis."

The night was long and bitterly cold. The snow came again in thin crystals, cold snow. After a few hours it ended. Morning came gray and squalid, overhung with dark clouds driven slowly by the north wind.

Seton had slept only fitfully. He looked around before the soldiers' rifles started up again. The creek, where he could see it, ran
black through some willow brush, bent with the weight of snow,
then circled through the white, empty flat. The new snow had covered the ugly smudges the shrapnel had carved on the surface. There
lay the small mounds of snow-buried horses. Such mounds also lay
on the slopes and bluffs where soldiers and their horses had suffered Nez Perce repeating rifles in their first and only charge. Seton
turned to the north where the pocket was open. A black-and-white
horizon, nothing hospitable about it; but if help was to come, it
would come from there.

The shooting started again when there was enough light to aim
by. It was long-range shooting as on the day before, and no one was
hurt. The twelve-pounder Napoleon cannon was silent that morning.
Around noon a voice called from southwest of the pocket. A man in a
soldier's coat, probably an Indian scout, appeared with a white flag on
a pole. He stood on a low rise south of the break in the bluffs through
which the bands had come onto the campsite. The firing stopped. The
man called in Chinook, then in poor English. "Colonel Miles wants to
see Chief Joseph!" he said.

Warriors watched from everywhere. Some on the Lamtama bluff
crawled out of their pits and stood around Wottolen, out of sight of the
enemy. "What is this?" one man said. "Are the bluecoats inviting the
chief to eat with them?"

"Maybe they're giving up," Kywis said.

"They probably want us to give up," Wottolen said.

A young man came from the Wallowa band area and walked
toward the man with the flag.

"Whis-tool," a warrior said. "He speaks some English."

"You should go," Allultakanin said, looking at Seton. "You speak
the suyapu language better than this boy."

Seton shrugged. "They called for Chief Joseph. If they had called for White Goose, the chief might have wanted me to translate. But they wanted Joseph."

"Colonel Miles," someone said. "Isn't that the man the Lakotas call Bearcoat? Bad Grizzly Bear Boy talked about him. He is said to have a new soldier fort on the Yellowstone River east of where we crossed." He paused. "How did he get after us?"

"Cut Arm," Wottolen said. "Cut Arm sent him after us."

They watched as Whis-tool reached the man with the flag and talked with him. Later, they both walked south through the soldier line and over a ridge and out of view to the army encampment on Snake Creek. Some of the warriors used the cease-fire to see their families. Seton and Allultakanin went. They found the women of the Lamtama shelters raising parts of the covers to let light in. Itsepit and Petolwe were working there.

"Dawn, how is she?" Allultakanin asked.

Itsepit shook her head. "Very weak. Talooth has stopped the bleeding. She needs good food, but we have none."

"Can I see her?" Allultakanin asked.

"Yes," Itsepit said. "But it's too narrow for both of you."

"I'll wait," Seton said. Allultakanin let himself into the trench and vanished.

Itsepit looked at Seton. Her pretty face was haggard and drawn, her eyes hollow. Mussed hair hung loose. Her leather dress, so carefully kept in other times, was sullied and stained from the wet and from huddling in the earth hole. Only in the dark could women dare to go to the creek and clean themselves. Looking at her delicate face with the marks of exhaustion on it, he felt a lump in his throat. "How is it?" he asked in a low voice.

She caught his worry and gave him a quick smile. "Hard," she answered. "I do better than many others. Our food is running out. We can't cook here. Much of the food we took at that depot, we can't eat without cooking it. The jerked meat and the soldier bread are almost gone."

She paused. "Most of the women haven't eaten for two days. We give the food to the children and the wounded. And a little to the warriors." She looked at the ground.

"The children cry in fear when the cannon balls explode. And they cry with hunger and cold. The old people suffer in silence. The wounded suffer in silence. Cold and dampness are everywhere." She looked away.

"The young warrior with the stomach wound died. Bobtail Horse. We buried him last night." She paused again.

"There is an old man, Alahoos, who counted everything that happened—who was killed, who was wounded, who is missing. He makes announcements every day. He tells us what is happening. Do you think we will ever get out?"

Seton considered it. "I don't know. Wottolen tells us we are waiting for the Lakotas. By now our scouts must have reached them. He says we have to hold on. Maybe two more days, maybe three. The Lakotas could be close. White Goose and Looking Glass think that too."

"What happens then?" Itsepit asked.

"We attack the soldiers. They can't fight us and the Lakotas at the same time," he said. "One more battle and we'll be free." He shrugged. "That's what Wottolen says."

Itsepit nodded. "Yes." But there was no conviction in her voice.

Allultakanin appeared in the trench and climbed out. His wife came behind him. Then came the children, pitiful to see, moles emerging from the earth. Tsacope, Ilsoo, Red Walker. Tsacope went to Seton and put her arms around his leg. He patted her tousled hair. She looked up, eyes huge. He bent and picked her up. "We will soon leave this place," he said, trying to say something good. She buried her face on his shoulder.

"When will we leave?" she asked, her voice almost inaudible.

"Soon," he said, looking at Itsepit.

"You can see Dawn," Oyipee said.

Seton nodded. He hugged Tsacope again and let her softly down into the snow. Itsepit took her hand. Seton slipped into the trench and bent and went forward. The pit had been widened where Dawn lay. Talooth sat across from her, her legs to the side. The cover of the shelter had been lifted so Dawn could see the sky. She was bedded on a robe, a deerskin under her head. She was covered with a black buffalo robe that left only her head free. Talooth nodded to Seton when he knelt by Dawn's side.

Her eyes were closed. Her hair was wet along the sides of her face. Her face was thin and worn, the eyelashes tiny black half-moons on the pale cheekbones above her sunken cheeks. She looked dead until she opened her eyes. She recognized Seton. She said nothing, just looked. Maybe she was beyond words. But she looked at him with black eyes that had no light in them. Maybe she didn't mind dying. Seton touched the robe where he thought her right arm would be. He looked straight into her eyes, trying to get in and swim in her consciousness as in a river, communicating his admiration for her, his pride in her strength, mostly that he wanted her to live. He did not know if he reached her.

In this nonverbal communication, it seemed that she understood something. Her eyes blinked and, almost imperceptibly, she seemed to nod. He looked again and nodded slowly and got up and walked away. Itsepit stood where he had left her. She held Tsacope on her arm. She looked at him for a moment, searching his face. She saw sadness in it, but also firmness and deep anger. She half turned and pointed. "Look," she said. "Joseph is going to meet with the soldier chief."

The Wallowa chief had come down from the rifle pits on the bluff and walked toward the break between the Wallowa and Lamtama positions. Two warriors were with him. The three men were unarmed. The chief's leggings and his leather shirt showed cuts from bullets that had scratched him without doing serious injury.

"I'm going back," Seton said. He touched Tsacope's cheek and left, casting a last glance at Itsepit. Walking was easy on the frozen snow. On the off side of the bluff a dozen warriors stood around Wottolen, watching the proceedings. In the enemy lines, many soldiers stood in the open, watching also.

Bearcoat Miles was standing with a few officers near the man with the white flag. Joseph and his companions met them and the adversaries shook hands. Blankets were spread on the snow, and the parties sat down.

"Why do the bluecoats want to talk with Joseph and not with the other chiefs?" Swan Necklace asked.

"They think he is our leader and speaks for all of us," Wottolen said.

When the meeting had gone on for half an hour, an officer on a brown horse came from a gully behind the enemy line and rode slowly past the bluff held by the Pekonan warriors and into the pocket. He wore a yellow-colored overcoat against the wet. He rode along the creek and seemed to look everywhere, spying on defensive positions on the bluffs and observing the locations of the shelter pits.

"What do we do with this man?" one warrior asked. "Should we shoot him?"

This question was probably asked by many. "No, let's wait," Wottolen said. Nothing was done, but they watched the officer closely.

The parley ended. Joseph and his warriors got up and started back. When they had gone a short distance, Bearcoat Miles called Joseph. He returned alone. When he reached Miles, he was taken prisoner. Two officers grabbed his arms and, holding him between them, hurried him toward their camp. The colonel walked behind. The white flag came down. The man who carried it followed the colonel. Joseph's companions, caught off guard, quickly returned to the Nez Perce lines.

All of the warriors and soldiers had seen this violation of the flag of truce. The Nez Perce retaliated. The yellow-coated officer was pulled from his horse and taken into custody. Each party had a prisoner now. The warriors watched in bitter silence.

Finally Wottolen spoke. "Bearcoat is the same as Cut Arm. Cut Arm took Toohoolhoolzote prisoner at the meeting in Fort Lapwai. Bearcoat took Joseph prisoner under a white flag before our eyes." There was a silence.

"None of these men can be trusted," he continued. "They break every promise."

"Watch out!" a warrior called. The soldiers had disappeared into their trenches. Their rifles started to bellow again, and the warriors returned to their pits. Firing was constant but not heavy. It ended at nightfall.

TWENTY-FIVE

TWO DOZEN WOMEN AND THREE OLD MEN WERE sitting outside the shelter pits in the snow. They were grateful to escape the confinement of the pits. The children and the wounded were safely asleep below. The night was cold and cloudy. The stars had gone somewhere else, run away.

They sat in silence. A woman next to Itsepit asked, "Why all this death in the east country? From the Big Hole to this place? Why? What did we do? What are we being punished for?"

Silence. Bear Shield spoke.

"I don't know. But it was from the east country where death came into our world. Old Man Coyote brought it." He paused. They were listening.

"We have a story about that. Some of you know it. I can tell it here. It's winter and it's dark. It's a winter story. Do you want me to tell it?"

The woman who had asked said, "Yes. Tell the story." Bear Shield began.

"Old Man Coyote's wife died in the east country. She had to leave him to go to ahkunkeneko, the spirit world. Old Man cried so hard that the death spirit, payawit, took pity on him. He lifted him into the spirit world where he saw his wife as a faint shadow. After some time there, Old Man was ready to stay, but payawit said, 'Tomorrow you will go home. You will take your wife with you. But you must guard against doing foolish things. I will advise you now what you are to do. There are five mountains. You will travel for five days. Your wife will be with you, but you must never, never touch her. Don't let any strange wishes possess you. You may talk to her, but never touch her. Only after you have crossed and descended from the fifth mountain may you do what you like.'

"'Yes, friend,' replied Old Man. When dawn came again, he and his wife started. At first it seemed as if he were going alone, yet he was dimly aware of his wife's presence as she walked behind him. They crossed one mountain, and now Old Man could feel more clearly the presence of his wife; like a shadow she seemed. They went on and crossed the second mountain. They camped each night at the foot of each mountain. They had a little tipi that they would set up each time. Old Man's wife would sit on one side of the fire and he on the other. Her form appeared clearer and clearer. The death spirit, who had sent them, now began to count the days and to figure the distance Old Man and his wife had covered. 'I hope he will do everything right and take his wife through to the world beyond,' he said to himself.

"Old Man and his wife were spending their last night, their fourth camping. The next day she would again fully assume the form of a living person. They were camped for the last time, and Old Man could see her as if she were a real person who sat opposite him. He could see her face and body very clearly, but he only looked and dared not touch her. But suddenly a joyous feeling seized him. The joy of having his wife again overwhelmed him. He jumped to his feet and rushed over to embrace her. His wife cried out, 'Stop! Stop! Coyote! Do not touch me! Stop!' Her warning had no effect. Old Man rushed to his wife, and just as he touched her body, she vanished. She disappeared—returned to the spirit land.

"When the death spirit learned of Old Man's folly, he became deeply angry. 'You incurable bumbler! I told you not to do anything foolish. You, Coyote, were about to establish the practice of returning from death. Only a short time away, the human race is coming, but you spoiled everything and established for them death as it will be. There is no coming back.' Old Man wept and wept, but the death spirit never talked to him again. The bones of Old Man's wife remained in the east country. All this happened a long time ago."

Bear Shield had finished. There was silence. Finally he continued. "Maybe our bones will remain in the east country too. It does not really matter. All trails, after we are dead, lead to ahkunkeneko."

A woman asked: "These lights we saw in the sky before we came to this place, was this the spirit world? Did the spirit world show itself to us?"

Bear Shield thought for a while. "I can't be sure. No one has ever spoken about something like these lights. I could think that it was the spirit world that opened itself to us." He paused. "Maybe we are supposed to cross over to it from here."

Another long night. At dawn on this fourth day of the siege, the light was poor and gray, as low clouds formed a dense ceiling that held the sun prisoner. Allultakanin brought the last rations of food for the three men left from Hemene's wi-ses: himself, Kywis, and Seton. Each got three pieces of hardtack. What little was left in the wi-ses shelter pit was reserved for Dawn and the three children. Everyone else would go without food from this day on. Hunger was not bad. After a few days, one would not feel pain anymore. Seton had learned this years ago on two wáyatin fasts. Thirst was much worse. On the bluff, Seton and the others satisfied that need by eating snow.

With the coming of daylight, long-range shooting resumed. At noon the bluecoats initiated another cease-fire. The same man stood with the white flag on the same rise southeast of the pocket. This time the call was to exchange prisoners, Chief Joseph for a lieutenant by the name of Lovell Jerome. He was the rider on the brown horse who had been held in one of the shelter pits during the night.

Once again the shooting stopped. Seton saw two officers and the Wallowa chief walk from the direction of the soldier camp toward the man with the flag. Three Wallowa warriors went to meet them. The lieutenant was with them, but without his horse. The horse had been seized. Seton watched as the officer and Joseph shook hands. Then each party returned to its own side, the chief coming back to the Wallowa section of the pocket. Between the lines the white flag came down, and the shooting started again.

A call went out by the chiefs for the warrior leaders to meet with them. Four men went from the Lamtama bluff: Wottolen, Allultakanin, Kosooyeen, and Lakochets Kunnin. They returned after an hour. The warriors gathered around them, leaving a few as guards in the rifle pits. The faces of the four were stolid. Seton sensed their anger, though they tried to remain calm.

"The officer the Wallowas took prisoner," Wottolen said, "he was treated well. He was given a good place to sleep. He was fed from the little the people have." He paused. "The Wallowa chief was not treated right. He was hobbled, hands and feet. Soldiers took a double blanket and rolled him in it like you roll a baby on a cradleboard. He could not use his arms, could not walk about. He was not put in a tent. He was put with the mules."

There was an angry murmur among the listeners. "What does Joseph say?" a warrior asked.

"He said he was treated worse than a horse thief or a murderer," Kosooyeen said.

He paused. "Joseph said we must fight more. The war is not over."

There was a silence. "What do the chiefs say?" someone asked. "What does White Goose say?"

"They all agree. We must fight on," Kosooyeen said. "We cannot trust anything Bearcoat says. You saw what he did."

Silence again. "Do they think the Lakotas will come help us?" someone asked.

"Yes," Wottolen said. "They think that." He paused. "Joseph saw many wounded soldiers in their camp, in tents over there." He pointed with his chin. "He thinks the bluecoats are not going to attack us anymore. I think that too. We killed too many of them. Bearcoat is afraid to get more of his men killed. What they will do is starve us. They think we'll give up for the children, women, the old people."

He paused. "Only a few days more. By now our people and our scouts must have gotten to the Lakotas. We must hold on for a few more days."

"Two men of my wi-ses have escaped with their wives and children," Allultakanin said. "They'll come back for us. They'll bring Sitting Bull."

Seton looked at the faces in front of him. Hard faces. Swan Necklace's face had become stone. So had his own, but Seton did not know it. The warriors listened, but the eyes of some contained no hope. They went back to their pits. The fighting continued. Shot for shot whenever a piece of a soldier was seen, whenever soldiers thought they saw a piece of a Nez Perce. Seton fired twice at a soldier in a trench across to his right, long shots. After his second shot, the man disappeared. Seton got a cut below his left eye from a stone chip that flew into his face after a bullet hit the edge of his shooting slit.

The shooting continued for the rest of the day. When darkness came, the rifles fell silent. The wind filled with snow. It grew colder. The warriors watched by turns throughout the long, frozen night.

Dawn on the fifth day brought no change. Gunfire continued, and the big gun of the bluecoats again threw shrapnel over the flats near the

Wallowa and Alpowai shelter pits. Perhaps Lieutenant Jerome, who had spent the night in one of them, had advised the gunners, though he knew only women and children were hidden there. Around noon a shell burst directly over one of the shelters and caved it in. Seton learned that six people were buried under the collapsed earth walls. Three women and a boy were rescued. A girl, twelve years old, and her grandmother perished. Their bodies were left in the ground where they died. Their names were passed around to be remembered. The girl was Atsipeeten. The grandmother was Intetah. These two were the only Nez Perce fatalities since the first day's battle, except for two warriors who died from wounds received that first day.

The warriors listened to the keening for the dead. The lament sung by the women could be heard from bluff to bluff, piercing through the noise of the soldiers' guns. Nez Perce rifles were silent through the burial ceremony, but spoke with renewed fury afterward. So the shooting went on as on the days before. New snow fell in the afternoon, thin white flakes floating down from the sky.

"North! Look! Are they Lakotas?" a warrior called, excited.

Seton half raised himself and tried to see through the dancing curtain of snow. In the north a dark mass moved, crossing from northwest to southeast. Animals? Horsemen?

"Buffaloes," someone called, filled with great disappointment.

A large herd of buffaloes passed unhurried before the wind. When they came a little closer, Seton saw that the backs of the animals were white from the snow that had settled on their fur. The soldiers' fire had died. Perhaps they, too, had thought they were seeing Lakotas. The herd drifted away, and the shooting resumed until dark.

Seton took courage from Wottolen in the pit next to him. Wottolen was a man unbending, stoic, unafraid, a leader of men in desperate times, a man like Teeweeyownah, Toohoolhoolzote, Ollokot, Rainbow, Five Wounds, Lean Elk, good ones, all gone. That was how he saw Wottolen. That was who the man was. If there were doubts in Wottolen's mind, no one was allowed to see them.

The sixth day, October 5, came gray and cold and gloomy as the days before. Occasional shots were exchanged, sometimes a flurry. In midmorning an outcry came from the bluff on the east side. Silence. Then a keening. The news ran fast along the bluffs. Looking Glass had been killed. Someone had shouted that Lakotas were approaching. The chief stepped from a rifle pit to look. As he stood unprotected on the bluff, a sniper's bullet struck him in the forehead.

A picture formed in Seton's mind. Looking Glass, a proud man, had been at times arrogant, self-assured. Perhaps too much so. After all, he had led them to the Big Hole and to this place. Now he was gone, too. Seton watched glumly as, across the pocket, men carried the body down from the bluff to the Alpowai shelter pits. Shrapnel exploded over the slough near there, and the men left the body and hurried back to their shooting pits. Women came out and took the body in. The keening continued—haunting, mournful sounds that had become all too familiar.

Wottolen called out. Seton turned and saw two men with a white flag on a long pole walk toward the low rise halfway between the lines. The shooting stopped. The only sounds were now the keening, echoing over the snowfields. The men walked across the rise toward the break in the bluffs between the Wallowa and Lamtama positions. They wore army jackets and white man's pants. Their black hair was short. Wottolen said in surprise, "Numipu. These are numipu. They look like Lapwai people."

As they watched, the two men passed through the break and were stopped by Lamtama warriors near the Lamtama shelter pits. Wottolen slipped out of his rifle pit. "I'll go see," he said, looking at Seton. He walked toward the small gathering surrounding the two men. Kosooyeen and Lakochets Kunnin went too. The rest of the warriors stayed. They saw Chief Joseph and some of his warriors come down and join the gathering. They saw White Goose there too. The cease-fire drew women out of the shelters. A few went to see the emissaries; most sat in the snow near the pits. Along the bluffs warriors relaxed and watched what was happening.

The meeting lasted for four hours. When it ended, the two men walked back to the soldier camp. When they came to the low rise of ground, they planted the flagpole in the snow and went on. Women and children had left the shelters and were huddled in the open. Seton saw Dawn lifted out and bedded among the women. Itsepit and Talooth were there. Where the gathering had taken place, chiefs and headmen held a council. They sat in a circle in the snow.

Kosooyeen came up to inform the men while the meeting went on. He spoke in a low, expressionless voice. "These men are Jokais and Meopkowit. They are downriver numipu, reservation people. They have come with Cut Arm. Cut Arm arrived last night. His troops are two suns behind him." The men were stunned. Some exchanged looks.

"These men have daughters with Chief Joseph's band. That's why they came with Cut Arm. That's what they said."

He paused. "They said Cut Arm promised to let us return to our homes. They said Cut Arm has said, 'No more war!' They said Bearcoat has said, 'No more war!' They said the soldier chiefs want peace." He looked along the faces around him.

"You mean the bluecoats have given up?" a warrior asked.

Kosooyeen shrugged. "Maybe. But these soldier chiefs are liars. We know that. How can we trust them?"

"If we go with Cut Arm, he will hang us," a warrior said angrily. "Or the suyapu settlers will hang us. Remember how the soldiers destroyed our homes, our property. The settlers and miners who stole from us were never punished."

"They'll hang me for certain," Swan Necklace said quietly. "I was with my cousins, Wahlitits and Sarpsis Ilppilp, when they killed the bad white men on the Salmon River." There was a silence.

"We should get something for the horses and cattle they stole from us," another warrior said. "And for our homes and lands taken from us."

Kosooyeen nodded. "Yes, that is what we want. I'll go back to that meeting now."

The warriors stood around, talking. Seton went down to visit Dawn. She lay on a thick robe, her body covered by another. Only her head showed, a face with hollow cheeks and burning eyes. She tried a brave smile, a flicker around her mouth when she saw him. He bent and looked over the buffalo fur into her eyes. Their eyes met and held for a long moment. He nodded solemnly and turned away. He sat down next to Itsepit. Tsacope was playing in the shelter pit with the other children. Itsepit asked what he knew. When he started to tell her, the women came over and sat and listened. There was silence when he ended.

Finally Talooth said, "I know these men. Jokais, that name means Lazy. Meopkowit, that name means Know Nothing. These men are worthless. Why are men like these telling us what to do?"

"Yes," Seton said. "They have daughters in the Wallowa band. They said they have come for them and that they want to help us." He felt awkward repeating information he had heard from someone else. No one could be sure whether these men had spoken the truth.

"What does White Goose think about this?" Oyipee asked.

"I don't know," Seton said. "They are talking there now." He pointed with his chin.

"What do the warriors think?" Oyipee insisted.

Seton shook his head. "We don't know yet. We know that Cut Arm and Bearcoat are liars. They have proven it. We cannot trust them."

"Does that mean we fight on?" Itsepit asked.

"Wottolen says we fight until the Lakotas come. Most of us think that."

"Will they come?" Talooth wondered. There was no answer to this question. Seton got up and went back up the bluff.

The meeting of the chiefs and headmen continued to early afternoon when the two reservation Nez Perces came back again. From the bluffs the warriors watched as they addressed the council. A debate went on for some time, then the emissaries left for the soldier camp again.

Shortly afterward a group of bluecoats marched through the snow to the rise with the white flag. Seton recognized Cut Arm. Beside him was an officer in a thick fur coat. That should be Bearcoat Miles, Seton thought. Now, from the Nez Perce side, Chiefs Joseph and Naked Head went to meet them. Three warriors were with the chiefs, but White Goose was absent. Joseph took the boy Whis-tool with him to interpret. The two parties met by the flagpole. The chiefs and officers shook hands and sat down on blankets thrown on the snow. The warriors around Seton watched with blank faces. No one knew what was going on.

They wondered about this meeting, Seton included. None of the officers understood the Nez Perce language. None of the chiefs understood English well. The interpreter, Whis-tool, a boy from Lean Elk's contingent, also called Delaware Tom, was the son of a Delaware father and a Nez Perce mother. He spoke neither Nez Perce nor English fluently enough to comprehend the intricacies of either language. The warriors worried what he would be able to translate. Would he recognize suyapu double-talk? How could each party understand the other? But something was resolved, it seemed. Both delegations got up and shook hands and returned to their lines.

Again the chiefs and headmen held council. White Goose was there, Bear Shield at his side, the band's warrior leaders around them. After a short time the meeting broke up to shouting. "The war is over! The war is over! It is done!" On the Lamtama bluff warriors shook their heads. They waited for Wottolen and the others. They came, frustration on their faces. Wottolen spoke first.

"Cut Arm and Bearcoat made an agreement with Joseph and Naked Head. The officers think this is for all of us." He paused.

"We have to give back the government guns and ammunition we captured, and what we took from the depot by the Missouri River. We go with Bearcoat to his Fort Keogh for the winter and return to our homes in the spring. We keep our own weapons. We keep our horses, the ones that were driven north by our people on the first day. Bearcoat says he has plenty of food. He will feed us."

He looked around, nodded, and looked to the ground. "This is what the chiefs agreed to."

"Who? What chiefs?" someone asked.

"Joseph and Naked Head and Cut Arm and Bearcoat, all of them," Wottolen said.

"White Goose, what did he say? What did you say? You spoke too, didn't you?"

Wottolen nodded. "We said these officers are liars. They say something now to keep us from fighting more, and when we stop fighting they will do something else. We said they try to trick us. We said Joseph and Naked Head are fools to believe them. We don't believe them."

"We said we do not give up our rifles, no government rifles either." Now Kosooyeen spoke.

"Why does Joseph believe them?" a warrior asked. "He was a prisoner in the soldier camp a few suns ago."

"He wants to believe them," Wottolen said. "He says the children and the wounded are suffering. The women go without food. We go without food. He says the suffering should end or more will die. He says we will be worse off when Cut Arm's soldiers arrive. They are two suns off. That is what they say."

He paused. "This is why he gives up, not for himself." There was a silence.

"What happens now?" a warrior asked.

Wottolen shrugged.

"What do you say?" Swan Necklace asked.

"I will not give up my rifle," Wottolen answered. "If Joseph and Naked Head give up theirs, that is for them to do. If they make peace that way, they make peace for the Wallowa people and the Palooses. They do not make peace for us."

He paused. "Cut Arm said no one will be punished when we are back in our homeland. He was asked about that. He said he gives us his word."

There was a silence. "If we don't go with Joseph and Bearcoat Miles, what do we do?" Allultakanin asked. "We can't stay here."

Wottolen nodded. "We leave tonight. We fight our way out if it comes to that. We go north to Grandmother's Land as we had planned." He looked around. "It will be hard. I think the Lakotas will meet us. I think they are on their way."

The men stood silently, mulling matters over. There was much to think about. The call went out to bring rifles taken from the soldiers. Not one of the Lamtama went. They kept the captured government guns. So did most of the Pekonan. Men of the Wallowa, Alpowai, and Paloos bands formed a single file and carried the Springfields and ammunition belts with .45-70 caliber cartridges out to the flagpole. Soldiers stood by and watched. These were rifles that had been taken in combat from the first fight at lahmotta to the repulsed cavalry charge six suns earlier. In the dreary light, the warriors came back empty-handed. There was no telling how they felt. An officer overseeing the capitulation counted 113 Springfields.

On the bluffs and on the flats by the creek, people were uneasy, agitated, disturbed. There was a great deal of talk. There was no joy that the fighting was over. And it was not over yet. A shot fell somewhere, followed by another and another. The soldiers jumped back into their trenches; the Lamtama and Pekonan warriors took to their rifle pits. Their lines blazed away at the soldier positions with a sudden fury borne from despair, frustration, and anger. Seton fired three shots and stopped. Wottolen and Kosooyeen called loudly to stop the shooting. They tried to calm the warriors. The soldiers' return fire slackened when the warriors' guns went silent. The firefight lasted only a few minutes but had put the peace arrangement in jeopardy.

An eerie silence descended upon the battlefield. Many eyes went to the stack of relinquished rifles between the lines. Soldiers and warriors on the south bluffs held their positions, uneasy, uncertain what would happen.

Chiefs Joseph and Naked Head took action to preserve the peace agreement. Joseph, on a borrowed horse, his Winchester across the pommel in front of him, dressed in a gray blanket with black stripes, rode slowly out to the soldier camp. Naked Head and three warriors were clinging to his knees and saddle blanket. They were unarmed. Eyes followed them from the bluffs and from the soldier trenches. They made it across the white flats and disappeared into the swalelike canyon that hid the soldier camp and Colonel Miles's headquarters. Everywhere people waited. Finally Joseph and the men with him came back. Behind them, officers appeared. The soldiers left the trenches and marched to their camp. The battle was over. Coming into the pocket, Joseph dismounted. He and those with him were quickly surrounded. From the bluff, Lamtama warriors watched. Seton looked at Wottolen. Wottolen shook his head. His face was grim.

Later, word came that Joseph had given his rifle to Bearcoat Miles. It was a personal gesture to validate the agreement made between him and the soldiers' chiefs. He offered the rifle to Miles as a token of his sincere intention to stick with the peace despite the exchange of gunfire that had just taken place.

That is what was said at the Nez Perce camp that evening. What Bearcoat and Cut Arm understood the gesture to mean, no one knew. There was no interpreter present when it happened, so it was unlikely either side truly understood the other. The warriors left their rifle pits on the bluffs and retired to their families, who were gathered by the creek. People settled down according to band. The general and the colonel wisely held the soldiers away from the Nez Perce camp. As a friendly gesture, they made food available to be picked up near the soldier camp. Many Nez Perces went. The Lamtama stayed back. Sullen and aloof, they would rather starve than take the white men's crumbs. Seton sat with the people of his wi-ses. Word came from White Goose and the warrior leaders. They would break away sometime after dark.

T W E N T Y - S I X

SOMEONE SHOOK HIS SHOULDER. SETON CAME TO slowly, back from dreams he had already forgotten. The face bent over him was Allultakanin's. He said, "We are leaving. Are you coming?"

Seton looked around. In the dark he saw Kywis and Petolwe standing together, the warrior holding Ilsoo bundled up in his arms. There was Oyipee, with Red Walker by her side. He saw Talooth sit with Itsepit. Dawn was lying next to them. "Are you coming?" Allultakanin asked again.

Seton pushed the robe off and stood up. Talooth and Itsepit were looking at him. He walked over. He bent over Dawn. She was asleep, perhaps unconscious. "I am staying," Itsepit said, looking at her sister.

"I am staying too," Talooth said. Seton looked at Allultakanin, then at Talooth. He did not have to think about it. He had made up his mind already.

"No," he said. "I will stay."

He nodded to Talooth. "You go. You have a grandchild, you have a daughter, soon a son-in-law."

He paused. "Go with them. This is my family here. You are needed by them." He pointed with his chin.

Talooth protested, but Seton looked to Allultakanin and called him with a motion of his head. He took Talooth's arm. Allultakanin understood. He took the other arm, and they both raised the woman up. She tried to struggle. "Grandmother," Ilsoo cried out. Talooth stood still. Her face fell. Tears streamed. Seton gently pushed her on. She started to walk.

Allultakanin nodded. He raised his hand. The gesture was one of respect, but it included a desperate sadness, a sorrow in the heart. Seton raised his hand in farewell. The snow crunched under many feet. He saw them walk away. There were dark figures ahead of them. The night swallowed them all. The faint sounds faded. Stillness.

Seton stood staring, searching for them. But they were gone. He turned and went and sat next to Itsepit. He noticed that the bundle of fur next to her covered Tsacope. Itsepit had tears in her eyes. She touched his arm. They were together but terribly alone.

The night was turning to morning when Dawn awoke. Seton heard a deep sigh and found Dawn's eyes were open. He touched Itsepit, who lay rolled into a robe, Tsacope almost on top of her. Itsepit came to slowly. She seemed to have traveled far in her dreams. She looked at Seton and recognized him. He pointed with his chin, and she saw Dawn. Dawn looked at both of them. Then she looked past them, here, there. "Where are they?" she asked. "Talooth." She coughed. "Oyipee, Petolwe." She looked at Itsepit. "Where are they?"

Itsepit looked at Seton. He shrugged, then nodded. "Tell her."

"They are gone," Itsepit said. Dawn blinked her eyes. A sharp wrinkle appeared above the saddle of her nose. She tried to comprehend.

"Gone?" she asked. "Where?"

"They went away. Walked out. North," Itsepit said.

Dawn laid back. She closed her eyes. After a while she said, "Why are we here?"

Itsepit looked to Seton. What should she answer? "You are in a bad way," she said. "We stayed here because we want a suyapu medicine man to help you." She did not say that she thought Dawn would not make it far beyond the camp.

Other people were listening. A Wallowa woman shook her head.

"Who is still here?" Dawn asked. "Of our people?"

"Tsacope and Seton."

Dawn opened her eyes again and looked around. "Is that all?"

Itsepit pressed her arm. "Yes."

"Where is my daughter?"

"She is here, asleep."

Dawn closed her eyes again. She breathed heavily. "I don't want to stay here. I don't want to be touched by a suyapu. They killed my father and my husband." She paused. "I want to leave."

Itsepit looked at Seton and shook her head. Seton shrugged. "We can't make it," she said. "You are too sick." She was close to crying.

"I'd rather die than be helped by the suyapu," Dawn said weakly.

There was a silence. "We have nothing," Itsepit said finally. "No horse. No tipi poles." She paused. "How could we move you? We have no food." She paused again. "Think about that."

Dawn nodded. She opened her eyes. "I know," she said. "We might all die there. I'd rather die in the snow by myself, or with you."

Itsepit looked at Seton again. "We might all die anyway," she said. "What do you think? Should we do it, follow White Goose's tracks?"

Seton thought for a long time. He looked at Tsacope, Itsepit. He looked over the people sleeping in the snow, the ones who were left of all the people who had started out on the Clearwater half a world ago. He looked to the two fires the soldiers had burned on the bluffs, dying down. Their pickets had been pulled in. The bluecoats were exhausted too.

He looked to Itsepit and shrugged. "Yes, we will leave. Perhaps we'll get through. Perhaps the Lakotas will find us." He tried a smile, but Itsepit could not see it. "I'll have to drag her," he said. "It will be hard on her. You have to carry Tsacope and the other robes." He bent forward and looked at Itsepit from close by. "Do we do this?"

Itsepit nodded. "We need a rope or a lariat," Seton said, "this long." He twice spread his arms, indicating a length of about twelve feet. Itsepit got up. She went among the Wallowa women and came back with a rope ten feet long.

"It's enough," Seton said. He took two cartridges from loops on the bandolier and pried the bullets off. Two smooth pebbles would have been better. He pushed the blunt base of the first bullet into the underside of Dawn's robe near the left corner, above her head. He pushed hard so the bullet made a bulbous dent in the upper side of the robe. Itsepit tied the rope around it. This was the way peg ropes were tied to the bottoms of tipi covers. They repeated the process with the second bullet near the right corner of the robe. Seton and Itsepit looked at each other.

Seton slung the rifle over his shoulder. He took kopluts, war whistle, and paint bag from the saddlebags. He tied the kopluts to his belt and slipped war whistle and paint bag inside his shirt. He saw that Itsepit carried her father's medicine bundle and a rawhide bag over her back. He shook off his robe, folded it, and tied it around Itsepit's waist. She nodded. He looked down at the saddlebags. There was no way to carry them. He was ready. Itsepit bent and gathered the robe with Tsacope and brought it up without waking her.

Seton stepped into the rope and laid it against his chest. He pushed lightly and tightened the rope. Itsepit walked and took the lead. Seton leaned into the rope and pushed. He took a step forward, another. The robe made a soft swishing sound in the snow. People watched from the dark but said nothing.

They followed the trail the feet of White Goose's party had printed in the snow. If Dawn felt pain, she did not say. They made their way below the bluffs on the eastern side of the pocket. The shelter pits were empty dark holes now that the covers had been removed. They went on until they had to cross the creek, their first difficulty. Seton stepped out of the rope. He stood and looked at the babbling water. He took his moccasins off. He walked to Itsepit and lifted her, light as a bird even with Tsacope rolled up on her arm, and stepped into the icy water. He carried them through to the west bank and went back for Dawn. He threw her upper robe across to the other side of the creek and, with the drag robe, lifted Dawn in his arms and carried her through. He sat her in the snow and sat down himself. He covered Dawn again and massaged his feet. He put the moccasins back on and stood. They could not stay here long; they were too close to the camp.

They moved on. It was hard work. Dawn said nothing. He was not sure if she was conscious. Or if she was alive. Or if the jolting had opened her wounds and she was bleeding to death. No sound came from her. They went on for four miles and came to Bean Creek, a stream the size of Snake Creek. Before they crossed they rested for a while. It was then that Dawn spoke. Her voice was barely audible. "I am grateful to you. I am glad to be away from those people." She coughed. "If I cannot go on, you go without me; take Tsacope with you."

"You are not going to die," Itsepit said, taking Dawn's hand. "You have the strength of a buffalo bull." Dawn nodded with a weak smile and closed her eyes.

They sat for some time. It was bitter cold and snow began falling again. Seton did not feel hunger, though he had not eaten for days. Itsepit had a few pieces of hardtack left for Tsacope and Dawn. After this day, there would be no food for anyone.

Seton's legs above the knees were numb. Before they went dead on him, he got up and they crossed this creek as they had the last one. They made two more miles to a gully and a hollow with a stunted larch. Morning was near, although the sun was still blocked by clouds. They made a camp in the hollow, piling snow around them and on top of the robes. They crawled together underneath and fell asleep.

In his sleep, in dreaming, Seton saw people and places he remembered and others he did not. He was walking, he was riding, he saw his mother, the white bandits' hanging in Lewiston. There was Hemene, the corral on Lolo Pass. They were catching salmon, he and Alex. He was young and he was younger. Finally a coyote came and stood over him. The huge gray animal opened its jaws, and a whining sound came from its mouth. He awoke, trembling. The whining was Tsacope; she was crying.

Itsepit talked softly to the little girl, but she kept moaning. Finally Dawn spoke. "Stop," she said. "The suyapu will come and get us if you don't stop." She turned to Seton. "We must go." He crawled out from under the robe and looked around. It was a gray, foggy day. No sun. He stood up and went to the edge of the hollow and looked over. There was no life in any direction. The snowfields lay empty. He walked a little way and urinated. He took a handful of snow and washed his face. He put another handful in his mouth. He mulled the snow around in his mouth until it melted. He swallowed and bent to get another mouthful.

From behind him Itsepit called. She had set Tsacope in the snow, tightly wrapped, and was trying to get Dawn up. Seton went to help her. Dawn was wobbly on her legs. He saw the bullet hole in the leather gown above her heart. "Help me," Itsepit said. She pointed with her chin. Together they walked Dawn a few steps. The women looked at him, and he turned around. With Itsepit holding her arm, Dawn squatted in the snow and relieved herself. When she was standing up, Seton and Itsepit led her back, Seton holding her firmly. Itsepit shook the robes out and placed the drag robe on the ground. They laid Dawn on it. They covered her with the other robe. Itsepit took four pieces of hardtack from her rawhide bag and gave two each to Tsacope and Dawn, who offered one to Seton. He shook his head. Tsacope sat quietly, watching Seton with her huge eyes. She munched the hardtack and asked for water. Itsepit pointed to the snow, eating a handful herself.

Itsepit checked the bandage Talooth had wrapped around Dawn's chest above the breasts. Seton did not look. "A little blood," Itsepit said. "Not much."

They went out, Itsepit taking the lead. The trail was still visible under the new snow. Seton leaned forward, pulling Dawn along. Later he heard her sing. It was not much more than a whisper. He did not know what she was singing. Perhaps a medicine song, or a death song. But her spirit was strong. It could be something good she was singing. After a mile they came to a place where about two dozen horses lay dead. They were covered with snow but recognizable. Most carried cavalry saddles. "There was a fight here," Seton said. "It must have been Short Bull and Thunder Eyes and the others. They stopped the blue-coats who came after them."

Itsepit and Dawn looked. It was a gloomy place, another little battlefield. Their people had gone on. They were in the gray mist ahead, perhaps already far away. They went on. It was hard walking. Every so often they rested. They made six miles that day and stopped for the night in the little valley of Black Coulee Creek, two or three miles south of Milk River. No one had followed them. They had seen no life on the plain. It seemed that buffaloes and antelope had gone away to their spirit caves. Above they had seen ravens and once a gyrfalcon, crossing the plain with a slow wingbeat, a large gray bird, speckled with dark brown dots.

That evening Dawn and Tsacope ate the last of the hardtack. They took to the robes early because of the cold and to preserve body heat. On the last few hundred yards before they reached a camping site among brush willows, Itsepit stumbled. She and Seton were spent. Their strength was almost gone. Dawn had been unconscious part of the day, but in their little camp her eyes were clear and filled with light. That night Tsacope slept with her mother. She had cried before Dawn bedded her next to her. The child crept close to her mother's body. Dawn softly talked her to sleep. Itsepit was silent, her eyes far away. Seton wondered how much longer the four of them would last.

Morning came, cold and gray as the ones before. They slogged on. Tsacope whimpered with hunger and cold as Itsepit carried her. Itsep-it had difficulty walking. So did Seton. Even though Dawn weighed almost nothing, the task of dragging her made him light-headed. Dawn was silent, barely alive. The few miles through the valley to the Milk River floodplain took them all morning. They came through the bluffs and saw the river before them. The floodplain was about four miles wide across the mouth of Lodge Creek, which ran in from the northwest.

Seton had hoped that the river would be frozen, but it was not. Along the banks, shore ice had formed, but there was water in the main channel. It ran free through dwarf willows on the plain. How could they cross? He sat down. He thought hard. What they needed most was food. Without it, in this weather, they would not live. He decided to search for game. He moved them into a small gully that ran down from the bluff. Where it made a turn, he bedded Dawn on the bottom of the gully. Itsepit lay next to her, Tsacope under the cover between them. Seton tucked them in. They were so weak they were asleep when he turned around.

They did not hear the coyote, but Seton did. The coyote called from the bluff directly above the gully. It was a single animal. Its calls were the bark-howls of long-distance alarm. They pierced the stillness of the white void of the floodplain and lost themselves beyond the river. Sometimes the sounds were like blasts from above the gully; sometimes they faded, directed elsewhere. Seton sat down. He realized that the coyote walked on the bluff in a circle. He wondered what it meant. He listened. Slowly he fell into a dreamlike trance. He was eleven years old on the bare, rocky ground above Lake Waha. A large male coyote stood before him, his head high above Seton's eyes. He looked down at him, huge before the red sky of morning. His coat was coarse and heavy. His amber eyes were slits. The coyote lowered his head and spoke. His face came closer and closer until it almost touched Seton's. The coyote kept talking, his eyes swimming in Seton's eyes. When the coyote withdrew, Seton awoke with a jolt. On the bluff above, the coyote no longer called.

Seton crawled up to the edge of the gully and peered over it. Itsepit woke. She heard a song. She looked around. It was Seton.

He sat nearby. He had stripped off his shirts and leggings. Sitting in the snow stripped to breechclout and moccasins he was painting himself. He followed Bear Shield's instruction. He took red ocher from the pouch and was painting his forehead red above the eyebrows. The kopluts hung from his right wrist. The eagle bone whistle was in place on his naked chest, above the bandolier with the last rounds for his rifle. He was singing the coyote song Hemene had taught him.

Itsepit sat up. "What are you doing?"

Seton turned to look at her. "Riders," he said. "Twenty, maybe more. They seem to know where we are. I don't know who they are."

He stood up. Itsepit heard the muffled sound of hoofbeats. Seton looked to the ground. It had finally come to this, in this distant place. Now they would live or die. He checked the Winchester and pulled the hammer back. He took a few steps and stood on the rim of the gully, facing out. He held the rifle in the crook of his left arm.

The dun horse of the first rider shied and snorted when the naked man with the red upper face stepped in front of it. The riders behind the first one had fanned out in a half circle. They were dressed in dark buffalo robes and held their rifles ready. A few wore feathers.

"Stop right there." Seton made the command in sign language with his right hand. The first rider backed the dun away. He was a middle-aged man with a single eagle feather behind his braids.

"What tribe are you?" the man asked in signs.

"Numipu," Seton signaled.

"What is your name?" the man asked.

It did not come easy for Seton to answer. He had not used the name before. But now, in this place, it had to be spoken. It had to be let loose on the wind, for his mother, for Hemene, for Bear Shield, for himself, for the coyote.

"Itsayaya pa'na." He said it clearly. Then he gave the name in signs.

The man nodded and smiled. He made the sign for "Lakota," holding the extended index finger of his right hand to the left of his throat and moving it across the throat with a cutting motion. He repeated it. "Lakota."

From the half circle of men behind him came friendly laughter. Seton stood motionless. The coyote had come. Death had hovered and looked and gone the other way. He made a step forward on shaking legs. The Lakota warrior saw him falter. He dismounted quickly to stand before the young man with the hollow face and hungry eyes filled with despair . . . and a desperate courage.

When Seton seemed to stagger, the man held him fast.

"Sioux?" Seton asked in English.

The man's face was close. Seton looked into dark eyes. The man raised his eyebrows and nodded. He touched the place on the thick robe over his heart. "Lakota."

EPILOGUE

The Nez Perces who laid down arms on Snake Creek, October 5, 1877, numbered 87 men, 184 women, and 147 children, a total of 418 people. In their understanding of the peace agreement made by Chiefs Joseph and Naked Head with Colonel Nelson A. Miles and General O. O. Howard, they believed that, after a winter spent at Fort Keogh, they would return to Idaho in the spring. Those of the Wallowa band thought they had been assured they would go back to their beloved country around Wallowa Lake in northeastern Oregon.

The officers negotiating for the military left the "homeland" question vague. They were most concerned with ending a war that had embarrassed the post–Civil War army, making it look incompetent and poorly led. Whatever the genuine intentions of Howard and Miles may have been, the final decision for a Nez Perce destination and placement was transferred to higher authority, which, against the agreement, placed the Nez Perces in the status of "prisoners of war."

General Philip Sheridan, at division headquarters in Chicago, ordered that all Nez Perce "prisoners of war" be moved to Fort Lincoln, whence they were to continue to Fort Leavenworth, Kansas. From there, they would go to Indian Territory, Oklahoma, after the army released them into the custody of the Bureau of Indian Affairs.

Moved from reservation to reservation, reduced by diseases for which they were not given medical aid, in April 1885, 268 survivors were allowed to leave Arkansas City, Kansas, by railroad for the northwest. On arrival in Idaho, 118 were allowed to settle on the Lapwai Reservation. Chief Joseph and 149 persons were sent north to the Colville Reservation in Washington because they refused to convert to the branch of Christianity practiced on the Lapwai Reservation.

Chief Joseph's famous "surrender speech," a staple in volumes on North American Indian oratory, must be considered a literary forgery. It was supposedly transcribed by Lieutenant C. E. S. Wood, Twenty-first Infantry, General Howard's adjutant. But Wood understood no Nez Perce, and no interpreter was present. The only white person in attendance who knew a few words of Nez Perce was Ad Chapman, the same man who had encouraged Captain Perry to attack the Nez Perce camp in White Bird Canyon. He had come with General Howard. He could not have been a source of information. But the "surrender speech" served both Howard and Miles well, and especially aided Miles's career.

A total of 233 Nez Perces escaped from the Bear Paws. This number included those who fled on the morning of the attack, a few scouts sent to contact Sitting Bull, and those who walked out with White Goose, mostly of the Lamtama band. It is historical fact that Nez Perce scouts did reach Sitting Bull and that the Hunkpapa leader went south with over half a thousand warriors to break the Nez Perces free.

When this force met with White Goose's band of refugees, they realized it was too late. The war party regretfully turned back, escorting the frozen and starving refugees to Lakota camps in Saskatchewan, only a little more than a day's journey from the border.

A party of Lakotas, with ten Nez Perce warriors led by Peopeo Tholekt, continued on and visited the battlefield. They buried the unburied dead they could find. If the Nez Perces had held out for two more days, as White Goose and most of the warrior leaders urged, Sitting Bull and his rested warriors would have reached them.

Some of the refugees remained in Canada, or went with the Lakotas to South Dakota reservations in 1881. Many drifted back across the Rocky Mountains and joined relations on the Lapwai Reservation or settled on the Colville Reservation.

The thirty Northern Cheyenne scouts, led by a minor military society leader, Two Moons, who guided Miles's forces to the Nez Perce camp and captured a third of the Nez Perce horse herd, were rewarded with five Nez Perce horses each for their service.

Of the eight men and two women of the Radersburg tourist party captured by White Thunder's scouts in Yellowstone Park, none was killed. Seven of the men were allowed to escape. Lone Elk and the noted warrior Seeyakoon Ilppilp protected the two female tourists, Emma Carpenter Cowan and her younger sister Ida, and their brother, Frank Carpenter, and sheltered them in the Nez Perce camp for one night. In the morning they were given horses and set free. Frank Carpenter described their experiences in a book, *Adventures in Geyser Land*.

SOURCES FOR FURTHER READING

Carpenter, Frank D. 1935. *Adventures in Geyser Land*. Caldwell, Idaho: Caxton Printers.

Coale, George L. 1956. "Ethnohistorical Sources for the Nez Perce Indians." *Ethnohistory* 3:246–55, 346–60.

———. 1958. "Notes on the Guardian Spirit Concept among the Nez Perce. *International Archive of Ethnography* 48:136–48.

Curtis, Edward S. 1911; 1991–95. "Nez Perces." In *The North American Indian*. Vol. 8, 3–76, 157–72, 183–85. Norwood, MA: Plimpton Press.

Haines, Aubrey L. 1991. *An Elusive Victory: The Battle of the Big Hole*. West Glacier, MO: Glacier Natural History Association.

Haines, Francis. 1955. *The Nez Perces*. Norman: University of Oklahoma Press.

———. 1963. *Appaloosa: The Spotted Horse in Art and History*. Austin: University of Texas Press.

Howard, O. O. 1907. *My Life and Experiences among Our Hostile Indians*. Hartford CT: A. A. Worthington and Company.

James, Caroline. 1996. *Nez Perce Women in Transition, 1877–1990*. Moscow: University of Idaho Press.

Josephy, Alvin M., Jr. 1971. *The Nez Perce Indians and the Opening of the Northwest*. New Haven, CT: Yale University Press.

———. 1983. "The People of the Plateau." In *Nez Perce Country: A Handbook for the Nez Perce National Historical Park*. Washington DC: National Park Service.

Lundsgaarde, Henry P. 1967. "A Structural Analysis of the Nez Perce Kinship." *Research Studies* 35:48–77.

Marshall, Alan G. 1977. "Nez Perce Social Groups: An Ecological Perspective." PhD diss., Washington State University.

McDermott, John D. 1978. *Forlorn Hope*. Boise: Idaho State Historical Society.

McWhorter, L. V. 1940. *Yellow Wolf, His Own Story*. Caldwell, ID: Caxton Printers.

———. 1952. *Hear Me, My Chiefs*. Caldwell, ID: Caxton Printers.

Miles, Nelson A. 1897. *Personal Recollections and Observations of General Nelson A. Miles*. Chicago: Werner Company.

Moeller, Bill and Jean. 1995. *Chief Joseph and the Nez Perces: A Photographic History*. Missoula, MO: Mountain Press.

Office of Nez Perce Indian Agency, Lapwai. 1862–1878. Reports, 1862–1877. In *Report of the Commissioner of Indian Affairs*. Washington DC: Government Printing Office.

Phinney, Archie. 1934. *Nez Perce Texts*. New York: Columbia University Press.

Schlesier, Karl H. 1975. "Nez Perces." In *Family of Man*. Vol. 6, pt. 74. London: Marshall Cavendish.

Spinden, H. J. 1908. "The Nez Perce Indians." *Memoirs of the American Anthropological Association* 2:165–274.

U.S. Congress. 1878. Report of the Secretary of War. 45th Cong., 2nd sess., December 3, 1877. Washington DC: Government Printing Office.

U.S. Department of Agriculture, Forest Service, Northern Region. August 1990 (revision 1995). Nez Perce (Nee-Me-Poo) National Historic Trail (map). Scale: 1:1,000,000.

Walker, Deward E., Jr. 1966. "The Nez Perce Sweat-bath Complex: An Acculturational Analysis." *Southwestern Journal of Anthropology* 22:133–71.

————. 1967. "Mutual Cross-Utilization of Economic Resources in the Plateau: An Example from Aboriginal Nez Perce Fishing Practices." Reports of Investigations, no. 41. Washington State University, Laboratory of Anthropology.

————. 1978. *The Indians of Idaho*. Moscow: University of Idaho Press.

————. 1985. *Conflict and Schism in Nez Perce Acculturation: A Study of Religion and Politics*. Moscow: University of Idaho Press.

Wilfong, Cheryl. 1990. *Following the Nez Perce Trail*. Corvallis: Oregon State University Press.

ACKNOWLEDGMENTS

I am deeply grateful to Judith Keeling, editor-in-chief; Karen Medlin, managing editor; Lindsay Starr, senior book designer; the staff of Texas Tech University Press; and John Mulvihill, copyeditor; for their meticulous work and their genial cooperation. Special thanks are due to J. M. and Barbara Hayes, who were always there when needed.